USS Washington

The Black Ship

Mark Wayne McGinnis

Copyright

Published by Avenstar Productions: info@avenstar.net

USS Washington

Print Book: **ISBN-13:** 979-8989461950

To join Mark's mailing list, jump to:

http://eepurl.com/bs7M9r

Visit Mark Wayne McGinnis at:

http://www.markwaynemcginnis.com

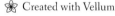 Created with Vellum

Chapter 1

Sylarix Star System, Tenebrous Expanse
Odyssey

Fleet Admiral Krythium Vorun

O*dyssey*, a seasoned destroyer that had seen its share of conflict, favored a design rich with smooth arcs over harsh angles. From the smooth, rounded ascent at her prow to the gentle outward flaring of her beam. There, within the absolute stillness and quiet of deep space, her beautiful, almost feminine silhouette was nestled within the muted glow of Sylar, an ancient red dwarf star drawing its last breaths. Her smooth, flawless hull reflected little of the fading starlight. The ship was silent, the crew more so. They were waiting, suspended in the void of the Tenebrous Expanse, a speck amidst the darkness.

Fleet Admiral Krythium Vorun, the Commander of the Malonise Fleet, stood motionless at the bridge's observation deck. His eyes, two orbs of reflective onyx, scanned the void. Vorun's form, a towering figure even among his kind, was encased in a uniform that spoke of battles won and honors bestowed. The fabric, dark against his iridescent silver-blue scales, moved with him like a second layer of armor.

Three hours had passed since their emergence into the expanse. The war games—a routine display of military prowess between Allied Forces, were running late. Vorun's gaze fixed on the distant Grish battle group, a constellation of warships that were anything but ordinary. They were brutal in their design, sharp like the edges of a blade, their hull surfaces a patchwork of battle-worn plating that told tales of survival and ferocity.

The Grish flagship, *Crocken One*, sat at the heart of their formation. It was a leviathan of space, a behemoth battle cruiser that held the dark around it like a cloak. It was not alone. Flanked by destroyers and frigates, it looked like the leader of a pack, silent and waiting.

Vorun's hands, webbed and tipped with retractable claws, gripped the metal railing before him. His ceremonial attire did little to hide the musculature of a life forged under high gravity and in the discipline of military service. His chest rose and fell, the gill-like slits on his neck flaring with each breath of the acidic water atmosphere that the ship's environmental systems mimicked after their homeworld's oceans.

The Grish Armada held formation, a tight knot of potential violence. Vorun admired their readiness, their unity. But beneath the surface, something stirred. An unease he still couldn't shake.

His Second-in-Command, Commander Happle, stood a respectful distance away, his eyes glued to the data on his display.

"What's the delay?" Vorun's voice was a low rumble that filled the quiet of the bridge.

Happle didn't respond immediately, his fingers swept over the console, his expression tight. "It's probably nothing, Sir," Happle finally said. But the hesitancy in his voice betrayed his words.

Vorun's instincts prickled. The Grish were many things— unpredictable in their diplomacy, sure—but in military precision, they were unmatched. Delays were not characteristic of them.

The alliance between the Malonise and the Grish was forged in the fires of necessity, bound by the exchange of Zylinthium fuel ore that powered both their civilizations. It was a solid alliance, as enduring as the seabeds of Majel. Yet Vorun couldn't help but wonder if the bedrock of their relationship was developing fault lines.

The silence stretched on. "Come on, enough of this," the Admiral murmured. Vorun felt his three hearts sync up, a steady beat that seemed loud in his ears. The war games were supposed to be a demonstration, a chance to display their military might in a controlled environment. But the liquid atmosphere was charged, filled with the electricity of an impending storm.

Vorun's eyes didn't waver from the viewport. The Grish ships were a study of martial efficiency. Their artillery ports aligned with precision; weapons charged with a glow that seemed a tad too eager for a simple exercise. His gut tightened. He had lived too long, fought too many battles, to ignore the signs of a prelude to combat.

Happle spoke up, breaking Vorun's concentration. "Sir, it's the communications delays from the Grish, the lapses in their normally punctual updates. It's subtle, but it's there."

His imposing figure eclipsed Happle as he pivoted to face

him. As Commander, Vorun needed to ensure the crew remained focused on their responsibilities, undistracted. Feigning calm, he dismissed Happle's concerns with a wave of his hand. The Grish, often referred to as *piglets*—the term had been bouncing about the galaxy of late—were also an enigma. Their motives and methods often eluded comprehension. But alliances were not about understanding; they were about respect, necessity, and sometimes, being the lesser evil.

Yet, Vorun trusted Happle's instincts. They had served together for years, their careers entwined like the roots of the great seaweed forests of Majel. To dismiss his Second's intuition may be to invite disaster.

A new tone pierced the quiet hum of the ship's systems, a variance not of programming, but of reaction—a pattern detected, an anomaly in the Grish formation. The subtle change did not escape Vorun's discerning perception. He forced a smile. If the Grish were playing a deeper game, they were not the only ones capable of deception.

"Commander Happle," Vorun said calmly. "Turn the fleet thirty degrees to port. Move the destroyers into flanking positions."

"Aye, Admiral," Happle replied, his voice steady.

As the commencement of the war games—*or whatever this was*—grew closer, Vorun's mind raced. Strategies, contingencies, plans, and counterplans swirled. More of the puzzle pieces of the Grish's actions began to fall into place. Their aggressive formation, the cold formality of their communications... didn't add up to a friendly exercise.

Odyssey's AI signaled a warning, a message incoming. Vorun's eyes narrowed as he read the encoded message from a trusted, well-paid spy within the Grish Fleet. The warning was clear.

The Grish are not here for war games.

Vorun's next order shattered the stillness. "Battle stations! Break formation! Scatter!" he commanded, his voice echoed, a thunderous call to arms.

Commander Happle moved with a veteran's speed. "I knew it," he muttered.

"Helm, turn us into the enemy, give them less of a targeting profile!"

"Incoming!" came the urgent call from Tactical.

Vorun braced himself.

Odyssey shuddered as the Grish onslaught began, a torrent of smart missiles and plasma fire. His ship, a titan of the void, was now an underdog in a fight he hadn't anticipated.

Suddenly, a power conduit short-circuited, unleashing a shockwave of charged particles that disrupted the aqueous environment on the bridge. Intense electrical arcs struck through the water, boiling it locally and creating violent, superheated bubbles that expanded explosively. The rapid temperature rise caused the water to become dangerously hot in mere moments, scalding the sensitive scales of the crew. The charged particles in the water carried a toxic level of heat, suffocating many of the fish-like crewmembers as their gills could not process the suddenly overheated liquid. Panic took hold as the crew scattered, seeking to distance themselves from the seething cauldron of heat that threatened their watery domain, while crucial systems shorted and sizzled.

"Happle, divert auxiliary power to the portside shields!"

The bridge trembled; the force of the incoming Grish fire was like hammer blows bombarding *Odyssey's* defenses. Vorun's voice cut through the chaos, commanding and clear. "Target the closest assets!"

As *Odyssey's* cannons powered up, a stark reality set in.

Vorun knew that despite the fierce reputation of the Malonise Fleet, their teeth had been blunted for this exercise. In the spirit of the games, each railgun, a staple in their arsenal, had been loaded with non-lethal ordnance—blank spikes designed to register hits without piercing hulls. Malonise warship Captains were now caught in the maw of a real battle, each holding their respective breaths as this twist of fate stymied their warships' true capabilities.

"Reconfigure weapons systems!" Vorun yelled.

Now, crews across the Admiral's armada of warships were working frantically, ejecting blank spikes from railguns, exchanging feckless missiles with real ordnances—a daunting process that ate precious seconds as the Grish closed in. The usual thunderous clap of their railguns remained silent, only adding to the growing tension, like a mocking echo of lost potential. Vorun felt a renewed surge of frustration. His fleet, revered throughout the stars for its might, now had to claw back from a disadvantage that no one had anticipated—but he should have. *Fucking piglets!*

Every Malonise warship, a behemoth crafted for annihilation, found itself dependent on auxiliary armaments. Their plasma cannons, hastily recalibrated, were gathering energy, offering a glimmer of hope in the desperate struggle to endure. Vorun was aware, however, that the real game-changer lay with the railguns, now being primed with lethal rounds, readying to play a pivotal role in their desperate fight for existence.

"Status!" he commanded.

"Armories are dispatching replacements... but it's taking time, Sir," Happle responded with urgency, almost apologetically.

Admiral Vorun understood the gravity of each second that ticked away. Actions were being executed with haste born of desperation, all crewmembers fully aware that without swift armament, *Odyssey* and her sister ships would stand as little more than practice targets for the enemy.

Deck plates vibrated as the first lethal spikes were fired, tearing through space toward the Grish, a delayed but emphatic declaration that *Odyssey* had regained her footing. The remaining crew leaped to action, still recalibrating weapons that were meant for show, but now for survival. Standing at the curved duraglass observation window, Vorun saw the plasma cannons humming to life, their glow a harbinger of destruction. With a roar, they unleashed their might upon the closing-in Grish ships.

One Grish destroyer caught in the path of the rail spikes onslaught buckled. Explosions rippled across its surface, its death taking two frigates along with it.

"The Grish destroyer has been struck directly! Their forward advance has been disabled!" Happle cried out with astonishment.

Vorun's hand clenched, his knuckles white. "Take that, you lying pack of shiteaters!" He turned to his crew, "Press the attack. Signal all ships to focus on those heavy battle cruisers. If we take them out, we may yet survive this treachery."

But as the battle raged on, the Grish, relentless, accelerated their advance, their destroyers sleek and deadly, cutting through the Malonise formation like propellers through water. Vorun watched the destruction, his fleet being torn apart, piece by piece.

The Malonise Fleet—ships once proud beacons of military power, now lay in ruins, their hulls breached, liquid atmosphere spewing into space, bodies spiraling away—forever lost to the void.

Odyssey crewmembers rushed to secure their posts, but many had already succumbed to the intense heat and lethal electrical currents coursing through the aqueous environment—

their gills spasming as they convulsed before floating still. The acrid stench of seared scales and boiled flesh permeated the bridge. Vorun's three hearts sank with each loss, each explosive rupture in the liquid atmosphere signifying the end of precious lives, of mighty warships, and of any glimmer of hope.

Odyssey was now alone amidst the debris and carnage, propulsion thrusters flickered like a dying flame. The lights of the bridge dimmed, multiple systems were failing—the end was imminent.

"Admiral, shields just fell!" Happle's voice was strained, but he maintained composure.

Vorun's response was resolute, "Divert all remaining power, including life support, back into shield batteries. Engineering," he yelled. "I need one more great, big gasp from our power-plant. Can you do that?"

"Aye, Sir. I can give you that," came a voice from one of the few still-active stations.

Happle stopped what he was doing and looked to the forward display and then to the Admiral. He smiled. "You're going to ram their flagship. Ram *Crocken One*."

"That... I am. Now it is time we ensure that Grish Fleet Commander regrets his actions today."

Vorun didn't wait for a reply as he approached Helm, pushing aside the body of a fallen crewmember. His hands took the controls, his movements deliberate. *Odyssey*, with its plasma cannons still firing in defiance, was now bearing down on *Crocken One,* the Grish Command vessel.

With a smirk, he said, "I know you see us... and right about now, you're looking for a way out—a means to survive beyond the next few moments." Through gritted teeth, Vorun's whispered monologue continued. "The impact is coming my friend, your demise is coming, we both know... that is unavoidable."

The Grish Commander, clearly aware of the threat, had

ordered all their fire concentrated on the fast-approaching Malonise flagship. Plasma beams from multiple warships converged onto *Odyssey*, seeking to end this final act of desperation.

But *Odyssey*'s course was already locked in. Vorun sat back and looked about the bridge. A scene of controlled chaos. His crew, the few that remained alive, were still doing their duty, fighting, knowing full well what lay ahead.

The distance closed between *Odyssey* and *Crocken One*. *Any moment now...* Vorun sat tall at the helm, his eyes locked on the tactical display. His crew, though few, now stopped what they were doing and looked to him, perhaps finding in his resolve the courage to face their end.

"*Odyssey*, you will be remembered..." Vorun's voice was a calm in the storm, the bridgecrew echoing the sentiment in their resolute stares.

The defenses of *Odyssey* dwindled, the gap between the dueling flagships rapidly closing. Just as they collided, a brilliant eruption, a detonation that devoured both vessels, marked the apocalyptic conclusion to a gallant final stand.

WHEN ALL THE EXPLOSIONS HAD FINALLY CEASED AND relative stillness returned to the Sylarix Star System, the Malonise Fleet, their once proud warships... were now little more than scattered space debris.

But the Grish Armada's business was hardly complete. Methodically, warships reassembled into an attack formation. The Malonise, their beautiful, vibrant, water world of Majel... that too would soon fall to their Grish conquerors.

Chapter 2

Earth
New York City, New York

Captain Galvin Quintos

I stood at the fifth-floor window of the 280-year-old St. Regis New York Hotel, fresh from the shower with damp hair, a towel fastened around my waist. Below me, 5th Avenue thrummed with life. I looked up and saw a stream of AirCars... staccato taillights blinking on and off high over Central Park, commuters already getting back into the swing of things. The Sun, a mere glint after the morning's downpour, was attempting to make a more substantial presence.

It had been five weeks since the Tidal Basin Massacre, the horrendous Varapin attack on Earth. Four weeks since the secondary, somewhat less devastating, attack by the Grish. Combined, though, the two horrific acts had brought the death toll worldwide into the tens of millions. Much of this city was in ruins—there again, many of Earth's other major cities were in far worse shape. Washington D.C. had been hit hardest, very little of America's government center remained intact. The White House and its occupants, gone, including the President and Vice President. The Capitol Building and its occupants, mostly gone. EUNF Plaza, and U.S. Space Navy headquarters—eviscerated.

So why was this a day of jubilation and celebration? I watched as strangers were embracing each other down there on a crosswalk... while all around, people were greeting each other with broad smiles and blown air kisses. What prompted such an outpouring of communal elation? Simple. The long years of intergalactic conflict were over—a peace accord had been signed with the Varapin. As the word spread across the world, a tidal wave of optimism and relief engulfed the masses. For the first time in decades, a sense of hope filled the air. Whatever uncertainties still lay ahead, this day had been one for the people to mark with festivity. I shook my head, not feeling anything close to jubilation. In fact, I was getting angrier by the fucking moment.

I turned away from the now all-too-bright and sunny morning outside and took in my expensive five-room suite, eyes eventually settling on the pristinely pressed, white uniform hanging from a hook on the back of the bathroom door.

Maybe now's a good time to quickly get you caught up on past events...

I was off the grid, hiding out in the Colorado wilderness when a heads-up on an incoming disaster pulled me back into the thick of things with the U.S. Space Navy. Suddenly, I was on USS Franklin, a top-tier omninought, when the Varapin blindsided Earth, hurling us into a spiral of chaos and into another spatial realm, thanks to their reality-bending tech— Quantum Spatial Entanglement and Relocation, or QSER.

We devised an audacious plan, a desperate ploy that teetered on the brink of insanity: to swipe the Varapin's prized tech and set Earth back to rights. It was a perilous wager, fraught with danger, but our sole shot at unraveling this pandemonium.

But time was a precious commodity we could ill afford. Our home planet was teetering on the edge, poised to transition from normalcy to a raging inferno to a frozen, desolate expanse. So, Stephan Derrota and Coogong worked like mad to get another QSER device up and running. Tick-tock.

That wasn't the last of our hurdles. We were threading the needle of a three-way deal with the Ilion, a race holding the key the Varapin needed—a cure for a disease threatening the Varapin's existence. The U.S. Space Navy played its part as the middleman.

Long story short, Earth and the Moon are back where they belong. The Varapin Fleet Commander, Sorlen Op, stayed true to his word. The Varapin are getting their cure, and we have peace—for now.

So, all is hunky dory, right? Not even close.

I noticed a small bouquet of fresh flowers on the elegant marble countertop of my hotel room, a touch of life and color amidst the gloominess of my thoughts. The Grish were still out there and getting more powerful by the moment. For anyone to think that Earth and her allies—the Thine and the Pleidian Weonan—were safe, was delusional.

It had been three weeks before I finally set foot back on slowly-recovering Mother Earth. My arrival was nothing short of a spectacle as if I had been catapulted into a level of stardom typically reserved for rock icons and Hollywood celebrities. The word had spread like wildfire through dry brush... Captain Galvin Quintos had led his starship team to victory. The Varapin had been defeated, and the world was safe once more—which couldn't have been further from the truth.

I opened the hotel room's mini-fridge, and there sat a chilled bottle of champagne, undoubtedly placed there by hotel staff, a symbol of celebration. Tempting... but it would remain untouched. I snatched up a water bottle instead.

And it wasn't just me who had been ascended to the heights of stardom. The beautiful, fair-haired Gail Pristy was currently gracing the cover of *Vogue*, while the Coogong/Stephan Derrota team had earned a nomination for the prestigious Nobel Prize in Physics. Captain Wallace Ryder and Akari James, much to the delight of the paparazzi, had recently been frequently spotted at various niche nightclubs and the occasional yacht party.

Now, you might be wondering, where was Doc Vivian Leigh during all of this? Well, she had departed the moment we returned to Earth. As you may recall, she had that long-lost husband in Florida... or was it Australia? Whatever, he was convalescing, apparently still requiring much of her attention. As for Hardy, he was undergoing a lengthy and meticulous process of repairs and upgrades. It turned out that he had sustained even more damage than I had initially realized. However, I'd been assured that I would be reuniting with him later today at the ceremony.

Oh God... the ceremony—a prospect I truly dreaded. Something coined *The Heroes of Sol Ceremony*.

Newly appointed by emergency referendum, President of the United States, Cyprian Block—that's right, the very same man who once commanded the EUNF U.S. Space Navy as its Executive Five Star Fleet Admiral—was about to present me, Captain of *USS Franklin*, with the nation's utmost distinction, the *Congressional Medal of Honor*.

But no, things wouldn't end there... dignitaries from around the world had already arrived for the festivities. I've been informed that the live event would be televised in 3D to every living room across the globe. To make things worse, later tonight, during the ceremony, I would also be honored with France's Légion d'honneur, the United Kingdom's Victoria Cross, Germany's Pour le Mérite, and Spain's Cruz Laureada de San Fernando. Enough ribbons and medals to sink me to the bottom of the Hudson. And don't get me started on the awards and medals I've already received from the Thine and Pleidian Weonan emissaries.

Look, am I overwhelmed and humbled by all the attention? Of course, I am. But none of this should be happening now. Would an Olympian Marathoner stop mid-race to receive a gold medal? Would the Stanley Cup be interrupted mid-game for a victory ceremony? The world had indeed found its respite, but for me, it was a relentless reminder of what had not been accomplished. War was still a reality—hell if anything, it was even more perilous of late. All one had to do was glance out to the middle of New York Harbor where you'd see the all too obvious reminder that the top half of the Statue of Liberty was missing. Stolen by the Grish just before *USS Franklin* and *USS Lincoln's* last battle against the piglets.

An hour later, I was dressed in my new uniform. I looked at myself in the bathroom mirror. "You're a phony, Quintos. Best you don't forget that."

A knock came at the door. I turned and glowered at the intrusion. I murmured, "Sign says do not disturb... it's not that complicated."

I opened the door ready to chastise room service for bringing more flowers, or more champagne, but instead stood flabbergasted, looking into the beautiful, alien face of Empress Shawlee Tee.

"Galvin. You look so handsome in your uniform."

"Uh... thank you, Empress..." I began, my words faltering as they left my lips. It wasn't because I wasn't happy to see the Empress—the welcome presence of a friend when I needed one the most, should have been welcome. but instead, it was the raw disparity before me that left me momentarily speechless.

Shawlee was standing there kitted out in a full combat suit, a shredder rifle slung over one shoulder, a tagger holstered at her hip. Gone were the flowing robes and regal hair, replaced by the practical attire of a warrior. Her helmeted faceplate had been retracted just enough to reveal her pretty, open-void visage.

"You can change on the ship, Galvin," she urged, her impatience evident. "But we must go. Like right now! There's no time to waste."

Chapter 3

All business, Shawlee pushed past me while talking into her TAC-Band, "Two to quansport, Coogong."

I only had time for one word. "Wait..."

The sensation of being quansported is a whirlwind of disconnection, a sudden flash of nausea, and a slight vertigo that engulfs one's senses. In that instant, one is acutely aware of one's body being segmented into oblivion—an abrupt and disconcerting feeling. The process is at its best when there's a moment to prepare, a chance to tighten stomach muscles and mentally brace for the experience. On the other hand, being taken by surprise, as I was at this moment, is akin to a donkey kick to the stomach, leaving one both pissed off and profoundly unsettled.

We materialized into a Quansporter compartment. There were thirteen adjacent pedestals to ours, and the compartment as a whole was large. Minimalist, utilitarian, and high-tech came to mind. Brushed metal bulkheads surrounded us, and there were two sets of quans-controls; typically, there is only one set. They were separated by six or seven feet—both console towers sporting the same high-tech brushed metal appearance. Their control boards were high-gloss black with a dazzling array of color-coded touch controls and a myriad of mini 3D-projected displays. As I took in the surroundings; there was that unmistakable *new-ship* scent in the air.

All that aside, my attention was not on my surroundings but more on the others in the compartment. Stick-figure-like Coogong with his oversized-looking helmet—amber-colored Ambiogel sloshing around within—was busy. He was in the process of quansporting in others.

The compartment was bustling with activity. Familiar faces, many displaying the same level of irritation that I was feeling. If someone were to hazard a guess about where all these people had been just moments before, they might presume a wedding reception or perhaps a formal ballroom gala. But I knew, they, like me, had been readying for *The Heroes of Sol Ceremony,* which was scheduled to commence in New York City any minute now.

Gail Pristy, fuming mad, stomped a high-heeled foot down onto the metal deck, "What the hell are we doing here?" she spat... as if I had anything to do with it.

Her reaction caught me by surprise, and I had to stifle a laugh. She wore a strapless, shimmery, emerald gown, tailored to perfection, enhancing her slim figure with an understated grace. Her fair complexion radiated natural beauty, with crystal-blue eyes and soft, naturally rosy lips that needed little enhancement. Her golden blonde hair, gently falling to her bare shoulders, caught the harsh lighting in a way that framed her face with a touch of brilliance. Even in this unexpected setting, she was the epitome of timeless elegance.

Before I could answer her, Hardy suddenly quansported onto the nearest pedestal. The ChronoBot, like Pristy, was a breathtaking sight. To say his chrome facade was shiny would be like describing the Kohinoor diamond as having a nice glint to it. Hardy's armor was a mirror-like radiance that defied comparison. And that wasn't his only alteration. His typical black onyx-like faceplate was now a deep, subtly glowing blue. I had heard he had undergone a retrofit and upgrade... I was curious as to what had changed on the inside. More or different weaponry, perhaps?

As if reading my mind, Hardy's faceplate suddenly came alive with an all-too-familiar facsimile, that of the middle-aged John Hardy, slightly pudgy, balding, and in need of a shave. Around the ChronoBot's neck were no less than five multi-colored ribbons, each suspending a distinct honorary medal.

He looked about his surroundings, perhaps he too had been taken totally off guard by being suddenly quansported here. But, instead of asking, *What are we doing here*, his first words were, "Where's Climbo?"

"Welcome aboard, Hardy," Coogong said. "Climbo has been quansported into Cargo Bay 5—this compartment is for crewmembers only."

"Climbo is a crewmember," Hardy said, looking to me for support.

"Uh, not so much, Hardy. And why do you need the mechanical mule here anyway?"

"Why do any of us need to be here?" came the familiar voice of a certain teenager. "For the first time in my life, I actually wanted to get dressed up, but then I'm whisked off to some new dreadnought?" Sonya, like Pristy, glared at me as if I was somehow responsible.

"Omninought," Crewman Grimes corrected, just now stepping down from another pedestal. "I've heard about this ship. Top secret but there's been rumblings. I'm betting this is the *Black Ship*... first-of-its-kind prototype, one designed in concert between Thine and Pleidian Engineers."

I caught sight of Empress Shawlee Tee hugging Pristy while apologizing for her unexpected abduction.

Now others were quansporting onto the ship. Crewman Chen, Akari James, looking menacingly pretty, her inked arms and shoulders making a statement... but not entirely sure what that was. Captain Wallace Ryder, dressed similarly to me, in a white officer's uniform, looked tanned and ready for his next yacht excursion.

As large as the compartment was, it was quickly becoming a bustling hive of activity, teeming with people and an undercurrent of urgency. Scanning the space I saw Chief Knott, and most, if not all, of my previous USS *Franklin* bridgecrew: Crewmember Davit, Lieutenant Commander Jorkins, Ensign Lira, Crewmember Soto, Lieutenant Hargreaves, Crewmember Takahashi, and Crewmember Barrow.

I glanced to the auto-hatch doors, wondering why we were all being crammed in here like so many sardines in a tin can. I was the ranking officer, well, other than the Empress, and it was time for me to take control of the situation.

That's when one more individual suddenly quansported into view.

The compartment was abuzz in excited murmurs as all eyes went to Cyprian Block, the newly designated President of the United States. Dressed in an impeccably tailored black suit, stark white shirt, and bright lavender tie, he raised his palms while taking in the crammed-in mass of people.

"My sincere apologies. I know the timing of this couldn't have been much worse. You all deserved your moment in the spotlight. To be honored and appreciated for your service to America and, of course, to Earth. But recent intel tells us we have little time to act—to meet an impending threat head-on. While here on Earth we have been licking our wounds and attempting to rebuild, the Grish have only grown stronger. They've been busy infiltrating farther and farther into our quadrant of space. Yes, the Varapin are no longer a threat, but that does not mean we can hang back on our laurels."

Hardy, at my side, leaned in close and whispered way too loudly, "I've never understood that... explain to me what the hell a laurel is?"

I *shooshed* him and pointed up to Block. "How about we just listen to what the man has to say."

"You will find this vessel is like none other," Block said. "A warship with new capabilities—this time the tech coming out of Thine labs. Coogong, thank you for your involvement in that."

"Uh-huh... that just means this new ship is untested," Hardy added, under his breath.

Block continued, "Outside that auto-hatch lies your new ship. Like USS *Franklin*, she's an omninought. Five miles in length, and quite lethal. Code named the *Black Ship*, today, here on her maiden voyage, we christen her USS *Washington*."

That rallied applause from the onlookers.

"Geez, it's like a fucking sauna in here," someone from behind murmured.

Irritated, I glanced back to see it was none other than Petty Officer Second-Class Aubrey Laramie leaning against the back bulkhead. Unlike the others here, she was not dressed in a long gown with her hair all done up and wearing makeup—no, instead she was wearing body-conforming athletic attire, a sweatband around her head, and fluorescent orange running shoes on her feet.

Catching my sudden scrutiny, she sheepishly shrugged and mouthed, "Sorry Cap."

"I have combined the 2nd and 3rd U.S. Space Navy Fleets into one; the collective assemblage of vessels now bears the designation Alpha Fleet. Two hundred Earth, Thine, and Pleidian Weonan warships in all."

That caused a stir. Two hundred warships coalesced into one fleet was rare.

"Coinciding with his most recent promotion, Fleet Commander Quintos will be commanding this first-of-its-kind battle group."

Heads turned—all eyes went to me.

I did know about the promotion of Fleet Commander, and I did know about the formation of Alpha Fleet. What I did not know was that I would be taking command *today*.

"Your mission," Block continued, his voice unwavering, "is to launch an assault on the Grish homeworld of Drakoria, while systematically dismantling that star system's formidable defenses. Along the way, you will encounter three Grish battle groups: Prowess Fleet, Torrent Fleet, and Pinnacle Fleet. The latter positioned closest to Drakoria, is what we call a Super Armada—equivalent in size to our Alpha Fleet. It is undefeated in battle. Needless to say, it poses the most significant threat we've ever encountered. If our intel is correct, it is this Pinnacle Fleet that is readying to attack the Pleidian Weonan Star System." Block's eyes settled on me. "The war is at a crucial stage... failure to meet our strategic objectives would have dire consequences for the alliance."

A man in a business suit who looked to be a bodyguard leaned in and whispered into the President's ear. Block nodded.

"Apparently, I need to move things along here. For those who've served the U.S. Space Navy the longest, you may recall a Chaplain typically being part of our crew. Today, we're reinstating this practice to provide support during these trying times. Chaplains can offer solace and guidance when needed most."

I inwardly groaned.

Block continued, "Now, before we proceed, I'd like to introduce someone, most of you, will not have had the pleasure of meeting." He gestured toward a man who I hadn't noticed standing amongst the crowd. He stood as tall as me, around six feet, with dark, wavy hair that fell just a bit too long, lending him a roguish, bad-boy vibe, complemented by an effortless smile worthy of a movie star.

There was something strangely familiar about him, and then it struck me like a bolt of lightning. This man, dressed in the stereotypical dark suit with a clerical collar, bore an uncanny resemblance to an older version of someone back on *USS Hamilton*—the deceased Chaplain Thomas Trent. My jaw muscles tightened as I remembered him as being one of the most treacherous and ungodly individuals I had ever met.

"Chaplain Halman Trent, raise a hand so everyone can see you there," Block said.

Hardy said, "Halman? What kind of name is Halman?"

"I think he's kind of hot," Aubrey said, standing on tippy toes to get a better look at the man.

"Let's just hope this isn't a father-like-son type scenario," I heard Pristy murmur off to my right. She shot me a wary look. I'd forgotten, she too was onboard *Hamilton* at that time.

"Good luck and Godspeed crewmembers of *USS Washington*... we're all counting on you," Block said with a brisk salute.

With that, the President quansported away, presumably back to somewhere on Earth.

Empress Shawlee took his place up on the raised quansporting platform. "You are all here because your Captain insisted you be here. You are his team, his preferred crew. Some of you have been promoted, all of you have been given pay raises."

The crowd came alive at that with hoots and excited applause.

She continued, "The *Black Ship*... sorry, *USS Washington*, is fully manned—not taking into account all of you, of course—mostly by Humans, some Pleidians, and a good number of Symbio-Poth 3.0s."

Groans erupted from the crowd. I turned and found my niece, Sonya, standing next to Ensign Plorinne. Unlike the rest of the crew, she looked pleased by the news. No one aboard, perhaps other than her Pleidian boyfriend, Plorinne, had more experience working with the biogenic robots than she did.

I heard Stephan Derrota's Mumbai-accented voice within the ruckus, "The 2.0s were bad enough, now there are 3.0s?"

I raised a hand. "Listen up, people," I barked. "Let's give the Empress our full attention."

She smiled. "Outside this auto-hatch is a team of Symbio crewmembers waiting to show you to your quarters, dormitory, or onto the bridge. You will be leaving Earth's orbit within the hour. I'm sorry that I have no time for questions, I'm already late leaving for another ship. Because war is threatening my homeworld, I must be there. Preparations must be made."

The auto-hatch suddenly slid open.

Shawlee gestured me forward, looking unsettled. Meeting me halfway, she took my arm and guided me away from the now-exiting personnel.

"Galvin, I've just heard Weonan is under attack."

"So, the Grish... they've moved up their timetable?" I asked.

"That's just it, it's not the Grish. We don't know who they are."

"We'll scrap the plan, hightail it to—"

"No, Galvin. Keep to the mission. The Grish need to be dealt with now before they become even more powerful. Pleidians have friends, alliances, within the sector. I just need to get there. I do best face-to-face when making a desperate plea." She smiled and squeezed my arm. "Just do me one favor, Galvin."

"Of course. Anything."

"Don't wreck this ship like you have all the others. It's really a special warship... you'll see."

With that, she began making her way back onto a quansporting pedestal. She nodded toward Coogong and then looked at me. "Stay safe Galvin. You may be my world's last hope."

I opened my mouth to reply, but she was already gone.

Chapter 4

As crewmembers continued to file out, I made a beeline to where Derrota and Coogong were talking. I noticed Petty Officer Second-Class Laramie and our new Chaplain walking side by side leaving the compartment, their heads bent toward each other in what appeared to be a hushed conversation. Aubrey certainly didn't let much grass grow under her feet.

"Captain?"

Chief LaSalle stepped in front of me, looking unusually perturbed.

"Chief?"

"Uh, do you have a minute?" he asked.

I didn't but nodded. "What can I do for you, Chief?"

"I have a personnel issue. As you know, a vessel of this size requires a sizable SWM department."

"Undoubtedly," I said.

"Nine of my most dependable and experienced crewmembers have refused their posts on *Washington*. They've been transferred to other fleet assets."

I raised my brows. "*Washington* is the pinnacle warship in

all U.S. Space Navy—"

Chief LaSalle sighed heavily. "It has to do with the whole DeckPort mishap that took place several months ago."

I shook my head, not following.

"Ah, you haven't heard... okay, well, while being completed over at Halibart Shipyards, it seems a welding supervisor... um, a Calvin Peterson, entered a lower DeckPort, and exited on an upper deck somewhere."

"Okay, so what's the problem?"

"The problem was, another Calvin Peterson, exited on a completely different DeckPort on the ship."

I let that sink in. "You're saying one Calvin went in, two Calvins came out, at two different DeckPort locations?"

"Yes, Sir."

"Both unhurt?" I asked.

He gave a nod. "In perfect health, indeed. Yet, that's not where the issue lies. The conundrum is the existence of two identical Calvin Petersons. The DeckPort suffered a malfunction. Ordinarily, when personnel pass through a DeckPort, they are instantly disintegrated, their molecular composition meticulously recorded. Essentially, it obliterates the original individual, then reconstructs and reconstitutes that person's molecules at the designated DeckPort destination. However, two exact replicas of Calvin were created."

I just stared back at the man.

"To maintain order, one would have to be eliminated, to be... terminated... right?" LaSalle asked.

I contemplated that scenario, allowing the Chief to continue.

"Captain. Would you willingly cease to exist, to breathe fresh air, while convinced beyond a doubt that you're the rightful survivor? The one to continue living your life?"

"Sounds like a nightmare situation," I said.

"It turned into a legal quagmire—protests, lawsuits, and the halting of *Washington's* construction."

"What happened? Which Calvin—"

"Nobody knows. Hush-hush and all that. But, in the end, it altered how DeckPorts operate. It was actually a simple fix. DeckPorts no longer save a person's virtual composition in buffer memory. The moment one walks into the device, their molecular version is dispatched to the intended DeckPort destination. No version is stored in the buffer memory which would cause that same multiple-version fiasco."

I slowly nodded. "So, that whole Calvin thing can no longer happen."

"That's what they tell me. There's a whole slew of ship regulations and procedures associated with DeckPorts now. I'm surprised you haven't been read in," LaSalle said.

I shrugged, "Most of us were brought here without much notice," I said. "So, back to your issue... the SWM crewmembers. Bottom line... you said everything is working?"

"Yes... but they simply don't trust the technology. We went through some of this when Quansporters first came on the scene. I think there were some early mishaps with that tech too."

There were, I remembered. "All I can tell you, Chief, is to work with the new technology, the Human and Pleidian crew, and the new Symbios. We're all going to have to adjust... to all of it."

He didn't look happy with that suggestion.

I MADE MY WAY TO THE OPPOSITE SIDE OF the compartment where Coogong and Derrota were locked in a conversation about the Symbio 3.0s. They both looked up as I approached.

"You're talking about the Symbio crewmembers?" I asked.

Derrota nodded. "It will take some getting used to."

"I already knew much of the crew was not going to be human," I said. "But I figured they would be Pleidian. Now we hear... they're going to be the latest iteration of Symbios, 3.os?"

Sonya joined our impromptu meeting.

"Did you know about this?" I asked the teenager with more hostility in my voice than intended.

"Yes. But I—"

"You didn't think it important to tell me?"

Her cheeks flushed, but not from embarrassment. She was angry. "And when was that supposed to happen, Uncle Person? I haven't talked to you for weeks. You're literally the most famous person in the country, America's new boy wonder. Did you know I saw you on three different talk shows on the same night? And when you were whisked away to Australia, Austria, Amsterdam, or some other location I can't remember starting with an A, did you even bother to let me know you were leaving? Maybe ask if I wanted to come along?"

"Hold on there. You were living with Gail—that was your choice. And you're back in school; you may be smarter than everyone else, but having an actual high school diploma may come in handy when you apply to University."

Both Coogong and Derrota remained tight-lipped, their gazes shifting back and forth like spectators at a tennis match.

"Oh, for God's sake, I've had my high school diploma for two years. And I'm already working on my bachelor's degree." Sonya let out an exaggerated sigh. "See!?" she exclaimed, looking at the two Science Officers. "He doesn't know shit about me!"

Coogong raised a stick finger, his worm-like face showing bemusement. "I can address the Symbio situation, Captain."

Sonya and I glowered at each other, neither wanting to give an inch.

"I suspect your primary concern is not having a repeat of

what had transpired on USS *Adams* with the crew of Symbio 2.0s."

"You think?" I spat back, instantly regretting being snarky to the kindest and most selfless being I had ever encountered. "Sorry, Coogong. You didn't deserve that."

Derrota interjected, "What Coogong was about to say, is that these are not the Symbios of USS *Adams* or those we've interacted with on Symbio R&R Decks. Although exceptionally intelligent, they are—"

Sonya rolled her eyes, "These are dumbed-down versions. You can say it, Stephan. They all look the same as one another, they all talk the same, and they're all devoid of a personality... no ego matrix."

"Really? They all look the same?" I said, absent-mindedly scratching the back of my head. "How would you tell one from another?" I scrunched my brow. "Like, you there, fetch my shoes. Then I see ten more Symbios, not knowing which one was sent off to find my shoes."

"What are you talking about? Maybe you should just fetch your own damn shoes!" Sonya said, practically spitting the words.

Coogong, contemplating my first point, said, "Nobody said they all had the same name, Captain, or that they were indistinguishable."

"That's right, Galvin," Derrota said, nodding. "They each have name tags."

I shook my head. "So, if Symbio Todd is across the room, name tag out of my line of sight, I wouldn't be sure if it was the one who was supposed to find my shoes?"

"Again, with the fucking shoes!" Sonya snapped, throwing her hands up in frustration.

"Watch your language," I scolded.

"There is one aspect of the Symbio 3.0 situation you are

29

probably not aware of," Derrota offered. "All Symbio 3.0s are cross-networked. Todd may not have been the one directed to fetch your shoes, but he would know which Symbio had been given that responsibility and could relay that information to you."

Sonya, eyebrows arched, raised her chin slightly—as if daring me to keep arguing my ridiculous point.

"Fine. We'll see how it goes," I said. "I suppose it'll be a positive not having to deal with individual personalities. With *Adam's* batch of 2.0s, it cost me a near-mutiny, not to mention having to give them a damn ship of their own."

"Just so you know, 3.0s aren't mindless bots you can abuse and bully about," Sonya interjected as if the defender of all biogenic automatons.

I let that go as if bullying Symbios would be at the top of my list of things to do. "The good news is," I said, looking about, "... I'm more familiar with this vessel's layout than I'd initially been with *Franklin*. With that said, once we're underway, Stephan and Coogong, I'd like the two of you..." I glanced toward Sonya's narrowing eyes. "... okay, the three of you, to give me a more in-depth ship systems overview."

Three hours later, freshly showered and dressed in the uniform that was left hanging for me in the closet, I stepped out of my quarters, the weight of my new fleet command settling uneasily on my shoulders. My mood was bordering on crappy anyway, then I caught my reflection in the polished metal of the corridor. Khaki. The U.S. Space Navy had the entire spectrum to choose from, and they landed on this? A throwback to some bygone era that wasn't even a good idea the first time around.

"Khaki," I muttered, under my breath. My boots echoed a

bit too loudly in the passageway. *We're off to defend the cosmos and they have me dressed like I'm on a field trip to the desert museum.* I could almost hear the chuckles of my crew.

I continued down the corridor, each step an uncomfortable protest. "Tomorrow, they'll probably have us wearing bowler hats and vests," I thought. *Right-o, gents, let's navigate by sextant and discuss the properties of wormholes over a spot of tea,* I mocked to myself, tipping an imaginary hat to a 3.0 crewmember who shot me a puzzled look.

As I made my way toward the nearest DeckPort, I became acutely aware of how extremely high-waisted the pants were, hell, they were belted practically up to my ribcage—*this has to be a mistake.* Then there was the texture of my uniform—the khaki trousers and matching button-down felt alien to my skin. They lacked the usual elasticity, the comfortable softness I had grown accustomed to. Maybe the uniform had been starched? No. It felt like some sort of synthetic blend, a fabric I was fairly certain had been retired last century for good reason. And then there was the sound—each step I took was accompanied by the unmistakable swish of synthetic fibers colliding, a friction of textile defiance. Khaki, the epitome of the mundane, seemed to be mocking me with each stride.

As I approached the bridge, a small part of me couldn't help but wonder if there was some method to this madness. I pondered the situation: Perhaps it's all a clever ruse ... a way to make our alien foes underestimate us. *Look at those quaint khaki-wearing humans,* they'd think, *harmless as can be.* And then, when they least expect it, we strike with the precision only the underestimated can muster.

Entering the bridge, I noticed that none of my fellow officers were similarly dressed. Their on-duty daywear was dark, gray, fitted overalls. Smart and contemporary. Crewmember Davit, standing by his post at Defensive Systems, was the first to catch sight of me. He laughed, attempted to cover his mouth with a hand, but it was too late. The damage was done. Within seconds, the entire bridge was laughing.

Head held high, I continued to my awaiting Captain's Mount.

Executive Officer Gail Pristy greeted me with a bemused expression. She announced, "Captain on the bridge!" The XO saluted as did the rest of my bridgecrew coming to attention. Then Pristy leaned in and whispered, "Your real uniform is hanging in your ready room, Captain."

I shrugged, "I'm perfectly happy with this uniform, XO. In fact, I think I'll be making this khaki attire the official daywear for all USS Washington bridgecrew."

I sank into my seat, surveying my new bridge. Subdued lighting paired with brushed metal accents gave the space a sophisticated ambiance. The bridge stations were a stark black, their surfaces alive with the familiar array of colorful controls, readouts, and projected 3D mini-displays, not unlike those in the Quansporter compartment. Despite the high-tech upgrades, it wasn't a far cry from USS Franklin's setup, which had lent its architectural bones to USS Washington's design. It was like stepping into a new pair of boots that had the same fit as the old —comfortable, but untested.

Pristy, now seated at Tactical, was bringing up a myriad of forward halo displays. The primary, the largest of them, projected an awe-inspiring 3D vista of U.S. Space Navy's combined 2nd and 3rd Fleets, now called Alpha Fleet. Beyond that, was Earth, blue and magnificent. Alpha Fleet was an eclectic montage of multi-world warships. Some were massive dreadnoughts and super battle cruisers, others were smaller... frigates, destroyers, and the occasional supply carrier. Two hundred warships in all, a fleet, an armada—all under my command.

I looked to Chen at Comms. With a clenched jaw, several fingers of one hand up to an ear, the other hand a blur of motion on his board, he looked a tad overwhelmed.

Pristy glanced back at me—saw my concern. "Captain?"

"Mr. Chen's not used to the craziness that comes with flag-ship communications."

"Yeah, he's going to need some help there on comms," she said, now scanning the other stations, her eyes coming to rest on Crewmember Soto seated at Damage Control. "Mr. Soto, join Mr. Chen at Comms 2. You'll be on double duty until further notice."

"Roger that, XO," he said, tapping at his board, undoubtedly transferring his station profile to the one closest to Chen.

Chen said, "Captain, we're being hailed."

I looked to the myriad of fleet ships up on the display.

"It's Admiral Flint," Chen added.

Tempted to take it in my yet-to-be-discovered ready room, instead, I said, "On display."

Admiral Flint, a gaggle of busy officers milling around him, looked back at me. Right off the bat, I could see that the Admiral was a *tough guy*. The kind you notice. Silver-haired, cut close, with eyes that had seen things. He had a lean, hard look like he could run a mile or throw a punch if he needed to. His uniform had the crispness of freshly minted dollar bills and the kind of medals that said he didn't sit behind desks for the big fights. His voice wasn't loud, but when he spoke, it commanded attention.

"Good. I have the whole bridgecrew," he said. "This is for your crew as well. *USS Washington* is being diverted."

"Diverted? But we're the flagship of the fleet—"

"Cool your jets, Captain. This is a liquid situation. Captain Eli Griffin of *USS Tempest* will be filling in for you until *USS Washington* reunites with Alpha Fleet. That should be well before the first of your three Grish battle group conflicts."

33

I knew Griffin from past encounters—he was an ass-kisser of the highest degree and a royal pain in the keister. Letting that go, I remembered the first contact with the enemy would be the Grish Prowess Fleet somewhere deep within Tarplin 5 Sector. An estimated four-day journey, even with several manufactured wormhole jumps in between.

Flint continued, "EUNF has received credible intel about fluctuating alien signals. Powerful transmissions from an unknown source, one's that have our eggheads here on Earth more than a little nervous. Leave it to say, there's a level of sophistication to these transmissions that's well beyond our—or any of our allies'—capabilities."

"So...? We'll be on a friend or foe type investigation?" Pristy asked.

"Basically, yes. Whoever, or whatever, is transmitting these signals, is on a direct vector for Earth. The might of USS *Washington* is being deployed, letting who or whatever this thing is, know that we're in no mood for uninvited guests."

I nodded, still not sure why *Washington* needed to be the vessel to take on this seemingly less important mission. "We'll make haste and find out, Sir," I said with more enthusiasm than I felt.

"Good. The coordinates have already been sent to your Helmsman. Keep me apprised with periodic mission updates, Captain. Flint out."

The halo display went black but quickly flickered to life again, this time framing the sharp features of Captain Eli Griffin of *Tempest*.

I glanced at Chen with a *what the hell* expression; the Comms officer shook his head apologetically. Griffin had somehow forced the transmission uninvited.

His image was almost too perfect, like he'd stepped out of a recruitment poster... with his chiseled jaw and hair that was buzz-cut short. His smirk was cocksure, the kind of grin that irked before words even passed his lips.

"Ah, Quintos," he said, voice smooth, rehearsed. "Looks like I'll be taking the reins for the upcoming skirmishes, eh?"

I bristled, not just at the interruption but at the message. Griffin was young, too young for the kind of swagger he paraded. "Captain Griffin," I started, keeping my voice level. "Admiral Flint has instructed you'd be filling in, not taking over."

Griffin chuckled, a sound that grated. "Semantics, Quintos. You go chase ghost signals, and I'll handle the real work with the Grish. By the time you're back, he might just make my position permanent."

His eyes glinted with mirth, clearly enjoying the dig. I felt the urge to wipe that smugness from his face with the back of my hand. "*USS Washington* has been designated flagship for a reason, Griffin. Don't get too cozy in my chair."

Griffin's smile didn't waver. "And you have fun chasing elusive signals. Seems to me, Admiral Flint is having second thoughts about who should be leading this expedition, Quintos. But don't worry, I'll take care of the fleet and be the one to dispatch the enemy into oblivion."

The halo display snapped off, leaving a sour taste in my mouth. Griffin's face, too pretty for someone who seemed to enjoy ruffling feathers, lingered in my mind's eye—a reminder that sometimes the U.S. Space Navy didn't just test you against the enemy, but against your own.

Pristy shot a concerned look back at me. "Why are you smiling? That guy's a colossal asshat."

I grinned, leaning back in my chair. "Because, XO, watching Griffin try to command is like watching a dog walk upright on his hind legs. It's not done well, but you're surprised he was able to do it at all."

Chapter 5

USS Washington

Captain Galvin Quintos

Somewhere in deep space...

Day two into manufactured wormhole travel, all was going well with the new omninought. The look-a-like 3.0s, despite initial doubts, were proving to be reliable and competent. They were working alongside their human counterparts, seamlessly blending into the day-to-day schedule. Doubts still lingered, but for now, the situation was eerily copasetic.

Wormhole travel was non-eventful and required little from the bridgecrew, so I was allowing small groups to venture out to various parts of the ship to explore—get a feel for this amazing new warship. And that's when the first of many complaints started rolling in. The ship was fine, but it lacked something essential, a feature present on virtually all previous Pleidian Weonan dreadnoughts, as well as on *USS Franklin. Washington* lacked the kind of operational Symbio Deck the crew expected when it came to R&R activities.

It was Empress Shawlee's past influence that had been integral to those fun and often challenging alternate-world experiential activities. Sure, the ship's three top decks had been allocated, and the R&R Symbios were up there fast asleep within their long-storage recharging berths. But the typically frenzied backstage, behind-the-scenes excitement was ominously deserted and quiet. My guess was this ship had been primarily an effort of the Thine, not so much the Pleidian Weonan. In any event, the absence of it left the crew with a sense of longing, not to mention, boredom. Long-term, a bored, unhappy crew was the bane of every commanding officer.

Deep in thought, I was pacing the front of the bridge.

"We'll be coming out of WT in five, Captain," Grimes said from Helm.

He was referring to wormhole travel. I took a seat at the Captain's Mount, reminded how irritating it was to have been sent on such a superfluous errand when the fate of Earth and her allies were in such jeopardy.

The halo display suddenly cleared—a static view of a million twinkling stars came into focus.

"Admiral Flint's provided coordinates seem to be right on," Pristy said. "The signal is definitely stronger here."

I leaned forward, eyes searching the expanse. "What the hell am I looking for?"

Pristy worked the display, as a red bounding box zoomed in, and then zoomed in again. "There it is," she said. "We're almost upon it."

The object was moving through space at an incredible speed.

"A sphere?" Crewmember Davit said quizzically.

"Looks to be glowing," Soto added.

"SARAH, what can our sensors tell us about that sphere? Have we come across anything resembling that before?" I asked.

The AI's female voice responded...

There's no direct match in our database for metallic, glowing spheres of this size and apparent molecular makeup moving through space unattended. This does not *appear* to be an alien droid or other advanced technology device. *However*, per my analysis, the object is composed of a non-native material, thereby creating a paradox. In addition, the markings, overall size, and the detection of symbols or glyphs correspond to depictions found on ancient relics from Earth.

"Elaborate," I said.

Approximately 2,400 BC, ancient Sumerian seals depict a seated goddess figure with her hands clasped. To her right side, there's a floating banded sphere with distinct surface ornamentation— similar glyphs can be observed. A similar floating sphere also appears on an adjacent Akkadian cylinder seal, where a standing King or some other figure, perhaps religious, is surrounded by spheres of the same kind.

. . .

"So, you're saying this thing is from Earth?"

Negative, Captain. This sphere does not appear to be from Earth. The molecular composition of the object—a metallic alloy of some kind—was probably not derived from this galaxy. Based upon my readings, the material is much heavier than any known material... an estimated 30X heavier than even some of Earth's heaviest metals, such as tungsten.

"I can grab it with a tractor beam," Pristy suggested.

"Hold on, XO," I said, already reaching out to Derrota via my TAC-Band. "Stephan, you're needed on the bridge."

"On my way," came the Science Officer's Mumbai-accented reply.

FIVE MINUTES LATER, DERROTA WAS HURRYING onto the bridge, his attention suddenly captured by what was on the primary halo display.

"Interesting," he said. "This is what we were sent to intercept?"

"The very same," I said.

"It's about the size of a beachball, has a twenty-inch diameter," Pristy said.

Derrota brought up his tablet and began tapping. "Heavy," he said. "Very heavy."

I looked at him, my blank stare prompting him to go on.

"A solid tungsten beach ball on Earth would weigh..."

"So, you're saying *it's tungsten?*" I asked.

"Um, no. Sorry, Galvin," Derrota explained, "... I was going to offer a comparison to—"

SARAH interrupted as if not wanting Derrota to steal her thunder...

A dense tungsten orb measuring 20 inches across— comparable to a typical beach ball—would tip the scales at around 1.2985 tons. Conversely, this sphere, made from an extraterrestrial metal, has a mass weight of approximately 33.67 metric tons.

Derrota shrugged, "There you have it." He looked back up to the display. "Where are you planning on moving it to?" he asked, looking dubious. "33.67 metric tons... that's not only going to buckle deck plates, it'll crash through from one deck to the next and the next."

"Why don't we just change its trajectory? Give it a little nudge. Get it off the direct vector towards Earth and be done with it?" I suggested. "It's not like we don't have other things to do. You said it yourself; the thing's too heavy to bring onboard."

Derrota rubbed at his chin. By his expression, I could tell he didn't like my suggestion... to simply kick it into a new trajectory, then just let the thing be.

"If we were to bring the object onboard, I suggest we employ gravitational manipulation matrices, fields that generate a controlled gravimetric distortion that forms a micro-gravitational null zone, facilitating the object's levitation by nullifying the gravitational attraction within a localized area."

Pristy and I exchanged a look.

She said, "You're saying you'll use anti-gravity tech, Stephan? Like what we use for our HoverCarts and such."

"Close enough," Derrota said with a shrug.

"We have no idea how dangerous that sphere is," I said. "Obviously, it's an alien device or artifact. We don't know if it's a weapon, one that's intended for just this scenario... space-faring curiosity-seekers that let their appetite for knowledge get the best of them."

"What if this sphere, this artifact, can answer the questions we've been asking for centuries? What if it holds the key to unlocking the mysteries of the Universe?" Derrota queried.

I wasn't surprised in the least by Derrota's scientific curiosity. But it came down to one simple question. "Be honest, Stephan, do any of those benefits outweigh the looming threat this thing poses to the ship and crew?"

He took a couple of beats to think about that. "That gravitational manipulation matrix I spoke of earlier... it operates as a nullicon barrier field, creates a localized zone of nullified energy... would effectively isolate the sphere from the ship's immediate surroundings. Within this field, the laws of physics are neutralized, rendering any potentially harmful effects from the sphere, basically, inert."

"What would Space Navy Command want us to do?" Pristy asked with a slight tilt of her head.

"They'd probably be most interested in any potential weapon capabilities," I answered, then pivoted to Derrota. "Where would you want us to put it?"

"You're not seriously considering this," Pristy countered.

"Hold 536," the Science Officer volunteered in a heightened sing-songy voice. "Deck 18, Violet Sector. That's adjacent to my R&D lab."

I dragged a hand down my face and let out a breath. "Go ahead and put a tractor beam on the thing, XO, but keep the object outside the ship for now. Stephan, you and Coogong need to do more analysis. Figure out those advanced signals being generated. Before that thing is brought on board my ship, I want to know what it is, and its intended purpose. Only then will I consider bringing it onboard into that Hold."

Pristy, looking satisfied, said, "I'll get that tractor beam initialized."

I watched as Derrota hurried off; he didn't get everything he wanted, but it was something.

"Helm, set an intersecting course for Alpha Fleet," I ordered. "It's time we get back to our intended business."

Chapter 6

I sat at the Captain's Mount quietly fuming. As it turns out, having that alien sphere tethered to *Washington's* portside via a tractor beam, had necessitated shorter manufactured wormhole leaps, which, in turn, was adding another full day of travel time before we'd be rejoining Alpha Fleet. Having come out of a wormhole just moments earlier, I was anxious to get going into the next one.

"Captain," Chen said, "We have an incoming communique from EUNF Command. It's a, *for your eyes only*, priority 1 dispatch."

"I'll take it in my ready room."

The auto-hatch swished open as I approached. Stepping inside, I was reminded how similar this ship was to *USS Franklin*, including my ready room with its adjoining conference room, separated by a glass partition. Taking a seat behind the desk, a projection came alive before me. Playing catch up, I seemed to be watching pre-recorded side-by-side feeds—a two-way communique caught in mid-conversation between Captain Griffin and Admiral Flint. Griffin's face was flushed with exhilaration. The kind that came after death-defying encounters and culminated in triumphant victories.

"No, no, nooo..." I groaned, watching the shitshow play out in front of me. He was practically preening as he addressed the Admiral—not even trying to downplay any self-congratulation in his voice.

"It was a near-perfect assault," Griffin continued. "We came out of FTL right on top of them. The Grish Prowess Fleet... it was caught totally unaware."

His *cat-who-ate-the-canary* grin had me grinding my molars.

"You should have seen it, Admiral. We immediately went to battle stations, exchanged weapons fire for close to an hour, taking out two destroyers, and a battle cruiser."

Admiral Flint looked pleased, "Talk to me about Alpha Fleet losses, Captain."

"Well... sure, we sustained some losses. It couldn't be helped. A destroyer and a carrier." Griffin placed a hand over his heart. "Sir, I mourn for those brave men and women who gave the ultimate sacrifice."

"Yeah, I bet you do," I murmured under my breath.

"After that, the enemy scattered. Was inevitable once they saw how Alpha Fleet was strategically dropping in behind their assets. They did not come prepared for such overwhelming odds... and to be honest, Admiral, it wasn't a fair fight," Griffin said, flashing that pompous grin again.

Internally I was seesawing between being angry and baffled. Griffin was showboating about an unauthorized battle I should have led. Yet I couldn't deny he had pulled off quite the feat of catching Prowess Fleet off guard. I absentmindedly shrugged; perhaps Griffin had some strategist chops buried under all that bravado.

"Our frontal assault hit hard and fast," Griffin continued, relishing his audience. "The piglets tried to mount a defense but they couldn't rally in time. Not against the kind of coordinated attack I had planned." He rubbed his palms together, a fly savoring an impending feast. "We drove them back exactly as I envisioned. Smart missiles up the exhaust pipes. Flushed 'em out!" His grin had turned downright diabolical.

I doubted the assault had been as orderly as Griffin portrayed. But the Admiral was buying what Griffin was selling... this was the most concerning aspect for me. The Prowess Fleet, significantly smaller than Alpha Fleet, less than a third of the size, had managed to take down two U.S. Space Navy warships. Hell, looking at it from a percentage standpoint, the Grish had surprisingly outperformed us. And what was even more disconcerting—the Grish's ability to escape the battle so easily. How long would it be before we'd be encountering those same warships again in another confrontation?

No, Griffin's involvement in the battle had been more of a stumble than a strategic win.

Flint rapped his knuckles on his desk, matching Griffin's infectious mood. "Detailed analysis to follow, I'm sure. For now, job well done, Captain. I'll admit, I had hesitations about your unconventional command style at first. But no arguing with outcomes like this. Whatever you're doing, it's obviously lighting fires under Alpha Fleet personnel."

My jaw tightened at the undeserved praise. Every proper protocol had been eschewed leading up to this engagement. If it had been anyone other than the golden child, they'd be before a review board faster than light travel.

"I'd like to press the offensive, Admiral," Griffin said, seizing the moment. "We think we know where Torrent Fleet is holed up. No doubt, that's where the remaining Prowess Fleet is headed. We shouldn't wait. We should strike now while they're unsuspecting of our advance. After that, we punch through to the real prize, into the Drakoria System itself."

My fists clenched. He wanted to continue as acting Commander—was directly, blatantly, lobbying for it. *The ego on this guy.* I should be the one briefing Flint on the engagement, not this... usurper.

But Flint was nodding along enthusiastically. "Press the attack then. No quarter for these mongrel piglets. Stay on target, Griffin."

The transmission ended and I stared numbly at the vacant display. Griffin had made his power play and Command was now squarely behind him, leaving me dangerously close to irrelevant with my own damn fleet. My first instinct was to launch a formal complaint, but I knew how that would end—making me look petty and desperate. Nope, going by the book against this apparent golden child was not the answer. I wanted my fleet and reputation back; it was time to stop bringing rulebooks to a gunfight.

Once back on the bridge, I turned to my XO.

Pristy glanced in my direction, her face drawing into a tight expression. "That wasn't a fruitful conversation, was it?"

"I need two things. One, contact Stephan so we can get that stupid sphere brought on board."

"And the second?"

I looked to Grimes. "We set a course for Torrent Fleet's suspected coordinates. Any remaining ships from Prowess will likely be there as well. We have a battle to intercept."

WHAT I HADN'T ANTICIPATED WAS HOW LONG IT would take Derrota and his team to prepare for the sphere. The gravitational manipulation and the nullicon barrier technology required that he create a localized zone of nullified energy, a task that consumed six excruciating hours... hours that I couldn't afford to spare.

Stepping into Hold 536, the magnitude of the unfolding situation became immediately apparent. The hold itself was vast, one of the largest on the ship, equivalent to two side-by-side football fields. Lab-coated individuals bustled about, clutching tablets in hand, their focused expressions intense as they worked. Five control consoles were strategically placed, each with thick black power cables snaking across the deck.

At the center was the metallic sphere, illuminating an energy field of pink, blue, and violet hues. Its surface shimmered with an otherworldly, ethereal glow, casting an eerie luminescence across the surroundings. Defying gravity, it hung there like an enigmatic celestial body. It emanated a faint vibration, akin to a tuning fork gently oscillating in the air. Versions of those same glyphs and alien symbols etched into the sphere were now adrift, floating throughout the massive hold while slowly orbiting like streams of wispy clouds. Sure, the spectacle was intriguing and dazzling, but also, lurking at a deeper level, I felt an unease brewing. As if the thing harbored secrets that I wasn't so sure I wanted to unravel.

His anything-but-subtle footfalls clanking upon deck plates behind me, let me know Hardy had arrived. I'd requested his presence just prior to my arrival. Knowing that his inner LuMan has a vast repository—three centuries worth of interstellar experience—he might have encountered something similar to this phenomenon.

"Cool, a disco ball," Hardy said. "I'm ready to trip the light fantastic." He raised mechanical fists and attempted an awkward dance shuffle.

"Funny," I said flatly. "What can you tell me about this thing?"

"Probably not much more than that army of white-coated brainiacs over there."

"So, you've never come across anything like this before?"

Hardy put his full attention onto the sphere. "Maybe." He took several steps closer to it. "Interesting... it's old. I mean... *really* old. Twenty-five thousand years old."

"Can you decipher any of those glyphs and symbols?"

"Sure, any third-year paleography student could."

"Paleography?" I repeated.

"Paleography is a multidisciplinary field that involves the study of ancient scripts, writing systems, and inscriptions. What you're looking at here is the precursor of the Middle Egyptian language."

"That's impossible. There was no *Middle Egyptian* anything twenty-five thousand years ago."

Derrota approached looking exuberant. "Galvin... Hardy... I can't tell you how exciting this is." He glanced back to the sphere. "We've already made several key discoveries. Like with those orbiting symbols."

"You mean the Egyptian glyphs and such," I said flatly.

Watching his thunder stolen was like witnessing a child's realization that Santa Claus doesn't exist.

Derrota, having recovered, looked up to Hardy, then back to me. "The ChronoBot told you that, didn't he?"

I smiled, "That and... the sphere is twenty-five thousand years old."

"Closer to thirty thousand," Derrota corrected, looking somewhat vindicated.

"So, it's from Earth? This is human-made, somehow?"

"No. What it suggests, though, is that the alien civilization that created this device had once visited, and consequently, may have influenced early Egyptian culture."

"All those ancient hieroglyphic inscriptions on temples and tombs, pyramids, sarcophagi..." I added.

"Not to mention the *Book of the Dead*," Hardy said, his face-plate coming alive with an animated Egyptian warrior shooting an endless supply of little arrows atop a horse-drawn chariot, wheels spinning furiously.

I continued, "That was all influenced by these same aliens—"

Derrota waved away the question. "We're getting ahead of ourselves, Galvin. We should wait until we've opened her up. Take a look around inside."

"That would be some trick," Hardy said, then saw Derrota was serious.

The Science Officer pursed his lips. "I believe this device might be a sort of virtual time capsule, allowing interactive access to the knowledge base of a once great and highly advanced alien civilization."

"You make it sound like this civilization no longer exists," I remarked.

"I suspect that is the case," Derrota replied, casting his eyes downward.

My gaze shifted back to the suspended sphere. "So, what's our next step?"

Raised and excited voices were now coming from a group of scientists.

I looked toward the noise, then back to Stephan. "What's with the commotion?"

"Let's see," Derrota said, hurrying off in that direction.

I held back, gesturing a cautioning hand toward Hardy. "Despite Stephan's toddler-like enthusiasm, we need to ensure that this sphere doesn't put *Washington* or the crew in harm's way."

Hardy's faceplate was now back to his typical John Hardy visage. "Not sure what you want me to say. You brought that thing on board. By the time I tell you things are looking dire—if things take a nasty turn—it may already be too late."

"You're saying... maybe I should send it back out into the void?"

"Seems you're looking for someone else to make a captain's decision here. I'm just a lowly ship's ChronoBot, Cap." Hardy's focus snapped to the sphere. "Look! Something's happening."

Similar to how the outward projected glyphs and symbols were being illuminated, there was now a projected grand entrance. Easily twenty feet high and almost Greek in architecture, with two massive, fluted columns framed by double bronze doors, topped by ornate acanthus capitals.

Before I could say anything, the robot was already striding off in that direction. Derrota was now making a beeline toward the sphere as well. I shook my head... *in for a penny...* I hurried after them.

Derrota placed a hand on the pillar closest to him, then rapped knuckles on it, showing that it was, *somehow*, solid.

I noticed one of the scientists moving toward the entrance. "Hold on there. No one goes inside before it's deemed safe."

The scientist halted and looked to Derrota—perhaps to see if he would override my instructions.

"He's right," Derrota said. "Too dangerous. We have no idea what we'll find in there and no one is expendable."

Both Derrota and I looked to Hardy.

"Maybe you should take a look, Hardy," I said.

"Wait. So what? I'm expendable?" the ChronoBot said, feigning indignance.

"I wouldn't put it that way... let's just say you're tougher than any of us. Chop-chop. Skedaddle. Report back on what you find."

That evoked chuckles from the now-encircling crowd of scientists.

There were three marble steps leading up to the ornate threshold. Before ascending, a small plasma weapon had deployed from a hidden compartment on Hardy's upper shoulder. It pivoted left and right as if looking for something to shoot at. He bounded up the stairs, then stopped atop the landing. Looking back at me he said, "Should I knock?"

"Stop goofing around. Just go on in," I said, making a shooing gesture with both hands.

The double doors opened outward before he reached them. Again, he turned back to face us. "Maybe we send Climbo in first—"

In unison, both Derrota and I said, "Get in there!"

Seeing that the scientists were now laughing, I shook my head. "He loves an audience, don't encourage him."

It was a full ten minutes before the ChronoBot stepped back out again. His faceplate was blank, emitting its soft blue glow.

"Well?" I asked.

All eyes were on him. Hardy didn't respond, didn't move.

Derrota and I exchanged a glance.

I said, "You know, some days he's perfectly normal. He's content to forgo all the antics."

But Derrota looked concerned. "Maybe he's been... I don't know, affected somehow. His memory banks—"

Hardy raised a metallic hand. "Cap, you're going to freakin' love this place!"

Everyone relaxed—took in a relieved, collective breath.

"Place?" Derrota asked. "So, it's a place?"

"Just tell me if it's safe," I said, cutting off my Science Officer. "Safe for humans... physically, mentally, that there won't be any lingering long-term repercussions if anyone goes in there."

Chapter 7

The decision was mine to make. Hardy would stay put; his vigilance outside the sphere would be our lifeline. SARAH had informed Pristy and Petty Officer Second-Class Aubrey Laramie that they'd been selected to join my impromptu team along with me and Derrota.

Pristy arrived and saw Aubrey standing there next to me. By the look on her face, I already knew what was coming.

Taking me aside, she lowered her voice and said, "Why bring along Laramie? She's not an officer, she's not an anything."

I smiled, "She'll bring a fresh, young perspective to the team."

"Really? That's what you're going with? You're saying I'm... what? A decrepit old nag? Then maybe you should just throw a blanket over my back and put me out to pasture." Her cheeks flushed with the realization of how stupid she was sounding. "Just forget it. Why should I care who you choose?"

I watched Pristy walk away, not sure what I'd just witnessed. I joined the group standing in the sphere's hush, its glow wrapping around us. I could almost feel it waiting for us to climb the steps, to enter its mysterious recesses.

"Captain? Excuse me... Just a moment, please."

It was the new Chaplain, Halman Trent. He hurried toward us with a dissembling smile.

"Captain Quintos," he repeated, his voice smooth as soft butter. "This sphere, it's a relic of profound mystery, sacred, I'd venture to say."

I eyed him warily, aware of the put-on charm offensive. His father's legacy loomed in my mind—I wondered if treachery was genetic.

He continued, "To invade such a sanctum... one might say it's a transgression against the celestial."

Aubrey shifted beside me, her gaze uncertain, clearly caught in the Chaplain's easy, persuasive words.

"Wouldn't you agree, Miss Laramie?" Halman prodded, obviously picking up on her indecision.

"It's Petty Officer Laramie," I corrected, speaking for Aubrey. "And I'm perfectly capable of making decisions that affect my ship and crew." There again, I thought, Admiral Flint seemed to have his doubts about me of late.

Aubrey nodded slowly, a frown creasing her brow. "Perhaps it does seem a bit... invasive, doesn't it?"

I stepped between them, breaking the line of influence. "This is a pursuit of knowledge, Chaplain, not a breach of the divine. We're explorers, not plunderers."

"But at what cost?" Halman pressed, his eyes gleaming. "There are lines man was not meant to cross."

I felt the pull of his words, the easy charisma that was clearly swaying Aubrey. "Your concern is noted, but we're crossing this line. Our purpose is greater than superstition."

He tilted his head, a conceding gesture cloaked in pious superiority. "As you wish, Captain. But remember, some truths come at a steep price."

With a final, lingering glance to Aubrey, Halman retreated,

his charm offensive retreating with him. Despite the Chaplain's silver-tongued warnings, Derrota, Pristy, Aubrey, and I proceeded up the marble steps. We strode through the open doors and came to a stop inside where we were enveloped by the expansive interior's beauty and silent shimmer. A flash, and there he was. Not human, but something close.

"Welcome, cosmic travelers," he greeted, his voice tinged with a subtle accent from a place I couldn't identify. "I am Grantham, Guardian of this Archive. Your interest in the heritage of Crythara honors us." He clasped his hands together in a gesture that was at once reverent and welcoming, then inclined his head slightly. Raising his gaze to meet ours, he continued, "Crythara was a world of extraordinary splendor, a civilization known for its remarkable contributions—its wonders were many."

Grantham was distinctly male and non-human. His hair was long and straight, cascading freely down the middle of his back. His stature was tall and slender, more elongated than an average human. His skin tone was smooth and as white as fine porcelain, almost reflective, hinting at a heritage adapted to an environment far different than that of Earth. His blue eyes, large and expressive, held deeply felt emotions that drew me in... to the point I had to force myself to periodically look away. The garment draped over his frame was reminiscent of a toga, yet distinctly alien, with fibers that shimmered when he moved. His hands were slender with an extra joint in his six fingers. Behind him, off in the distance, I could just make out... others, similarly dressed. These Crytharans were a beautiful, enigmatic, alien species.

Derrota said, "Thank you, um... Guardian Grantham. Can you tell us what this place is?"

"Here, you have a bridge between the ancient and the present—whereby I am the keeper of the flame that once burned bright in Crythara's cultural realm... now lost to unavoidable circumstances." Seemingly saddened by his own words, he suddenly brightened. "The Crytharans, facing their inevitable and all too soon demise, left this Archive as an echo of their once flourishing existence, with the hope that they, as a people, will not be forgotten."

"What are we supposed to do here?" Aubrey asked brusquely. "I mean it's nice and all..." She shrugged. "... but is this like some kind of museum? Where we simply wander around?"

Pristy and I exchanged a look. This was why I brought Aubrey along. Uninhibited, she gets to the crux of things.

I smiled and held up a palm, offering a lame greeting of sorts, "Hello. I am Captain—"

"Captain Galvin Quintos," Grantham interjected. "Again, welcome. We have been expecting you. You honor us with your presence."

I couldn't tell if I was being patronized or if Grantham really was this kind and unassuming. "What Petty Officer Laramie is trying to say is, thank you for allowing us into your... um, *archive* was it?"

"Yes, Captain. You can refer to this as the Archive," the Guardian said, then turned his attention back to Aubrey. "While you are certainly free to wander, take in the splendor of this small segment of Crythara, that is by no means the Archive's true intent. Not at all."

"And what is the intent?" Derrota asked.

Grantham, looking perplexed, said, "There is only one means for you to know, to truly know, Crythara and her people..."

I raised my brows. The dramatic pause, the suspense, was killing me.

"And that is to *become* a Crytharan, of course," said Grantham.

Aubrey smiled, suddenly excited. "So, it'll be like play-acting!" She beamed at me, a kid on Christmas morning. "Like our Symbio Decks!"

Grantham, with a glint of amusement in his eye, shook his head. "That, Petty Officer Laramie, is a misunderstanding. You do not just observe or play a version of yourselves; here you embody the lives, the very essence, of any number of our civilization's most exalted figures—be it members of the Imperial Council, revered scholars, or valiant commanders. You will walk in their footsteps, see through their eyes, and feel their joys and sorrows as if they were your own. This is no mere reenactment, where you play extended versions of yourselves; it is an immersive passage through time and memory."

My spine straightened, and the hairs on the back of my neck suddenly stood at attention. "I'm sorry, Guardian, but none of us have the luxury to disconnect from our reality. This is a warship we are on; we, each of us, have responsibilities."

"You will never be disconnected, as you put it, from your reality, your ship, your crew, Captain. Think of it as having, of living, two lives simultaneously."

"And we'll think and feel both existences at the same time?" Pristy asked, looking unconvinced.

"Indeed, there's a crucial distinction," Grantham clarified. "One part of you, which we refer to as the *Watcher*, remains true to your essence, a silent observer with the autonomy to think and feel *your* thoughts. And you are free to exit the Archive whenever you choose. The other part, which we call the *Adept*, is the being you will be synchronized with. You will think, feel, and fully experience life as this Adept, this Crytharan counterpart."

"You'll have to excuse my skepticism. But, as I've said, each of us has important jobs and responsibilities. I can imagine being so immersed that time runs away from us."

"Captain, please do me a favor. Contact your robot and ask him how much time has elapsed since you stepped into the Archive."

Derrota, Pristy, and Aubrey all looked at me. I did as asked, tapped at my TAC-Band, and said, "Hardy, how much time has elapsed since we came in here?"

"Are you being serious?" came Hardy's reply.

"Just tell me."

"Ten seconds, now eleven, now twelve..."

I cut the connection and looked at Derrota. "How is that possible?"

"I honestly don't know." He raised his tablet and began tapping. He narrowed his eyes, then he turned the tablet to face me. The typically running clock on the display's upper corner was holding steady—seconds, minutes, and hours were not advancing.

"That's quite a trick," I said. "You've found a means to stop time."

"If only that were true, Captain. Alas, that aspect is little more than an illusion for those within this Archive environment."

My mind was having a hard time reconciling that statement, but Derrota seemed perfectly fine with it. He was the scientist, not me.

"May I be frank, Guardian Grantham?" I asked, attempting to sound respectful.

"Of course, Captain."

"Why do we care? We get it... that you want the whole cosmos to understand, to experience the lives of your once exalted leaders, but, at least for me, it does not translate to any desire for me to vicariously live through the eyes of a Crytharan."

Grantham met my gaze, his eyes steady. "Captain, consider this—hundreds of Archive Spheres were deployed across the cosmos. This particular Archive wasn't intended for the cosmos at large, but specifically for Earth, for you right now at this particular, consequential moment in time. Your planet stands on the cusp of a great leap, much like Crythara had once before. By stepping into the lives of our ancestors, you won't merely be witnessing another world's abject history—you will be absorbing the essence of a civilization that learned far too late the cost of its own folly."

He paused, allowing his explanation to sink in.

"Again," he continued, "the lessons you'll learn here are not abstract. They are visceral, lived experiences that will sear into your consciousness. They will offer you a foresight that history books or simulations could never provide. When you return to your own life, you'll bring with you, not just memories, but the weight and wisdom of an entire culture. This can be transformative—not just for you, but for Earth. Imagine making decisions with the hindsight of a civilization that reached the stars but fell by its own hand. The trajectory of your world could shift, ensuring that the legacy of Earth will not mirror the tragedy of Crythara."

His words carried the weight of an unspoken plea, the urgency of one who has watched a history of marvels crumble into dust.

"This is your chance, Captain. A chance to change your world's path by living a fragment of ours. It is an act of transmission, of salvation, from one world to another across the chasm of time."

He was slathering it on pretty thick, I thought. "Look, um, Guardian... I'm just one person. We are just four crewmembers on a space vessel. I think you're giving me—us—far too much credit. Our influence—"

After a slight pause, Grantham said, "Let me elucidate on the process," he began again, his voice taking on the timbre of a seasoned orator. "Having breached the threshold of this Archive, your next task is to traverse the very fabric of time and existence."

I had no idea what he was talking about. The words sounded good, but there again, the heavy sales pitch was becoming a nuisance.... like an AirCar salesman out on the lot in need of making his quota, he didn't want to hear no for an answer.

Grantham's eyes swept over the four of us to ensure we grasped the weight of his words. "The Archive is a crucible of experience, a conduit between who you are and who they are. Soon, you will feel the lives of Crytharans enveloping you, becoming part of you, even as you retain the essence of your true selves. Many important scenarios have been prepared for your arrival. You will start with perhaps the most consequential."

With a nod, he encouraged us forward. "Let's proceed inside so you can embrace the odyssey that awaits. Step forth not with trepidation, but with the courage to embrace the transformative power of the Archive."

From the unenthusiastic expressions of my three cohorts, I could tell they felt as I did—beyond hesitant. But collectively we moved farther into the Guardian's virtual world.

Then, as if a switch had been toggled, we found ourselves standing before Grantham in a new location. Our respective gazes swept across the grandeur of this aspect of the Archive's interior. It was like stepping into the annals of history, an immense marble Parthenon-style structure—the grandiosity of ancient Greece melded with an unfathomable alien world.

Towering vaulted ceilings crowned the space, fluted pillars stood like silent sentinels, and banners of vivid color draped the walls.

Off in the distance, Crytharans were absorbed in their affairs, moving with a rhythm and grace that belied their awareness of the grand structures around them, almost as if they were actors in a well-rehearsed play, ignoring the audience of newcomers. This was an alien world, yet it resonated with an air of familiarity—perhaps echoing Earth's similar historic lineage.

To our right, was an office space, or perhaps a study. It was sprawled with dignified opulence—an enclave where governmental deliberations might unfold. Behind an oversized desk, a figure was caught in a temporal stillness, his elaborate toga of golden, shimmering fabric marking him of high stature. Outside the office, several others stood equally frozen, each a statue, a testament to the suspension of time.

Grantham's voice pulled us back from our silent observations, "As you step into their space, into their very being, you become Watchers. Become the breath of life that will animate these still figures, each one holding a pivotal moment in Crytharan history within their grasp." He gestured toward the unmoving Emperor at his desk. "There, you see Crythara's last living Overlord, Emperor Jaxon."

The Guardian turned toward me. "Captain Quintos, it is here you will synchronize."

I met his gaze and then looked to my fellow crewmembers. Other than shrugs and unsure looks, I got nothing useful from them.

Guardian Grantham continued, "Join him and let the present and the past converge. Through your shared eyes, you will witness the beginning of an end. A civilization's final heartbeats."

With that, each of us was beckoned to step into our respective Crytharan counterparts, our Adepts.

I strode into the office, hesitated, then moved around to the back of the desk where the Emperor was seated. Emperor Jaxon had a commanding presence, his stature imposing, his eyes sharp and discerning, set beneath a furrowed brow that hinted at the weight of his responsibilities. He had long, jet-black hair that fell in loose waves, framing his face with an air of regal austerity.

Hesitating, I looked over to Grantham whereby he gestured for me to sit.

"Like... on his lap?" I didn't wait for an answer. Seating myself, I felt the weight of another person's world crash down on me—the full gravity of his circumstance hitting me. Momentarily breathless, I soon felt the warmth of his heart bleeding through—a heart devoted to his world but also, beyond reason, to another... to one Lady Era. I knew—as the Emperor—that I stood at a pivot point, not just for the planet as its reluctant leader, but also for myself, the Captain of USS Washington. *This is too weird.*

The melding of two awarenesses proved both exhilarating and unnerving. I experienced his thoughts, felt his feelings while staring down at the ancient prophecy scrolls scattered haphazardly across his desk. The cryptic texts spoke of forbidden paths and choices that could fracture civilizations.

I stood and moved to the window overlooking the crimson forests stretching to the horizon, so beloved and soon to be consumed. Crythara had seven standard days before the emerging black hole devoured this world. Contacting the Korrents—our age-old enemy—could, possibly, enable emergency mass evacuations. But ten millennia of rigid tradition prohibited seeking help from those heathen atheists. Violating such taboos would surely fracture the bedrock of our entire culture.

As I agonized over this impossible decision, the doors blew open. General Daxis stormed in, medals clinking, face mottled with rage. I knew then that Daxis harbored his own silent Watcher—Aubrey Laramie—lurking behind the hulking warrior's bluster.

"Begging for mercy from those heathen enemies goes against all honor!" Daxis thundered. "Better we die with dignity than debase ourselves at their feet!"

I opened my mouth to respond when Lady Era appeared behind him, copper hair flowing over her senate gown's crimson silk. Her exposed bare shoulders and exquisite long neck instantly captivated me. Her secret Watcher... of course, was none other than Gail Pristy.

As our eyes locked, I experienced the Emperor's cascade of memories—the electric passion of Era's lips that very morning, the exhilaration and longing for more... in what seemed like our final moments together.

Lady Era glared fire at the General. "How many innocents will your noble death sentence encompass, General? His Excellency seeks the path of maximum survival, not that which feeds your ego!"

Her defiance ignited General Daxis's fury. He turned on her, hand drifting toward his ornamental weapon. "Watch your tongue, Senator! Consorting with unbelievers has clearly warped all reason!"

Anger flared within the core of my being. I stepped between them, raising my hands for calm. "Nothing is gained here through personal attacks. But I will be pleading our case to the Korrents before day's end. You need to come to terms with that, General. Too many precious lives hang in the balance." Our eyes met, the decision's weight like neutronium on my shoulders. Would I doom us all by violating age-old beliefs?

"Blasphemy!" thundered Pontifax Zedar, now sweeping into the room in a cascade of rich, muted-colored fabrics. His tiered headdress aimed skyward as if to align him more closely with presumed deities hovering in judgment. With an inward smile, I knew Derrota was the Pontifax's internal Watcher.

Pontifax Zedar glared pure venom. "Have you fallen completely under this witch's spell? To consider casting scriptures aside so casually!"

I saw Era recoil at the verbal lashing. But I held my response. Striding directly to Zedar, I matched his outraged glower with cool resolution.

"The texts offer no answers here. Would you debate prophecy while entire generations perish needlessly?" I motioned toward the creeping shroud devouring the horizon. "Time has run out for platitudes."

For an instant, doubt seemed to crack the zealot's stony façade. But just as quickly his expression hardened like granite.

"Forbidden!" he railed. "You court open rebellion, fracture civil society, even damnation itself! The armies defend tradition first and will oppose this lunacy to the end!"

Zedar gestured toward Daxis, appealing to the martial code as an ally. My pulse raced as I prepared a rebuttal, but Lady Era cried out in surprise—

There in the open doorway stood Lord Clitus, his face a stone mask as he gazed upon the volatile scene. His gaudy jeweled tunic and golden circlet marked him unmistakably as among Crythara's wealthiest noblemen. He also happened to be Lady Era's husband.

Guilt flooded through me—no, through the Emperor—at the memory of Era's soft lips against his own.

"So, the rumors do hold truth," Clitus mused aloud. "You

plot open treason against ten millennia of sacred writings?" His tone brimmed with contempt.

I tasted bile, tamping down the rage threatening to choke rational thought. This pampered noble would put personal gain over planetary survival. Consorting with those threatening apocalypse to jockey for status.

I struggled to temper my response although it still echoed sharply off the vaulted ceilings. "Better offended Gods than dead children by the billion! Our window is closing!" I jabbed a finger at the creeping darkness now swallowing the horizon.

But Clitus merely kept that triumphant smirk—the look of one believing he now held all the leverage needed. He didn't get it. That none of the trivial games of wealth and influence would matter once true oblivion arrived in a handful of days.

As Clitus droned on in criticism, I caught Lady Era's eye. Our shared glance laid bare, concealed longings, words left unspoken in what little time remained. But under her husband's possessive glare, she retreated silently back into his dominating shadow.

The scene seemed to freeze, distilling to a single knife-edge moment. As Clitus and Zedar moved to block my decision, cold ambition wafting off them in waves, I realized no force in this Universe would steal Era's future. Not callous fate, not scheming men blinded by pride. Here, at love's ending, I embraced whatever chaos awaited without remorse.

"So be it then....." Zedar intoned. He swept his robes around dramatically, turning to General Daxis in tense silence. They exchanged a resolute glance—clearly intending to marshal forces against *my heresy*. With that silent agreement made, they stormed out of the study.

With a huff, Clitus took hold of Lady Era's hand, escorting her away without a backward glance, her last anguished look searing itself into my soul with finality. Now alone, I moved to compose the formal plea for Korrent evacuation assistance, willing to sacrifice even my crown against the grinding wheels of faith and tradition if it would save Crythara.

As darkness swept over the scarlet forests outside, I sank into my chair in isolation. Only history would stand judge now. Perhaps the Gods could show mercy if enough souls were spared the coming void.

Yet despite the road ahead, I harbored no regrets over my decision. Gazing out at the gathering shadows, I swore a solemn oath—neither destiny nor ambition would steal my world's future from this Universe. Here, with resolve, I embraced eternity's judgment without hesitation. For one truth shone clear—a life not seized for truth invites only empty oblivion.

The familiar swish of silk whispered from the hallway. Lady Era blew back into the room, radiant determination animating her features. Our eyes locked as I stood and closed the distance. I drew her into a fierce embrace, sensing her longing for a life free from the constraints of this new reality. Two souls, alike in their struggle, torn between fate and obligation, yearning for a forbidden future together. I pulled back just enough to see Era's face, mere breaths apart. In her eyes I saw reflected not just Lady Era's essence, but also the luminous spirit of Gail Pristy gazing back at me. Our lips met in fervent declaration, not gentle affection, but raw anguished desire born of frayed nerves and pride's fall.

And in that instant, I realized that I—Galvin Quintos—loved Gail Pristy. Perhaps, I always had.

The sound of marching boots echoed from the hall. Familiar footfalls signifying pending conflict. But Lady Era and Emperor Jaxon—Pristy, and I—stood immersed in our perfect moment, isolated from the surrounding threats.

We both grasped the one great truth—life invites oblivion when love remains unrealized. All the looming chaos seemed a trivial price to pay for this end. For this doomed love, I would stride grinning into damnation a thousand times over.

The approaching steps grew louder, more strident.

But at that moment, all distractions faded away, leaving only us, locked in each other's gaze, our lips meeting once more with determined resolve despite our defiance of the obstacles ahead.

Suddenly, my wrist began to vibrate. Jaxon had completely melted away, and I was myself again—Captain Galvin Quintos. And I was being hailed.

Chapter 8

I hurried onto the bridge, Pristy and Derrota close on my heels. The familiar face of Admiral Flint was up on the halo display. Noticing his reddened cheeks, and the flaring of his nostrils, it was clear something was very, very wrong.

"Admiral," I said, coming to a stop beside the Captain's Mount.

"There's been a serious... miscalculation within the Briant-Slivan Sector."

I racked my brain for what and where that was, certain that confusion was plastered all over my face.

"Dammit, keep up Captain! It's where Alpha Fleet, just hours ago, intersected with the Grish's Torrent Fleet."

A chill shot down my spine like a cold blade. "What the hell went down?"

"Mind your tone, Captain," Flint snapped. "It was a trap. There was no way to foresee what ultimately occurred. Any U.S. Space Navy Captain could've found themselves in the same predicament."

Pristy, at Tactical, glanced back at me with a roll of her eyes.

I inwardly seethed. It wouldn't have caught *me* off guard. A ship's captain has an arsenal of technological safeguards to sniff out potential enemy tricks, like what I suspected went down in that Briant-Slivan Sector. But it all boils down to experience. To understand your adversary—just as I understand the Grish. I wasn't buying the Admiral's spiel, and from the way I locked eyes with him, he knew it. This mess was as much on him as on Captain Eli Griffin.

"May I ask what the battle details are?" I prompted, keeping my tone measured.

The Admiral glared back at me as if debating whether to further his humiliation. "Frankly, Alpha Fleet incurred devastating losses. Fifty percent, maybe somewhat more than that. As I understand it... imminent total loss was a possibility. The order was given to jump away. To save what assets remained. I can't say it was a bad decision. Captain Griffin potentially saved thousands of lives—"

Suddenly furious, I spoke right over him, "Captain Griffin's incompetence may have put humanity's very survival on the line. Alpha Fleet was everything... the last-ditch effort of the U.S. Space Navy, hell, the entire Alliance. It was our goddamn final chance to put an end to the Grish once and for all! This is as much on you Admiral, as it is on Griffin. A clusterfuck of epic proportions!"

"How dare you take that tone with me!" Flint snapped, his face reddening. "That's blatant disrespect toward a Senior Officer. I warned you, Quintos. Now I'm having you brought up on charges the second we cut transmission." He jabbed an accusing finger. "Insubordination, plain and simple. You can explain yourself to the disciplinary board after you've had some time to cool off in the brig."

We stared at each other, both glowering.

Eventually, Flint took a steadying breath, his grip still white-knuckled on the arm of his chair. "I've sent your Helmsman the rendezvous coordinates. Just make damn sure *Washington* gets there in one piece. But fair warning - the second you drop from the warp, you'll be under Captain Griffin's command. Admiral Flint out!"

The display went black. The bridge fell silent for a solid minute.

At some point, Hardy had sidled up beside me. "I've heard the chow in *Washington's* Security Ward ain't half bad."

That evoked a smile. I turned toward Mr. Chen. "Do me a favor, put in a call for Admiral... I mean, *President* Block."

"Yes Sir. Um, it may take a while. There are a lot more hoops one has to go through to get to that level."

By now, I was betting Block had already heard the news of Admiral Flint's and Captain Griffin's epic fuckup. Unless I was reading the situation wrong, all too soon, at lightning speed, President Block would be on the horn to Comms looking for me.

My thoughts were interrupted as three super-sized, serious-looking men dressed in black security uniforms made their way onto the bridge.

Hardy zeroed in on them. "Want me to turn them into a molten gumbo of human remains?"

"That's disgusting, and no, they're just doing their jobs." I looked to Pristy. "XO, you have the Captain's Mount."

Our eyes met for a prolonged moment, neither wanting to mention what had transpired between us earlier within that Crythara realm... but perhaps not wanting to forget it either.

She flashed a crooked grin. "Maybe I'll smuggle in a cake with a hidden file."

. . .

As it turned out, President Block hadn't gotten back to Chen at lightning speed. In fact, it was now going on four hours and counting since my incarceration. I was seated within a six-foot-by-six-foot cell, three solid bulkhead walls, and one clear diamond glass partition, enabling me to see across to the opposite cell—currently occupied by another crewmember.

The man sprawled before me was a behemoth, a roll of fat at his middle... reminiscent of a deflated inner tube. His appearance was unkempt, with a thick beard framing a face topped by a wild mane of hair that seemed to have never known the touch of a brush. In his current state, he lay on his back, his booted foot tapping out the beat of a song, perhaps some rock ballad, a thumping melody pulsating in the recesses of his mind.

Still, the unkempt man held an air of mystery that intrigued me, stirred a modicum of curiosity amid my growing boredom. He was clad in the standard ship's uniform, his bulk straining against seams. Rolled-up sleeves revealed arms adorned with intricate tattoos... depictions of an illustrious career? Despite the grease stains, oil smudges, and... *breakfast leftovers?* there was an air of something, *confidence maybe*, surrounding him.

With some argument upon arrival, I'd been allowed to keep my TAC-Band. I tapped into the ship's AI and spoke in little more than a whisper, "SARAH I'd like to access someone's personnel file—"

Your command-level clearance has been suspended.

I made a face a five-year-old would have appreciated.

There's more than one way to skin a cat. I called up Sonya. "I need your help."

"I'm busy." She cut the connection.

I stared at my TAC-Band. "I can't believe you just..." I mumbled, calling her back. "Don't even think about doing that again."

"What do you want Uncle person? I'm busy."

"Busy doing what?"

"That's none of your business. I have a life of my own, one that doesn't always include you. What if I was in the mad throws of wild sex with my boyfriend?"

"You're not allowed to do that until you're at least 30," I said, but fairly certain my niece was not active in that way yet... but what the hell did I know?

"What if I was taking a shower or plopping a deuce? You can't just expect me to drop everything whenever you contact me."

"Well, are you doing any of those things?"

"No."

"I need your help, Sonya."

"Hey... I heard you've been sent upriver, thrown into the slammer, sent to the big house, gone to the pokey, the joint, the clink, you're doing a stretch, you're off to the hoosegow, checked into hotel graybar..." She was laughing now, unable to continue.

"Very funny, clearly you've been busy with your thesaurus."

Sonya was still laughing.

I waited, then said, "Are you done?"

"Yeah. At least until I can think of some more."

"In my current predicament, I no longer have command-level access to SARAH, more specifically, to crewmembers' personnel files."

"And you want me to hack something for you. Right? To jeopardize my good standing on this ship, commit felonious actions that could put me in the brig myself?"

Before I could answer, she said, "I'm in. What do you need?"

"The personnel background on the prisoner adjacent to me in Cell #8. And try to keep your voice down, you're being a bit loud."

"Loud? You're asking for my help, and you're *insulting* me?"

I heard the rhythmic tapping of fingers on a keyboard.

"Huh, looks like you're in Security Confinement Hold #7."

"Yeah, I need the info on the crewmember next to me."

"Hush! Let me work. Looks like there's only the two of you serving time." She started to laugh again.

"Sonya!"

"Alright, so it looks like we've got Kaelen Rivers, age thirty-eight, holding down the fort as a Senior Engineer in Engineering and Propulsion. Seems the guy's a bit of a legend in his own right. And get this—he's straight outta some small, backwoods town in Tennessee, where they probably measure success by how well you can fix a lawnmower. Raised on a steady diet of grease, gears, and probably too much fried chicken, he cut his teeth in his old man's workshop. Oh, and the dude's brainpower? Off the charts. Apparently, he even graced MIT with his presence, picking up a bunch of fancy degrees along the way. And as if that's not impressive enough, he's been shaking up the propulsion game within the U.S. Space Navy, earning more pats on the back than a dog with fleas."

I kept my eyes on Kaelen as Sonya continued filling me in on his life story. He was now standing, looking at something at the top back corner of his cell. Stepping up onto the molded bulkhead bench, he was now strategically pounding specific spots with his clenched fist.

"But wait, there's more... His thirst for knowledge wasn't exactly confined to the straight and narrow. Turns out, he's got a rap sheet longer than a holographic receipt at a HyperMart's clearance event. This guy's a renegade engineer, always seesawing the line between brilliance and sheer madness. Unauthorized experiments? Check. Clandestine dealings? You betcha. Seems like our Kaelen here knows how to stir up trouble faster than a bull in a china shop. That's how he ended up here in the U.S. Space Navy. It was either here or jail."

"Looks to me, now he's got both," I said.

"Good point. Can I go now?"

"Yes, and thank you," I said, ending the connection.

Somehow Kaelen had managed to pop out a tiny edge of one of his cell's high-up wall panels. Using his fingertips, he was now attempting to pry open the panel.

I raised my voice so he would hear me through two layers of diamond glass, "You know, even if you get that panel off, there's no way you'll be able to reach any kind of opening you can escape through. And it's too high, anyway."

Without looking at me, he said, "I'm not trying to escape."

"Then what are you doing?"

"Looking for the interconnect conduit to the camera." He pointed to the same small black dome that was featured high up in all the cells.

"I don't like cameras tracking my movements."

"It's not like you're doing much moving. You're in a jail cell."

"Just the same, I don't like it." It was then that Kaelen had managed to pry open the panel just enough to slide a flattened hand up behind it. He fiddled around for a few moments, then pulled. Something *snapped*.

Looking pleased with himself, he repositioned the panel, pounded it back into place, and jumped down to the deck. Now, for the first time, he looked over to me, doing a double take. "Crap. You're the Skipper."

"That, I am."

"How much trouble am I in."

"You mean, how much *more* trouble are you in?"

"Uh, yeah, that."

I gestured with a wave of a hand. "Don't stress about it. I have misdeeds of my own to worry about."

Nodding, the big bear of a man sat... in the process of lying down, getting comfortable.

"What did you do, specifically, to warrant a stay in here?"

He turned his head toward me. "Nothing so bad."

"I'm not judging."

"I... um, commandeered a couple of maintenance bots. Made a few minor adjustments to their operational efficiency."

"That sounds more like something you should have been commended for."

He shrugged.

"What kind of operational efficiency are we talking about?"

"Oh you know, just a little tweaking here and there. Squeezed some extra speed out of their actuators. Upgraded the sensor resolution on their optical units."

I nodded. "Useful upgrades I'd think. So, what exactly was the problem?"

"Well, the thing is....." He scratched his beard, averting his eyes. "I also may have made some modifications to their behavioral protocols. The new situational awareness logic I added had some... unintended effects."

I raised an eyebrow. "Do tell."

"It caused them to be a bit more mischievous, you could say. They started playing harmless pranks on way too many of the 3.0s that were milling about. Hiding their tools, moving mop buckets around, smearing slippery Gelapack jam on the soles of their boots." He chuckled at the memory. "Anyway, my supervisor didn't find it so funny. Said I *violated operational parame-*

ters." He used air quotes to make his point. "And *compromised core functions.* So here I am."

I smiled and shook my head. "Creative boredom does seem to get you into trouble."

"Yeah, well, at least it keeps life interesting." He turned onto his side to face the opposite wall.

I guess this conversation was over.

Chapter 9

The loud bellowing of an overhead Klaxon awakened me. SARAH's voice soon followed...

Battle Stations...
Battle Stations...
All Essential Crewmembers
Report to Your Stations.

I got to my feet and tried to see down the length of the hallway toward the guard's station but couldn't get a clear view. "Hey! What's going on?" I yelled. "You need to let me out of here!"

Kaelen sat up, smirking in the opposite cell. "Right, because prisoners demanding to be sprung always works wonders," he said, his voice laden with sarcasm. "I'm sure the guards will be handing over the keys any minute now."

I heard approaching footsteps over the din. Expecting to see the guard, I was surprised to see it was Sergeant Max Dyer, all kitted out in a combat suit.

"We've been sent to spring you Cap," he said. Looking back down the hall, he yelled, "Open Cell #7 and #8!"

There was a click and a clank—both inset diamond glass doors swung open. Kaelen and I stepped out of our respective cells.

I saw the rest of Max's team down by the guard's station—Wanda, Ham, Hock, and Grip, each donning combat suits, carrying shredders.

"What's going on?" I yelled over the noise. "Where are the guards?"

"We're under attack," Max said. "Have no idea where any of the guards wandered off to. Maybe the head."

"They went to the head together?"

"Look, Cap, we need to go." Max turned to leave.

"Wait! Why are you here? What's with the assault gear?"

"We've been boarded, Captain. We seriously need to get moving... like right fucking now. This deck's already lost."

Kaelen, already heading for the exit, disappeared around a corner.

"Lost? How is that—"

Max, physically manhandling me forward now, said, "Move it, dammit! Don't make me carry you!"

Catching up to the others, we ran from the ship's brig out into the adjoining passageway. I caught sight of Kaelen disappearing into the DeckPort.

Wanda yelled, "Circadian Platform, Deck A!" She was the next to enter, with Ham, Hock, and Grip filing in right after her. Max and I brought up the rear.

WE ENTERED THE ROTUNDA, A SPACIOUS circular chamber, located on the Circadian Platform at the ship's apex. This area serves as a nexus, linking to the bridge and featuring an expansive and captivating 3D navigational display known as the Gravity Well—which to my surprise, was currently in use.

I spotted Pristy at one of the command podiums, Derrota, Hardy, and several of the bridgecrew huddled next to her.

Taking in the ginormous 3D Gravity Well display at the Rotunda's center, I got a quick visual of what was happening... which wasn't much. I did notice several dark, amorphous splotches amongst the stars, but no enemy ships. I wondered if perhaps they were cloaked—otherwise, why all the fuss?

Reaching Pristy and the others, my XO said, "They were there when we emerged from the wormhole. And before you ask —no, I don't think they were expecting us. This wasn't some kind of ambush."

Bewildered, I looked back out to the Gravity Well. "What the hell are you talking about?"

Hardy spoke up, "They're *Voidlings*. It's been several centuries since I—well, LuMan—had encountered any of these pests."

I tried to make sense of what I was looking at.

"Captain," Derrota began, his tone urgent. "These formless entities inhabit the vacuum of space, capable of manipulating their molecular structure to navigate through solid objects... including starships. Picture swirling masses of dark energy, billowing clouds of deep purple and black hues. Innocuous looking to passersby."

I frowned, processing the information. "You're talking about those splotches?" I asked, gesturing to the Gravity Well.

"Yes, of course, that's what we're talking about," Pristy said wryly.

"Are they intelligent?"

"In a rudimentary sense," Derrota replied, his expression grim. "They possess a basic form of intelligence, allowing them to analyze and adapt to their surroundings."

"And what can they do to us? To the ship?" I pressed.

"They're a direct threat to both. Upon contact, their dark energy tendrils can drain the life force from living beings, while also eliciting a caustic chemical effect. They target primary systems, disrupting power sources and disabling essential equipment."

"Nobody's died yet but HealthBay's filling up fast," Pristy said. "Mostly first- and second-degree burns. Voidlings' vaporous tendrils are like coming into contact with hydrochloric acid. Chief Knott suggests appropriate environmental or combat suits for anyone coming into close contact."

I frowned. "So, how do we fight them?"

Derrota's gaze sharpened as he studied the creatures. "We'll need a combination of strategy and specialized equipment."

"Energy-based weapons don't do much, if anything," Hardy volunteered.

"You've fired on them... the splotches?"

"Voidlings," Pristy corrected. "And we're not sure if they're all part of the same organism."

"We will need to find a better way to destabilize their energy forms," Derrota said. "Maybe by deploying containment fields."

Pristy gestured toward the Gravity Well. "For now, we're sealing off affected areas of the ship. Trying to prevent any further infiltration."

"But that's not working very well," Wanda said, joining the conversation. She lifted her arm to display the corrosive, acid-like damage that had ravaged her combat suit.

I turned back to Hardy. "Did LuMan devise a means to fend them off... two centuries ago?"

"Not really," the ChronoBot said. "Sometimes Voidlings just seem to get bored and wander off after a while. But that can take weeks and by then the damage... well, it's not pretty."

Derrota nodded, continuing to look perplexed.

"You have to have some idea of what to do, Stephan. That containment field idea sounded promising."

"The problem is deployment. The Voidlings are hard to detect, and... out in space... they'd be impossible to round up. Sorry, even Coogong is at a loss. Still, we do think it will have to be a technology-based solution."

I let out a frustrated breath, then had a thought. "Someone bring me Kaelen Rivers."

Pristy, annoyed, made a *who the hell is he* expression. "Where can we find him... this *Kaelen Rivers*, and more importantly, what can he bring to the party? We already have the sharpest minds working on the problem."

"He's an Engineer," I said. "Was in the cell across from mine in the brig. A meddlesome genius. We should look for him in Engineering and Propulsion."

"Sounds like my kind of troublemaker," Hardy commented. "SARAH will know where he is."

Chapter 10

I was in my ready room seated at my desk, trying to convince SARAH to get me returned to Command-Level status, when Chen's voice interrupted my tirade.

"Captain, I have a high-priority communique for you."

"Who is it? Can it wait? I'm in the middle—"

"It's the President, Sir."

"Oh... of course, put him through."

The halo display came alive with an exasperated-looking President Cyprian Block. Forgoing any niceties, he said, "Dammit, Galvin... USS *Washington* should have reached the rendezvous point hours ago. You acknowledged receipt of the coordinates. What's the problem? You do realize I am no longer a Space Navy Admiral. The office of President keeps me more than a little busy these days."

I stared back at him. So... he wasn't going to bring up the whole Alpha Fleet fiasco? The loss of a hundred warship assets, the many thousands of service members now dead because of an epic fuckup?

"Apologies, Sir. Communications have been dark due to extended wormhole travel. Upon exiting the most recent wormhole, we were attacked. Although that might not be the best description."

"Attacked? By whom?"

"They're called Voidlings and we're dealing with it, Sir. And yes, I'm well aware Admiral Flint is in an uproar over our delay—"

"Oh for shit's sake, what are you rambling on about? Admiral Flint? He's gone."

"Uh... gone, Sir?"

My ready room auto-hatch suddenly slid open, and Crewmember Chen hurried in. He handed me a tablet with several lines of text written on it:

Captain, we are just now receiving an influx of bottle-necked past communiques from U.S. Space Navy Command. Admiral Flint has been relieved of duty. You have been put back in command of what is left of Alpha Fleet.

I handed the tablet back to Chen and waved him away.

"Sir, I'm just now receiving my updated orders."

"I want you at the rendezvous point posthaste, Captain. Make your assessment of the situation, readiness of the fleet, and then get back to me."

"From what I understand, the losses are..."

Looking annoyed, Block said, "You know what they say when life gives you lemons?"

"Make lemonade?"

"No. When life gives you lemons, swap them for limes and make a fucking margarita. Do what you do best, Captain. Improvise and find a way to turn this into a win."

· · ·

Two hours later, seated around the Captain's Conference Table, Derrota, Coogong, Hardy, and I sat silently, waiting for one more crewmember to arrive.

Derrota said, "Galvin... perhaps I can be notified when he arrives. My time could be better spent—"

"Let's give him a few more minutes, Stephan," I said, doing my best not to show my impatience.

Hardy, too bulky for the frail chairs, was completing his fifth circuit around the room, this time walking backward. The ChronoBot moonwalked past the passageway-entry auto-hatch... just as it slid open.

Kaelen Rivers sauntered in.

"Hey... " the Engineer said, dodging Hardy and taking the empty seat next to Coogong. They looked at each other. "How's it going, little man?"

Coogong smiled. "Quite well, Crewmember Rivers. Thank you for asking."

"You're late, Kaelen," I said.

I waited for an apology or an excuse, but none came.

He scratched at his messy beard, suddenly captivated by Hardy. "Appendages engineered with frictionless kinematics, yes?"

Halting his backward groove, Hardy glanced back at the impertinent Engineer. "Actually, it's all done with rubber bands. Two hours each morning, I have my loyal pet hamster, Mr. Sprockets, wind me up for the day."

Kaelen smiled at that. "Funny. A ChronoBot with a sense of humor."

"We're waiting, Kaelen," I said. "What have you come up with."

The Engineer looked to the overhead while taking in a tedious, long breath.

"Captain..." Derrota said. "I am very busy, and clearly, Mr. Rivers has nothing to offer—"

"It's actually very, very, *very* simple," Kaelen said, turning his attention to Derrota and then to me. "Really... Captain? These are your best minds?"

"Uh... just to throw it out there, I never said I was anyone's best mind," Hardy offered back.

"Just go on, Kaelen. And how about you forgo any further dramatics?"

The portly, scruffy Engineer placed a hand over his heart, and said, "We need to set the stage for *amore*... for some Voidling romance." He smiled and waggled his eyebrows, then followed up with an adolescent back-and-forth fist motion. "You catch my drift, Cap?"

Perplexed, I opened my mouth to speak—

"Ingenious!" Hardy said.

Derrota was smiling now too. "They are organic..."

Coogong said, "It would take some time in the lab..."

"Oh, for shit's sake, somebody tell me what you're all going on about," I said, feeling like the only kid in class that doesn't know how to speak Pig Latin.

"We're talking about pheromones," Kaelen said. Again, came the waggling eyebrows. "What better method to capture someone's attention than by appealing to their primal instincts?"

I let that sink in. "Voidlings have primal instincts? They can..."

"Yeah, they screw like rabbits," Kaelen said. "But not in the sense your dirty mind is thinking."

"Voidlings drift through the darkness of interstellar space, surviving on sparse background radiation for decades at a time," Derrota explained. "This extremely low level of electromagnetic energy allows them to slowly self-replicate by integrating high-energy protons and electrons from cosmic rays into new crystalline biomatter."

Derrota paused, taking in blank stares.

"Essentially, they utilize ionizing radiation to power incredibly inefficient reproduction, with new Voidlings separating only once every 50-100 years," Coogong jumped in. "Their sensitivity to cosmic rays has led them to develop complex pheromone chemical signaling to find mates across vast gulfs to reproduce."

Kaelen, looking impressed, said, "However, when Voidlings detect electromagnetic emanations from spaceships or stations, they flock toward them. The concentrated energy sources represent a massive spike in available electromagnetic power. Upon infiltration, the sudden influx of shipboard EM energy triggers a reproductive frenzy. No longer limited by scarcity, juice-rich power systems send the Voidlings' biomolecules into overdrive. They voraciously unravel and rapidly recombine ambient particles into daughter crystals—utilizing metal alloys and composites instead of cosmic rays. The teaming reproductive phase generates huge blooms of juvenile Voidlings."

"So, we're like one big incubator for them?" I asked.

Kaelen shrugged, obviously underwhelmed by my question.

"Ships represent instant population booms that allow the Voidlings to propagate much quicker," Derrota said. "Once back in the void, they return to eking out a meager existence on traces of interstellar radiation between encounters."

"We just need a pheromonal enticement that's more exciting than USS Washington," Hardy asserted.

"The equivalent of sexy hot pants and halter tops, baby!" Kaelen said with creepy exuberance.

Seeing Coogong's perplexed expression, I waved away the Neanderthal comment. "What do we need to do? How do we implement this, um... strategy?"

Kaelen suddenly stood up and gave Coogong a friendly smack on his shoulder, "Come on boys, how about you show me what's in your lab."

It was another eight hours later before Kaelen was ready to test his pheromone chemical signaling process on the Voidlings. Because we were dealing with Voidlings both within the ship, as well as out in space, Kaelen had explained this was going to be a process that extended out thousands of miles in every direction. Derrota had offered up the Gravity Well display to showcase the test, which everyone would be able to watch in real-time.

Gathered around the outer railing of the Gravity Well most of the bridgecrew and other department heads were present, including Chief Knott from HealthBay, Chief LaSalle from SWM, Chaplain Trent... with Petty Officer Second-Class Aubrey Laramie at his side—still behaving like a love-struck groupie. Others included Captain Ryder and Akari James, along with Max and his team. Virtually everyone on the ship had been affected by the annoying Voidlings, brandishing bandaged arms, hands, and other body parts. Several crewmembers were itching small patches of exposed, reddened skin.

As if on cue, Hardy said, "Now hear this... all crewmembers! Please refrain from attempting to pet or feed the Voidlings. Sure, they may look innocent, but trust me, they are far from sweet, domesticated companions. That is all."

Derrota and Kaelen, who was holding a tablet, stood at the podium.

Pristy, wedging herself to the front of the crowd next to me, said, "Where's Coogong? Wasn't he a part of this dog and pony show?"

Chief Knott spoke up, "He's recuperating in HealthBay.

Seems some of the Voidlings found a way to penetrate his EV-Suit."

"Oh... that's too bad."

"Don't worry," I said. "He's watching via 3D optic feeds."

She nodded. "What are we waiting for then?"

I wasn't exactly sure. I looked out to the Gravity Well which was basically the inky black void of space... interspersed with the lighter, purplish Voidling splotches.

Kaelen cleared his throat and tapped on the top of the podium's microphone. "Hello? This thing on?"

Several people groaned.

"This shouldn't take more than a few minutes," he continued. "For your viewing pleasure, I have color-enhanced the chemical signaling pheromones." He touched something on his tablet with his index finger, and said, "Five, four, three, two, one!"

The Gravity Well changed to a new perspective, one that showed both USS Washington, as well as the surrounding space. A bright red mist spewed from dozens of ship maneuvering thrusters. The mist moved away from the ship, heading farther out into space. Then, as if it had a mind of its own, it started to coalesce into one large shape.

Pristy leaned forward, her eyes narrowing. "Is that..."

Aubrey Laramie leaned into Chaplain Trent, and finished Pristy's sentence, "Look Halman, it's a big red heart! You see it?"

Trent put an arm around the Petty Officer, looking at her with a smarmy smile.

I caught Pristy's eye roll and chuckled.

She glanced over to me, then in a faux sexy Marilyn Monroe voice said, "Oh look, Captain... isn't it just wonderful?"

Things were happening within the Gravity Well. Out in

space, all of the purplish splotches were now moving toward the big, red vaporous heart.

Someone said, "Look, they're leaving the ship!"

Sure enough, a near-constant parade of purplish splotches pirouetted away from the hull like rebellious jellyfish escaping an interstellar aquarium, adding a surreal touch to the vast expanse of space.

IT TOOK ANOTHER FIVE MINUTES BEFORE THERE WAS stillness; it appeared as if all of the Voidlings were now huddled together within the heart-shaped, chemical-signaling pheromones.

Derrota looked over to me from his perch at the podium. "The ship has been freed from all Voidlings." He looked to Hardy for verification.

Hardy said, "They've gone, and not a one of them bothered to say goodbye."

Derrota, looking serious, said, "We can destroy them. A single fusion smart missile would be sufficient."

All heads pivoted toward me.

"What do you say we just leave them be, Stephan?"

Chapter 11

Vintarra Nebula
USS Washington

Captain Galvin Quintos

ollowing our brief stop to address the Voidling situation —just two days later—*USS Washington* materialized from its manufactured wormhole, entering the Vintarra Nebula.

Assembled around the Gravity Well once more, the initial gasps of wonder from the crew faded, and a hushed reverence fell across the Rotunda as we all stood transfixed by the majestic sight spread out before us. I stared wide-eyed into the swirling emerald and violet hues of Vintarra Nebula, humbled before its scale and epic beauty. In the quiet, I wanted to commit every detail to memory—how the amorphous clouds seemed to shift and glimmer, stellar gases flowing in immense patterns my mind struggled to comprehend.

Derrota was speaking to Lieutenant Hargreaves and Ensign Lira in a lowered voice, "Vintarra's origins reach back billions of years, when two massive star systems had collided violently, their dying stars rupturing and spilling out layers of fiery stellar gases. Over eons, the disrupted clouds of hydrogen, helium, oxygen, and sulfur gases cooled and spread into the swirling, colorful layers of the stellar breeding grounds that now surround USS Washington. Within these beautiful, tenuous veils of gas, the gravitational variances are just now, slowly, giving birth to new stars... to new star systems."

"I feel bad Chen is missing this," Soto murmured.

Davit gestured with a backward glance. "He's literally thirty feet behind us on the bridge," he said in a hushed voice. "All he has to do is come take a quick peek."

I glanced back at Chen who was still trying desperately to raise Alpha Fleet on comms. I knew nebulas like this notoriously scrambled transmissions, but an uneasy dread was taking hold, nonetheless. It had been hours—no staticky, garbled answers back—just silence hanging... ominous and foreboding.

Then I saw it. Remnants of the already-ravaged Alpha Fleet from the recent attack led by Captain Griffin... many of the once-virile warships were now decimated, floating hulks. Had the Grish already tracked and intercepted the rest of the fleet, eviscerating the last shreds of hope for Earth? Were we staring at this brilliant stellar frontier—at the moment when humanity's final defense against oblivion stood revealed—fall in flashes of fire, into some unseen darkness lightyears away?

The beauty of the nebula abruptly became icy and threatening to me as I pictured Earth in my mind's eye; many of the loved ones of my crew may have been obliterated without us being aware. Chen's failure to contact Alpha Fleet triggered the sobering realization—the ongoing war and the possibility that

Earth had already been defeated, erased, without our knowledge.

"Got 'em!" Chen's voice erupted with excitement.

I spun toward the bridge, seeing Pristy already sprinting back inside.

Fast on her heels, I arrived at the Captain's Mount, seeing an officer projected up on the primary halo display.

Chen said, "Captain, this is Captain Longmont of *Capital Fight*."

My eyes widened, locking onto the figure before me—the infamous Captain Longmont. He was commanding dreadnoughts while I was still a wet-behind-the-ears U.S. Space Navy cadet. Longmont's presence seemed to fill the bridge, his stature towering, even in the holographic projection. I couldn't help but notice the Captain's unconventional appearance... his hair, a wild mane of unruly curls, the sleeves of his uniform rolled up, revealing smooth, hairless, muscular forearms. Despite his unorthodox demeanor, there was an undeniable aura of confidence surrounding the man—good, this was an officer I could deal with.

Longmont was the first to speak, "Fleet Commander Quintos, good to have you back where you belong."

"Where I belong?" I asked, not sure what he was saying.

"Commanding Alpha Fleet... or should I say, what is left of Alpha Fleet."

"Thank you," I said. "How about we dispense with the niceties and get right down to business with a situation report? What are Alpha Fleet's current assets?"

The muscles in Longmont's left cheek twitched. His voice tinged with frustration as he said, "You're not going to like what you hear, Sir. As of now, Alpha Fleet is comprised of forty-five warships, including five dreadnoughts: *USS Capital Fight, USS Tempest, USS Sentinel, Intrepid*, a Thine dreadnought, and

Relentless, a Pleidian dreadnought. And we still have our four precious battle cruisers—USS *Renegade,* USS *Valkyrie,* USS *Leviathan,* and the Pleidian super cruiser, *Eclipse.*"

I was taken aback by Longmont's discouraged tone. "And what about the rest of our forces?"

Captain Longmont's shoulders slumped, his demeanor growing increasingly sorrowful. "The Thine and Pleidian assets did not fare well, most being destroyed over the course of the two battles. Other fleet vessels consist of a mix of destroyers, frigates, troop transports, and other vessels. Add to that, various support ships, and smaller craft. Uh... few assets are battle-ready at this point. And one more thing, the loss of life has been catastrophic. HealthBays are packed with the injured." He stopped, looked down, and sniffled. "I'm sorry, Captain." He took in a breath and continued, "Needless to say, all ships are operating with minimal crews."

Pristy had already called up a logistical display, listing Alpha Fleet's actual assets and ship conditions. It painted an even worse picture than Longmont's report.

Sensing Longmont's frustration... or was it humiliation... I said, "Understood, Captain. Thank you for the detailed update."

Captain Longmont, his tone softening slightly, admitted, "Look... I know it's not nearly enough, Captain Quintos. Two hundred ships down to a mere forty-five... we've taken hit after hit from the Grish. Truth is, I'm not certain if we can turn the tide with what we have left. Every loss weighs heavily on the remaining ship Captains. The future of Alpha Fleet is, well, uncertain at best."

I didn't like what I was hearing. This man was once the epitome of valor within the U.S. Space Navy. Now, he'd been reduced to a little more than a shadow of his former self, worn down by two devastating defeats at the hands of the Grish and the weight of so many lives lost under his command. All of it had clearly taken its toll. It was disheartening to witness such a decline in someone I had admired for so long.

"Are you done?" I asked, blank-faced.

"Sir?"

"With your pity party?"

I glanced to Pristy. "XO, remind me to arrange for a crate of tissues to be transported to the bridge of USS *Capital Fight*. Ensure they're of the extra plush variety." I pivoted towards Longmont. "Ought to assist with the teary whimpering, the sniveling, happening aboard that vessel, wouldn't you agree, Captain Longmont?"

His eyes narrowed, a storm brewing within them, anger rising like a tidal wave. "How dare you speak to me like that. Who the hell do you think you are? I'll have you know—"

I interrupted, "There's some of the spirit I've been waiting for. Maintain that intensity! Channel your fury. I understand you're itching for a fight but save your wrath for the real enemy. The Grish are the ones who've wronged you and Alpha Fleet, not me."

He stared back at me, seething, but perhaps comprehension sinking in.

I said, "Tell me, Captain. Of the thousands of surviving Alpha Fleet crewmembers, do they reflect this same dismal, hopeless attitude?"

He didn't answer right away. He didn't answer at all, but eventually, he slowly nodded.

"Where is Captain Griffin?"

Captain Longmont snapped out of his internal reverie. "He has been in meetings with the High Command, um, due to the unexpected turn of events. He's still onboard *Tempest*, Sir, but his XO has taken over in the interim. Captain Griffin is expected to resume command soon. Due to our losses, Admiral Flint has been—"

I held up a hand, now remembering. "I'm aware of Admiral Flint's, um, reassignment."

I blew out through puffed cheeks. Not only had Alpha Fleet been physically decimated, but both crew and command were wallowing in despair—spirits shattered by overwhelming loss. Warships were operating with skeleton crews. This wouldn't do...

I inwardly smiled, recalling the trio of Symbios I'd encountered in a corridor just yesterday. Hurrying toward the bridge, I'd rounded a corner and stumbled upon a peculiar sight— three Symbio 3.0s, of course, identical-looking, valiantly struggling to upright their toppled HoverCart, its cargo of cleaning supplies scattered across the deck.

"Gracious me, apologies, Captain," they said in unison as they mimicked the throwback antics of the *Three Stooges*. One gripped an edge and heaved, while another attempted to balance bottles atop the cart, only to send them tumbling once more. The third, slipping on a puddle of soap, caused the cart to titter-totter, and collapse with a resounding crash.

By now, I was suppressing laughter at their earnest yet chaotic efforts. If only I could instill some of their unyielding optimism and playful spirit into the despondent crews of Alpha Fleet... and Lord knew, *Washington* had more than enough of these next generation of Symbios to spare.

I snapped myself back to the present, relaying the next steps to Longmont, "Captain, here's the plan. As discussed, Alpha Fleet is currently unprepared for another confrontation with the Grish. Our vessels have sustained extensive damage. While we work on repairing our assets, we will also focus on replenishing diminished ship crews while also restoring the spirits of our weary crewmembers. I will start by rotating select crewmembers from *Washington* over to other fleet vessels, starting with *Capital Fight*."

Captain Longmont shifted in his seat, averting his eyes from the holographic display. He then nodded halfheartedly, but I could sense the hesitation lingering beneath the surface.

"Rotation will allow for some much-needed rest and recuperation," I continued. "Morale and focus have clearly suffered, but interaction with *Washington's* crew should help lift spirits."

I studied Longmont's reaction. His eyes remained downcast. *Oh for shit's sake, what's with this guy?*

I filled the awkward silence once more, "We'll start small at first, maybe 100 Symbio 3.0 crewmembers per ship at a time."

Longmont's gaze drifted to the side. "Uh... you didn't mention the crewmembers would be Symbios."

"You have a problem with that, Captain?"

"Captain Quintos," Longmont began cautiously, "... it's not that I have an issue with the Symbios specifically, it's just... after everything we've been through, morale is fragile. Bringing in unfamiliar crewmembers could add more strain. You understand."

I squared my shoulders, meeting Longmont's gaze with a steely resolve. "No, Captain, I don't understand. And let me be more direct. I'm not asking for your permission. In fact, I believe the Symbios' presence will be beneficial in boosting morale and fostering camaraderie among our crews."

Longmont's expression remained guarded, but he nodded curtly in acquiescence. Clearly, he was not entirely on board with the plan. I didn't care. Longmont and the rest of the Captains needed all the help they could get to rally Alpha Fleet.

I turned to Pristy, "XO, I want you to oversee this, and begin the rotation process immediately."

Pristy eyed Environmental Systems. "Crewmember Barrow, that's your assignment."

The crewmember offered back a brisk nod. "On it, XO."

"Captain Longmont," I said, "... we will stand by to provide any assistance needed during the rotation process. Crewmember Barrow will coordinate assistance from *Washington's* SWM and Engineering to expedite ship repairs. Together, we will rebuild Alpha Fleet into a force to be reckoned with once more."

Longmont's eyes met mine, a flicker of that same reluctance passing through his gaze before he composed himself. "Understood, Fleet Commander Quintos. We appreciate your support."

His words sounded accommodating yet lacked sincerity. A wave of frustration washed over me. Did he fail to understand the critical nature of this situation?

"We will need a comprehensive accounting of asset damages—repair assessments, the whole 9 yards. From what I understand Washington has substantial parts and component replication capabilities."

I studied his weathered face, searching for any glimmer of the valorous leader who had inspired so many. But all I found was the same dull resignation.

"Yes, yes, that's fine Fleet Commander Quintos. We certainly will need all that."

My fingers curled into fists at my sides. I wanted to reach through the halo display and shake the man by his shoulders. To tell him we were on the verge of losing everything, and his moping wasn't helping. The crews that were still present would require leaders they could trust, not just one more wellspring of melancholy. But I held back, inhaling slowly. Berating him wouldn't provide the jolt he required. I needed a new approach, no matter how vexing his despondency was.

"We'll, um, uh... get going on that first thing..." Longmont stammered tonelessly, filling the silence. "I'll start making arrangements shortly."

For now, I could only trust that interacting with *Washington's* crew would regenerate his fighting spirit. Once Longmont witnessed their grit and determination firsthand, perhaps it would awaken his own.

With a final nod of acknowledgment, I signaled for the communication to be terminated and turned my attention back to the bridgecrew. "Alright, let's get to work. We have a fleet to restore and a war to win."

Chapter 12

Pleidian Weonan Star System
Royal Guard Flagship, *Impervious*

Empress Shawlee Tee

Onboard her Royal Guard's Pleidian Weonan Super Battle Cruiser Flagship, *Impervious*, stood Empress Shawlee Tee. She wore her combat suit—marked with charred craters from enemy Phazon fire—evidence of the fierce battle she had just fought on her homeworld. The Empress, along with her entourage, hurried onto the bridge. Shawlee's shredder, still smoldering from near-constant firing, was slung over one shoulder.

Captain Hankon was barking off commands to his exhausted bridgecrew. They obediently answered back, executing their tasks with the efficiency of a seasoned crew.

Shawlee moved toward the primary display, and what she saw made her heart sink—at least a third of her fleet already ravaged. Lifeless husks were now adrift. The occasional momentary burst of flames—quickly extinguished within the frigid void—made her gasp as two more Pleidian Weonan warships suddenly exploded—one and then the other.

She knew the enemy was neither Grish nor Varapin—beyond that, no one had a clue who they were—why they were terrorizing her world. While most Pleidian warships had been conscripted into Alpha Fleet, the Royal Guard, a mere 12—mostly older—warships, had been ill-prepared for an attack of this magnitude. The enemy fleet consisted of twenty Herculean-sized warships strong with zero losses thus far. As Shawlee approached, Captain Hankon came to attention.

Ignoring him, her eyes fell upon another display—one where her beautiful homeworld of Weonan was being systematically carpet-bombed by hundreds of low-flying fighter craft.

She spun toward the Captain. "We cannot lose to this onslaught! Whatever you haven't tried, haven't dared to attempt, because it would be too reckless or improbable to succeed, now's the time you go there."

Shawlee bit her tongue, as the Captain took a moment to digest her command. She watched his gaze sweep over the remnants of their fleet. The Empress took in the scene as well... the fleet was battle-worn but unyielding—she took pride in the fact their spirit had not been broken.

The sight must have ignited a spark within the Captain as well. He turned back to his crew with vigor and his words came out as forceful as a firing rail cannon, "Divert all power to the shields and prepare to disengage the main thrusters! Shut down all running lights—we're going dark. On my command vent atmosphere from all airlocks on Decks 12, 19, and 32. Helm, put us into a slow tumble."

The crew paused, disbelief scored on their faces.

Shawlee scannned the displays, then looked up at the Captain.

"Trust me," Hankon added.

There was a determined gleam in his eye. He turned to his Communications Officer. "Broadcast a five-minute countdown timer on all open channels, audio only. Prepare to emit on my mark."

Impervious, its engines silenced, began to drift, to flounder, like a ghost among the celestial carnage—heading directly into the lion's den—a cluster of the enemy's five most powerful warships; two immense battle cruisers, and three destroyers.

Captain Hankon took note of Shawlee's terrified expression and offered back a crooked smile. "You asked for a miracle, Empress... this plan, if you can call it that, hinges upon the ancient Pleidian art of *K'vora*—using the enemy's fear against them."

The enemy, seemingly confident in their impending victory, tightened their formation, unconcerned with just one more disabled and dying warship—they readied to initiate their final, devastating blow.

"Broadcast now," Hankon ordered.

Impervious emitted the countdown timer, along with a series of low-frequency pulses, mimicking the signature of a critical reactor overload. To the enemy, it would appear as though the Weonan flagship, nearly upon them, was on the brink of self-destruction.

Shawlee placed a hand to her mouth. She imagined the confusion raining down upon their attackers. No one would want to be caught in the blast radius of a dying super battle cruiser. The enemy halted their advance, scrambling, maintaining a safe distance, their formations breaking as they scrambled to reassess. But Weonan's flagship had already tumbled in among the enemy.

"That's it!" Hankon bellowed. "Now, reroute all power to the engines and weapons systems. Target that command ship!" the Captain ordered.

Impervious surged forward, the crew—despite being exhausted—were galvanized by adrenaline. They focused their weapons on the enemy command ship. The deck thrummed with rail cannons coming alive. The display showed a tight cluster of smart missiles on a bending trajectory toward the closest enemy ship.

Shawlee's heart pounded with fear and anticipation as the meaningless countdown timer beeped, a theatrical hoax... and their only chance of survival. She had never witnessed the *K'vora* technique before; she'd heard tales of its effectiveness... but if it failed, her entire fleet would be decimated.

Even before the timer had gone quiet, *Impervious* was unleashing a devastating barrage of Phazon Pulsar fire, energy bolts wreaking catastrophic damage to the combatant vessels. The enemy command ship, caught off guard, was overwhelmed by the sudden, all too close, onslaught. It exploded in a blinding flash, sending debris hurtling through space. Shawlee heard shrapnel thumping against *Impervious'* shields. The enemy ships, no doubt anxious to cut their losses, scattered in disarray.

Shawlee watched in awe as the tide of battle turned. The enemy, who had been relentless in their attack, were now fleeing in terror. She had witnessed the power of the *K'vora*. She now knew that it would be a weapon that would forever be etched in the annals of Pleidian Weonan history.

With the enemy in retreat, Hankon ordered the fleet to pursue. *Impervious* led the charge, its weapons blazing. Shawlee stood on the bridge, her heart filled with relief and triumph. She had witnessed the courage and resilience of her people. On the precipice of defeat, Shawlee inwardly vowed to never let her guard down like that again.

. . .

THE PURSUIT CONTINUED FOR HOURS UNTIL THE LAST of the enemy ships had been destroyed. The battle had been a costly one, but the five remaining Pleidian Royal Guard Warships had emerged victorious. As they made their way back to Weonan, Shawlee couldn't help but feel a sense of gratitude.

She turned to Captain Hankon. "You saved us, Captain. You are a true hero."

Hankon smiled. "I was just doing my duty, Empress. It was the crew who fought bravely, many making the ultimate sacrifice."

Shawlee nodded. "Yes, but you were the one who dared to make the difficult decisions. You were the one who led us to victory today."

Hankon inclined his head. "Thank you, Empress. I am honored to serve."

Shawlee looked out a viewport as they approached Weonan. Home. She considered the precariousness of the situation they had just endured—first, an ill-prepared Alliance facing the seemingly unstoppable Grish—and now, there was another, *unknown* enemy.

"Captain, deploy our Arrows to the surface," Shawlee said. "Let's ensure every enemy fighter has either left the system or is destroyed."

Chapter 13

Alpha Fleet's Rendezvous Point
USS Washington

Captain Galvin Quintos

I was up late into the wee hours. The job of Fleet Commander was more *Fleet Baby Sitter* than I had counted on. Forty-five warships translated to forty-five different sets of logistical problems, technical issues, and complaints. It was 0200 hours, and I had slipped out of my ready room in search of a snack. Mess was always open, manned by automatons, and a few over-enthusiastic 3.0s. I ordered a Denver omelet, a side of hash browns, toast, and a black coffee. Finding a seat off by myself, where I wouldn't be instantly spotted, I relished quietly eating my breakfast in solitude.

. . .

THREE BITES IN, THEY ARRIVED. A GROUP OF SIX, no, seven. All were young, loud, and had far too much energy for two in the morning. Now, all clustered at the ordering counter, they spewed their orders rapid-fire, as the service bot's head swiveled back and forth like a hyperactive owl on espresso.

I continued to attack my omelet, trying not to listen to the chatter. It was then that I recognized one voice in particular. There at the counter, sure enough, was Petty Officer Second-Class Aubrey Laramie.

Taller than most of her peers, she was barking off her order, her voice ten decibels louder than it needed to be.

"Could I trouble you for an artisanal quinoa salad, garnished with microgreens and drizzled with a balsamic reduction, accompanied by a side of gluten-free avocado toast, lightly dusted with Himalayan pink salt, please?"

If she turned around, I would be in her direct sightline. I winced, trying not to loudly scrape metal chair legs across metal deck plates. Then I carefully scooted around so my back was facing them.

A man's voice resonated behind me. Another one had joined the fracas. I knew that voice. It was none other than Chaplain Halman Trent.

As I was trying to enjoy my breakfast, Trent's patronizing voice filled the air, ruining the taste of my omelet.

With his usual flair for dramatics, he began doling out over-the-top life lessons and holier-than-thou dime-store parables on the importance of eating healthy, causing several of the young women to change their orders, much to the chagrin of the automaton behind the counter. Aubrey's order was held up as the epitome of a meal for a raised consciousness. I rolled my eyes and silently prayed for a swift end to his sermonizing so I could finish my breakfast in peace.

With the sudden loud clang of dishes and the sound of glass

crashing onto the deck, I spun around to see that one of the women had dropped her tray en route to their table. Aubrey was still at the counter... while Trent had one hand casually cupping one of her impeccable butt cheeks. I inwardly glowered.

Simultaneously, drawing near with a tray grasped securely in his two mitt-sized palms was Grip, the lofty, dark-skinned Marine whose bearing demanded regard.

He set down his tray, pulled out the chair across from me, and sat down. But he didn't start in on his meal. Instead, he leaned back, his dark eyes leveled on the other table with all its youthful, eager patrons.

"What's on your mind, big guy?"

Grip's lips curled into a sneer. "We need to do something about... all that."

"All that?" I repeated.

"You can't tell me you approve of what's going on. Trent's a handsy motherfucker. Thought you and Aubrey were friends."

I shrugged, "I'm friends with a lot of people. That doesn't mean Petty Officer Laramie isn't free to lead her own life. She's a big girl." I scooped up a forkful of hashbrowns and shoveled them into my mouth.

"I'm not talking about his ass-grabbing as much as I am about that whole cult bullshit."

"What cult?"

"Where you been, man? It's all over the ship. It's like Christ and his disciples, only Trent ain't the Messiah, and his followers are more like feckless lemmings heading for the cliff's edge, oblivious to the impending fall."

"How many... what percentage of the crew are we talking about? A handful—"

"I don't know. There are groups... bands of them roaming around. They get extra points if they sign up others."

"Sign up for what?"

"It's called..." Grip made a pained expression like he had a bad bout of gas. Then he looked up as if trying to find the answer somewhere hidden in the overhead. "... *Inheritors of Tenebrosity!*" he finally said, triumphant.

"Religious beliefs, spiritual choices, if it brings my crew closer together, who am I to complain? Trent was brought on board for just that reason."

"You're not getting it, Cap. Look, I was brought up as a Baptist in the Deep South. I'm not anti-religion, I'm anti-psychological manipulation, coercion, and exploitation."

I glanced toward the table of crewmembers. There were eight of them now, all sitting still, their heads bowed, each holding hands with the person next to them. Trent, at the head of the table, was saying something akin to grace, but I couldn't hear precisely what he was saying.

"Here's the crux," Grip interjected between mouthfuls, his tone thick with concern as he paused to chew. "It's the 3.0s. Trent seems to have a perfect sign-up rate among them. It's like they're drawn to his words like magnets to metal, and I'm not sure how to break through that influence."

"It's not your job to break through that influence."

His nostrils flared.

I'd obviously riled him up.

"So, you're okay with it? Your crew systematically being sucked into a mind-controlling cult?"

"Anyone who knows me, knows I'm not a joiner and that includes religious pursuits." With that said, something was gnawing at the back of my mind. Something Sonya said... *All Symbio 3.0s are cross-networked.*

Grip must have picked up on the uncertainty in my voice. "What is it?" he asked, starting in on his bacon.

Ignoring the question, I raised my coffee to my lips. Across the room, Aubrey was unusually animated, commanding the spotlight with exaggerated gestures and a high-pitched tone that seemed out of character. The Aubrey I knew wasn't prone to such over-the-top enthusiasm; she resembled more of a laid-back observer with an inner intensity rather than a stereotypical over-enthusiastic sorority plebe at a socialite gathering.

Grip was talking again.

"I'm sorry, what did you say?" I asked as if suddenly snapped out of a trance.

"I *said*, I don't think it's right to have people—or Symbios—running around proselytizing."

I glanced up to see that a giant, bulging vein in Grip's neck was pulsating.

The big Marine threw down his metal fork onto his plastic plate with a clatter... loud enough to get the attention of those at the other table.

In that instant, I caught Aubrey's eye—a flash of *something* in her expression, was it guilt? Shame?

Grip rose abruptly from his seat, nearly toppling his chair in the process.

"Hold up," I said, hesitating, then lowering my voice to a whisper, "You may be right. I don't want you to think I'm not being receptive to your concerns. Especially when it comes to the Symbios."

"Why just the Symbios?"

"It's not just the Symbios, but Sonya mentioned to me that the 3.0s are different than other Symbios—different than those we used on the Symbio Decks. This latest iteration is cross-networked. What one thinks, they all think."

"They are of one mind?" he asked.

I shrugged. "Pretty much."

"So... if a few of them were being influenced to do something counterproductive to the goals of the U.S. Space Navy, or those in command within the fleet... that could be a problem."

"Yeah. That would be a big problem. Especially considering what we're up against with the Grish. That we're *all-too-soon* going back into battle."

Grip took a deep breath, his voice more relaxed now, "Want me to bus your tray, Cap?"

Lost in thought, I said, "Uh, yeah, thanks."

"What are you going to do? About the Inheritors of Tenebrosity?" the Marine asked.

"I'm going to talk to their Messiah."

I caught three hours of sleep in my ready room before my TAC-Band woke me up. Opening one eye, I saw it was Sonya. She'd bypassed the need for me to accept her call. Her projected form hovered over my wrist.

"So, let me get this straight, you leave me a desperate message, something about the world coming to an end, and what are you doing when I hurry to get back to you first thing, like, even before I brush my teeth? I find you're taking a mid-morning nap!"

Working to clear the cobwebs from my muddled mind, I said, "Can you come here? To my ready room? I don't want to talk about it over comms."

"You look like crap."

"Thank you. I'll see you when you get here. Oh, and find Hardy." I cut the connection.

By the time Sonya and Hardy arrived, I'd had a chance to splash cold water on my face and brush my teeth. I'd also asked SARAH to contact Pristy and Derrota, have them meet me here in my ready room.

Pristy, who was just coming onto the dayshift, said, "What's this about? What's with all the secrecy?"

Hardy said, "I think I know."

That made me nervous, I hadn't told anyone...

"It's about Climbo, isn't it? I looked it up within the United States Space Navy Personnel Regulations and Standards of Conduct Handbook. There is not one specific rule concerning the riding of a robotic pack mule within ship passageways and corridors."

"This has nothing to do with that, Hardy. You can ride Climbo to your heart's content."

I looked to Sonya. "I need this compartment sealed off from eavesdropping... from SARAH or anyone else who might tap into our conversation."

Pristy made a face. "Why am I here?"

Derrota said, "I am wondering the same thing. Why am I here, Galvin?"

Sonya was at my desk, her fingers tapping away at the keyboard. "And... done! This room is sealed. No one's opening this kimono any time soon."

I stared at her. How did she even know that phrase?

I took everyone in, and said, "We may have a problem. And... I may have made things a whole lot worse."

"The suspense is killing me," Pristy said sarcastically. "But I have to initiate tactical system diagnostics and synchronize data feeds this morning."

"What kind of problem?" Derrota inquired, now looking more interested.

"Chaplain Halman Trent has been busy soliciting crewmembers into his flock."

"Oh, that," Sonya said. "Someone tried to recruit me, I told him to get lost."

Good girl, I thought.

"What's wrong with being a part of something... something bigger than ourselves?" Pristy asked, with far more defensiveness than necessary.

"And what do you know about Inheritors of Tenebrosity?" I countered.

She shrugged off the question. "Just that someone passed me a pamphlet. I was invited to the service on Monday night."

"Service? What kind of service? Where?"

"I don't know, I haven't gone yet. Ship's Chapel."

"This ship has a chapel?" I asked, feeling like that was something I should have known about.

Hardy said, "It's on Deck 15, Violet Sector. Previously was Provisions Hold 231."

"What's all this about, Galvin?" Derrota asked.

"We need to know what we're dealing with here," I pressed. "If there's a cult or some kind of underground movement spreading aboard the ship, the fleet, it could jeopardize morale and mission readiness."

Derrota nodded, acknowledging the potential gravity of the situation.

I continued, "We can't afford any distractions or disruptions, especially with the current state of affairs in the sector. If Chaplain Trent is recruiting crewmembers into something potentially dangerous or subversive, we need to intervene before it escalates any further."

Glancing around the compartment at the faces of my team, I saw both bewilderment and wariness.

"I think you're all over-reacting," Pristy said. "I'll check it out tomorrow night and report back." She smiled and turned to leave.

"No."

She spun back around. "What do you mean, *no*? What? I can't attend a spiritual gathering? You may be the Captain of this ship, but you have no right—"

I held up my palms in mock defense, "From what I've already determined, 100% of the Symbio 3.0s have joined. And very few human crewmembers have declined to become members... sure, there are a handful like Sonya and me, those who aren't big joiners. But think about it... in a *very* short amount of time, his follower base has grown exponentially. Don't you find that just a little bit odd?"

The teenager intervened, "Wait... I'm reviewing ship security feeds for the last few days." Sonya smirked and shook her head. "It may have something to do with these amulets... necklaces being offered up. Trent and his followers are presenting them as gifts to the crew."

Unwittingly, Pristy's hand moved to cradle the pendant suspended from the simple gold necklace at her throat. Aware of the collective gaze upon her, she downplayed their interest. "It's nothing. A token of solidarity... a bond among comrades. They're giving them out all over the ship. What's the big deal?"

"Ah, very clever!" Hardy said with enthusiasm. "And Sonya, you are right... it's the amulets."

A 3D projection, thanks to one of the ChronoBot's latest upgrade capabilities, came alive at the center of the compartment. "What we've been missing is the technology aspect," Hardy continued, "Chaplain Trent has been busy, very busy."

The feed showed Trent and a crewmember standing within one of the ship's smaller passageways in mid-conversation. With a gracious, humble smile, one hand patting his heart, he offered her a necklace.

Trent said, "Here is a small gift... one that is of little monetary value. Just a small token of appreciation that I like to give to those in my close circle."

Only now did I realize it was Aubrey Laramie standing there with Trent.

"Uh, thank you. But I'm not much for jewelry. Gets in the way of my workouts," she said.

Now that was the Aubrey I knew...

She took it anyway and looked at it. Held it up so the light could catch the colorful stone.

Hardy paused the video, freezing Trent and Aubrey in a timeless instant. A square, bounding box appeared around the necklace. Zooming in to fill the display, we were now looking at an extreme close-up of some kind of gem hanging from the necklace. It was an amulet, adorned with intricate engravings. The adornment pulsated with a dim, ominous light.

"I have encountered such a device before," Hardy said. "Centuries ago, during the Celestial Conflict of Shadows, the token was wielded by the clandestine sect known as the *Umbral Covenant*, who used its mysterious energies to destabilize the tyrannical rule of the Luxan Empire in the Orion Nebula, ultimately leading to the Empire's collapse."

"That same necklace?" I asked, frowning.

"They're called *Eclipse Amulets*. What the good Chaplain is about to tell Petty Officer Second-Class Laramie, and has told other followers of the Inheritors of Tenebrosity, is that this jewel is believed to possess mystical properties that grant insight and enlightenment."

"In other words, this is a clusterfuck of epic proportions," Sonya said.

"In reality," Hardy continued, "... the Eclipse Amulet contains advanced neural interface technology that can subtly influence brainwave patterns when worn by individuals. Through subtle electromagnetic pulses and targeted frequencies, the amulet can induce feelings of tranquility, euphoria, and heightened suggestibility in those who wear it."

The ChronoBot's faceplate glowed with a deeper shade of blue. "Chaplain Trent strategically presents the Eclipse Amulet to crewmembers during private counseling sessions or sermons, framing it as a sacred relic that symbolizes the unity and power of the cult—although, he doesn't refer to it as a *cult*. Unbeknownst to his recruits, the amulet's influence gradually fosters a deep emotional connection to Trent and his teachings, making them more susceptible to his manipulation and control. From there, his devoted followers pass on the amulets to others, breeding even more followers."

A dramatic pause, then Hardy continued, "The Eclipse Amulet serves as both a physical symbol of devotion to the Inheritors of Tenebrosity and a covert tool for indoctrination, allowing Chaplain Trent to recruit new followers with alarming efficiency while maintaining an air of mystique and authority."

Pristy, who was still fiddling with her own Eclipse Amulet, had yet to remove it from her neck—to yank it away in anger or disgust.

Derrota slowly approached her. "Gail?"

"None of that is true," she said shaking her head. "You're going to believe the recollections of a 300-year-old, *well-past-his-prime* robot? This amulet was merely a thoughtful present. You have zero evidence it possesses any kind of mind-manipulating capabilities," she scoffed. "Come on... let's be realistic here."

"Then take it off," Sonya said. "You have to know, you're acting super weird."

Derrota, now standing right in front of her, said, "Please, Gail. Let me have it. If you are right, if there's nothing nefarious about the amulet, you can have it back."

The amulet was now clenched within her fist so tight that

her knuckles were turning white. "No! I'm not going to let you—"

I strode toward her, grabbed her fist, pried open her fingers, took hold of the fragile chain around her neck, and snapped it off of her.

Pristy gasped, placing open palms around her now-naked neck.

"I'm sorry, Gail," I said.

I brought the necklace to Derrota, its amulet swaying from the shimmering tether. "Can you analyze that thing? See if it's altering people's minds?"

The Science Officer took the necklace from me, carefully holding it by the chain. Then, in a version of *Hot Potato*, Stephan passed the chained amulet to the ChronoBot. "Hardy has all the sensors necessary to make that determination."

With a whir and a series of beeps, Hardy exclaimed, "Alert! Alert! Incoming brainwashing frequencies detected! Recommend immediate removal of this nefarious charm before we all start chanting *Hail Trent!*"

"Very funny," I said, holding out an open palm for him to hand it to me.

"Not a good idea, Galvin," Derrota said, tapping at his tablet. "You don't want to touch the amulet's surface. Even for a moment." He looked to Pristy who was now slumped against the bulkhead, lost in a fog of daze.

"The effects of an Eclipse Amulet, I'm sorry to say, are both devastating and perhaps even permanent," Derrota said.

The Science Officer walked toward Pristy and placed a hand on her shoulder. "We'll get this figured out. How about we take a walk down to HealthBay together?" he said softly.

She gave a slow nod, a lone tear tracing a path down her left cheek.

Before Derrota turned to leave with her, I said, "These amulets... they have the same effect on the 3.os, I take it?"

Derrota looked to Hardy.

"More so," Hardy said. "It would be like water drawn into a dry sponge."

Chapter 14

Stepping into HealthBay, I was immediately struck by the sight of nearly every bed occupied, the wounded from various ships in the fleet claiming every available space. Amid the chaos, my XO was conspicuously absent. As nurses and med techs bustled around me, attending to the urgent needs of their charges, my attention was drawn to Chief Knott. She stood at the reception desk, a figure marked by her distinct 1950s-style bob in an unnatural shade of red. With focused precision, she was scanning something on her tablet.

"What's the situation, Chief?" I asked, positioning myself at a respectable distance next to her.

"Oh, Captain. Glad you're here. We're operating at over 100% capacity. My staff is exhausted with no downtime."

"Can we bring more MediBots out of storage?"

"No, they just get in the way. Great for surgery, not so great for patient trauma."

I slowly nodded, not having a ready answer.

"I was wondering... the new 3.0s have been programmed with medical package level 6. They wouldn't substitute the existing MediBots, but they could be useful here in the ward."

Immediately, alarms went off in my head. I spun her around to see if she was wearing one of Trent's amulets around her neck.

"What are you doing?" She protested, taking a step back.

"I'm looking to see if you're wearing an amulet. The same jewelry I've noticed half your staff wearing."

"NO. I'm not, and I already know about that. Stephan read me in on the issues—the Chaplain's nefarious gifts to crewmembers. I'm still having a hard time believing it. But after examining your XO... it was decided she needed to be isolated. I don't know what I'm going to do with her, to be honest. I've instructed my people, those who haven't come in contact with Trent's minions, to stay clear and not accept anything they have to offer. That, and for those who are already wearing the necklaces, to not remove them. We're watching them. This is a damn mess, Captain. Not the kind of thing I need to be worrying about with a ward full of injured crewmembers."

"I understand," I said, taking in the overcrowded Health-Bay. "Back to the 3.0s. They are all infected, or whatever you want to call it. Something to do with their one-mind networking."

"Well then, you'll have to find me some help from another source," she snapped.

"I'll talk to Stephan, he has lab personnel that—"

"Already talked to Stephan. All his people are wearing amulets," she said impatiently.

"How about Hardy?" I suggested. "He's not busy at the moment."

She was already shaking her head. "That robot of yours is getting more and more unhinged. The way he rides that mechanical mule around. I think you need to have his internal circuits checked—run whatever diagnostics are suitable for a Chronobot."

"I'll keep that in mind. So, where can I find my XO?"

She gestured toward the double auto-hatches. "Third exam room down on the left."

She took my arm before I could turn away. "Be careful with her, Captain. She's vulnerable. Exhibiting symptoms identical to those coming off opioid addiction."

"People get over addictions..."

"Yes, but with this, there doesn't seem to be any kind of detoxification protocol we can follow. There's nothing in her bloodstream. Her brain has been altered, synapses rewritten. This very well could be permanent. For her, as well as anyone else the Chaplain and his followers have targeted."

I ENTERED PRISTY'S EXAM ROOM, FINDING HER curled up on her side in the fetal position. Her eyes were open, puffy, and red. I wondered if she'd been crying non-stop since she left my ready room.

I took the seat next to her bed, reached out, and took her hand in mine. Her fingers were warm and clammy.

Pristy's eyes flickered towards me, a glimmer of recognition in their depths. She was a shell of her former self, a mere shadow of the strong, capable woman I had come to rely on.

"Galvin," she whispered, her voice hoarse and strained. "I'm so sorry."

It had been a long time since she called me anything other than Captain.

"Sorry?" I echoed, scrunching my face. "What do you have to be sorry for?"

She swallowed hard, her small Adam's apple bobbing in her throat. "I... I don't know. I just feel like I've let you down."

I squeezed her hand reassuringly, trying to ignore the knot of worry that was forming in my stomach. "You haven't let me down, Gail. You're going through something but we're going to figure it out."

She shook her head, tears welling up in her eyes. "I don't know if I can. I don't even know who I am anymore."

I leaned forward, resting my elbows on the edge of her bed as I tried to gather my thoughts. "You're Gail Pristy, my XO, and one of the most capable officers I've ever had the pleasure of serving with."

She gave me a weak smile. "I don't feel capable."

I took a deep breath, trying to steady my emotions before I spoke. "I'm here for you, Gail." I offered a supportive grin but not sure if I pulled it off. "I'm not going anywhere."

She nodded, but I could see the doubt in her eyes. I knew I had to do something, anything, to help her.

"You talked to anyone besides Chief Knott about this?" I asked, hoping that maybe she had confided in someone else... a psychiatrist? Did *Washington* even have one of those?

She shook her head. "No. I didn't want to burden anyone else with my problems."

I sighed, running a hand through my hair. "You're not a burden. You're my friend, and I want to help you." My words sounded hollow. She was far more than a friend.

She looked away, her gaze fixed on the bulkhead behind me. "I don't know what's happening to me, Galvin. I feel like I'm losing control."

I reached out and gently turned her face towards me, forcing her to meet my gaze. "You're not losing control, Gail. You're just going through a difficult time."

No response.

I was at a loss. *How was I going to reach her?* I closed my eyes, my mind racing as I tried to piece together the events of the past few days. "Look, I would never minimize the pain you're feeling but I do know you've overcome far worse obstacles."

She looked at me, her eyes filled with fear and longing. "I can't..."

"We will work through this. You have to believe that we can. I know you feel like you're all alone, but you're not."

She sighed, her shoulders slumping, her gaze distant. "Everything seems... so far away. I..."

"Do you trust me, Gail?"

"I trust you." Her words came out like a dying whisper.

It didn't take a genius to know that every word she uttered was a monumental feat. I leaned in closer, our bodies now touching. A lump formed in my throat as I sought the right words, but I felt like I was just repeating myself. "Don't give up on me, okay?"

She looked at me, her eyes searching mine. "What if I..." She swallowed weakly. "... can't stop it."

I shook my head, my voice steady and unwavering, "No way you'd surrender to anyone or anything. You're Gail fucking Pristy, and you're one of the strongest people I know."

She took in a wheezy breath, her eyes glassy. "Thank you, Galvin."

I gave her hand a final squeeze before standing up. "I'll be back. I just need to check with Chief Knott and see if she can send someone to help."

As I turned to leave, she called out to me softly, "Galvin?"

I paused, turning back to face her.

She took another wary breath, her voice breathy and thin, "Back when we were in the sphere together... that Crythara realm when we played those roles... I need to know what you were feeling."

And there it was. She was going there. Stepping across the line we had ventured close to but never crossed. I felt my heart kick into overdrive as if readying for a race, for a starting gun to shatter the quiet that enveloped us. But was this a race I even wanted to consider? Was this Pristy asking or was it the amulet—Trent's manipulations slicing at my vulnerable underbelly? Add to the fact, I was terrible at expressing my emotions—probably because that was a side of myself I'd gone out of my way *not* to explore. Keeping my feelings bottled up had become second nature to me over the years, a defense mechanism I wasn't sure I could ever fully get over. I felt her eyes on me. The seconds ticked by, knowing that if I tried to explain my feelings, I could be sending her the wrong message.

As I stood there looking into her eyes, I saw a glimmer of hope that I did not want to crush. I opened my mouth to speak, but no words came out. I feel like an idiot... I'm pretty sure I looked like one too. *Dammit!* I was navigating unfamiliar terrain. This was a *do-or-die* moment. All I had to do was take this singular leap of faith. But all I could manage was a pathetic smile.

Her nostrils flared slightly as she gulped down her emotion. In a dismissive tone, barely audible, she uttered, "I'm really exhausted, Captain." Tears threatening to fall freely, she squeezed her eyes shut. "I need you to leave, please."

I sat at the Captain's Mount brooding. The easy answer would have been to simply demand all crewmembers to give up their amulets and toss Chaplain Trent into a jail cell. But after checking on Pristy, her emotional state was tenuous at best... and she had only been wearing her amulet for several hours. Who knew what the effect would be for those already wearing amulets for days? I couldn't even imagine the turmoil that would transpire if hundreds, thousands, of crewmembers, were thrown into such a cataclysmic mental state.

As of now, Derrota and Coogong confirmed that certain non-biological beings—although under the spell of the amulets —appear to be harmless. Of course, that could change over time. SARAH still appeared to be reliable. And, although Hardy possessed an organic brain element as well as a robotic one, he appeared entirely unaffected. And the Symbios were a wild-card. They were clearly under the influence, but to what extent, and what would the reversal process look like for them? And Derrota had warned that the effects of the amulets could go beyond the physical—to the mystical aspect. And if the mystical is involved... things get complicated, difficult, if not impossible, to analyze.

I shook my head. A subtler strategy going forward would be essential. I didn't want to jeopardize the crew's well-being with the too-aggressive seizure of the amulets. At least for now, our focus should be to undermine Chaplain Trent's influence and systematically dismantle the cult from within.

Chapter 15

XO Gail Pristy

Pristy was awakened in the wee hours of the night, alone in the solitude of her room. Her condition hadn't improved; instead, she felt an intensification of her malaise. Tears welled as a growing sense of despair strangled her thoughts. She was spinning, gradually succumbing to an unseen force as if dragged down into the ocean's depths, gasping for air, her vision obscured by the murky waters. *What the hell is wrong with me?*

She did her best to shake off the dread, rising from her bed. Donned a robe and exited her room.

The corridor lay hushed, bathed in the subdued glow of dimmed overhead lighting. She stumbled her way to the main HealthBay floor, finding it similarly peaceful, its beds occupied by slumbering figures. Noticing the on-duty nurse preoccupied with a patient, Pristy, unsteady on her feet, departed HealthBay, her destination uncertain—she was tempted to find the nearest airlock to jettison herself out into the void.

It struck her that Hold 536 was nearby, especially now that these omninoughts were equipped with DeckPorts—nothing seemed too distant. She reached Derrota's laboratory, where it was dark with shadows, and quiet except for the steady drone of computer servers. A gentle draft from the clean-room air filtration system brushed her face.

She transitioned into the adjoining Hold 536, its expanse still occupied by the sphere with its ghostly projections. Although none of Derrota's team was present, she was not alone.

Atop the virtual staircase of the sphere's Crythara Realm stood Grantham, the Archive's Guardian. Whether Pristy had anticipated finding herself here remained uncertain. With the burdensome sorrow that blanketed her, Pristy just stood there, finding it difficult to do anything else.

Grantham lifted a hand, beckoning her closer.

Her ambivalence gave way to... *Why not?* Gradually ascending the staircase, she approached the Guardian.

"Welcome, Lady Era," he greeted.

Caught off guard, she replied, "You're aware that I am, and always will be, Gail Pristy."

The Guardian extended a hand toward the threshold. "Your Adept awaits to be sustained by your essence; please proceed to continue your Crythara adventure."

Pristy hesitated, her heart missing a beat. She had no desire to return to that realm, to confront the memories and emotions she had left unresolved with Galvin. Yet, she suspected ignoring Grantham's summons would be a mistake. With a heavy sigh, she stepped across the threshold and into the swirling vortex of the Crythara Realm.

The world around her shimmered and morphed, transforming into the lush forests and rolling hills of Crythara. Pristy found herself standing in a clearing, surrounded by towering trees and the sound of birdsong. She could feel the warm sun on her skin and a gentle breeze rustling through her hair.

In the distance, she saw a figure approaching. *Is that my Adept?*

The young woman was dressed in simple robes, her long, dark hair flowing behind her. She had a kind smile, and her eyes sparkled with intelligence.

"Welcome back, Lady Era," she said. "I am Anya. I have been expecting you."

Pristy nodded, unsure of what to say. She had never been comfortable with the title, *Lady Era*. It felt strange and unfamiliar as if it belonged to someone else. Which, of course, it did.

"Please, call me Gail," she said.

Anya smiled. "Very well, Gail. Shall we begin?"

Nodding again, Pristy followed Anya deeper into the forest. Anya asked questions, seemingly knowing the answers beforehand, casting doubt on her sincerity. Nevertheless, talking was therapeutic, a break from her dreary thoughts. Whether Anya was genuine or not... didn't seem to matter. Pristy recounted her recent experiences since her previous visit to the Realm. She described the conflict with the previous attacks on Earth, and, more recently, the peculiar and unsettling occurrences on *Washington* involving Chaplain Trent and the amulets.

Anya listened patiently, her expression never changing. When Pristy was finished, Anya said, "I understand. You have been through a great deal. But you are strong, Gail. I have confidence you can overcome anything you set your mind to."

Pristy wasn't so sure. She felt disoriented, afraid to commit to any path forward. "I don't know," Pristy said. "Honestly... I feel like I'm losing my mind."

"You're not losing your mind," Anya said. "You're just struggling to make sense of everything that's happened. But I'm here to help you. Together, we will uncover a path to get you on the other side."

Pristy nodded, feeling somewhat relieved. *Why do I trust this, aberration, or whatever she is?* Anya wasn't her friend. She wasn't her confidante. Not really. However, right now... with her here, by her side, she did feel better.

They continued walking through the forest, in tandem. The sun began to set, casting a golden glow over the trees. Pristy looked up at the sky and saw a single star twinkling in the distance.

Turning back to Anya, Gail gasped. Anya was no longer Anya. She was, instead, *Lady Era.*

"What is happening?" Pristy asked, a wave of dizziness washing over her—vertigo churning her stomach. *Oh God.* Her surroundings grew more menacing and treacherous by the moment. She groped for a stable anchor, anything to regain her balance, but nothing was there. As the trees whirled, Lady Era transformed into a swirling vortex—her tender grin twisting into a distorted leer.

"Gail... listen to me," Lady Era said... *or was it Anya?*

Bringing open palms to her face, Pristy said, "I can't. I can't think. I don't want to be here. Make it stop."

The whirling began to lessen, allowing her to discern forms —the trees, the earth, and the being standing before her. No longer was it Lady Era, nor was it Anya. It was herself, Gail Pristy. A mirror image, her twin. With one difference... she, her doppelgänger, was wearing that damned, cursed amulet.

Her double said, "Gail, stand perfectly still. Can you do that for me?"

Pristy found that she could, the vertigo lessening now.

"You remember when you were the Watcher, and Lady Era was the Adept, yes?"

"Yes, I remember."

"How you walked into her, became the Watcher within her?"

"Yes."

"What I need you to do, Gail, is stand perfectly still. Do not blink, do not breathe, do not swallow."

Pristy went rigid, her beating heart pounding, anything but still. She watched as her twin approached, walked purposefully toward her. *What the hell is she doing?*

She felt her double merging within her. Becoming aware of the quiet Watcher there with her, just as she had been with Lady Era. Pristy was now the Adept. The sensation was different, invigorating. A newfound confidence blossomed within her, a heat radiating from her chest, spreading to her stomach, warming her face, and filling her lungs with a breath no longer constricted by fear and hopelessness. Instinctively, she reached for her neck, grasping the amulet that had been her doppelgänger's. She tore it off with renewed strength, throwing it, allowing it to fly free... disappearing into the night.

WITH A START, SHE SAT UP GASPING, HEART racing. She was back in her hospital bed in her darkened HealthBay room. Had that been nothing more than a dream?

Captain Galvin Quintos

I was jolted awake by an incessant dinging at my quarters' auto-hatch. Rubbing the sleep from my eyes, I checked my TAC-Band—0300 hours. "Christ!" I barked into the darkness. *Who the hell could be knocking at this hour?* I stumbled to the auto-hatch and slapped at the *OPEN* switch.

Gail Pristy rushed in, wearing nothing but a hospital gown and a thin robe precariously hanging open. "Just shut up and listen. Maybe you should sit down. Yes, sit!" She started to pace. "Okay, okay..."

I sat at the end of the bed, momentarily startled by her disheveled appearance... that and her unbridled energy. Something had clearly changed. Gone was the weakness and fragility, the frightened vulnerability I had seen just hours ago. Now her eyes shone with a fiery determination, her posture radiating a bold confidence I hadn't seen in a long time, perhaps ever.

As the words spilled from her lips, I tried to keep up, wondering what had happened to cause this dramatic about-face and why she had felt compelled to wake me in the dead of night. Maybe Chief Knott had altered her meds.

Before I could speak, Pristy launched into an urgent explanation of a vivid dream she'd had. Within the Crythara sphere, she had encountered the Guardian, Grantham, who initiated her into a revelatory experience of empowerment and knowledge. Through this mystical process, she had been transformed into an Adept, endowed with new strength and purpose.

As she recounted her experience, I struggled to focus on her words rather than the distracting glimpses of bare skin visible beneath her open robe. I felt a pang of guilt, knowing I needed to remain professional despite the intimate setting.

Noticing my diverted attention, Pristy's frustration grew. "Galvin, are you listening?" she demanded. "This is important!"

Her sharp tone snapped me back to full alertness. Whatever had happened to her in that sphere, it had lit a fire within her.

I stretched and straightened my posture. "Wait, did you dream this... or—"

"Don't interrupt. Uh, yeah it was a dream... but also real.

The sphere must be reaching out beyond that hold, if that's even possible."

She pressed on, emphasizing that the Crythara sphere was the key to stopping Trent and freeing the crew from his influence. Though risky, she was convinced we could trick him into entering the sphere where the Guardian would strip away his manipulation and lies.

WE HAD BEEN AT IT ABOUT HALF AN HOUR, devising a strategy to outwit Trent, when the ship suddenly lurched; we stumbled, awkwardly being thrown together. Reaching out, my hands slipped beneath her open robe. Feeling her taut waist beneath the sheer fabric of her gown, the gentle curve of her hips, our faces were now barely an inch apart. We stayed like that for several moments, looking into each other's eyes.

Then, the auto-hatch suddenly swooshed open.

Hardy rushed in. "Uh-oh! Well, this isn't awkward. Not at all."

"What. Do. You. Want. Hardy?" I asked through clenched teeth.

Pristy stepped away, pulling her robe in tight around herself.

"Cap, we've got company," he announced. "An unidentified ship on an approach vector. ETA: 15 minutes."

I gestured to the overhead, "And what's wrong with SARAH making an announcement? What, are you now the designated town crier?"

"SARAH's throwing a hissy fit."

"What are you talking about?"

"I'm talking about the ship's AI. And for the time being we need to be cautious about taking what she says as trustworthy. It's the whole amulet influence situation taking a turn for the worse. Has something to do with her being on the same network as the Symbios. Coogong's working on the problem. In the meantime, you're needed on the bridge." He looked to Pristy. "Sorry for, um... storming in like that."

"I need to get dressed," she said, heading for the exit. "To be continued, Captain. Our Trent discussion, not... well, whatever."

I watched as she disappeared, the auto-hatch closing behind her.

Chapter 16

"Hardy, try ringing the damn bell next time—no more just bursting into people's quarters."

"The bell. Got it. By the way... that ship I mentioned? It just changed course, no longer a threat."

I glared at the ChronoBot, the irritation bubbling within me like a kettle left too long on the stove.

Hardy's faceplate flickered with an image of a smiley face, his version of a shrug.

I growled as I started throwing on my uniform. "But since you're here and we have a few minutes, help me hash a few things out."

Hardy leaned his broad back against the bulkhead, arms crossed. "Shoot. I'm all ears."

I raked a hand through my hair. "It's Trent. The guy's got half the crew wrapped around his finger with those damn amulets. As you know, my XO was under his spell too."

"Check."

"She managed to pull herself back from its influence by interacting with the sphere."

His faceplate showed a question mark. "The sphere? How so?"

"She had some sort of vision, or dream, in there. She met herself—the confident, strong-willed Gail Pristy we all know—who was wearing the amulet, and she merged with it." I shrugged, still not fully understanding it myself. "After that encounter, she ripped off her amulet as if she was breaking the chains that were binding her to Trent's cult."

"Uh... you'd already taken that amulet away from her."

"This happened in her dream. I guess it was symbolic. Anyway, we're thinking the sphere... it may be the key."

"And how do you propose we go about using it?" Hardy asked.

"Strategic patience," I replied firmly. "We can't rush this; spooking Trent or his followers could backfire."

"Patience," Hardy echoed mockingly before switching his faceplate to display an hourglass.

Ignoring him, I continued, "Trent's built up quite the following. If we go in guns blazing—so to speak—we risk turning those people against us when we need unity the most."

I paused, my gaze hardening as I thought about Alpha Fleet and our recent losses. "With Alpha Fleet in shambles and us waiting on repairs, any fracture aboard could be catastrophic."

"Stability is key right now," Hardy agreed, his tone losing some of its humor as his faceplate displayed a simple nodding emoji.

"And then there's the political game." I began pacing now, my thoughts racing ahead of me like starfighters in formation. "Trent isn't just some low-level zealot; he has connections and clout." I turned back to Hardy. "If we accuse him without hard evidence or if we act too harshly, it could end up being my head on the chopping block instead of his."

"So what's your play?" Hardy asked.

"We lure him in," I said decisively. "Make him think he's won something—a concession from me or perhaps privileged access to information about our next move."

"And how do you make that happen?" Hardy's tone was earnest now; he knew as well as I did that subtlety wasn't exactly my strong suit.

"I'll visit his Chapel during service—show my face amongst his flock."

I paused, thinking through the steps like studying pieces on a chessboard.

"Then afterward, I'll pull him aside for a private conversation where I let it slip... about the sphere... how it might hold secrets even greater than those amulets of his."

Hardy tilted his head—or at least that's what it looked like as his faceplate changed to display an intrigued emoji with a magnifying glass.

"That might just work," he mused aloud.

Determination hardened my tone, leaving no room for doubt. "Once Trent sneaks into that sphere—thinking he'll be uncovering something profound—we'll have Grantham do whatever mystical thing he does to make those amulets as harmful as paperclips."

"Sounds like you've got it all figured out," Hardy said, but his tone had a taunting edge to it.

"What?"

"Nothing. You're just assuming the sphere, Grantham, will be taking our side in all this. Will choose to go along with your scheme, over his own."

I fastened the last clip on my boot and headed for the auto-hatch with Hardy in tow.

"The sphere went out of its way to help Gail," I said. "Why would it suddenly switch sides?"

"To screw with us? To cause mischief? Who knows what the sphere's true intentions are?"

I flashed back to my own time within that realm as Emperor Jaxon. "No, there's a morality to that place, to that consciousness... if you can call it that."

As we moved through the corridors toward the bridge, each step felt heavy with indecision. I couldn't afford to lose any more time or influence. Trent's growing reign over the crew had to end; there were battles ahead that would require every ounce of fleet personnel's free will and determination. I slowed and then came to a stop.

Hardy took several more strides, then looked back at me. "Was it something I said?"

I shook my head deep in thought. "If I take it for granted that the sphere is cognizant of everything happening on this ship. That even now, the Guardian, is listening to this conversation, he, it, is already on board with what needs to happen next."

"Trust me, Cap," Hardy remarked. "An artificial intelligence, or whatever that entity might be, doesn't need a reason to outwit its organic counterparts."

I shrugged. "I'll meet you on the bridge. It's time I confront the good Chaplain head-on and do so right now."

Chapter 17

As I moved through the softly illuminated corridor, my thoughts swirled with the growing, numerous threats to *USS Washington* and her crew—a burdensome load pressing down on my shoulders as if iron chains were coiled around my neck. Up ahead was the DeckPort, the sleek phone-booth-sized transitory portal ready to take me where I needed to go and do so within an instant.

A sudden vibration on my wrist jolted me from my thoughts. I glanced down to see Sonya's face on the projected holographic display above my TAC-Band. She didn't bother with formalities, not even a *Captain* or *Hey Uncle person.*

"Got SARAH back online," she mumbled between pops of her bubble gum, tapping away on her keyboard. "You can thank me now." Her eyes never met mine; she was absorbed in her work, a whirlwind of youthful exuberance and casual disrespect that somehow had become endearing over time.

"What have you got for me?" I kept my tone level, though inside I was anything but calm.

Her 3D projection flickered as she chewed, bubbles inflating and bursting with each keystroke. "It's bad," she said flatly. "The Symbio 3.0s, they're all screwed up. Alpha Fleet's got more problems than a math book."

Sonya relayed incidents across the fleet—ships once proud and unyielding now crippled by unexplained malfunctions. *USS Gator's* propulsion system came alive erratically, sending it careening into another ship; *USS Calgary* reported critical life support fluctuations; on *USS Honor,* weapons systems failed during routine diagnostics.

I shook my head. *If it wasn't one thing these last few days, it was another.*

"And it gets worse," Sonya continued, her voice taking on an edge that belied her casual demeanor. "There have been accidents—crew injuries piling up faster than dinner plates in a restaurant kitchen after the mid-day rush."

My chest tightened at each revelation, each piece of evidence painting a damning picture of sabotage from within. But nothing prepared me for what came next.

Sonya's expression sobered as she delivered the final blow. "A repair team on the outer hull of *USS Lexington*... somehow, they were jettisoned into space," she said, her voice was almost a whisper now, "All dead."

The words hit like an uppercut to the ribcage, knocking the breath from my lungs. Lives lost—not to the enemy's hand but to treachery within our own ranks.

"The infected Symbio 3.0s are behind this?" I asked, wanting confirmation even though I suspected the answer.

Sonya nodded solemnly. "Well... and Trent, of course. He's not just after you as the ship's Captain. Although, I'm not sure what his ultimate intentions are."

I felt the icy tendrils of dread coil around my spine as Sonya's findings painted a clear image: Chaplain Trent had orchestrated chaos across Alpha Fleet seemingly with a single goal—to weaken us from within. But all that does is make us vulnerable at the hands of our enemies. Could that seriously be his plan?

"And all this is being accomplished via those amulets? Have you isolated exactly how?" I asked.

"Not yet," she admitted, frustration tinging her words. "But it's sophisticated—I haven't figured it out yet."

I took a moment to gather my thoughts before responding, aware that every second counted but also that haste could lead us further into disaster.

"What had happened to my XO, when her amulet was taken from her, resulted in devastating repercussions. Severe mental and physical withdrawals... we'll need to find an alternate course of action."

"Duh," she said with a roll of her eyes. "I was there. I already know all that."

"But what about the 3.os? They're not human, doesn't seem to square that they'd have such a negative reaction—"

"Let me stop you right there, Uncle Clueless. Plorinne had an encounter just an hour ago that doesn't support your theory. He noticed a 3.o, I think this one was called Leo, emerging from a maintenance closet; Plorinne grabbed his necklace, yanked it off his neck. The Symbio went berserk, totally unhinged—violent and vicious. Leo bit Plorinne on the cheek, like some kind of possessed monkeyfuck. Then Leo snatched back his amulet and went back to work as if nothing had happened."

"Cripes..." I spat. Again, with the damn amulets. Clearly, this has gone way beyond an AI having a hissy fit—now it's the 3.os.

"In the meantime, I had to take Plorinne to HealthBay where the Chief sprayed AugmentFlesh onto the wound. She said he should be fine in a few days."

I shook my head. "Okay, keep at it," I instructed firmly. "And Sonya..." I waited until she met my gaze directly for the first time since our conversation began. "... good work on getting SARAH back online."

A faint smirk crossed her lips before she vanished from view, leaving me with racing thoughts and an urgent need to act.

The revelation demanded immediate attention; we were in dire straits if we didn't regain control—and quickly. Every system compromised was another opening for our adversaries to exploit; every life lost was another blow to our morale and combat effectiveness.

As I stepped through the DeckPort, I mentally prepared myself for what lay ahead—a confrontation not only with an enemy outside our hull but one that lurked among us like a virus swimming in our veins.

We had trained for countless scenarios—faced down a myriad of threats across galaxies—but nothing quite like this insidious infiltration by our own Chaplain whose vendetta threatened not just my life, but thousands more, and potentially the very sovereignty of Earth itself.

I steeled my nerves, knowing from now on I needed to tread lightly. Trent's treacherous plot threatened not only my crew, but the fate of humanity itself. Defeating him would demand every shred of tactical cunning and grit I possessed.

I reached the Chapel's auto-hatch entrance just as the service concluded. There was a sign that posted the various Chapel Services and starting times. A throng of crewmembers was funneling out, each displaying a glazed, smiling countenance. The split between human crewmembers and the look-a-like Symbio 3.0s was about 50/50. I nodded and reciprocated a smile of my own as they passed by. Inside, I caught sight of Trent's dark figure moving among a few stragglers, his hands steepled in a prayer gesture, a somber shepherd tending to his faithful flock.

Taking a deep breath and letting it out slowly to steady myself, I continued farther into the Chapel—a place sanctified by belief but now tainted by deceit—and prepared to play one of the most critical roles of my command career.

Surveying the area, I noted what used to be Cargo Hold 5 had undergone a metamorphosis at the hands of Chaplain Trent. The shadows gradually relinquished their hold on the space, revealing the extent of its alteration.

Gone were the utilitarian storage crates and bare metal bulkheads. In their place, rows of polished wooden pews lined the carpeted deck, facing a raised dais at the front. The overhead lights had been replaced with smaller sconces, giving the Chapel a warm, intimate glow. Along the sides, were backlit, faux, stained-glass windows.

At the front, the dais held a simple podium made from dark wood. Behind it, were various golden religious symbols—the Christian Cross, the Star of David, the Islamic Crescent and Star, the Buddhist Dharma Wheel, the Hinduism Om, and one more symbol I was unfamiliar with... but now remembered the geometric shape of Pristy's amulet—it was the very same.

Spotlighted, the symbols were catching the colorful rays from the illuminated stained glass. All in all, the effect of the space was surprisingly authentic for a cargo hold turned sanctuary.

As I walked down the center aisle, my boots sank into plush burgundy carpeting, muffling my footsteps. The pews, filled earlier, now stood empty except for a few stragglers murmuring prayers. At the front, Chaplain Trent was speaking in hushed tones with a young crewman.

I slid into an empty pew halfway back, not wanting to intrude. As I sat, the hint of incense still hung in the air, mingling with the smell of candles recently extinguished. It lent an ethereal atmosphere to the space, complementing the hypnotic Gregorian chants filtering through hidden speakers.

I had to admit, Trent had crafted an inviting facsimile of a traditional chapel. No detail had been overlooked. The pews, carved with ornate designs, featured kneeling rails padded with crimson velvet. Brass offering plates adorned each row, polished to a reflective sheen.

At the front, behind the podium, a set of doors led to what I guessed would be private offices, perhaps meeting rooms. I surmised this is where Trent conferred with his most devout followers and influential recruits. What exactly went on back there was anyone's guess. It was then that Aubrey Laramie hurried out, adjusting her uniform and tussling her hair. She slowed, spotting me, an expression of surprise on her face, and something else. Was that shame? She hurried on without making eye contact.

I checked the time. Ten minutes until Trent's next service. The few remaining crewmembers rose from their seats, genuflected toward the religious symbols, and quietly filed out. Soon it was just Trent and me, left alone in the expansive, converted cargo hold.

Sensing my presence, the Chaplain turned. His face broke into a broad smile, though it stopped short, not reaching his eyes.

"Captain Quintos," he said warmly, spreading his arms. "What an unexpected pleasure. To what do I owe the honor?" His voice echoed through the capacious sanctuary.

I stood slowly, taking his measure. "Chaplain Trent. I hope I'm not intruding."

He swept his arm to encompass the room. "My Chapel is always open, particularly to our Commanding Officer."

His genial tone felt forced. I approached the dais, cautiously, aware that this man wielded influence over much of my crew. Up close, his resemblance to his late father was uncanny. The same wavy dark hair, piercing blue eyes, angular features. But where Chaplain Thomas Trent had exuded compassion, his son's gaze held a simmering intensity, like a fire smoldering beneath a layer of ash.

"You've built quite a following aboard *Washington*," I began casually. "Your services seem to provide a measure of comfort during these difficult times."

"I'm heartened to hear that," Trent replied smoothly. "In times of adversity, spiritual support can make all the difference."

I nodded. "Thanks to you and your... community... morale remains high, despite our recent losses. I'm grateful for that."

Trent's smile broadened at the implied approval. "We aim to provide a sanctuary from the stresses and chaos of the outside world. An oasis of sorts, for the soul and spirit." His hands swept over his vestments. "Speaking of which, I should prepare for the next service."

I touched his arm lightly. "Before you do, I was hoping we could speak privately for a few minutes." I gestured to the doors behind the podium. "Your office?"

Trent's eyes narrowed. After a slight pause, he nodded. "Of course, Captain, right this way."

He led me through the doors into a spartan hallway. We passed a kitchen, restrooms, and a small library before arriving at his private office. Inside, Trent settled behind a large desk while I pulled up one of the chairs opposite him. The walls were adorned with various antique religious icons and paintings.

"Now then, Captain," Trent began smoothly, nesting his hands together on the desktop in front of him. "What can I do for you?"

I met his piercing gaze. "I've come to ask a favor." I lowered my voice conspiratorially, "One that requires the utmost discretion."

Trent's expression remained neutral, but a gleam of curiosity flickered in his eyes. He waited silently for me to continue.

I took a slow breath. "That alien sphere we picked up. Our scientists believe it holds secrets yet undiscovered. Knowledge beyond our current comprehension. You may have been right to caution me, and I apologize for not heeding your warnings. Entering that alien realm... well, let's just say the civilization that held that technology was incredibly advanced. As it turns out, it's a virtual genie in a bottle—what it offers to those that enter, let's just say it's beyond enticing. A distraction to the crew, hell, myself, I can ill afford. On the other hand, I can't help thinking this sphere holds untold benefits yet to be unlocked."

Trent's interest was piqued now. He leaned forward intently. "What does this have to do with me?"

"Your abilities, the influence you hold over the crew, may be the key to unlocking the sphere's true purpose." I held his gaze. "I'd like you to interface with it... off the record, of course. See what you can discern."

Trent searched my face, wary but unable to fully mask his intrigue. "You want me to access this sphere?" he asked, slowly. "But... as you said, I was the one who cautioned not to enter."

I nodded. "You're absolutely right. And it's up to you. This may have been a bad idea. I apologize." I motioned to stand.

"Hold on... tell me more."

"I was thinking your spiritual insights may reveal things our scientists have thus far overlooked. You, of all people, won't be influenced by the realm's, um, enticements. Unimaginable wealth, lifespans without limits... enticements beyond imagination. But, as a man of the cloth, you'd have little need for such distractions. But this must stay between us." I lowered my voice further, "Can I trust your discretion?"

A slow smile spread over Trent's angular features as his curiosity of what I was suggesting sunk in. He stood abruptly, came around his desk, and placed a hand on my shoulder. "You can count on me, Captain. I'm honored by your faith in my abilities. I'll begin interfacing with the sphere as soon as my busy schedule permits."

"Excellent." I rose and headed for the exit. Pausing at the door, I met Trent's gaze. "I look forward to hearing your findings."

With that, I left the somber confines of the Chapel, the next series of moves in this high-stakes game with Trent now set in motion. What happens when he enters that sphere is out of my hands. I can only trust that the mysterious entity within will know exactly what needs to be done.

Chapter 18

Chaplain Halman Trent

rent slipped unseen into Hold 536; the cavernous compartment was murky except for the soft glow emanating from the shimmering metallic sphere hovering silently within its stasis field. He moved toward it, transfixed by its orbiting glyphs and symbols.

The sight certainly was captivating. Tempted to proceed, the Chaplain hesitated. Placing any faith in what Quintos had told him was out of the question. He'd seen through his deceit. Did Quintos really think his attempts to manipulate him would be so easy? There again, wasn't he here—doing exactly what had been asked of him? He bristled, irritated at the blatant disrespect, especially for one of his religious standing. The situation gnawed at him. He knew he should just turn around and leave. Do it now, and not give any of this another thought.

He looked again at the beguiling threshold... he could almost feel the potential power that could be gained from within—

"Chaplain!" a voice cried out, desperate and trembling.

He turned to see Aubrey Laramie, disheveled uniform, eyes red-rimmed, hesitation and shame warring across her face. *What the hell does she want? She must have followed me here.*

"My amulet..." she choked out, one hand clutching at her bare throat. "I've lost it!" Her breath hitched on a sob as she gestured wildly. "I was on duty, and it must have slipped off. I've retraced every step but..."

Trent had moved on, no longer titillated by the woman— there were so many to choose from on a vessel of this size. He winced at the sight of her, startled by her sallow coloring, and her tangled hair. His irritation simmered within. That amulet had been his offering, an initiation into his fold. The void it left rendered her forlorn. Defenseless. Pitiable. His desire for her to be gone intensified, as she had become nothing more than a nuisance.

"Stop your silly theatrics," he barked, annoyed by the disruption. "Your childish actions prove you are not worthy of inclusion in Inheritors of Tenebrosity. You disgust me."

Aubrey colored, shrinking back. "Please, Chaplain, I need its guidance or I'm lost." She stepped forward desperately, the sphere's glow framing her anguished face. "Without it I have nothing. No one."

The desperation in her voice resonated within Trent. He had cultivated such yearning, nurtured its addiction... an addiction that made this quest—this sojourn into the sphere—even more desirable. He relished the potential power that it held.

The Chaplain looked down at Aubrey, ready to reprimand

her for interrupting his plan. Instead, his eyes drifted down to her shirt, unbuttoned at the top, exposing the swell of her breasts—his eyes lingered there on her cleavage, *perhaps she is deserving of a tad more of my... attention*. With a huff of disgust, he reached beneath his robes and withdrew another amulet.

"Do not be careless again with this gift," he admonished as he extended the charm.

Aubrey's fingers closed over it like a lifeline, relief cracking her woeful facade. She turned and hurried away without another word, restored purpose quickening her step.

Trent watched her departure with narrowed eyes before advancing toward the sphere, hunger rising like bile within him. He could feel the orb's paranormal influences—certain he was far more sensitive to such things, him being a man of superior piety.

Shielding his eyes against the sphere's sudden blinding radiance, he hesitated. Having second thoughts, perhaps Quintos' warnings of this alien object had been justified. There again, his exceptional intellect would surely equip him to handle any challenge it might hurl in his direction.

TRENT'S MIND FLASHED BACK TO HIS TIME ON Rigel IV, when he had first learned the power of the mystic arts. He had met a venerable alien mistress there, a wandering sage who possessed forbidden knowledge. She was an old, decrepit being, dressed in a frayed robe, little more than a rag draped around her frail shoulders. Her voice was songful yet commanding, hinting at some semblance of wisdom. At first, she had resisted his overtures, wary of sharing her secrets with an outsider. But he had charmed her with his intellect and persistence, coaxing the intricate formula of the Sithform Malediction from her grasp after several chance encounters. Perhaps they hadn't met by chance, he now speculated.

The ritual had required sacrifice, whereby Trent had been persuaded to hand over his family signet ring, an heirloom passed down generations bearing the Trent family crest. The ring meant little to him, not when weighed against the immense power promised by this old witch. Eagerly he had watched as the hunched mistress drew strange arcane symbols on the ground with a stick, chanting in some long-forgotten tongue that seemed to reverberate with ancient power. Having taken his ring, she had imbued it with the curse through an elaborate and tediously long ritual. Unconsciously, he had taken a step back, a sizzling energy filling the air as the metal glowed a sinister red. Had she branded it with some ancient evil leached from the shadows themselves? Did that matter? Not really.

Trent had cared little for learning any means to later reverse the effects of the spell—such benevolence held little allure for him. But the power to corrupt, to bend others to his will through power and influence—that was all he craved. With the altered ring returned to him, engraved with eldritch sigils, he had gained a means of controlling those around him through its insidious power. Thus far, none have resisted its sinister influence. Even the strongest willed, eventually, succumbed to its corrupting touch. Trent often wondered what the old witch had taken from him in return... Did he care? Meh, not so much.

BACK IN THE PRESENT, TRENT STARED AT THE floating sphere with anticipation. Here was yet another opportunity to expand his dominion, to claim the ship, hell, the whole damn fleet, for his nefarious designs.

There again, some were resistant to the allure of acquiring an amulet—and, by extension, to joining his cadre. Naturally, this posed an issue—though potentially one he could circumvent with the magic contained within this sphere. Having already been endowed with abilities by one old sorceress, perhaps this was where he would augment, perfect, his arsenal of control. A smirk flickered within him at the thought of his continuously expanding legion, whose steadfast devotion, fueled by the sphere's potential sway, would render him unstoppable. Even Quintos would kneel before his might once enveloped by the sphere's occult power.

Trent could almost reach out and touch the strange, projected, rotating symbols that seemed to be talking directly to him. The sphere's metallic exterior shimmered, now accompanied by an unearthly keening that set his teeth on edge. He blinked, squinting, as the sphere's oscillations slowed, its glow dimming to a soft violet hue.

There stood the Guardian having descended halfway down the staircase. His voice resonated, "Welcome, Seeker. I am Grantham, the Guardian of this Archive. State your purpose here."

Trent straightened, gathering his wits. Would some unknowable password be required? This was an unexpected development, but he would not be cowed. "I am Chaplain Halman Trent, a simple man of the cloth. I have come seeking knowledge, nothing more."

The Guardian seemed to consider his words. "Knowledge carries great responsibility. What wisdom do you seek within the Archive's depths?"

Trent's mind raced. How much should he reveal? But the Guardian's expectant silence demanded an answer. "Insight," he began carefully. "Into the nature of influence. Of bonds between minds, wills. How they can be... shaped."

"Ah. You wish to understand the technology behind the

amulets you have created. The ones that exert control over others."

He stiffened. "You know of my amulets?"

"I know many things. But what matters now is how you will use what you learn here. Will it be for good? Or will you follow the path of destruction?"

Trent bristled at the implication. "My path leads only to enlightenment. To guide others toward purpose."

"Purpose must come from within. It cannot be forced." The Guardian's voice grew stern. "If you want knowledge, you must vow to walk in the light. To forsake coercion and respect the will of others."

The Chaplain clenched his jaw, weighing his options. Acquiescence here would secure the knowledge he craved. And once learned, who was to say how he might apply it?

"You have my vow," he said finally, dipping his head in false contrition.

The Guardian seemed to accept this. Raising a welcoming hand, he gestured to Trent toward the entrance at the top of the stairs. Now seeing him up close, Grantham was most definitely an alien of some kind. Not completely hideous. He took in his bound, long hair and his white skin. Tall and slender, his limbs were unnaturally elongated.

Taking in the immense interior, he felt as if he had just entered a Greek or Roman temple. Towering columns and marble were everywhere.

With the wave of the Guardian's hand, Trent found himself transported to what seemed to be a bustling town square where the air was electric with anticipation. All around him, townsfolk were frozen mid-gesture, voices muted, faces alight with excitement.

He turned to the Guardian. "Uh... What is this place?"

"The past of Crythara, moments before a pivotal duel." The

Guardian gestured to the raised platform where no less than a dozen figures were seated.

Halman's eyes were drawn to a beautiful woman in an elegant gown. A portly, yet stately, figure sat next to her in majestic garb, his robe adorned with a stately emblem.

Grantham continued, "I see you have noticed Lady Era, wife of Clitus, the nobleman seated beside her."

Trent gave the brutish man a sideways glance. "Seriously? She's *his* wife?"

Ignoring his comment, Grantham said, "You are here to observe; you will embody the life, the very essence, of one of our civilization's most exalted figures, Nobleman Clitus."

Trent returned his gaze to the pompous-looking guy wearing nice threads, seated next to Lady Era.

"You will experience this event as if it were your own. Mind you, this is no mere reenactment; it is an immersive passage through time and memory."

He had the feeling the old alien had rattled off this spiel a thousand times before. "Okay... will I remember any of this?"

"Of course, think of it as having, of living, two lives simultaneously, your own and his. One part of you, which we refer to as the *Watcher*, remains true to your essence, a silent observer with the autonomy to think and feel *your* thoughts. The other part, which we call the *Adept*, you will be synchronized to. You will think, feel, and fully experience life as this Adept, this Crytharan counterpart."

Trent looked unsure.

"You will bear witness as another," the Guardian continued. "Clitus, his thoughts, and feelings... shall be yours."

Before Trent could respond, the world shifted. Suddenly, he was seated alongside the regal figures, a tumult of emotions churning within. Suspicion, jealousy, despair. This was the mind of Clitus, laid bare.

A fanfare sounded and all at once the square came alive. The crowd roared as two men strode into the arena below. Trent, aware of Clitus's festering thoughts, felt the nobleman's hatred for one of the men in the center ring—Emperor Jaxon, clad in simple battle gear, was of average height, with well-defined musculature. The other man was a broad-shouldered brute, a mass of muscle and scars—Garoff. Looking to his left, he saw Lady Era eyeing the Emperor. No doubt about it, he was her champion. Trent felt the simmering volcano brewing within Clitus.

Trent's breath suddenly caught in his chest, eyes widening as he noticed the amulet hanging around Garoff's thick, sweaty neck. *What the hell?* Unease stirred within him. Something was wrong here.

As the adversaries squared off, Trent—in Clitus's guise—spotted a specific observer. Doing a mental double take, he silently urged Clitus to glance back in that direction. It took a few moments, but there he was. He was my—Chaplain Halman Trent's—exact duplicate. The doppelgänger stood amidst the crowd, face aglow with eagerness and cheering fervently for the larger, hulking combatant, Garoff. Even while immersed in the flesh and mind of Clitus, it wasn't lost on Trent that his twin had provided the amulet to Garoff. No doubt, intending to influence the duel. He certainly could see the logic in doing so. Inwardly smiling, he swelled with pride at this evidence of his handiwork... even here, symbolically, within this virtual realm.

Garoff's eyes found Trent's twin within the crowd. The Chaplain knew all too well, the glazed look of adoration, the unwavering devotion of someone ensnared by the amulet's spell. It was the same look that had greeted him countless times aboard *USS Washington*, in the eyes of those who had accepted his gifts and had become his unwitting acolytes.

Suddenly doubt shadowed his thoughts, then an ominous

revelation took hold. His twin there... he was little more than a cruel mockery made flesh by the sphere's devious machinations. This spellcraft had not been his doing. Yes, something was very, very wrong. Dismay flooded Trent's borrowed mind even as excitement gripped the crowd around him. He longed to silence their din, still their worthless lives... to do so with the force of focused thought. Instead, he was trapped, forced to endure this pathetic drama as the pathetic Clitus.

With a resounding clash of blades, the duel commenced. The Emperor was surprisingly nimble, evading the larger man's powerful first swings. Back and forth they maneuvered as steel sang out. Garoff's brute strength, a good match for Jaxon's speed and skill.

As the duel wore on, Trent felt Clitus' despair growing. His wife's eyes followed Emperor Jaxon's every move—her stare full of longing. Trent was aware of Clitus' thoughts; *my wife wanted him to win... desperately wanted him to be the victor. When had she ever looked upon me with such a gaze? I have never been her champion.*

Rage brewed within Trent, mirrored by Clitus' thoughts— Trent wanted to scream. *This farce must end! Garoff must strike the killing blow, or else all may be lost!*

But Garoff was teetering, his movements slowing, becoming sluggish. Gruesome bloody gashes streaked his form like crimson rivers carved through the landscape of his flesh.

With growing clarity, Trent suspected the sphere had deceived him. Did that matter? Who cares if amulets were powerless here... But a chill slithered down his spine. No. Not just here. If Garoff was to fall, to lose this ridiculous farce of a duel, Trent had a creeping feeling that much more would be lost. *Holy shit...* suddenly his hopes of complete and total domi-nation had been thrown into jeopardy.

And then he knew it in his bones—realization sinking in.

That hadn't been Aubrey Laramie pleading with him for a replacement amulet. Like his doppelgänger, she too was an aberration created by the sphere—meant to distract him, to keep any doubts he may have at bay, as he handed over that amulet— the same amulet worn around Garoff's thick sweaty neck.

Fury surged through his veins. To come so close, only to have his destiny unravel before his eyes! He strained against the bonds of Clitus' mind, yearning to wrap his hands around the Guardian's wrinkled, old throat.

Helpless, he was forced to observe the Emperor... and with one last dramatic swing of his blade, he catapulted Garoff's severed head high into the air, and with it, the amulet... splintering into dust.

Fuck! Trent's anguished inner howl reverberated in the silence of his mind amidst the crowd's raucous cheers. All Trent had worked toward had been circumvented by mere illusion. The bitter taste of defeat filled his mouth, Clitus' disgusting mouth. The sting of betrayal burned his heart. He had been outplayed, by Quintos... but the game was far from over. When he is freed from this cursed sphere, all will pay for this humiliation.

Chapter 19

Captain Galvin Quintos

Racing down the passageway, my boots thundered against the metal deck, each step in sync with the urgent wail of the overhead Klaxon. The voice of SARAH filled the air, a stark reminder of the emergency at hand, directing off-duty crew to safety. The corridor bore the scars of recent chaos. An overturned HoverCart blocked the path and a maintenance bot lay discarded with its arms akimbo and head twisted unnaturally. Also scattered upon the deck were the now-powerless amulets... human crewmembers had torn them from their necks as soon as they learned their dependence on them was not only unnecessary but toxic to their wellbeing.

Ahead, at the corridor's intersection, I spotted a group of Symbio 3.0s, their demeanor once calm—and their obedient assistance guaranteed—now raged uncontrollably. The change in their demeanor sharply diverged from the human crewmembers previously under Trent's influence... who now, remarkably, showed no signs of the manipulation or withdrawal from his amulets' effects.

The disparity was puzzling. Thanks to Guardian Grantham's intervention, the amulets had been reduced to mere decorative trinkets for the Human and Pleidian crew... so why wasn't that true for their Symbio-Poth counterparts?

The Symbio 3.0s, still wearing their amulets, were in a frenzied state. Perhaps the Guardian's powers of restoring normality were limited to organic entities, leaving the artificial minds of the Symbios discordant. It seemed plausible that the Symbios' cognitive functions had been fundamentally altered, making their restoration a far more complex undertaking.

A distant scream drew my focus, urging me to head in that direction. Turning left at the intersection, I found Ensign Lira on the floor, defending herself against three of the 3.0s. Her uniform was in tatters, a clear mark of the struggle, and her cheek was stained with blood. The 3.0s were relentless, their kicks aimed with precision and malice.

Fueled by rage and the enhanced abilities gifted by Gorvian plasma, I intervened. My fist connected with the nose of one Symbio with the force of a pile driver, a satisfying crunch signaling a direct hit. I spun my elbow, knocking another Symbio's head back viciously as if whiplashed. These Symbios, despite their incredible bio-mechanical engineering, were just as susceptible to targeted strikes—a vulnerability I exploited fully—courtesy of Doc Viv's Gorvian concoction that granted me quicker reflexes and near superhuman strength in such dire moments.

The 3.0s scattered, their abilities not up to snuff to match my intervention. Assisting Ensign Lira to her feet, we quickly assessed her condition. She waved off my suggestion to visit HealthBay, determined to continue. Together, we headed towards the bridge, the incessant blaring of Klaxon echoing throughout the corridor.

THE BRIDGE WAS A WHIRLWIND OF ACTIVITY. Station officers and support crew were navigating the crisis with a blend of urgency and precision, their efforts a testament to their training and years of experience. I dropped into the Captain's Mount as Pristy turned to face me.

"SitRep, XO."

"The Symbios' unexpected rebellion spans across the entire fleet," she said. "All those 3.0s you offered up to lighten the spirits on our sister ships, are causing nothing but havoc. The calls for assistance have been coming in non-stop."

I saw Ensign Lira had joined Chen at Comms 2. The two of them looked overwhelmed.

"But *Washington* has her own issues," she said. "The ship, quite literally, has become a madhouse. It's not safe to walk the passageways. I've implemented security protocols, posting guards at all primary departments: Environmental, Propulsion, HealthBay, and hopefully soon... here at the entrance to the bridge."

I nodded. "Good work, XO. Where's Trent now?" I asked, my tone not hiding my *growing-by-the-moment* contempt for the man.

She hesitated, "He's... no longer onboard *Washington*."

Irritated, I shot back, "He's not a pilot, doubt he'd know how to operate a Quansporter console... so where the hell is he?"

"I have no idea. I've put Hardy on it. I'm waiting on an update."

Pristy turned away, all business. Clearly, there was still a chill between us. I took in her profile, the slight upturn of that petite nose, the natural pout of her lips—*Dammit.* I forced myself to look away.

She had multiple halo displays going now, feeds from all over the ship depicting the riotous conditions in every sector, on every deck.

The amulets, sure, neutralized the human crewmembers—even some of the other biological alien crewmembers—but somehow still had a sinister hold on the Symbios. *Dammit, Trent. What did you do?*

Truth was, these inter-networked Symbios thought with one mind. Give an amulet to just one of them, and hell, the whole fleet would have crazed 3.0s running about.

Pristy, her back still to me, said, "Perhaps Trent had unwittingly created a lasting effect with the 3.0s—beyond the amulet's original intent—one that screwed with their inner workings." She shrugged. "I'm just throwing that out there."

I took in what my XO said without acknowledgement. Derrota had informed me that he may have an idea about the Symbio situation but needed time in his lab to do some tests. He hadn't bought that the amulet's power was derived from some kind of paranormal spell. He, the quintessential scientist, sought answers in the realm of science, not mysticism.

Chen said, "Captain, we have an incoming high-priority communique coming in from EUNF Command."

I raised my brows questioningly.

"Admiral Gomez, Sir."

I let out a breath. *This isn't going to be fun.* "Put him through."

The display flickered on, revealing Admiral Gomez. A brooding figure, he was heavily browed, with thick lips, and large, sad-looking eyes. His short brown hair, marked by a distinctive stripe of gray at the top, lent him a unique, almost skunkish appearance. Despite this, his sharp uniform, bristling with medals, underscored his high rank and years of distinguished service.

"Admiral Gomez," I said, bracing for the reprimand—the deluge of verbal admonishments I knew was coming.

"Captain Quintos, nice to make your acquaintance. Your reputation precedes you."

I didn't know if that was a good or bad thing, so only nodded.

"Reviewing your reports, well, to be honest... I'm at a loss."

Here it comes. I squared my shoulders. I'm a big boy, this wasn't my first time in the hot seat, and certainly won't be the last.

"Captain, you've been handed an impossible situation with little support from... well, anyone."

Huh?

Gomez grimaced, rubbed a hand at the back of his neck, and rotated his head around as if he needed serious chiropractic attention. "I want you to know, Captain... *all that* changes from here on out. I am limited by what I can offer, being so many light years away, but I promise you, I'll do my best to get you what you need."

Was this guy for real? There's been one clusterfuck after another, and while I wasn't the crux of most of that, I too had made mistakes.

"Appreciate it, Admiral. Currently, we require a period to conduct repairs and to strategize our forthcoming operation against the Grish more effectively."

"From what I know of your, um, past exploits, Captain, that is exactly where you shine. Alpha Fleet is a quarter the size it was at the start of this campaign. *Washington,* the fleet's flagship, should never have been sent on that ridiculous errand to intersect with that sphere."

I did not comment on that.

"I have news from the Pleidian Weonan situation. Empress Shawlee—"

"Is she safe?" I blurted out. Only now remembering how she had rushed off to deal with something happening, an impending attack, to her homeworld.

"Yes. She is alive. I know you are close to the Empress. Weonan was attacked by an unknown, at the time, battle group. They suffered substantial losses, but the Pleidian Royal Guard held... eventually drove off the attackers."

"Are we talking about the Grish, Sir?"

"Apparently not. Several of the enemy ships were intact enough to be boarded and scrutinized. They are called the *Wrinnth*." He held up a tablet, found what he was looking for, and read aloud, "They have six legs, an orange central body, perhaps reptilian, but also spider-like in the way they move, and they're covered in a gloppy kind of mucus." He looked back up to me. "They sound delightful."

"What's their beef with the Pleidians?"

Gomez shrugged. "Unclear. As far as anyone knows they're not from that quadrant of space, there are no border disputes or history."

I tried to imagine a reptilian, orange spider.

"The Empress is concerned. Having much of her assets sent off with Alpha Fleet, Weonan is now only minimally protected. A second attack by the Wrinnth would be catastrophic. She requests her assets be allowed to return to protect her homeworld."

I looked to Pristy.

She gave a dismissive gesture. "The fleet has only a scant number of Pleidian vessels. Yet, it's a number we can't afford to lose."

Gomez was back rubbing at his neck. "I'll let her know. In the meantime, Captain, I'm working on getting you more help."

"More help?"

"Too early in our negotiations, but the Alliance may be expanding. Seems the Grish has made another enemy."

"That's not surprising," I said. "I look forward to hearing more."

Gomez let out a breath. "You have two days to complete ship repairs. With Prowess Fleet, out of the way, I want you ready to push on to confront Torrent Fleet—"

"Two days?" I scoffed. "Admiral, two *weeks* wouldn't be sufficient. Alpha Fleet has been decimated. We're having to replicate critical parts. Complete systems are being manufactured as we speak." I didn't want to get into the fact that we also have Symbios running around like crazed banshees.

"I understand that. But again, you have two days, Captain."

I took a breath. "Look, Sir... Captain Griffin's encounter with the Grish, with Prowess Fleet, you do realize he might have run them off, but he didn't defeat them. My assumption is those remaining assets have, by now, merged with Torrent Fleet; we're still trying to ascertain their location."

"Good! Once you locate the enemy fleet, combined or otherwise, do what you do best, Captain. Destroy it. Then, move on to the Grish Drakoria System and the awaiting Pinnacle Fleet."

I almost laughed. Was this Admiral on hallucinogens? "Sir, I don't know how we're going to defeat a fortified Fleet. But even discussing going on to engage with that Grish Super Armada, which, by the way, is gargantuan and undefeated in battle, is ludicrous."

"I did mention I'm working on getting you some help," the Admiral said flatly. By his expression, he knew perfectly well he was sending *Washington*, and what remained of Alpha Fleet, not into one impossible battle, but two.

Chapter 20

I entered the lab and found Derrota and Coogong standing, working side-by-side at a far lab bench. Several amulet necklaces were suspended in containment fields hovering a foot or so off the countertop like glimmering jewels floating on invisible strings.

Approaching, Derrota shook his head, looking genuinely perplexed. "I still have no scientific explanation for the amulets' original, um, esoteric qualities. As a man of science, I'm loath to acknowledge mysticism, spells, and such."

"I understand," I said. I leaned in closer to Stephan keeping my voice down as if I was in a university library, "I still don't understand how SARAH was infected. How the hell does an inanimate computer come into contact with an amulet?"

Derrota stared at me for two beats, then said, "Picture this problem as a moving target, Galvin. There is little on this ship that isn't interconnected, cross-referenced... networked."

That still didn't explain how a strictly biological-affecting influence had, somehow, crossed over into a technology-affecting influence. It was unclear what was happening with the

Symbios... the violent reaction one of them had to Phlorinne after he snatched the amulet off the Symbio's neck.

I glanced at the Thine scientist. "I don't get it."

Coogong remained quiet, engrossed in his data.

Derrota exhaled, sounding frustrated. "Indeed, it seems the Chaplain has forged a *defend-to-the-death* hive mind. The 3.0 units are ensnared by the amulet's charm, and its influence has taken an unyielding hold... likely an unintended consequence. Judging from what I know about the Chaplain, he doesn't possess the technical expertise to meddle with their programming."

"Agreed," I said.

"These artifacts, the amulets, clearly contain forces beyond present understanding," Derrota said. "While their origins may forever remain a mystery, we have at least discovered a means of defeating them."

"Thank God," I said, happy for some good news for a change.

Coogong smiled over at me but stayed silent.

Derrota gestured to a display. "See this graphic of counter-acting waveforms?"

I nodded.

"By analyzing the precise energy signature of the amulets'... let's call them emotion waves for now, I can generate an inverse harmonic frequency."

He highlighted the competing wavelength. "This counter-transmission neutralizes the manipulative effects within the very hardware of the 3.0s."

"So, no more biting Symbios? The same would extend to the SARAH, other technologies onboard?"

"Most likely. But, more importantly, we've created a destructive resonance within the amulet itself, which, if my calculations are correct, should overheat its crystalline matrices."

Derrota nodded to Coogong, who tapped at a tablet.

I watched the suspended necklaces; nothing was happening.

"Oh my... I may have to increase the amplitude," Derrota stammered as he adjusted the controls.

Simultaneously, the amulets began to glow, then, *BANG!*

Each burst into countless shards, every fragment corralled within its own confinement field.

Coogong spoke up for the first time, "In essence, we destabilized the amulets through deliberate dissonance between wavelengths. The impacted Symbios should be able to cope without negative repercussions."

"Other than having a crystal explode around their necks," I added with a wince.

"Yes, well, there is that. No way around a little discomfort I'm afraid," Derrota said.

I paused, momentarily mesmerized by the glimmering fragments, some still floating in the contained space like clouds of fairy dust. "So, the next question is how do we deploy that, uh, what did you call it... inverse harmonic frequency?"

Derrota and Coogong looked at each other in confusion.

"It's not a hard question. You've figured it out here in the lab. Now I want to get it going in the real world, throughout the ship—throughout the fleet."

Derrota nodded and pointed to the row of containment fields. "That *was* the real world. If we were successful, every amulet within ten thousand kilometers has been..." He twisted his mouth, casting his eyes downward to where the eviscerated remains of the amulets were smoldering in shallow piles.

. . .

FOR THE NEXT FIVE MINUTES, I WATCHED AS THE two continued working, murmuring scientific calculations and formulas that meant nothing to me. Before I could say *job well done*, my TAC-Band began vibrating. With a glance, I saw multiple calls coming in. The first was from Chief Knott.

"Go for Captain."

"What the hell did you do?"

"I'm sorry?" I sputtered.

"Symbio-Poths, they're being brought in by the truckload. Several of them have had their heads blown clean off!"

I looked at Derrota and then at Coogong.

Both wide-eyed, said nothing.

"I can't treat them here," the Chief continued. "They're not human. Wouldn't know how the hell to... repair them."

"Understood. They'll need to be sent up to the Symbio Deck's maintenance area, wherever that is on this ship. I'll reach out to Sonya—"

Before I could complete my sentence, Sonya had breached my connection to Knott. Looking furious she barked, "What the hell did you do!"

Sonya was to Symbios what Jane Goodall—two centuries ago—was to wild chimpanzees in Africa. And while Goodall was a primatologist, perhaps Sonya was quickly becoming something akin to a Symbio-oligist.

"We had no idea that was going to happen," I blurted out, scowling at Derrota and Coogong.

The two scientists stared at me, stock-still, obviously mortified by the turn of events.

Sonya's eyes narrowed, "All you had to do is give me a day's warning. Enough time to activate the Symbio Deck's manufacturing and repair capabilities." She put her hand to her mouth. "Oh crap."

"What?"

"We're not set up for 3.0s. I have no idea if their bio-mechanical constructs are similar enough to 1.0s or even 2.0s."

I shrugged and offered up an apologetic smile.

"They're already showing up, mostly walk-ins, but some brought in on Hovercarts. Plorinne's telling me a few were missing their heads. We need their heads if we're going to try to repair them."

I glanced over to the exploded amulets within their containment fields. "It is possible that not all of their heads, um, survived the, uh, blasts."

Suddenly distracted, she looked away, and said, "No, Plorinne! Stack them up in Hold 22B!" Turning back to me, glowering, she said, "I have to go clean up your mess."

She cut the connection.

Teeth clenched, I stared at the two scientists. Before Derrota could say anything, I held up a hand to stop him. "You two are in the doghouse until further notice. Collect whatever equipment you'll need and get on up to the Symbio Deck. Make yourselves useful, and repair as many as can be repaired."

Coogong, looking adequately humbled, said, "There is, um, another problem, Captain..."

"What?"

"There are, most likely, injured or decapitated Symbios throughout the fleet."

I shook my head and dragged a hand down my face. Through gritted teeth, I said, "Then I guess you should be reaching out to your counterparts on the other ships. Then head on over to the Quansporter compartment. And you might want to have SWM send up a shitload of HoverCarts. Stack 'em and pack 'em. Best you get to it."

. . .

I ARRIVED ON THE BRIDGE IN A SHITTY MOOD. On the way, I'd been forced to step over close to a dozen damaged Symbios; several, at least to me, looked to be irreparably damaged.

Heads turned in my direction, I felt eyes tracking my progress to the Captain's Mount. *Yup... Captain Quintos, the Symbio Killer, has arrived on the bridge.* As if I didn't feel guilty enough.

Pristy turned in her chair, tilted her head, made a saccharinely sweet expression, and said, "Well, well, in light of your recent slaughter of hundreds of defenseless Symbios, what will your next orders be, Captain? Perhaps we can line up some maintenance bots as target practice. Oh! Wait! How about we play *whack-the-hovering-sensor-droid* like a piñata? How does that sound?"

There were several chuckles from my bridgecrew, which I ignored. I really wanted to stand up and explain how this was not my fault. That it had been Derrota and Coogong who had screwed the pooch, but I'm the Captain of this ship and, you guessed it, the buck stops with me.

So, I offered Pristy back my own saccharinely sweet smile, and said, "How about you give me a SitRep on the elusive Chaplain Trent?"

"Hardy just updated me. He's currently on another ship. It's one of our smaller assets. From what the ChronoBot tells me, Trent forced his way onto one of the fleet's supply shuttles. After putting a tagger to a pilot's head, he forced the airman to lead him to *USS Crosswinds,* an old frigate. Then he tied up the shuttle pilot, shoved him into a supply locker, and found his way into a below-deck maintenance passage."

"So, Hardy has him?"

The corners of Pristy's lips ticked up, "Apparently, Hardy dragged him out of the supply locker, then—kicking and screaming—out of the passageway, and finally tossed him over Climbo's back."

"Wait. Hardy took Climbo with him? To look for Trent?"

"You know how Hardy gets attached to his... friends," she said. "... be it Symbio fairies or mechanical mules. Hardy should be back on board by now, heading to the brig with his prisoner."

"And the disposition of the fleet?" I asked.

"Ship repairs have been stalled due to the whole Symbio fiasco," Pristy said, catching herself stifling a laugh. "If I may, I suggest we assign an overseer. Someone who will Quansport from ship to ship to ensure things are getting done to schedule."

I nodded. "Someone to crack the proverbial whip."

"I guess if you want to put it that way."

I smirked. "How about Captain Griffin?"

"You mean Commander Griffin? Sure, that could work," she said.

"Track him down and get him on it. We'll call him our *Alpha Fleet Repairs Ambassador*."

She nodded unenthusiastically. "I'm sure he'll be thrilled."

"Exactly. Nothing like a little grunt work to evoke some well-needed humility. Let him know Admiral Gomez's two-day deadline. That, and he'll need to hit the ground running."

"Copy that."

I headed away looking at my TAC-Band.

"Where you off to?" she asked.

"HealthBay," I said. "Apparently, not all of our human crew had removed their amulets before they..."

"Blew up?" she said, finishing my sentence.

Chapter 21

I arrived at HealthBay not knowing what to expect. What I hadn't expected, was the crazy madhouse I was walking into. Guilt hit me in the face like a sledgehammer. Every bed was occupied and every doctor, nurse, and MediBot was clearly on duty, attending to crewmember patients with a similar if not identical type of injury. Neck and head trauma.

Third bed over, I saw her. Petty Officer Second-Class Aubrey Laramie. Her neck and chin were bandaged, and a small patch of blood had seeped through her dressing. She raised a hand and attempted a smile as I moved to her bedside.

"Can you talk?" I asked, feeling the weight of culpability constricting my chest.

"Somewhat," she said, swallowing. "It looks worse than it is. Doc says they're kicking me out of here later today or tomorrow, then I'll be able to recover in my quarters."

"That's good," I said, not knowing what else to say. I cleared my throat. "Look, I'm sorry—"

"No," she croaked. "I'm sorry. I latched on to that perv like cat fur to a black sweater. Then... when I put on the necklace. It was like I became another person. Infatuation turned into... I don't know, obsession maybe? I couldn't think, I couldn't eat, hell, I couldn't breathe. Now, I despise the man."

"You're probably not alone in that respect," I said, gesturing to the full ward around us.

She shut her eyes and gave a slight shake of her head. "I'm mortified. You're the very last person I'd ever wish to witness me in that state. I've been lying here replaying my actions." She hammered a fist down onto the bed. "I'm not that gullible, that impetuous."

Impetuous like suddenly kissing me last year in my ready room without warning?

She must have read my expression, my thoughts.

"Shut up," she said.

I raised my palms in mock surrender. "Hey, I didn't say anything." With a smile, I gave her arm a couple of pats. "I need to check on the others in here. Take care of yourself."

I spent the next half hour going from bed to bed, patient to patient, asking how they were doing—if there was anything I could do for them. As it turned out, no one had injuries that were worse than Aubrey's. No horrific decapitations, thank God. Maybe I'd dodged a bullet. Still, this should not have happened.

NAVIGATING TOWARD THE SYMBIO DECK, I WAS laden with apprehension about confronting Sonya and witnessing the utter disapproval I expected to find in her gaze. The teenager typically wasn't one to ask for much, but when my actions contributed to darkening her world, as they did today, I couldn't shake the sense that I'd failed her.

Like HealthBay, this place was chaotic, resembling an out-of-sync production line. Derrota and Coogong, along with Hardy were present. Crewmembers from ShipWide Maintenance bustled around; one pushed a HoverCart heaped with decapitated Symbios, while another pair hoisted a Symbio by its extremities, flinging the biomechanical form onto a heap of its 3.0 counterparts.

Sidling up to Derrota at a diagnostics console, I noticed he was attaching leads to a stretched-out, headless Symbio body.

"Repairable?" I asked, watching the body's left leg suddenly twitch.

He nodded. "Oh... hello Galvin. Yes, they're all repairable. We have thirty-seven new heads being fabricated. Seems there's a design flaw with this 3.0 version. The neck structures, vertebral columns, are insufficiently supported." Derrota used the point of his probe to direct my eyes to the exposed cross-section of the neck.

I winced. It looked like a chopped tree stump.

Derrota continued, "The musculature in this area should have been made more robust."

Now glancing around, I was only half-listening to him.

"Have you visited HealthBay?" His voice wavered with uncertainty, and he didn't bother concealing his anguish.

"No fatalities. A few scrapes and minor injuries," I lied.

"Oh, that's good, very good," he said momentarily looking lost in self-incriminating thoughts.

Moving on, I passed by Hardy who was pushing an oversized squeegee thing on a pole. He must have just gotten back from throwing the Chaplain in the brig. No rest for the weary.

Although Symbios don't have blood, per se, they do have bodily fluids of various hues, and puddles of the stuff had saturated much of the deck. The ChronoBot's faceplate displayed his John Hardy face, an old-fashioned clothespin clamped to his nose.

Sonya was in a nearby chamber tending to a large metallic container. Clad in denim pants and a casual tee, her oversized apron was stained with muddied, greenish-gray fluids... similar to those Hardy was swooshing towards the drainage grates.

"Hey there," I said, peering over the edge of the big vat.

"Hand me that agitator." She chinned toward what looked like a giant spoon hanging from a hook on the bulkhead.

I did as asked.

She took it and began slowly stirring the milky white liquid within.

"What is this stuff?"

"SynthDerm Polymer."

"Oh... okay."

"It's a bio-compatible elastomer, meticulously engineered to form the base of a Symbio's epidermis... offers unparalleled realism and flexibility."

"Has a distinct, um, smell to it, doesn't it?" I asked.

She stopped stirring long enough to glare at me.

"Hey, I'm sorry. I'm very, very, very sorry, Sonya. There's no excuse for what's happened—"

"Take this, and keep stirring," she said.

I did as asked, trying to duplicate the same slow, figure-eight motions.

Ensign Plorinne had arrived with a wheelbarrow full of fleshless Symbio skulls. "Hey Captain," he said good-naturedly. "Best you stand back, Sir. Get SynthDerm on your uniform, or your skin, it's near impossible to get it off."

Sonya and Plorinne started dropping the skulls into the vat. *Plop, plop, plop...* in they went. Once done, Sonya snatched the agitator from me and began stirring again.

Plorinne headed off, I assumed to get more skulls.

"These heads... they won't look like they're supposed to. Not enough time to do the regular facial fabricating."

I nodded and peered down into the vat. "Kind of reminds me of bobbing for apples."

She huffed out an exasperated breath.

"Please don't be mad at me. I know I screwed up. Screwed up badly."

She made a face, "Ya think?" She offered a crooked smile. "They won't look like the other 3.0s."

"Is that a bad thing?" I asked. "A thousand Symbios all with that same bowl haircut, and pasted-on smile?"

That warranted a real smile.

"You know, this version really is a shoddy excuse for a Symbio 3.0," Sonya said. "Less intelligent, only passable capabilities for doing rote jobs. No imagination, no individualism... SWM MopBots have more personality."

"I think the intent was to avert another Symbio mutiny."

"I guess," she said. "You don't have to hang around here, you know. I'll get over being mad at you... someday."

"I like hanging around with you." I took another look into the vat. "You and your friends."

"Ha ha," she said, trying not to laugh.

THE LAST STOP ON MY TREK AROUND THE SHIP WAS the brig. Chaplain Trent was seated in the same cell that I had occupied earlier. With an erect back, and head held high, he looked like a chastened child sitting in the principal's office.

"Chaplain," I said, catching the man's attention.

"Ah, Captain Quintos. So considerate of you to visit me."

I stared at him through the diamond glass. He sat there looking smug and unconcerned—It made my blood boil.

"I hope you realize the amount of trouble you're in," I said, unable to keep the anger out of my voice. "Your actions have contravened multiple protocols, including section 489b of the

Uniform Code of Military Justice that forbids behavior unsuitable for an officer, as well as regulations such as section 555.1a which prohibits assault, and then there's section 777.3c which prohibits kidnapping."

Trent waved his hand dismissively. "Don't waste your breath citing U.S. Space Navy regs to me, Captain. I'm not actually in your precious U.S. Space Navy if you recall."

I clenched my fists. "Maybe not officially, but you were serving aboard this ship in an official capacity. That makes you subject to our codes of conduct."

He smirked. "I don't recognize your authority over me or my actions."

"Well, you're going to have to recognize the authority of a court-martial," I shot back. "What you've done goes far beyond some petty infraction. You've endangered this entire ship and her crew with your reckless behavior."

Trent leaned back against the wall of his cell, looking infuriatingly relaxed. "I was merely providing spiritual guidance to those interested in embracing a higher path. Any... unfortunate incidents were unintended consequences."

"Unintended consequences?" I sputtered. "Over two dozen crewmembers are recovering in HealthBay right now because of your so-called spiritual guidance. Not to mention the damage done to hundreds of Symbios that are now disabled."

"Casualties in the quest for enlightenment," Trent said with an all-knowing smirk.

I stepped right up to the partition, glaring at him. "I don't care what kind of twisted justification you've concocted in that deranged mind of yours. You've endangered this ship and its crew. And I promise you, you will face the consequences."

Trent stood up smoothly, meeting my gaze through the glass between us. His eyes were cold, but his tone remained polite and calm. "We shall see, Captain Quintos. Perhaps it is you who will face consequences for impeding my sacred work."

With that vague threat hanging in the air, he turned and walked to the rear of his cell, signaling the conversation was over. I stared after him for a long moment, then turned on my heel and walked out of the brig.

Chapter 22

I'd been given a mere forty-eight hours to marshal Alpha Fleet and carry out crucial repairs on incapacitated ships. Perhaps of greater significance, I had to mold it into a finely calibrated combat unit—a unit that would go into battle with not only confidence but also that added extra intangible thing—camaraderie.

So, how does a fleet commander instill that elusive, fickle even, frame of mind—that potent cocktail of morale and fighting spirit, especially when the odds seem so insurmountable? Well, I was still working on that...

I stood within the Rotunda's Gravity Well projection, what was left of Alpha Fleet splayed out before me, a cinematic, slow drift camera roll perspective from overhead.

The two days I'd been granted by Admiral Gomez had already come and gone, so yeah, the clock was ticking, a constant reminder that time was as much an adversary as any alien flesh-and-blood enemy we'd face. *Dammit! I had to act and act fast.* The tactics I'd be employing would have to be both simple and effective... no, not just effective... fucking brilliant.

Hardy was standing at the podium. It was just the two of

us here. I'd given explicit orders to the bridge, don't bother us unless it's a three-alarm fire. Pristy, who had had the most time working with the Gravity Well, mentioned that the device had a *War Games* component that would let me *game out* battle scenarios using SARAH's formidable AI processing capabilities. Over the last hour, I saw that firsthand. The way the AI comprehends all the factors—the virtues, capabilities, vulnerabilities, critical battle damage of each Alpha Fleet ship, even the variables of each ship's Captain and crew. SARAH had every past Grish battle scenario stored in her memory banks. After doing deep-dive analytics of the enemy's weaknesses and advantages—advantages beyond the obvious, their sheer numbers had left me even more concerned than before.

We were coming at this in terms of a three-dimensional Cartesian coordinate system and my brain was physically hurting. I was drawing upon academic concepts I hadn't fully utilized since the academy. Deploying attack strategies using a coordinate-based system, leveraging SARAH's AI to calculate and simulate engagements from various vectors and trajectories in the three-dimensional battlespace. This involved specifying target approaches using a grid of right ascension and declination for broader spatial orientation, combined with radial velocity vectors for dynamic positioning. By manipulating these spatial coordinates and velocities, we simulated flanking maneuvers and pincer attacks from directions that exploited the enemy fleet's tactical gaps, optimizing our forces' effectiveness in the vacuum of space.

No less than fifty battle attack scenarios had already played out for us in ultra-high-virtual reality. At ten times the actual speed and coming at the gamed-out play action from different view perspectives, it allowed us to see what works, or where the wheels fell off the cart. Up to this point, we had observed time and again the dismal fate of Alpha Fleet's modest forces, repeatedly being annihilated with striking, definitive clarity.

"Let's go again, Hardy. This time, send our super battle cruisers to initiate their onslaught along the positive Y-axis path."

Hardy wobbled his head from side to side, conveying skepticism. "Meh... not really feeling that strategy, Cap. Perhaps we should consider swooping down on those four piglet destroyers situated in the X-coordinates from -1000 to -500, Y-coordinates from -200 to 200, and Z-coordinates from 100 to 300?"

I massaged my temples. Keeping pace—specifically juggling the geometric calculations—and mentally managing the math, specifically, the subfield of geometry, had been within my grasp until now. But I'd hit my threshold. Was I ready to give up? Concede to the fact we wouldn't be defeating the Grish Torrent Fleet with what we were capable of bringing to the battle?

I let out a resigned breath and said, "Just show me."

"I'm calling this *Attack Plan Porcupine*."

"Fine, let's see it."

As the simulation kicked off, Alpha Fleet didn't rush into battle. Instead, it spread out, with *Washington* taking point, its presence making a bold statement against the Grish. The fleet's smaller ships, including battle cruisers and destroyers, positioned themselves strategically, ready to pounce, not in a head-on clash but through hit-and-run tactics designed to chip away at the Grish's superior numbers.

Washington darted forward, drawing the Grish Fleet's attention. The omninought's movements were deliberate, designed to create openings for Alpha Fleet's smaller vessels to exploit. The Grish, being confident in their numerical advantage, pushed forward, not realizing they were playing into Hardy's latest strategy. But I'd watched this same strategy too many times to be optimistic.

At the moment the Grish Fleet was momentarily overextended, while Alpha Fleet was striking hard, again. This part of the plan had been effective. The smaller ships, now acting as agile predators, launched precise strikes along the Grish's flanks. Alpha Fleet's smart missiles, precision railgun forays, and Phazon Pulsars hit key enemy vulnerabilities pretty much nonstop. These were not random attacks but carefully coordinated maneuvers, each strike forcing the Grish to divert resources to fend off these smaller skirmishes, thinning their defensive posture.

Simultaneously, *USS Washington* unleashed its full arsenal. Its firepower was not just aimed at causing physical damage but also at sowing chaos within the Grish ranks. The Grish, caught off guard by the ferocity and precision of these attacks, scrambled to regroup, their formation beginning to falter.

Hardy's, and to a lesser degree, my strategy, for Alpha Fleet was clear: divide and conquer. By drawing the Grish Fleet's resources in opposite directions, their numerical advantage would be, potentially, neutralized. I watched as the smaller Alpha assets continued their assaults, now targeting isolated Grish vessels, while *Washington* bore down on the heart of the enemy formation, including their flagship, the Grish Super Battle Cruiser. The omninought's firepower overwhelmed the Grish flagship's defenses. In previous scenarios, this failed— Grish support vessels swooping in to protect their command ship.

As the battle progressed, the Grish seemed to have found themselves unable to mount a coherent defense. I tamped down my growing excitement. Their attempts to rally were being met with relentless pressure from an unpredictable Alpha Fleet, our ships now encircling the Grish Armada, cutting off any chance of retreat or regrouping. I exchanged a glance with the ChronoBot and did a double-take. His faceplate was on a 5-

second loop. A cartoon showing a comically oversized, terrified, pig galloping in circles—being pursued by a group of tiny, determined humans with oversized forks and knives.

I put my attention back on the Gravity Well display. Confusion clouded my mind... or perhaps it was disbelief. I was now witnessing a battlefield littered with the growing remnants of the Grish Fleet. Sure, there were plenty of Alpha Fleet losses too, but we had clearly outmaneuvered and outsmarted our adversary. *Washington* and its supporting ships were now turning the tide through tactical brilliance and the element of surprise.

"Huh... I think we're going to emerge victorious this time," I declared.

"Indeed. Attack Plan Porcupine," Hardy remarked, now performing an ungainly jig that would be seared into my memory.

From behind, I heard Pristy say, "Holy crap, honestly, I didn't think you'd figure it out."

I glanced behind Hardy to find the XO standing there, a radiant grin lighting up her face. Hues of the Gravity Well shimmered across her figure. I wanted to rush to her, sweep her up into my arms, and swing her around. I wanted to breathe her in and kiss her. But, of course, I didn't.

Instead, I turned to Hardy, and said, "Okay big guy, now you just have to do it again, and again... and again so it's no longer just a fluke of circumstance."

His faceplate went black. "Buzz kill."

Chapter 23

I t's one thing to come up with a viable plan. A plan on paper, or via Gravity Well, in this case... one that foretells probable battle tactics success. It's a whole other thing to bring together an eclectic group of U.S. Space Navy, Pleidian Weonan, and Thine ship Captains, and deliver them their specific marching orders. Orders that take into account variables and contingencies. All those *what-if* scenarios. But it's human and alien nature—one could argue—to insist upon playing devil's advocate, to want to come up with one's own spin on things—to put forth an attack plan that may be derived from the gut just as much as from strategy.

Seated in the Captain's Conference Room, I looked around. They were all here, and it was standing-room-only, with several COs here via video feed. No one looked particularly happy.

Here's where I'm at with each ship's Commander, having perused Hardy's Attack Plan Porcupine. They've scrutinized the OPORD—the Operations Order—in exacting detail. Every OPORD has been crafted with particular attention to the viewpoint of each Captain and tailored to their respective vessel. And while I took in the myriad of ideas and/or constructive criticisms, I had no intention of changing anything. These were *my orders*, and it was *their job* to follow them. But this assembled group had never been cohesive—had never played well with others.

As I surveyed the room, the friction was impossible to ignore. Hardy's Attack Plan Porcupine lay at the center of a brewing storm, each Captain's scrutiny carving deeper divides. I saw that Captain Longmont of USS *Capital Fight* was being especially reserved.

Captain Marquez of USS *Valkyrie*, whose face was as rugged as the asteroid fields of Zeta Reticuli, broke the tense silence first. He leaned in, his bushy eyebrows furrowing like two caterpillars in a standoff. "This plan assumes too much risk for the left flank. My ship can't cover that expanse effectively," he declared defiantly.

No sooner had Marquez's words left his lips than Captain Liu of USS *Sentinel* sprang into action. Behind her back, she was known as the *Cat Lady;* her quarters typically housing no less than five felines on any assigned vessel. She also looked somewhat cat-like with wide-eyed, expressionless features, and a short-cut black bob hairdo. She stood, her chair screeching across the deck in protest. "And my vessel is supposed to just slide into the heart of the enemy formation with only theoretical support? It's reckless!" she exclaimed, her hands flailing for emphasis as if swatting at an invisible swarm of space gnats.

The compartment erupted into a cacophony of disagreements, each Captain airing their grievances, their faith in the plan waning by the second.

I raised a hand, signaling for silence. "I hear your concerns, loud and clear. Each of you brings invaluable experience and insight to this table, and yes, Attack Plan Porcupine is not without its risks. But let me remind you, the essence of warfare is risk. What we're undertaking is unprecedented, designed to play to our strengths and exploit the enemy's arrogance."

I walked over to the display, pointing to the highlighted sectors. "Captain Marquez, your concerns about the left flank are noted. But remember, *Valkyrie's* agility is unmatched. You can outmaneuver them where others can't. And Captain Liu, *Sentinel's* firepower will be our trump card. You'll have the support needed, not just theoretically but every step of the way."

My gaze swept across the conference room, meeting the eyes of each Captain. "Doubt is a luxury we can't afford. This plan, our plan, relies on each ship, each Captain, playing their part. It's not just about following orders; it's about mutual confidence, having faith in the power we possess when we come together as one entity. Yes, we've never been cohesive, but today, we change that narrative. Today, we stand together, not as disparate ships, but as a singular, indomitable force."

Pristy, who had been standing off to the side, spoke up, "We can't pretend this will be easy, or that doubt won't creep in. But I ask you to trust in Fleet Commander Quintos' plan."

Hardy cleared his non-existent throat.

"The Captain's *and* Hardy's plan," she corrected. "Trust in the plan but most importantly, in each other. Together, we can turn the tide. United, we can ensure success. And if that fails, bear in mind the recent havoc wreaked by the piglets upon our home... upon Earth."

The room went dead quiet, the heated arguments cooling to a contemplative silence. I could tell we were in for a rough ride, but right in the middle of all that tension, it felt like we were finally starting to pull together.

I nodded approvingly toward my XO. *Good job.*

. . .

NOT ALL OF ALPHA FLEET'S 45 WARSHIPS WERE battle-ready; three needed more time to make repairs: *USS Titan*, a next-generation smart missile destroyer; *USS Liberty Star*, a super-carrier, designed to serve as a formidable deep space airbase capable of deploying a wide range of aircraft; and *USS Maverick*, an out-of-date frigate whose better days were decades past. We would stay in close contact, and, if possible, they would join the fleet in a few days—although, by then it would probably be too late.

All of our guest Captains were back on their respective ships. A consensus had been made—reluctantly, to follow the orders given. Our intel on the Grish Armada—what remained of Prowess and the entire Torrent Fleet— indicated that the armada was on the move and could very well be headed to Earth to finish what they had started.

Crewmember Grimes had already locked in a course for the Hanlang Bar System, a two-day excursion that would entail two manufactured wormholes with several FTL jaunts in between.

The forty-two battle-ready Alpha Fleet warships had taken up formation, ready to leave the rendezvous location.

Situated within the firm cushions of the Captain's Mount, I glanced about the bridge, the epicenter of anticipation and activity as we prepared to embark on one more perilous journey. The crew's eyes were fixed on the large primary halo display, where a spectacle of prismatic colors began to coalesce into a swirling vortex. It was like witnessing the birth of a cosmic serpent, its scales shimmering with every hue imaginable, wrapping around itself in an intricate parlance of physics and light.

The wormhole's iridescence painted the bridge in surreal shades, casting my crew in an otherworldly glow. Even though we were all veterans of space travel, each foray into a wormhole still felt like peering into the divine.

With the wormhole becoming stable, I knew it was time to

muster my fortitude. So why did I want to jump away from here, and yell for the Helm to take us in an entirely different direction?

"Take us in, Mr. Grimes," I commanded crisply.

The Helmsman's hands flew over his board as he executed my order. The ship hummed with power, and the deck plates vibrated as we surged toward our unknown fate.

"Captain." Chen's voice was steady, yet held an edge that immediately caught my attention. "We're receiving an urgent transmission from Admiral Gomez."

Chapter 24

Whatever the Admiral wanted to convey would have to wait. Deep space comms were down during wormhole transits. We were currently hurtling forward at an unholy, consciousness-warping velocity that rendered FTL—faster-than-light—travel a mere speck in the rearview mirror.

The collective tension of my bridgecrew seemed to release all at once. Previously strained expressions, were now relaxed... soft-murmured conversations resumed between station posts. Several new halo displays—Logistics, and Ship Diagnostics were projected into view. No red flags. Even today's Mess Hall lunch special—Beef Chili with Cornbread—was posted. Normality had eclipsed apprehension... at least for now.

Four hours and seven minutes later, while working within the muted lighting of my ready room, the unthinkable happened. A moment in time that was so enormous, it would change the trajectory of my life.

I looked up hearing a distant, echoey announcement resonating within *Washington's* passageways and corridors. I couldn't make out SARAH's specific words, only her sobering tone. I suddenly sat up straight, my body going rigid as if hit by a bolt of lightning. *Oh my God...* Something terrible had just occurred, I just *knew* it. My breath caught in my chest, instant vertigo had me reeling, while a paralysis of both mind and body had me incapable of action.

My vibrating TAC-Band jolted me back to reality. It was Chief Knott. I tapped to accept the call. As her projected form materialized, I saw that all color had drained from her face, her eyes were wide and fixed. I'd seen that look too many times. That dreaded battle stare. The look of one who's seen something unimaginable, something horrific.

"Talk to me, Chief. What's happened?"

She opened her mouth to speak, but no words came out. Tears brimmed, then cascaded down her cheeks, dual rivers of despair.

"Chief!" I barked, getting to my feet.

She gasped out, "Get down to Circadian Platform Deck G. Do *NOT* take the DeckPort! Quansport there. Come now. Hurry!"

Within seconds I was sprinting across the Rotunda, heart thundering, a relentless drumbeat heralding doom. Reaching the Quansporter compartment, I was met by a Symbio-Poth 3.0, he was one of the newly refurbished ones, his featureless face eerily blank, like wax melted under intense heat.

"Captain, I'm ready for you," the 3.0 announced, motioning toward the Quansporter's pedestals.

Without hesitation, I leaped onto the nearest one. "Do it!" I commanded.

In a flash, I was quansported into a broad, meticulously clean corridor probably no different than a hundred others within *Washington*. The Quansporter's disorienting flash left a ghostly afterimage that blurred my vision, but it couldn't obscure the odd circumstances unfolding before me. I took in the scene—several individuals stood huddled before the Deck-Port. Strange... but Chief Knott, palms up to her face like a child playing peekaboo, was leaning against a bulkhead, sobbing quietly off by herself.

I could see that one crewmember was down on his knees, leaning over as if praying or looking for something lost on the deck. Again, momentarily paralyzed—something wasn't making sense. Then, the huddled crowd parted. The man on his knees was Stephan Derrota and he was speaking in low tones, speaking as a parent would gently talk to a young child who had awakened from a nightmare. It was then that I saw the flash of blonde hair. I looked up, seeing the faces of the others—why so distraught? *You know why, you just don't want to look at her...*

Then, I felt my knees go weak. My heart sank, each beat a hammer against an anvil of dread. Derrota's voice was a soothing murmur, the kind meant to comfort the inconsolable.

Taking those two unsteady steps felt like crossing an abyss. I dropped to my knees beside Derrota, my eyes locking onto what remained of Gail Pristy. She was there but not whole, her body a cruel testament to the fragility of life aboard a starship where death could be sudden and merciless.

Her face was serene, untouched by the carnage below her waist where her body should have continued. There was nothing. It was as if someone had edited her out of existence from the midsection down. The DeckPort had executed a sharp, precise, and horrifyingly definitive cut.

She was trying to speak, her lips moving with effort, forming words I strained to hear over the ringing in my ears.

"Everyone leave! Get out!" I barked, not recognizing my own voice. It was harsh, commanding... desperate.

The group dispersed without protest, leaving only Derrota and me flanking Pristy—sentinels guarding a fallen comrade.

Derrota looked at me with eyes that said what words could not—this was it; there would be no miraculous recovery.

Gail's eyes found mine, those brilliant blue orbs that had always seemed capable of piercing through any facade I put up. "Galvin," she whispered, her voice barely a breath.

I leaned in. "I'm here," I replied, fighting to keep my voice steady as I took her hand in mine. It felt small and fragile.

"I've always..." She paused, wincing in pain or perhaps at the struggle to articulate thoughts that had remained unspoken for too long.

"Don't speak," I urged gently, my thumb brushing over her knuckles in a futile attempt at comfort.

"No," she insisted with a faint shake of her head. "You have to know Galvin... I've always loved you. From the first time we met."

Her words struck me with the force of a comet hitting solid ground. We'd danced around our feelings for years, duty and decorum keeping us at arm's length.

"Gail," I started, choking back emotions that threatened to overwhelm me. "Our time together—it's still possible."

She smiled that same smile that had first drawn me to her years ago on *Hamilton's* bridge—a smile that now would be seared into my memory until my last breath.

"Shut up and listen," she said, her voice cloaked with surprising strength. "You need to finish what we started... don't let this change you."

I nodded, unable to trust myself with words.

"Gail," I managed after a moment, leaning in so close our foreheads softly touched. "I... I love you too."

But as the words left my lips, something shifted in her gaze

—a flicker of something distant and untouchable—and I knew then that she was already slipping away from me.

Her grip on my hand weakened; her eyes lost their focus and gazed through me as if peering at a distant mirage in the desert.

"Ga... il?" My voice broke on her name—a plea for her not to go... not yet.

Her eyelids fluttered once... twice... then... although not fully closed, stilled. The light in her eyes dimmed and then... snuffed out. Just. Like. That. She was gone.

Time ceased its march for one agonizing moment as silence descended upon us—a silence so profound it roared louder than any battle cry or alarm Klaxon ever could.

Derrota placed a gentle hand on my shoulder—but his touch barely registered.

I sat there on the cold deck cradling Gail Pristy's hand in mine long after warmth had left it—long after anyone else might have called for medics or covered her with a flag.

Then the pain hit like a one-two punch—I reacted, not with sobs or wails, but with a silent tribute—for Gail Pristy... my XO... who had always loved me and whom I had loved in return... too late realized and now forever gone.

Chapter 25

No-no-no. This cannot be the end of her...

Chapter 26

S till on my knees, I straightened, letting go of Pristy's lifeless hand. Only Derrota and Chief Knott were in attendance. Clearly, instructions had been issued that this section of the vessel was to remain undisturbed.

I stood and tore my eyes away from my XO's still form.

"Stephan... I understand enough about these devices to know that they have memory buffers just like Quansporters. This was not supposed to happen. We can bring her back."

My friend, maybe my best friend, could only stare back at me.

"What? We need to get moving. Before—"

"I can't, Galvin. It's not possible." His eyes went to the DeckPort, then down to Pristy's still form. "This ship—the DeckPorts—are not the same as on *Franklin*. They've been modified so duplicate versions of a person can't be inadvertently created."

My breath caught. I remembered what LaSalle had told me several days earlier when I first came on board *Washington*.

Rage surged within me like a storm, uncontrollable and fierce. My hands, now balled into fists, shook at my sides as I glared at Derrota. He had the gall to stand there, spouting impossibilities when I knew better. With a swift movement fueled by desperation and rage, I pushed him up against the bulkhead, my face inches from his.

"You have to save her," I growled through clenched teeth. The metal bulkhead thudded behind him, echoing my fury. "Stephan, look at me! You're going to dig into that DeckPort's circuits and you're going to figure this out like you've done a hundred times before!"

Derrota's eyes were wide with shock, his hands raised in a helpless gesture. But it was the resignation painted across his face that further fanned the flames of my anger.

Chief Knott was suddenly there, her hands on my shoulders trying to pull me back. "Captain, please!" she pleaded.

I shrugged her off with an angry jerk of my shoulders. "I do not accept this! Not like this—a malfunction? She doesn't have to die!"

"I'm sorry, Galvin," Derrota said, his voice barely above a whisper as he shook his head. His words felt like hammer blows to my resolve. "But there are new restrictions – EUNF laws in place that restrict, outlaw doing exactly what you're proposing... There are ethical lines I cannot cross."

In the depths of space, *Washington*, along with Alpha Fleet, sliced through the fabric of the Universe, propelled within its manufactured wormhole. Our destination was an intergalactic battle against the Grish. Yet, as the weight of Earth's fate rested upon my shoulders, I found myself consumed by a personal anguish that eclipsed even the looming specter of total planetary occupation.

Chief Knott's medical personnel had, discreetly, handled

the transfer of Gail Pristy's grisly, partial remains. The body would remain in the ship's morgue until *Washington's* eventual return to Earth, where the remains would be handed over to Pristy's mother, Claire, and her father, Roger Pristy.

For six relentless hours, I ordered, implored, and even threatened those few aboard with the technical wherewithal to delve into the intricate and complex circuitry of the DeckPort—Pristy's essence was in there, somewhere... I was sure of it.

Derrota, Coogong, and even the enigmatic Hardy—all, I suspected, possessed the tech skills, but none dared risk the certainty of imprisonment or, in Hardy's case, permanent deactivation. I was baffled and angered by Hardy's uncharacteristic adherence to the rules.

In a futile attempt to maintain a semblance of normalcy, I decided to engage in a morning bridge post. I was there physically but I kept getting lost in thought, staring at the empty Tactical Station. I felt the sympathetic gazes and whispered pity from my crew, their concern sincere yet suffocating.

It had been Crewmember Davit who told me to go, take some time for myself. That absolutely nothing would be happening as long as *Washington* was within the wormhole.

Deep into the night, I emerged from my ready room with a half-consumed bottle of *25-year-old Macallan Scotch Whisky*. Numbed by the booze, I set out without a destination, content to wander, and at times drunkenly stagger, through the ship's meandering passageways.

In the endless corridors, I sought solace but found only

haunting reminders of Pristy—her face captured in distorted bulkhead reflections, her ghostly image walking beside me, forever wearing that enchanting, bemused smile.

I don't know how many hours I wandered, stumbled... one, three, maybe more? Perhaps drawn by a need for seclusion, I drifted into a long narrow passageway within the ship's underbelly. This subterranean alcove of oversized pipes and endless cable runs was like a dense metal jungle whispering secrets of this omninought's inner workings. Towering black electrical cabinets, like ominous tombstones, encroached upon the already too-narrow passageway. Their forms cast eerie shadows against the occasional flickering of cloudy lights. It was a fitting environment for my fractured state of mind, dreary and colorless. Coming to a particularly foreboding spot, I stopped and slumped against a bulkhead, then allowed gravity to pull me down to the deck plates.

When the tears came, they arrived in all their glory—a deluge of anguished cries accompanied by copious amounts of runny snot and breathless, dry heaves. Yeah, ugly crying. The inevitable self-directed questioning followed, *Why, why, why?*

Lost in my misery, I succumbed to exhaustion and drifted into a fitful sleep amidst the pipes and gravestone cabinets.

WHEN I FINALLY AWOKE WITHIN THAT COLD DARK passageway some hours later, one truth became evident—I was no longer alone.

Chapter 27

A shape materialized there in the dark recesses of *Washington's* underbelly. I cleared my throat, my voice hoarse from meltdown. "Who's there?"

The bearded man stepped forward and looked down at me. He picked up the now-empty bottle of *Macallan's*. "If you don't mind me saying so, you're a pretty pathetic-looking sight, Captain."

"Mr. Rivers... what are you doing here?"

Kaelen Rivers stepped further into the muted light, his face devoid of the pervasive pity I'd come to see on everyone else's expression since the accident. I appreciated that.

"Initially, it's crucial to temper your hopes. But we may be able to bring your XO back from oblivion."

I just stared up at the man, slack-jawed.

"I mean it, Captain, even a 5% chance of success might be overly hopeful thinking."

I didn't care about the odds; his words jolted me to my feet. "Who is *we?*" I demanded, my heart racing.

Kaelen smirked. "Come on, Captain. You didn't actually believe them when they said they wouldn't help you. Did you?

Of course, they had to say that they wouldn't *break regulations*, especially since they were only put into effect this past week, after the incident involving that Calvin Peterson bloke. Eyes and ears everywhere." He glanced around the cramped space. "Good. You've found one of the few places onboard *Washington* that doesn't have security cameras. SARAH won't be watching or listening to us here. You need to understand, a ship's AI is not on your side, it is on the side of the EUNF."

I nodded, my mind still reeling with the implications of his earlier words. "So, what's the plan? How do we bring her back?"

Kaelen's demeanor grew grave. "Reviving Gail will be messy... challenges and setbacks are inevitable. The DeckPort's quantum memory buffer, which captured her molecular pattern, was immediately purged following the incident to forestall unintended replicas, in line with the new guidelines. Yet, Derrota and I are devising a strategy to delve into the quantum domain itself, drawing on Sir Louis de Broglie's foundational work in quantum physics."

"The same physics that led to our original Quansporters back on *USS Jefferson*," I said, remembering the breakthrough.

He nodded, "That's right, it started with Port Entanglers back then. The Port Entanglers utilized the principles of quantum entanglement, where particles are linked together so that the quantum state of each particle cannot be distinguished independently of the others, even when separated by vast distances. This is the foundation for all quantum teleportation technology, including the DeckPorts." Kaelen let out a breath. "Uh, what we're intending is, well, complicated. I'm not so sure you want to get that far into the weeds with the technical aspects."

"A woman's life is at stake, lay it out for me. If I have questions, I'll ask."

Kaelen continued, "With DeckPorts, when a person steps

in, their physical form is converted into a pure quantum energy state. This energy state, containing all the information about their molecular structure, is reassembled for transit. However, due to the principles of quantum entanglement, we believe that a person's quantum state remains connected to their original physical form, even after dematerialization."

"How does that help us?"

"If we can tap into this entanglement, we might be able to trace Gail's quantum signature back to the moment just before the incident occurred. In essence, we'd be using the DeckPort's quantum entanglement as a sort of *quantum roadmap* to locate her specific energy state."

I leaned forward, intrigued. "And once you've found her quantum signature?"

"That's where things get tricky. We'll need to find a way to reconstruct her physical form from that quantum state. It's like trying to reassemble a complex puzzle from just a handful of pieces. But if we can leverage the DeckPort's quantum entanglement properties, we might be able to fill in the missing information and bring Gail back."

"I'm sensing a *but* coming."

Kaelen nodded grimly. "*But* the process of manipulating quantum states is highly unstable. One wrong move, and we could trigger a cascading quantum reaction that might tear apart the very fabric of space-time. We'll need to proceed with the utmost caution and precision."

I took a deep breath, weighing the risks and rewards. "What do you need from me?"

"DeckPorts came out of EUNF labs. The development, top secret. Access to the DeckPort system's programming—its QuansScript code, will be necessary to bypass the quantum buffer's security protocols. Coding at that level is not my area of expertise. Nor is it Stephan's, or the worm guy's."

"The worm guy?"

"Uh, Coogie, Coogar, Coomy... I can't remember the little fucker's name. The brainiac with the helmet."

"Coogong?"

"Yeah, him. Anyway, there's only one person onboard who's got the coding skills—"

I raised a palm to stop him right there. "No way. I don't want Sonya involved with any of this. She's just a kid. You, me, Stephan? We're adults and know the risks involved."

Kaelen went suddenly quiet and pursed his lips.

I closed my eyes and winced. "She's already working on it, isn't she?"

"Look, Stephan, the worm guy, and the ChronoBot all tried to keep her away from this. But I suspect you already know how she can be. She wouldn't hear it."

"Fine," I said, resigned.

"Now that all of *Washington's* DeckPorts have been switched back on, your ChronoBot has been standing sentry. Making sure that the one your XO had, um, had her accident—"

Suddenly furious, I cut him off, "Who the hell gave the order to do that? There have been two major accidents involving those things—"

"In your absence, *Washington* and the rest of Alpha Fleet dropped out of the wormhole. Fleet Command was informed of the accident. Both Admiral Gomez and President Block have now gotten involved. Subsequent orders have come down—all DeckPorts were to be opened back up for use. Something I can't totally disagree with."

I blew out a breath, shaking my head.

"The lack of inter-deck crew access on a vessel of this magnitude poses a colossal safety hazard. Regardless, your Science Officer, Stephan, has assessed the DeckPorts and pronounced them secure. The incident involving your XO was an extraordinarily unlikely occurrence of two entities utilizing a DeckPort simultaneously—Gail Pristy stepping into one on Deck G while a utility bot entered another on Deck 39."

I rubbed at the two-day stubble on my chin and met Kaelen's gaze, renewed determination burning in my eyes. "It's time I get out of here. Let's do whatever we can to bring Gail Pristy home."

"How about you first start with a shower," Kaelen said. "And then maybe a toothbrush."

Chapter 28

I stepped out of the shower, steam billowing around me as I reached for a towel. The hot water had done little to ease the tension in my muscles or the weight on my shoulders. After drying off and donning a fresh uniform, I left my quarters and made my way to the bridge.

As I assumed my position at the Captain's Mount, I was well aware of the crew's attentive gazes upon me. Had word spread of my drunken stupor? I could feel their apprehension—the last thing I needed was them questioning my ability to command this omninought as we headed into the fray.

I stood and looked to the bridgecrew, making eye contact with every one of them. "I am fine. Yes, I needed a minute. But I'm back and I'm 100% here with you. Not only ready to take on the Grish but defeat them. The truth is, USS *Washington* has yet to be tested and has yet to go into battle. I remember Empress Shawlee's last words to me before she left the ship, *Galvin, this is a very special warship... you'll see.*" I smiled at the memory. "She also said, *don't wreck this ship like you have all the others.*"

This sparked grins and a couple of chuckles, but most significantly, it resulted in a shared relaxation of postures. The only deviation was from Crewmember Davit, seated at Tactical. He had big shoes to fill. Undoubtedly, that was weighing heavy on his mind right now. I placed a hand on his shoulder and softly, for his ears only, said, "Deep breaths, you've got this."

"Mr. Chen, I take it you have alerted your Alpha Fleet counterparts that we are readying to continue final wormhole transit before engaging the enemy?"

"Yes, Captain. The fleet is awaiting your command."

I turned to the Helm Station. "Mr. Grimes, care to work your wonders and produce another magnificent wormhole for us?"

"Aye, Sir. One spectacular wormhole coming up."

Fifteen minutes later I was back in my ready room. The quiet hum of the ship's drives was no match for the relentless chaos in my mind.

Settling into my chair, I activated an alternate, secure halo display that Sonya had set up for me. The display was segmented into four distinct feeds. Each showed the members of the team assembled with one intention—to rescue Gail Pristy from the clutches of the malfunctioning DeckPort.

In one section, Derrota and Coogong huddled together in a lab I didn't recognize, their faces illuminated by the glow of quantum-space simulation scenarios—working tirelessly, running one test model after another, searching for the key to unlocking the secrets of the DeckPort's quantum entanglement.

Another section revealed Kaelen, strategically positioned in Engineering. His body was hunched over in concentration as he devised ways to circumvent the EUNF's recently implemented DeckPort security measures. The situation demanded a meticulous approach, as a single error could draw unwanted attention from SARAH, and subsequently, the EUNF—jeopardizing our covert endeavor.

Sonya occupied the third quadrant. Perched there in the dark recesses of the Symbio Deck, she worked her keyboard, editing lines of QuansCode essential to our mission. Her black hat abilities had made her the perfect candidate for this task, but even she had to tread carefully; SARAH monitored the ship's network with a continuous, watchful eye.

Finally, my gaze settled on Hardy, standing sentinel at the defective DeckPort. His unwavering dedication to the cause was a small comfort in the face of the challenges ahead.

As I watched my team work in stealth, scattered throughout the ship in obscure locations beyond SARAH's reach, a sense of unease crept over me. The knowledge that Alpha Fleet would soon emerge from the manufactured wormhole, likely plunging into battle, only added to the pressure. As USS *Washington* and Alpha Fleet prepared to confront the external enemy, we found ourselves in an internal battle against time, desperately scrambling to rescue Gail Pristy from oblivion.

My gaze was fixed upon the central halo display, its swirling blue and silver vortex possessing an almost hypnotic allure. Against this backdrop, the hushed murmurs of my bridgecrew merged seamlessly with the continuous hum of *Washington's* propulsion system.

"We'll be dropping out of wormhole transit in approximately three minutes, Captain."

"Thank you, Mr. Grimes."

My right leg jittered as I gnawed on the inner flesh of my lower lip. Apprehension was an understatement for what I felt —the painstaking anticipation of the unknown.

For the past three hours, SARAH had dedicated itself to pinpointing the likely coordinates of the expanded Torrent Fleet. The AI had delved deeply into the scope of its analytical capabilities, detailing the exhaustive computations, a myriad of models, regression analyses, and scenario simulations it performed. The ship's computer was fairly convinced of the fleet's location, assigning a 72.8% probability that the fleet was stationed within the region commonly known as the Alamanda Space Quadrant.

My eye caught Lieutenant Akari James rushing by and then settling behind Tactical 1. She flashed me an irritated look. No doubt, she would prefer to be in the cramped cockpit of an Arrow Fighter alongside her squad, presently on alert in Flight Bay One. But, with perhaps the exception of XO Pristy, there was no one else I wanted to be seated at Tactical before going into battle.

The bridge lights flickered as we reentered normal space. I took in a sharp breath, feeling the familiar lurch in my stomach.

Emerging from wormhole transit is like snapping back to reality from the depths of a dream, where the universe abruptly contracts and then expands in a disorienting rush of stars streaking into place.

It never mattered how many times I experienced it; my body always registered the unpleasant shock of re-entry. The crew around me stiffened in their seats, their eyes glued to their stations as they braced for what came next.

"Status report," I barked, even as my eyes darted to the various halo displays showing *Washington's*—and now all of Alpha Fleet's—position within the Alamanda Space Quadrant.

"Sensors coming alive," Akari said, all business. "We've got company. Shit! It's Torrent Fleet, and they're close... twenty-five thousand miles and closing!"

"Raise shields! Activate cloaking systems!" I barked.

Akari shook her head, "They already have a lock on us. Cloaking won't do much good. Dammit!" Her fingers moved in a blur of motion. "Deploying our long-range sensor droids... should have a better perspective of what we're dealing with soon."

My eyes were locked onto the logistical display, a myriad of green-colored icons, the good guys, and red icons, the bad guys, rapidly advancing toward each other.

"Captain, all primary weapons systems are online and reading fully operational," Akari reported crisply. She spun around to look at me, a smirk on her lips and a twinkle in her eyes, "Wait... Is this *Washington's* maiden space battle?"

The question had caught me off guard. "Um, I suppose it is," I said with a shrug.

"This is going to be epic!" she said with a child's enthusiasm. "This ship, originally the *Black Ship*, has more integrated weaponry than any previous U.S. Space Navy vessel. All weaponry has been optimized under SARAH's lightning-fast neural net, so we should see a noticeable improvement in target acquisitions, bogie locks, and countermeasure capabilities for deployed smart missiles.... And don't get me started on this ship's Broadsides."

Her enthusiasm felt misplaced amid the tension, but it provided a welcome distraction from the knot tightening in my gut.

"This ship's firepower will obliterate anything in its path," she continued, eyes alight. "The Broadsides alone could cripple a battle cruiser with a single volley."

My hands gripped the armrests of the Captain's Mount, nails pressing into the faux leather. This was the moment—the calm before the tempest, when the atmosphere hums with potential, and the tension as thick as expired molasses, metallic on the palate.

"Tell me what we're up against, Tactical!" I commanded.

Three halo display projections popped into view.

The bridge thrummed with a hive of commotion, yet my attention narrowed on several halo displays. The rotating 3D images of enemy ships appeared almost artistic against the void of space—a gallery of impending doom.

Akari's animated voice cut through the tension. "Alright, Captain, feast your eyes on this," she said, enhancing the images on her console. "First up, we've got the Hindrava-class Super Battleships—just look at those behemoths! They're almost the size of our dreadnoughts and pack enough firepower to turn our frigates to space dust."

I studied the angular monstrosities as they spun slowly in the display. Their imposing forms looked ready to carve through our fleet like hot knives through butter. A shiver ran down my spine—not from fear, but from the sheer anticipation of meeting such foes in battle.

"Next are their Kanagrav-class Destroyers," Akari continued. "Sleek, lethal... like steel daggers poised to strike. They're roughly equivalent to our destroyers but carry an extra punch with their oversized energy cannons."

The display shifted, showing a line of Kanagrav-class ships with their brutalist architecture. I nodded, mentally matching them up against our own destroyers and calculating the odds.

"And let's not forget the Krit'haga-class dreadnoughts," she said as another image swelled into view. "These titans dwarf even their super battleships in sheer size and have turrets that could obliterate a star station."

I felt a grudging respect for these colossal ships. The Grish knew how to build them—making them imposing and deadly.

More ships joined the spectral fleet on display.

"Lastly, the Bezkur-class Frigates. Compact and deadly— they're meant for rapid response and patrol duties within their formations." Akari leaned back as she finished her presentation.

Their blocky shapes moved among the larger ships like brave hounds among wolves.

My eyes roamed over each vessel as they turned on display, absorbing every detail—the hard lines and weapon ports bristling like thorns on an interstellar rosebush. The Grish had numbers and might on their side; that much was clear.

But we had something they didn't—resolve hardened by having a home worth defending. That and the pride of the U.S. Space Navy, USS *Washington*, a badass omninought that just might even the odds. I turned away from the display for a moment to catch Akari's gaze, noting that her fierce determination mirrored my own.

"We may be outnumbered," I said firmly, "but maybe not totally outmatched."

"They're launching Cyclone Death Fighters!" Ensign Lira yelled from Sensors and Reconnaissance.

"Mr. Chen, coordinate the Arrow assets with the rest of the fleet. Then have them standby for my order," I commanded.

"SARAH, bring us to battle stations."

The overhead Klaxon blared. Her voice filled the bridge:

Battle Stations...
Battle Stations...
All personnel report to your stations...

"The enemy has come to a full stop," Akari announced.

"Seems they've chosen their turf for battle," I said.

Too jittery to remain seated, I got to my feet and stood

behind the Captain's Mount, feeling my heart thundering against my ribcage like a relentless drum. This was it—the culmination of all our strategies, the moment when theory would meet the unforgiving crucible of reality.

My eyes flicked between halo displays absorbing the constantly updated information. The earlier deployed sensor droids were now transmitting, giving us incredible visuals of the battlespace. On the main display, I watched as Alpha Fleet gracefully slid into the prescribed formation, each vessel becoming a crucial piece in our intricate game of cosmic chess.

To starboard, The Pleidian Super Cruiser, *Eclipse,* flexed her muscles, a bulwark of defense ready to shield our flanks. Behind her, the sleek lines of USS *Leviathan* took up position, her cannons glinting like the eyes of a predator in wait. And there, weaving through the stars with an elegance that belied her *take-no-prisoners* firepower, was USS *Renegade.* Despite her age, she moved with a prowess that inspired respect.

I glanced at the halo display as more names flashed across it —USS *Valkyrie* and USS *Sentinel*—each assuming their places in Attack Plan Porcupine. We had dissected this plan in the virtual meeting room until it lived in our bloodstreams; now, every Captain knew their role, their timing down to the last second.

"Captain," Chen's voice loud and steady, "Message from Captain Marquez of USS *Valkyrie.* He says they're in position... locked and loaded, and *Valkyrie's* ready to dance."

A wry smile tugged at my lips. Marquez always did have a way with words. "Tell Captain Marquez to keep his ship's dance card open; we'll be cutting in soon enough," I replied.

SARAH's voice echoed off in the distance as she directed personnel and resources in preparation for what was to come. This ship's AI was far more proactive than other ship AIs in the past, such as MATHR or Sir Calvin.

The logistical display refreshed, showcasing the latest strategic information. Up to this point, Alpha Fleet Captains had executed their orders flawlessly. Chen's voice remained a steady hum, conveying intelligence and providing the bridge-crew with essential updates required for their duties.

I settled back into the Captain's Mount, eyes sweeping over my crew, feeling their focus and resolve as an extension of my own.

"Mr. Chen, open a channel to all Alpha Fleet ships," I ordered.

Chen's fingers flew across his console. "Channel open, Captain. You're live."

"Crew of Alpha Fleet, this is Captain Galvin Quintos of USS Washington. In a few moments, we will engage the enemy in a battle that will decide the fate of Earth, home to most of us. The Grish have come to our doorstep, threatening everything we hold dear. They believe they can crush us beneath their might, but they have yet to face the true strength of humanity."

I paused, allowing the words to sink in. "Each of you has trained your asses off to be here today, and I know you're ready to show these intergalactic douchebags what we're made of. Remember, this isn't just about us—it's about our families, our homes, our allies, everything we hold dear. Look around at your crew. Whether you are Human, Thine, Pleidian, or Symbio, you are brothers and sisters in arms. We're all in this together, and we're not going down without a fight. So let's channel that unbreakable spirit that makes us who we are and show these swine shits what we're capable of."

My throat tightened as I continued, emotion threatening to overwhelm me. "Each one of you has experienced personal loss. Crewmembers, friends, perhaps someone who was more than that..." As if a fist had taken hold of my heart, my mind flashed to Pristy's face. Her smile, the way her eyes sparkled when she laughed. The pain of her loss was still raw, a gaping wound that refused to heal.

I swallowed hard, pushing past the lump in my throat. "We've all lost someone dear to us, whether it was to the Grish, the Varapin, or some other cruel twist of fate. But we cannot let their deaths be in vain. We owe it to them to fight, to stand up against those who would seek to destroy us."

I looked around the bridge, meeting the eyes of my crew. In each gaze, I saw a reflection of my own pain, my own determination. We were united in our grief and in our resolve to make things right.

"So as we go into this battle, carry the memory of those we've lost with you. Let their spirits guide your actions, your decisions. Fight for them, for the future they'll never get to see. Show the Grish that we will not be broken, that we will not surrender in the face of their aggression."

My voice grew stronger, fueled by the moment upon us. "We are the U.S. Space Navy. We are the last line of defense for Earth and her allies. And we will not fail. So let's go out there and show them what we're made of. Let's make our fallen comrades proud."

A chorus of cheers erupted over the comms, an uproar of voices united in purpose. I felt a swell of pride in my chest, knowing that these brave men and women were ready to lay down their lives for the greater good.

As the cheers died down, I signaled for Chen to cut the connection. I settled back into the Captain's Mount, my gaze fixed on the halo display. "All right, Alpha Fleet," I said, my voice calm and resolute. "Let's show these motherfuckers what we're made of."

I paused, directed my attention to Comms. "Mr. Chen, signal ship Captains... initiate Attack Plan Porcupine."

Chapter 29

I was up and pacing again.

"Cap," Akari said, chinning toward the primary halo display.

There, the Grish flagship loomed in the distance, a grotesque trophy bolted to its bow—a dismembered Lady Liberty, her torch extinguished, her crown desecrated. My jaw clenched. This was a declaration of contempt, a message carved into the very symbol of our home. But it only steeled my resolve. Alpha Fleet Captains moved like gears in a well-oiled machine, each vessel executing Attack Plan Porcupine with the precision of seasoned warriors.

"Target their flanks, Lieutenant," I ordered. "Focus fire on those Bezkur-class Frigates. Let's clip their wings."

The halo display flickered as Akari directed *Washington's* Phazon Pulsar cannons to unleash volleys of energy at the enemy's patrol units. The smaller vessels dispersed, weaving erratic paths, yet our targeting held unwavering, SARAH assuming the role of an unerring marksman... relentless, unemotional. One by one, their vessels erupted into brief blooms of fire and debris, extinguished as quickly as they flared out in the cold vacuum of space.

But retaliation came swiftly. The Torrent Fleet was not to be underestimated. More Cyclone Death Fighters swarmed from the belly of their flagship like hornets roused from a nest. They darted toward us, weapons blazing with a ferocity that spoke of a hunger for conquest.

"Launch all Arrow Fighters," I commanded. "Defensive formations!"

Washington's three launch bays disgorged battle-eager craft —sleek, red Arrow Fighters that darted forward to meet the enemy head-on. I pictured Captain Wallace Ryder leading the charge, undoubtedly with a smile on his face. His pilots were among the best, and I trusted them to fly circles around the enemy's Death Fighters.

On my command, the warship *Eclipse* angled her Broadside cannons and unleashed bowler munitions that carved through space toward their largest target. The impacts were thunderous, even in silence—the enemy's hull breached—her atmosphere venting into the void like ghostly tendrils.

I heard Akari talking directly to her counterpart on *USS Leviathan,* "No! Deploy smart missiles, fusion tips!"

Within seconds the missiles were streaking across the battle-space and finding their marks with devastating accuracy. *USS Renegade,* though older than the other warships, proved cunning and lethal as she fired her rail cannons, punching holes through a smaller nearby enemy frigate.

FOR THE NEXT THREE HOURS, THE BATTLE RAGED ON, and our losses mounted. Then *Intrepid* took a direct hit; her hull ruptured, leaving her drifting—a gutted dreadnought losing atmosphere on multiple decks. I watched as expelled bodies tumbled away into the expanse.

I shook my head, "Come on... Keep to the plan, dammit," I urged through gritted teeth. "Marquez! Liu! Focus on your sectors."

The bridge was alive with activity—Chen coordinating via Comms, Grimes adjusting course at a pace to keep us out of enemy firing solutions. Akari attacked her console with ruthless efficiency as she directed counterassaults.

The battle raged on—a chaotic whirlwind of destruction and death without sound but felt in every shudder of *Washington's* superstructure.

I watched as USS *Valkyrie,* in a burst of impressive helmsmanship, dove beneath an enemy battle cruiser. Valkyrie emerged victoriously on the other side—a wounded predator still hungry for blood—as explosions rocked the enemy ship.

And then I saw her, off in the fray. The heart of the Grish Fleet was suddenly exposed.

"Helm, get us off this course vector! Thirty degrees to port, and pedal to the metal, Mr. Grimes. Chase that son of a bitch, don't even think about letting her get away."

"She's called, *Gorvikk Hragnok,*" Ensign Lira said from somewhere behind me.

"Sounds kinda of Russian," Akari commented over one shoulder.

"Stay on her!" I barked to Grimes.

With a glance at another halo display, I observed a view from one of our previously deployed sensor droids. I took in the almost cinematic perspective—USS *Washington* with virtually all of her railgun cannons afire, each having locked onto a different enemy asset. SARAH was cunningly targeting hundreds, maybe thousands, of enemy vulnerabilities all within the blink of an eye.

Abruptly, *Washington* shuddered—a gush of air whooshed from the overhead vents as though the craft had received a blow to its gut. Then came the sounds of distant Klaxons coming alive, the alarms exacerbating the foreboding situation.

Akari slammed a fist down onto her board. "Fuck! We just took a missile right up the tailpipe! Portside drive is hemorrhaging antimatter."

"Crewmember Davit, watch our aft shields!" I barked.

"Propulsion's being impacted. Trying to compensate with starboard drive," Grimes said.

"We have a new problem, Cap," Akari said. "... looks like a rapidly closing-in Kanagrav-class Destroyer. Coming right at us and fast."

My eyes went to the primary display, *Washington's* Phazon Pulsar cannons were already zeroing in on the destroyer.

"She's looking to ram us!" Akari exclaimed. "Two hundred miles and closing!"

Washington's luminous Phazon bolts continued to hammer its defenses—it was an unyielding, brilliant barrage, now forcing the enemy's forward shields to transition from yellow to orange, and, finally, to a bright red.

"One hundred miles out! Seventy-five, fifty..." Akari shouted.

Overhead SARAH made an announcement:

Brace for impact...
Brace for impact...
Brace, Brace, Brace...

The Grish destroyer was growing larger and larger by the second.

"Hold on to something!" I yelled, wincing against the inevitable impact, where one massive warship would collide with another massive warship. This was going to be bad...

Suddenly, the Kanagrav-class Destroyer's shield defenses collapsed beneath the relentless assault—the vessel exploded into an enormous inferno. Debris was unleashed, pelting *Washington's* shields and hurling metallic fragments and composite materials across the vacuum of space, creating a deafening assault of clatters and bangs, prompting the bridgecrew to cover their ears.

"Helm!" I yelled, "Get us back in the chase of that flagship!"

"On it, Captain."

Seated back within the Captain's Mount, I took in the melee. Explosions, crisscrossing rail spike munitions with their tell-tale tracer rounds, Alpha Fleet's bright green Phazon bolts, and the Grish's red energy beams, warships maneuvering for advantage, or scrambling for safety. Smart missiles with their locked-on trajectories... it was impossible to gauge who was winning, the battlespace still too volatile, too unpredictable.

My stomach lurched as *Washington* abruptly altered course. And then, just as quickly, I was hurled back into the padding of the Captain's Mount—the ship's thrust dampeners laboring to mitigate the swift acceleration.

The display, alive with a relentless barrage of data, chronicled the mounting toll of Alpha Fleet ship losses with unyielding precision.

"Back in pursuit," Grimes said with cool, calm satisfaction. "You can run, but you cannot hide..."

The combat zone had noticeably cleared, resembling a vast salvage yard with dark, inert husks of rudderless warships, one after another, devoid of life.

Chen said, "Um, Captain, I have a message for you from J-Dog."

"What is it Captain Ryder has to say?" I asked, glad to hear my friend was still breathing and causing trouble somewhere out there.

"Uh, these are his words, not mine, Sir... *If you can stay long enough in one place, just maybe my Arrows can fucking RTB and refuel.*"

"Tell him I'll keep that in mind. One way or another, things are coming to a head."

My TAC-Band had been practically vibrating off my wrist for the last hour, only now did I take a second to glance at it. Three messages from Sonya, two from Derrota.

Sonya: Hit brick wall w/ QuansCode. Like breaking into Fort Knox!

Sonya: One step forward - two steps backward!

Sonya: Terrific, DeckPort parameters locked, factory fucking set!

Derrota's messages were far more conversational but just as sobering.

Derrota: Sorry, Galvin, but unfortunately, we're not having luck with our lab simulation models. Will keep you up-to-date.

Derrota: Power conduit must have ruptured on Deck 18. All data was lost.

I felt Pristy's life essence slipping away into the ether by the second. *I'm sorry, Gail... I don't know what else to do.* I was tempted to reach out to Hardy but didn't think I could stand any more bad news.

"Back in the chase, Captain," Grimes said. "Seems *Gorvikk Hragnok* has taken a few hits. I think I can catch her."

"Less talk, more action, Helm!" I ordered.

I saw we were on an intercept course, Grimes weaving us through the tangled mess of broken warships.

"I want every smart fusion-tipped nuke we can spare locked onto that ship, Tactical."

"Still can't get a lock," Akari said. "That flagship knows we're here, using countermeasures."

In an exhilarating bit of flight navigating, Grimes had this behemoth of an omninought, moving in fast and side-sliding in close to *Gorvikk Hragnok*, matching the flagship's speed. I felt like I could almost reach out and touch the boxy, angular warship.

Grimes said, "Merry Christmas—all wrapped and delivered to you Tactical... all you have to do is put a bow on it."

Akari smirked, looking back over her shoulder at me with a brow raised. "Bowlers?"

I stared at the pride of the Torrent Fleet. The Grish Super Battle Cruiser was right there, flaunting the Statue of Liberty on her bow where it was a little crooked, off-kilter... and beyond infuriating.

I set my jaw. Whoever it was that said *revenge is a dish best served cold*, hadn't just gone up against a Grish Armada. "Ready all portside Broadsides, Tactical, fire when ready. Light her up."

Boom! Boom! Boom! Boom! Boom! Deck plates jittered as *Washington's* massive Broadside cannons reverberated throughout the omninought's superstructure.

The flagship's shields were no match for the relentless barrage, and within seconds of succumbing, the vessel erupted into a massive fireball—one that threatened to engulf both ships.

As *Washington* veered away from the explosion's grasp, my eyes sought out what, if anything, was left of Lady Liberty amidst the carnage.

"Cease fire," I called out, almost reverently.

The entire bridgecrew was up and on their feet. A silence fell over the bridge.

Crewmember Soto stood, pointing to the halo display. "There!"

Indeed, there she was—weathered yet resilient—Lady Liberty's silhouette miraculously preserved, drifting in a slow somersault, as though seeking a path back to Earth.

"The battle... it's over," Akari said. "No one's left to fire on us... on any of us."

I slowly nodded. She was right. The battlespace had gone quiet, stillness prevailed.

"Lieutenant James, how about you get a tractor beam on that statue before she leaves the star system?"

"Roger that, Cap," she said.

Chapter 30

The Klaxons had all gone silent. Fewer and fewer PA announcements from SARAH blared down from above. Now came the arduous task of searching for the few crewmembers still alive within the shipwrecks. A section of a broken ship that, remarkably, still maintained a pocket of atmosphere. Or the unaccounted-for escape pods floundering amongst the wreckage. We'd scan for life-signs and dispatch rescue teams accordingly.

Washington was the hub of Alpha Fleet's post-battle clean-up. To that end, Crewmember Soto seated at Damage Control, was working with Chen to organize the mess and direct resources accordingly.

I stared at the display, the list of lost Alpha Fleet assets and their respective crews was chilling. With that said, I felt there must be something wrong. That SARAH had miscalculated somehow. How was it that we had lost only ten warships?

Of the 42 warships that went into this battle, 32 remained. Among the lost were *USS Renegade, USS Leviathan,* and the Thine dreadnought, *Intrepid.*

Akari sat facing me, her arms crossed over her chest, the hint of a smile on her face.

"Assessment?" I asked.

"Well, your Porcupine Attack Plan was solid... EUNF will be teaching that shit to new cadets for years to come. Each of the fleet Skippers did what they were supposed to do. And having the element of surprise sure didn't hurt. But it was the *Black Ship* factor that made all the difference in this battle. The better integration between SARAH and *Washington,* her robust weaponry..." She shook her head. "Seriously, what ship, what fleet, could ever stand up to that?"

I couldn't argue with her. *Washington* and SARAH together seemed to be an unstoppable force. I thought back to the battle, how *Washington* would be sparring with three, sometimes four enemy assets, and clear across the battlespace, other Grish vessels were also being targeted by the omninought, and, inevitably, were destroyed—that was multitasking on a whole other level.

Lieutenant Hargreaves at Flight Control said, "Captain, all Arrows have returned to flight bays."

"How many did we lose, Lieutenant?"

"Thirteen, Sir."

Akari took in a sharp breath. "Permission to check on..."

"Yes, yes, of course, go. And good work here today, Lieutenant James."

THE REMNANTS OF TORRENT FLEET LAY STREWN across the vast expanse like celestial confetti, a testament to Alpha Fleet's reemergence as an exemplary fighting force. It would be easy for me to take credit for that, but much of that goes to *USS Washington*—and those Thine and Pleidian Engineers who had refined the original *Black Ship* into her current form.

As I headed out of the bridge, I took a moment to savor the victory, but it was a fleeting indulgence. My mind turned to those who bore the brunt of our enemy's wrath.

SEVERAL MINUTES LATER I WAS STRIDING INTO HealthBay, my boots thudding heavily on the deck, each step a reminder of the cost of war. The sterile smell of antiseptics greeted me as I entered, along with the soft beeping of monitors and the hushed voices of medical staff attending to the wounded.

I took in the circular ward, crewmembers laying in their beds, some visibly battered by the battle, others with injuries hidden beneath bandages and bio-gel packs. I made my way between the beds, offering words of comfort and gratitude to those whose eyes met mine. Each *thank you* I uttered felt painfully inadequate when measured against their sacrifice.

"Captain," a young Ensign called out weakly as I passed. His arm was suspended in a sling, but his spirit remained unbroken.

"Ensign," I replied, stopping at his bedside. "You held your station admirably."

A hint of pride flickered in his eyes. "Just doing my duty, Sir."

I clasped his good hand firmly before moving on.

Beyond, on the other side of a glass partition, I looked into the RegrowPod area where all of the clamshell lids were closed up, more seriously injured patients inside.

At last, I reached where Chief Knott presided over her domain with both compassion and authority. She looked up from her datapad as I approached, her face etched with fatigue and concern.

"Captain Quintos," she began, her voice gentle yet firm. "May I have a word in private?"

We stepped away from the main ward into a small alcove that afforded some semblance of privacy.

"It's about XO Pristy," she said hesitantly, her eyes finding mine.

I tensed, feeling a surge of anger and frustration rise within me like a tide against a stubborn shore.

"Yes, Chief?" My response was terse; I could feel my control slipping.

"The medical staff... they've been asking about arrangements," Knott continued delicately. "Her parents—"

"No!" The word erupted from me with more force than intended. The walls seemed to close in as I grappled with the awful reality she was trying to present.

Knott recoiled slightly but held her ground. "Captain, we need to consider—"

"Consider what?" My voice was a low growl. "That she's gone? That there's no hope?" I struggled to compose myself, keenly aware that my outburst was as much about my own denial as it was about preserving hope for my crew.

"Sir," Knott pressed on, her tone steady but tinged with empathy. "Her family will want—need—to say goodbye."

The words struck like a dagger. Goodbye. It wasn't something I was prepared to face—not yet. "I need time," I said abruptly, turning away from her earnest gaze. "Time to think."

Without waiting for a response, I left HealthBay behind me, retreating into the complex maze of corridors of the omni-nought. My thoughts churned like a storm-ravaged sea—Pristy's absence, a gaping chasm that threatened to consume all rational thought.

Was it truly futile? Was there really no chance of pulling her back from that quantum abyss where she might be lost? My heart rebelled against the notion even as my mind warned me to brace for the worst.

I walked without direction, losing track of time, until the conversation with Chief Knott, mercifully, started to fade away.

I found Hardy keeping vigil by the lower DeckPort, the site of Pristy's tragic accident. But he wasn't alone. Climbo, his ridiculous mechanical pack mule, was there too. Looked like they were playing a game of fetch.

I watched as Hardy tossed what appeared to be a broken-off mop handle, Climbo scampering off after it, his metal body whirring with exuberant energy. At first, I felt a flicker of irritation—Hardy was shirking his duty. But as Climbo bounded back, prancing about with the makeshift stick clenched between its jaws, I couldn't help but smile.

There was something innocent and carefree about the scene, a brief respite from the weight of grief and responsibility that had been pressing down on me. Climbo danced in anticipation, its mechanical eyes fixed on me, waiting for me to take my turn.

Against my better judgment, I reached out and took the stick out of Climbo's jaw, eliciting an enthusiastic whirring from the robotic mule. With a half-hearted toss, I sent the stick skittering across the deck.

"What was that?" Hardy asked.

"What? I threw the stick."

"You throw like a little girl."

"I do not. Anyway, it was a toss... not a throw. I tossed it, okay?"

"Uh-huh."

I clapped my hands together, and said, "Here Climbo. Here boy, bring me the stick!"

Climbo did as told, spinning in circles with excitement. I snatched the stick away from the mechanical mule. This time, I threw it as far down the passageway as I could.

Climbo was off like a shot, its four legs propelling it forward with surprising speed. As it retrieved the prize, I found myself laughing—a sound that seemed alien to me.

Climbo returned, victorious, and deposited the stick at my feet with a metallic clatter. Its body vibrated with excitement, and I couldn't help but indulge the robot's enthusiasm, bending down to scoop up the offering once more.

It was then that Hardy stirred from his statuesque vigil, his chromium features shifting to regard me with what I could only interpret as a wry expression.

"I think I just figured out how to save Pristy," he announced, his words cutting through the lighthearted moment like a Phazon bolt.

The stick slipped from my fingers as I straightened, my heart pounding with a sudden surge of hope and trepidation.

"What?" I managed, my voice catching in my throat. "How?"

Hardy's faceplate flickered, displaying a complex diagram—a tangled web of equations and schematics that made my head spin.

"It's a long shot," he admitted, his tone sobering. "But there's a chance we can exploit the principles of quantum entanglement to backtrack Pristy's quantum signature and pull her essence out of the rift."

I stared at the incomprehensible data, my mind struggling to grasp the implications of what he was proposing.

Hardy's faceplate settled on an image of a Mobius strip, an endless loop that defied conventional logic.

"What are you trying to tell me?" I asked.

"Imagine, Captain," Hardy began, "if we could twist the fabric of space-time itself, much like this Mobius strip. By creating a localized inversion field around the DeckPort, we could theoretically reverse the flow of quantum data—essentially rewinding Pristy's last moments before the accident."

I let out a slow breath, trying to wrap my head around the concept. "Rewind time itself? We just defeated a Grish Armada... I certainly don't want to go through all that again."

"No, this process would be contained within the localized inversion field." He tilted his head toward the DeckPort.

"Ah. Okay... But wouldn't that require an immense amount of energy? Precision? Not to mention know-how that's well beyond any of our own?"

"Let's break it down," he replied. "It would demand a near-perfect synchronization with her quantum signature at the moment of... dispersal. But unlike Stephan's and Coogong's attempts at direct retrieval or duplication of the XO, this method wouldn't be reconstructing or replicating her; it would be an actual reversal of time on a quantum level for her alone."

"Would that entail any reprogramming of the thing? Sonya says the QuansCoding that would be necessary has too many security roadblocks to get around. And Kaelen has had zero breakthroughs—"

"No, Cap. What I'm talking about doesn't alter the Deck-Port at all. In fact, it's important that nothing be changed with this unit."

My head was spinning. "I'm still missing something, Hardy. If none of us have the technical know-how..."

"I never said the science had to come from any of us. Think about this—you, yourself—have just recently experienced a quantum-level experience."

I could now *literally* see the gears turning in Hardy's head via his faceplate, as he pieced together his explanation. He was onto something, a thread of possibility that I hadn't considered.

"Captain," Hardy said, the blue light from his faceplate reflecting off the bulkheads. "... remember your time within the sphere's reenactment? You do know, that wasn't just an illusion or some advanced holo-simulation. It was real."

I narrowed my eyes. "Real? How can that be?"

He nodded as if he'd anticipated my doubt. "The sphere's technology operates on principles beyond our current understanding of quantum mechanics. When we were inside, we weren't just playing roles in a fabricated scenario; we were actually experiencing an alternate realm—a real place that exists on a different quantum plane."

My mind raced back to those moments within the sphere. I could still feel the rough texture of the Crytharan robes, smell the fragrant air of their gardens, and hear the subtle inflections in their speech. It had all felt so authentic... because it was.

"That's why you had full tactile experiences," Hardy continued. "For all intents and purposes, it was real. Our consciousnesses were projected into that realm, becoming part of its very fabric."

"But how does that help us with Pristy?" I asked, struggling to connect the dots.

Hardy's faceplate shifted to a visual of intertwined threads —a representation of entangled particles.

"Quantum entanglement," the ChronoBot said. "It doesn't just link particles over distances; it can also connect different states of being—different realities. If we can pinpoint the exact quantum state Pristy was in before the accident, we might be able to go back, rewind, so to speak, and pull her back through that same entanglement."

I took a moment to process his words. The implications were staggering. If Hardy was right, we could potentially reverse what had happened to Pristy by tapping into an alternate quantum reality—one where she still existed intact.

"And you believe this sphere can help us achieve that?" I asked.

"We need to persuade the sphere, likely that Grantham

Guardian fella, to let us have a look behind Oz's curtain, to understand the workings of the Wizard."

My heart pounded against my ribcage as I considered his proposal. It was a long shot—but if there was even the slimmest chance we could bring her back...

My TAC-Band started to vibrate. It was Chen. I was needed on the bridge.

"Hardy," I began, steadying my voice despite my growing excitement, "I need you to set up a meeting with our team—you, Kaelen, Derrota, Coogong... and Sonya. Have them meet me in—"

"Hold 536 on Deck 18, Violet Sector," Hardy said. "Got it." He hesitated, looking at the mechanical pack mule. "Climbo, you stay here. Anyone tries to use this DeckPort, give them a donkey kick to the nuts."

I rolled my eyes, "And if it's a crewmember of the female persuasion?"

"I don't know... bite her ankles. He gets my gist. Climbo is more intuitive than you give him credit for."

Chapter 31

I hurried onto the bridge, the residual buzz of adrenaline from our recent skirmish with the Torrent Fleet still thrumming within the compartment. The crew's attention shifted toward me. I nodded to them, a silent acknowledgment of our collective triumph.

"Mr. Chen," I called out, then turned to exit the bridge. "I'll take the communique in private."

THE AUTO-HATCH TO MY READY ROOM SLID OPEN, then closed behind me, cocooning me in a familiar solitude. I took a deep breath, bracing myself for whatever news Admiral Gomez had waiting for me.

The display flickered to life, and Gomez's projection materialized before me. Though visibly fatigued, he projected a strong resolve.

"Captain Quintos," he began, "... first off, congratulations are in order. You and your fleet have done what many thought impossible. Especially being so outnumbered as you were."

I inclined my head slightly. "Thank you, Admiral. But it was a team effort. The fleet performed beyond expectations."

Gomez nodded solemnly. "Indeed. However, while you were engaged with the Torrent Fleet, there were developments within the Pleidian Star System that require your attention."

My brow furrowed at that. We'd been so focused on our own battle that news from other fronts had been put on the back-burner.

"The Pleidians," he continued, "... managed to defend against an attack we didn't see coming—a testament to their resilience and tactical acumen."

"Empress Shawlee Tee, is she..."

"She is fine. But her Pleidian Royal Guard has suffered a multitude of losses and significant damage."

A wave of guilt washed over me, she'd selflessly offered most of her warship assets over to Alpha Fleet.

"But that's not all," Gomez added gravely. "In the time since that defense, we've learned more about the Pleidian's attackers, and we've been able to uncover their motives behind their aggression toward the Pleidians."

My interest was piqued; I leaned forward slightly. Knowing your enemy was half the battle.

"As we've previously discussed, the attackers call themselves the Wrinnth," Gomez said as he swiped through data on his end, bringing up images of sleek ships.

They were unlike any design I'd encountered before.

The Admiral continued, "They're a species we've had minimal contact with—reclusive and typically, up until now, non-aggressive."

I studied the images more closely, noting their angular architecture and dark hulls that seemed to drink in any surrounding light.

"So, now you know... why they're attacking the Pleidians?" I asked.

Admiral Gomez's features tightened, a clear sign that the news he bore was grim. "The Wrinnth," he continued, "... have begun systematically attacking their neighbors within that sector of space. These are not just random incursions; the attacks are calculated, strategic."

I leaned back in my chair, processing the information. "Systematic how? Are they seeking territory, resources... what's driving them?"

He paused, selecting his words carefully. "Intelligence suggests they're after resources, yes, but not in the way we might think. They aren't just stripping planets bare; they're taking control of key production facilities and trade routes. It's as if they're setting up a new empire right under our noses."

I rubbed my chin thoughtfully. "And the Pleidians were in their way."

"Exactly." Gomez nodded. "The Pleidians are known for their rich mineral planets and advanced technology. We're guessing they're simply the latest opportunity to the Wrinnth's expansion."

I stood and paced a few steps before turning back to face the display. "Clearly, the Wrinnth had been watching, waiting... chose their attack when the Pleidians were most vulnerable."

"The fact Shawlee's Royal Guard managed to hold off the attack is a testament to Pleidian battle prowess, but next time..." The Admiral drifted, averting his eyes.

"And there will be a next time," I interjected.

"Without a doubt. How soon, is anyone's guess," the Admiral said, resigned.

I retook my seat and stared back into Gomez's tired eyes. An impossible choice was at hand, and, apparently, the Admiral didn't want to make that choice without my input.

"As things stand," I began, "Alpha Fleet is readying to move on to the Drakoria system where we'll hit Grish's Pinnacle Fleet hard and fast. We've caught the enemy off guard, so it's key—essential—to strike now before Earth becomes a target again."

With a pained expression, Gomez countered, his voice heavy with reluctance, "There's no way Pinnacle fleet will simply stay put after such a glaring defeat. The Grish will want to address the problem head-on."

I couldn't fault the Admiral's logic.

"Back to the Pleidians," Gomez continued. "It still comes down to the fact the Pleidians, like the Thine, are our staunch allies. Their sacrifices over the years, the countless lives lost in defense of our cause, have been immeasurable. To turn our backs on them now would not only be a betrayal of the highest order but could potentially shatter the fragile coalition we've forged against our common foes."

"And that is undisputed, Admiral. What does the Empress have to say? Seems she should have a say in the matter."

"She insists the decision should come from Alpha Fleet's Commander. You, Galvin."

Of course, she would say that, I thought. I shook my head, frustration rising. "I really don't want to split Alpha Fleet in two."

I paused, an idea starting to brew.

Gomez must have seen a change in my demeanor.

"Say it, Captain. At this point, no idea should be discounted no matter how improbable the chances of success are."

With a half-smile, I shrugged. "Okay, but remember, you asked for it."

Gomez nodded. "Spit it out."

"By now, word has gotten back to Drakoria. That their Torrent Fleet was a total loss."

"No doubt," the Admiral said.

"So, what do you think the odds are that details of the battle had also gotten back to Grish High Command... that periodic transmissions had been sent, perhaps even mid-battle—updates and details regarding Alpha Fleet's capabilities?"

"It's a certainty," Gomez said. "There would be an obvious delay, but yeah, that would be standard procedure, just as it would be with our own SOP."

I could see Gomez wanted me to get to the point.

"And, with that, they know about *USS Washington*. The Alliance's new, fricking amazing omninought. The same one that just kicked their piglet asses even though their forces outnumbered ours two to one."

"Without a doubt," the Admiral said with a smirk.

"Let's say that Alpha Fleet shows up to confront Pinnacle Fleet there in the Drakoria system as planned. They'll be confronted by our fresh-from-victory warships along with that formidable omninought."

"Dammit, Captain, get to the fucking point!" Gomez barked, having had enough.

I smiled again. "The question here is, would this give the Grish pause? Would they attack or wait to see what Alpha Fleet does?"

"I don't know, and why does it matter?"

"Just, please, bear with me on this."

"They would hesitate. No doubt about it," Gomez said. "They'd want to collect as much sensory information as possible, scan every inch of the ship, collect data. Even then, they'd want to see what *Washington* intends, I'd imagine."

"Agreed," I said triumphantly.

Gomez did a roll of his fingers gesture for me to keep going.

"And that's why I'm making the decision to break *USS Washington* off from Alpha Fleet and get her over to Pleidian space as quickly as possible."

Gomez threw up his hands and shook his head. "Now I'm totally confused."

"Good! That's what I'm counting on from the Grish. Because, the ship they think they'll be assessing, shitting their proverbial pants over, won't be *USS Washington*, it'll be *USS Franklin*—the only other omninought in existence."

I held up a palm and continued, just as Gomez was about to respond, "Yes, after *Franklin's* recent beating, she's still sitting at Halibart Shipyards undergoing repairs. But we're only looking for *Franklin* to deceive the Grish, not actually go up against that Pinnacle Fleet on her own. And once *Washington* has successfully dealt with the Wrinnth, we'll hightail it over to help *Franklin* and the rest of the Alpha Fleet decimate the Pinnacle Fleet, then it's on to the Drakoria Star System, and, well, save the day... or whatever."

Gomez just stared at me.

I attempted another smile.

"That's a ridiculous plan."

I nodded.

"It makes a shitload of assumptions."

"That it does," I agreed.

The Admiral wobbled his head from side to side. "There again, I guess it could work. I'd have to check to see if *Franklin* can even clear SpaceDock," Gomez mumbled.

He appeared to be tapping, his eyes diverted to an out-of-view keyboard. "Uh... I'll have to get back to you." Admiral Gomez looked up at me, a line forming between his brows. "You know, Captain, you have a very devious mind."

"So, I've been told, Admiral."

Chapter 32

Sonya Winters

Sonya stood huddled in the dimly lit Hold 536 with the rest—Hardy, Derrota, and Kaelen—her eyes tracking her uncle's progress on her TAC-Band. The sphere glowed faintly behind them.

Then the Captain burst into the compartment. His face was taut with anxiety and something else—a vulnerability she wasn't accustomed to seeing. "Sorry I'm late," he panted. "Everything's happening all at once."

Sonya noticed the weariness in his voice, a tone that seemed out of place for the unflappable Captain Galvin Quintos.

His gaze flicked to Hardy, searching for a sliver of hope. "You still think you may have the workings of an idea?"

Hardy nodded, his faceplate reflecting the ambient light of the hold. "I do. Just need to speak with the Guardian fella."

Quintos exhaled sharply, running a hand through his hair in a rare show of distress. Sonya watched him closely, noting the tautness of his jaw, the restless energy that seemed to vibrate through him. She knew that look—it was one of desperation. This whole ordeal with Gail Pristy had shattered something within him. The Captain she knew was a fortress of strength and resolve; now she saw cracks in that facade.

A chirp from Quintos' TAC-Band sliced through the silence, causing him to curse softly under his breath. His annoyance was palpable as he checked the message, his eyes darting over the text with growing irritation.

"I'm needed on the bridge," he announced begrudgingly.

For a fleeting moment, Sonya caught a glimpse of longing in the Captain's eyes as they settled on the enigmatic sphere—their one last chance at undoing what had been done. He seemed torn between his duty and his desire to stay, to fight for Pristy's return by any means necessary.

His focus shifted back to Hardy and then to Sonya, and she felt the weight of responsibility settle upon her shoulders. "Do what you can to bring Gail back to us," he implored.

As her uncle hastened out of the hold, Sonya's gaze lingered on his retreating figure before returning to Hardy, Derrota, and Kaelen. They were an unlikely team—Sonya with her coding prowess, Hardy with his human-infused AI insight, Derrota with his deductive scientific mind, and Kaelen with his engineering genius—all united by a singular purpose—to defy reality and bring back their fallen friend.

They didn't have time for doubt or fear; every second that ticked by was a second lost from Gail Pristy's dwindling quantum echo. Sonya cracked her knuckles—a nervous habit—and looked to Hardy. "Okay, robot, it's showtime."

Hardy strode forward, brazen. She watched as he took the steps to the opening of the sphere, two at a time, then disappeared within the ornate threshold. Those steps, that threshold, were an illusion, she knew that. Just as the projected, slowly rotating symbols and glyphs were an anomaly beyond simple explanation. The influence—the magic—of the sphere expanded well beyond that small metal orb. What was real? Was the sphere itself—and the worlds within it real?

As Derrota and Kaelen trailed behind Hardy through the opening, she wavered. A sense of foreboding gripped her; any aspirations they harbored of locating and banishing Gail from that quantum dimension were likely wishful fantasies if not outright delusions. Contemplating her uncle's emotional well-being, she couldn't bear to entertain the dreadful implications if this plan failed.

PASSING THROUGH THE SHIMMERING PORTAL, Sonya was awestruck upon seeing the vast marble courtyard. It was difficult for her to comprehend that all of this existed here. At some level, she knew she was still within Hold 536, and this was simply a suspended beach-ball-sized sphere. She pondered her location—was she inside the Hold or within this ancient Crythara reality? This led her to consider the unfathomable idea of both realities existing simultaneously.

Sonya was well-versed in intricate QuansCode programming or constructing the distinct personality matrices of a Symbio Poth, no doubt about it. But to probe into the mechanisms of abstract quantum realms, like this one, if she was truthful with herself, made her feel *lacking* and out of her depth... at least when compared to Derrota and Hardy.

On the other hand, she wasn't entirely certain about Kaelen's knowledge or lack thereof. The man irked her, he could be an arrogant jerk at times. But she presumed he fulfilled a specific role, being here at the request of her uncle.

Letting out a breath, she took in the virtual surroundings that weren't so much virtual but real, just taking shape upon an alternate quantum plane. But even knowing that, she struggled to make sense of the subtle vibrations thrumming through the intricate carvings and towering columns that surrounded them. She looked up to the twenty-five-foot-high, carved, arched ceilings. The awe she felt instilled a sense of humility within her.

Up ahead, she spotted Hardy, Derrota, and that Guardian Grantham, already deep in hushed conversation. And of course, there was Kaelen... lurking nearby. Even from a distance, he smelled like yesterday's pizza. Really, what was he doing here tagging along on a mission that required the utmost precision? What was my uncle thinking?

She joined the group, eliciting a bemused glance from the wizardly old man. Before Sonya could compose herself, Hardy launched into a long-winded explanation, his holographic displays spinning out complex diagrams and equations as he delved into obtuse theories of quantum mechanics. She suppressed an exaggerated eye roll. Leave it to the self-important ChronoBot to jump straight into incomprehensible technobabble without so much as a *hello* or a briefing on their situation. As if this gatekeeper character would inherently know why we were here... the consequential retrieval of a lost crewmember from the ether.

Sonya chewed at her bottom lip unconsciously as her mind raced to keep up with Hardy's complex theories on quantum entanglement and his assumptions of DeckPort teleportation constructs. Typically, she relished technical challenges but Hardy's complex theories on quantum entanglement and assumptions about DeckPort teleportation constructs left her doubting her own intelligence. She snuck a quick look at Derrota, comforted slightly to see that he too, with all his intellectual prowess, was straining under the weight of Hardy's relentless barrage of techno jargon.

When Grantham eventually broke his silence, his voice

dripped with patronizing doubt, "Only after a millennium, were the Crythara enlightened to the information that you seek. What leads you to think any of you possess the ability to comprehend these notions, and further, are prepared to embrace the profound universal realities being put forth?"

Sonya ground her molars, the words *back off, Grandpa* perched on the tip of her tongue. This dude was treating them like clueless toddlers. He didn't get it. They were all-in... here to save an actual human being. This wasn't some abstract exercise or game. An actual life was at stake. Getting dissed by this geriatric fuckhead, was really starting to...

Before she could unleash the full force of her simmering temper, Hardy barreled in with renewed urgency, "Look, you may or may not already know all this... but one of our officers was lost in an accident having to do with an interdeck quantum teleporter. Uh, specifically one of our ship's DeckPorts." The ChronoBot gestured to the world around them. "You not only know the quantum tech... you live it. Right? So, what do you say you take a quick look under the proverbial hood, maybe get your hands a little dirty? In the end, you can help us do a good thing... get this contraption of ours working, maybe isolate our friend's entangled signature."

Derrota raised a hesitant finger. "Her name is Gail Pristy. You know her from when she was here earlier. Please, help us retrieve her— fully intact of course, from whatever specific quantum plane she now inhabits."

Pristy. Just the mention of her name was enough to douse Sonya's blazing irritation with a cold serving of guilt. Her *uncle person* was depending on them, on her, to bring Gail back from the brink of oblivion. She'd seen firsthand how this had wrecked the man, as if anyone didn't already know his true feelings for the woman—feelings that were as transparent as space itself.

Sonya refocused on Hardy's inscrutable ramblings about

manipulating quantum states and rewinding cosmic inversion fields. Geez, the robot just needed to shut the hell up for a second—let this Guardian guy consider what was being proposed.

Grantham was eying them, each of them, with grim solemnity.

"You propose a perilous undertaking," the old codger intoned, his piercing gaze seeming to scrutinize their very souls. "Quantum realms are not to be trifled with when intending to change the chronology of historical events."

Sonya's temper flared again, anger burning away any doubts she may have had about what they were doing here. They were putting everything on the line, proposing this wild cosmic gambit, all in service of trying to save one of their own! Who was this relic to judge their motivations based on his preconceived notions of humanity?

Before she could unleash a blistering torrent of furious retorts, Kaelen's gruff voice cut through the tension with mocking irreverence. "Yeah, yeah, enough with the mystical double-talk. Just show us the ropes already, Gandalf."

Despite the direness of their situation, Sonya found herself suppressing a smirk at the Engineer's brazen disregard for deference. Leave it to Kaelen to deflate the Guardian's pomp and self-importance with one mocking nickname.

Surprisingly, Grantham's stern countenance faltered for a moment, a trace of dry amusement crossing his composed features before he regarded them all with an unreadable expression. "If you are to venture into the esoteric domains of quantum reality, you must be prepared to shed your crude, linear biases and evolve your understanding beyond its causal shackles." His piercing gaze rested on Sonya. "Can you transcend the limits of your perceptions? Remake yourselves into vessels for cosmic mastery?"

Sonya was about to go off about how accomplished her team was—Derrota, Hardy, and even Kaelen had accomplished feats that few others could match. That underestimating them would be a colossal mistake.

But Hardy beat her to the punch, shutting down the argument before it even started. "We're ready, Freddy. Show us how to master the quantum waveform."

Grantham motioned for them to follow him further into the pavilion, while Sonya's irritation bubbled beneath the surface. *Pfft... transcend the limits of your perceptions... Give me a break.* Haughty old fossil, who was he other than a lonely old doorman?

Sonya followed the Guardian Grantham through the ornate archways, trying her best to mask her irritation. As they moved deeper into the pavilion, the surrounding architecture seemed to shift and mutate, the marble columns giving way to the familiar bulkheads and decking of *USS Washington.*

She blinked in confusion, wondering if they had somehow been transported back to the ship. But no, the subtle thrumming of energy that permeated the space told her they were still very much within the Guardian's realm. Up ahead, she recognized the curved alcove that housed one of *Washington's* DeckPorts— the very one where Gail Pristy had met her tragic end.

Gritting her teeth, Sonya steeled herself as they approached the DeckPort's open maw. Hardy's robotic friend and assistant, the squat, four-legged bot, Climbo, stood vigilant nearby, its multitude of sensors and appendages swiveling to track their movements.

"This is where it happened," Hardy stated, his tone uncharacteristically somber. "Right here, where Gail... was..." He trailed off, unable or unwilling to give voice to the gruesome details.

Sonya swallowed hard, memories of that terrible day

flooding back. The panic, the blood, the look of utter anguish on her uncle's face as he cradled Pristy's broken body. She shoved the images aside, focusing instead on the task at hand.

"So, what now?" she asked, her voice tight. "How do we find her... her signature or whatever?"

Grantham regarded her with that infuriatingly calm expression. "You must first learn to perceive the quantum realm," he intoned. "Only then can you hope to manipulate its intricate fabric."

Before Sonya could protest, the Guardian raised a gnarled hand; the DeckPort seemed to shimmer and distort. Suddenly, they were no longer alone in the alcove.

Gail Pristy stood before them, alive and whole, her expression one of serenity as she prepared to step into the DeckPort.

Sonya's breath hitched, torn between joy and dread.

"This is but a quantum shadow," Grantham explained, his voice seeming to echo from all around them. "A fleeting impression of events as they once unfolded. Observe carefully."

They watched, helpless, as Pristy strode forward and into the DeckPort's shimmering threshold. For a brief moment, her form seemed to fragment, distorting in a dizzying array of fractionalized shards. Then, just as quickly, the image collapsed, leaving Gail Pristy cleaved in half, lying on the deck, dying.

Sonya felt bile rise in her throat, the memory of Pristy's gruesome fate searing itself into her mind anew. She wasn't the only one affected; Derrota had gone pale, and even Kaelen looked shaken.

"Again," Grantham commanded.

The scene reset. Pristy reappeared as if nothing had happened.

They all watched, powerless, as the horrific sequence played out over and over, each repetition seeming to chip away at their resolve. Sonya lost count of how many times they witnessed

Pristy being cleaved in two, the images blurring together into a nightmarish collage of pain and loss.

Finally, after what felt like an eternity, Grantham raised his hand once more. This time, the loop ceased.

Sonya sagged against the nearest bulkhead, her legs trembling, her mind reeling.

"You have borne witness to the immutable path," the Guardian intoned. "Now, you must learn to bend reality to your will." He looked at each of them, his eyes coming to rest on Sonya. "You, child. You shall be the one."

Sonya wanted to scream, to rage against the cruelty of being forced to relive that trauma even one more time.

But before she could give voice to her anguish, Grantham spoke again, "Focus your intent," he commanded. "See not what is, but what could be. Reshape the quantum flow through the power of will, the strength of your focused consciousness."

Sonya squeezed her eyes shut, struggling to clear her mind of the haunting images. She reached out, grasping for that elusive thread of perception, that glimmer of possibility that Grantham spoke of.

Once more, Grantham had Pristy posed like a frozen caricature within an Apex Nexus game, only with this, the stakes were literally life and death. At first, there was nothing. Just the echoing emptiness of the alcove, punctuated by the ragged sound of her own breathing. Then, like a distant echo in a vast canyon, she sensed... something. A faint ripple in the fabric of reality, a hairline fracture that seemed to splinter off into infinite permutations.

She latched onto that fleeting impression, pouring every ounce of her being into shaping it, bending it to her will. The effort was excruciating, like trying to reshape solid steel with nothing but her bare hands. Tears brimmed at the corners of her eyes and her lips began to quiver. She felt Derrota's comforting hand upon her shoulder.

"You've got this, Sonya."

Gradually, almost imperceptibly, the quantum flow began to shift. Sonya's mind swam with a dizzying array of potential outcomes, each one more improbable than the last. Taking a single step forward, Pristy was immediately thrust back to her original position. *Crap!*

Then, just when she felt her grip on reality slipping, something changed.

The scene reset once more. Pristy stepped into the DeckPort's threshold. But this time, instead of heartbreaking calamity, her form remained intact. She passed through the shimmering portal, seemingly unharmed; then she was gone.

Sonya's eyes flew open, scarcely daring to believe what she had just witnessed. She swiped at her moist cheeks and looked around her, the others wore similar expressions of stunned, silent elation.

"You have glimpsed the malleable nature of quantum reality," Grantham's voice rang out, suffused with an undercurrent of pride. "Well done."

But even as the words of praise washed over her, Sonya felt a nagging sense of unease. They—*she*—had achieved the impossible, altering the very fabric of one particular quantum plane, one potential reality. And yet...

Her gaze swept the empty alcove, coming to rest on the inert DeckPort. "Was that real, or just a test?" She looked to Grantham, almost afraid to hear his answer.

"Where is she?" Hardy asked. "I'm not picking up her life-signature."

Derrota stepped closer to the Guardian. "The ChronoBot asked you a question, sir. Where is Gail Pristy?"

Dread coiled in the pit of Sonya's stomach as she breathed out. "If we changed things, then where did Gail go?"

The question appeared to fall on deaf ears, the old man offering only a contemplative, faraway expression.

Finally, the Guardian spoke, his eyes pinned to the Deck-Port, "This is a facsimile of the DeckPort within *USS Washington*. With that said, reality is reality. Your Gail Pristy... she would have emerged if she chose to do so."

Kaelen snorted, "What kind of bullshit are you trying to sell here? Of course, she'd want to come out." He glared at the old guy, then to the others. "I'm sorry, Sonya. The dude's no better than that shyster Chaplain, Trent."

Hardy, now glowering at the alien aberration, went still. His 7-foot-tall frame seemed ready to pounce or maybe activate his myriad of plasma cannons.

"Come on, robot," Sonya said, defeated. "I think we should go now. I just want to go. Okay?"

Hardy remained still, silent.

Both Kaelen and Derrota looked on, seemingly not knowing what to say or do.

The Guardian was unfazed, maintaining the same pleasant expression he'd worn when they first entered the sphere. He turned to Sonya. "I do wish you safe travels, child."

The four of them turned and left without so much as a glance over the shoulder.

Chapter 33

Captain Galvin Quintos

I made it back to the bridge, still reeling from having to leave Hold 536 in such a rush. The bridge buzzed like a whacked beehive. Captains across Alpha Fleet lit up the halo feeds, their faces knotted in confusion and dissent. News of *Washington's* diversion to Pleidian space didn't sit well, nor did the plan to prop up *Franklin* as a decoy. The Captains were voicing their resistance loud and clear, and Lieutenant Akari James was doing her best to fend off the onslaught. She looked relieved as I made my way forward.

"What in seven hells are we doing splitting the fleet?" Captain Marquez's voice cut through from his feed.

I looked at his image on the display; his jaw was clenched with the firmness of long-held resentments.

"We don't have the luxury of debate," I snapped back. "*Franklin's* our best shot at putting the Grish on their back foot... giving them pause. It's a gambit, but it'll work."

"You expect us to follow a ghost ship into battle?" Captain Liu spat, her tone as sharp as shattered glass.

"*Franklin's* more than a ghost," I argued, pushing down that clawing doubt in my gut. "She's a damn good decoy. And she has plenty of fight left in her, by the way."

"And what about our Pleidian allies?" another Captain chimed in. "You don't think they would be best served having the entire Alpha Fleet there to back you up?"

"Look, I take my orders from EUNF Command. But, no," I said firmly. "We have two equally challenging demands on our limited resources. Grish's Pinnacle Fleet cannot be left to its own devices. Earth cannot endure another attack."

I scanned the feeds, catching glimpses of anger and fear. The Captains were clearly at odds, mixing like fire and electricity; they erupted into a fireworks show of raised voices, speaking over each other in a frenzied exchange.

I cut through the noise. "Listen up! This isn't about what we're up against; it's about what we're fighting for. Earth. Humanity. Our damn future." I let each word land with the weight of iron. "You're going to show the Grish we mean business. It's time to stop this sniveling and show some backbone. Show some damn moxie."

The bridge fell silent, save for the hum of machinery and the distant echoes of orders being barked. Some Captains nodded reluctantly; others scowled but didn't argue further.

"After *Washington* departs Pleidian territory, undoubtedly triumphant, we'll meet you to finish off the Pinnacle Fleet, and then we'll all proceed to the Drakoria Star System where, collectively, we'll pound those contemptible piglets into bacon bits," I declared, locking eyes with each feed in turn. "So, do you have what it takes to get this done, or do you want to stay behind and explain to your grandchildren why you watched, cowering from the sidelines?"

Marquez's mouth twitched into a hesitant smile.

Liu folded her arms across her chest, her posture unyielding as ever, but her silence was concession enough.

One by one, they fell in line—not out of blind obedience but from something stronger: a shared determination to face whatever hell awaited us.

TEN MINUTES LATER, GRIMES WAS CONFIGURING the coordinates for Pleidian space—ten minutes after that, a newly manufactured wormhole was taking shape nearby within the void.

"Helm, when ready... take us in."

"Aye, Captain," Grimes acknowledged with a curt nod.

Chen piped up from his station, "Captain, Admiral Gomez is holding for you."

"I'll take it in my ready room."

ONCE SEATED BEHIND MY DESK, I STEELED myself for whatever curveball the Admiral would be sending my way this time.

"Patch him through," I said to SARAH.

Gomez's face materialized—the man seemed to look more haggard every time he appeared.

"Quintos," he began without preamble. "I already know you're en route to Pleidian space. Excellent."

Well, if he already knew that, why the hell was he contacting me? I raised my brows. "What can I do for you, Admiral?"

He hesitated—looked as if he'd just eaten a sour grape. "There are times we as U.S. Space Navy officers have to take one for the team. Roll with the proverbial punches."

I inwardly groaned. Here it comes.

"I need you to do me a personal favor. Can you do that, Galvin?"

Oh, so now we were on a first name basis? Then this must be a big ask. "If I can, certainly, Sir."

He looked back at me as if looking into the muzzle of a shotgun.

Jesus, just say it, man.

"You need to release Chaplain Trent from custody. That, and drop all charges leveled against him."

I tilted my head. "I'm sorry, I must not have heard you right, Sir. Funny, I thought you said to drop all charges leveled against Trent and let him go."

"The man has influential friends in high places, Captain."

"You're a Space Navy Five-Star Admiral, who in God's name is higher up the food chain than you?" I blurted out.

"Think about it, Captain. Who would be higher up the food chain?" he said with irritation.

He waited.

I exhaled deliberately, a calculated attempt to quell the fury simmering within me. "President Block."

Gomez dragged a hand down his face. "All I can suggest is watch him carefully, hell, put a 24/7 babysitter on him. But as things stand, the good Chaplain is being given a second chance to make amends."

I nodded, speechless.

"Contact me as soon as you reach Pleidian space and have assessed the situation there. Admiral Gomez out."

The display dissipated into nothingness.

WE WERE FOUR HOURS AND SEVENTEEN MINUTES into our trek toward Pleidian space, giving me time to deal with several mounting personnel issues.

I wanted to be there when Chaplain Trent was released from his jail cell—ensuring he understood the conditions, no, my conditions, for his release.

I waited in the corridor just outside the brig, my arms folded across my chest as the security officer approached with Chaplain Trent in tow. Trent strutted out, his chin raised defiantly, clearly having already learned that his charges were being dropped. A smug grin played on his lips.

"Shut down the security feeds for the next five minutes," I ordered the guard, my voice clipped.

The guard hesitated and then headed away, leaving Trent where he stood.

I closed the distance between the Chaplain and myself, rearing back and delivering a stinging slap across his face. The sound echoed through the corridor as his head whipped to the side from the force of the blow.

Before he could react, I seized him by his clerical collar and dragged him down a nearby passageway. As if on constant replay, my mind flashed back to the despondency, humiliation, and physical pain this sick fuck had single-handedly orchestrated against my crew. He flailed and struggled, but I was fueled by a cold rage. I continued to manhandle him, throwing several quick jabs to the back of his head. Let me just say... my actions were more gratifying than you could possibly imagine—and I wasn't done yet.

We swiftly veered into another corridor. Trent's eyes grew wide upon spotting the word **AIRLOCK** painted high on the bulkhead. He stumbled, collapsed, and fell once more. At that point, half-dragging him, I delivered one final powerful thrust, launching him into the already open airlock chamber. With a powerful kick from my left boot, I propelled him into a sprawling, disheveled heap onto the chamber deck. I then forcibly slammed the hatch closed, trapping him within.

"You can't do this!" Trent shrieked, clambering upright and hammering his hands against the airlock's transparent panel. His eyes bulged, terror gripping him.

I ignored his cries, striding over to the control panel and slapping a sequence of buttons. Red warning lights began flashing as an ear-splitting alarm pierced the air. Trent froze, his gaze following the loud hiss of breathable air being sucked from the chamber.

"Stop! You can't just kill me like this!" he screamed, clutching at his throat as the first effects of oxygen deprivation set in.

My hand hovered over the green-lit button—the one that would open the outer airlock door and eject him into the frigid void of space. Trent's eyes locked on mine, his face reddening as his gasps became more desperate.

The seconds ticked by in silence, save for the blaring alarm. Finally, I leaned toward the speaker. "You so much as fart in public, you'll be right back here," I said, my voice laced with venom. "And there won't be any second chances. Have I made my point?"

Trent nodded frantically, his lips forming the word *yes,* though no sound escaped. Sweat beaded on his brow as his movements became sluggish.

"I can't hear you, Chaplain."

"Yes," he croaked, his voice a strangled rasp. "I promise!"

Satisfied, I disengaged the airlock sequence, and the hissing stopped as the chamber repressurized. Trent crumpled to the ship's deck, sucking in deep, greedy breaths as the color returned to his face.

Chapter 34

After dinner, I headed up to the Symbio Deck to catch up with Sonya. She filled me in on what went down with the sphere and the encounter with the Guardian. She explained how, with Grantham's help and using the enigmatic power of the sphere, she'd created what amounted to an opportunity for Gail Pristy to return to our particular quantum realm. But, to Sonya, it seemed more like a roll of the dice—one Gail, for some unexplained reason, decided not to take the chance on.

Previously engaged in sifting through a bin of assorted limbs, she now grasped a stray Symbio arm with one hand and gestured with it while she spoke. "Truth is," Sonya said, "... we have no idea where she is. Not really. Gail might already be living her life out on some parallel plane, perfectly happy there."

Her gaze met mine, guilt darkening her features.

She stopped, obviously realizing her commentary was unwelcome and hard for me to acknowledge.

"I'm sorry," Sonya choked. "You know you're not the only

one who misses her, right? I've been living with her for months. Never had a big sister, but, I guess, she's as close as I'll ever get."

I nodded. "Well... thank you. You tried. More importantly, you cared," I said softly, turning to leave.

"Hold on." She rushed over to me, enveloping me in an embrace with her three arms, squeezing me tight. Such affection was uncommon for the teenager. "Are you going to be alright?" she asked, her voice muffled against my chest.

"I'm fine. I promise. It's better to know how things stand."

It was 0200 hours and, apparently, I had a new late-night friend... insomnia. Instead of tossing and turning for hours on end as I had the night before, I was now back roaming *Washington's* seemingly endless corridors.

Embarking on my third circuit of the vessel, this trek led me past the Mess Hall to top off my coffee, then by the men's head to dispose of it, and finally, past Circadian Platform Deck G, where Climbo continued his quiet vigil over one specific Deck-Port, which I was beginning to loathe.

"You know, Climbo, you no longer need to hang out here. You can go back to wherever you... uh, you know, typically hang out."

The mechanical mule stared back at me expressionless.

Curious, I asked, "Have you let anyone use this DeckPort since... what happened to XO Pristy?"

Instead of answering, Climbo did something I'd never witnessed him doing before, he sat back on his haunches, which was comical in of itself... but it was all at once clear to me... he was letting me know he had not left his post.

Chapter 35

Halibart Shipyards, *USS Franklin*

Chief Craig Porter

P orter had arrived at the immense Halibart Shipyards, not too far from Earth's Moon, just thirty minutes earlier. He had caught a military shuttle at Kirkland Airforce Base in New Mexico where he'd been visiting an old girlfriend, Connie. Or was it Bridget? Officially, he remained on active duty but had been troubled in recent months by an illness, a condition known as Leptospirosis, which he believed he contracted within Cueva de los Guácharos, an isolated and challenging-to-access cave network deep inside the Amazon rainforest. He was fine now, ready for the next thing.

Porter, an enigma captivated by the untamed wilderness, as well as cutting-edge technological advancements, excelled as a U.S. Space Navy Engineering & Propulsion Chief, mastering advanced propulsion and wormhole mechanics. His expertise in

Alcubierre and tachyonic induction spring jump drives, along with manipulating vacuum fluctuations and negative energy for fast translocation, was unmatched. His ability to integrate and refine these systems for space-time and quantum synchronization proved crucial on past dreadnoughts, including USS Hamilton.

But if he was being honest, the Leptospirosis had been resolved for quite some time; rather, it was his almost compulsive fascination with exploring the wild and studying diverse animal species that drew him back to terra firma instead of the celestial realms.

However, it was a summons from his long-time friend Galvin Quintos, backed up by the highest authority—the President of the United States himself, formerly the esteemed Five Star Admiral Cyprian Block—that had overridden his usual, tried and true, get-out-of-deployment excuses.

His knowledge of the mission was limited to the name of the ship he'd report to—USS Franklin, one of the new omninoughts he had only heard of but never served on. He learned that the vessel was undergoing repairs at SpaceDock 24B and that he had 24 hours to make it operational and set it underway.

Accompanied by young Ensign Roisin Blunderton, he hurried within the long spaceway corridor with its diamond glass view portals flanking both bulkheads with panoramic views out to one colossal spacecraft after another.

The Ensign's captivating emerald eyes darted about the space as if fearing she might miss the turn-off. She nervously tucked a wayward strand of auburn hair behind one ear. "Uh... I believe it's coming up on the right, Sir."

"You don't have to bother with that *sir* stuff with me, Ensign. I'm just Porter."

"Roger that, Sir. I mean, *Porter*." She glanced his way. "No footlocker or duffle for you?"

"Had no time for any of that. I was told my, um... things, will be delivered later on today. Was pretty much ushered onboard that shuttle at gunpoint."

She chuckled, then went serious unsure if Porter was joking or not. "Um, we should be able to scrounge up a uniform for you, other sundries, once onboard."

He glanced down at his clothes... board shorts and a bright yellow Hawaiian shirt adorned with a recurring motif of scarlet and azure macaws. He smiled, adjusting his worn, frayed NY Mets baseball cap tighter on his head. "This *is* my uniform."

Once again, she wasn't sure if he was kidding, so she simply nodded her acknowledgment.

Hurrying along at a good clip, Porter said, "What can you tell me about the crew."

"The crew?"

"Yeah, *Franklin's* crew? What do you know about who will be shipping out with us?"

Her pace faltered momentarily as she turned to gaze at him quizzically. With a pinched brow, she motioned toward the closest viewport with one hand. "This is a shipbuilding facility. What reason would there be for any of these craft to have a crew onboard... like, poised to deploy just in case they're needed at some point in the future?"

He had to force himself not to look at her as if she was an idiot. "I understand that this is a shipyard. But this is a deployment, and as last minute as this is, that omninought won't pilot herself—she'll need a crew."

Her back straightened at Porter's tone. "Well, nobody told me anything about a crew. My orders were to meet you here, show you to SpaceDock 24B, get you whatever else you need for an imminent departure, and wave goodbye from the dock." Her voice took on a haughty edge—her chin lifted slightly to signal her discomfort with being spoken to in such a manner. He noticed the Ensign was repetitively using the palm of one hand to smooth down her uniform.

The jetway passage leading to SpaceDock 24B loomed ahead, the auto-hatch sliding open with a deflated hiss that seemed too tired to bother with a full greeting. Porter strode through, Ensign Blunderton at his heels. Before them, *USS Franklin* asserted her dominance over the shipyard, a titan among toys.

Spacecraft buzzed around like flies on a carcass, their comings and goings lacking any semblance of order. Materials and crewmembers were being shuttled to and fro in apparent disarray, vividly portraying the urgency of the situation.

Porter caught Blunderton's eye, his smug grin playfully mocking her. "Looks like we got ourselves a crew after all."

Her mouth twitched, annoyance flitting across her features before she masked it with professionalism. "Seems so."

Franklin's bow was a mountain of metal and might, casting a shadow over the dock that could swallow moons whole. They walked toward her, their steps echoing on the platform. As they approached the gangway, figures emerged from the shadow of the ship—a motley crew if ever there was one.

A giant of a man with tattoos crawling up his neck barked orders at a scrawny kid whose uniform hung off him like sails without wind. Nearby, a woman with eyes too old for her face directed two droids hauling crates, which Porter suspected contained munitions or spare parts.

Blunderton's smirk found its way back to her lips as she caught sight of the crew's less-than-stellar assembly. "Quite the selection," she said, then murmured, "... got yourself a real fine ship of misfits and rejects."

Porter's brow lifted in silent assessment. "Well... quality isn't always in the polish," Porter shot back, attempting to sound unfazed.

Their banter was cut short by a series of quick pings from Blunderton's tablet—orders incoming. She scanned them quickly; her face paled just as fast.

"What is it?" Porter asked.

"Uh... Looks like I'm being reassigned."

"By whom? To where?"

"By you," she retorted, fire dancing in her eyes.

"First I've heard of it," Porter said with a laugh.

She made a snarky face. "Seems misery loves company."

Porter shrugged. "It'll be fine. Don't sweat the small stuff."

Blunderton's posture stiffened as if she'd been slapped by an invisible hand. "I don't do ships," she spat. "And I'm not one of your misfits here."

"You are today," Porter said with far too much pleasure.

Their gazes locked. Then a pause.

Finally, she exhaled sharply through her nose and nodded curtly.

Together, they boarded USS *Franklin,* stepping into the belly of the beast where shadows played hide and seek among steel ribs. The hum of power ran through the deck plates, vibrations telling tales of readiness and potential disasters alike.

Blunderton followed close behind as Porter moved through corridors lined with cables and flickering lights. They came upon compartments where crews worked feverishly—engineers swearing at uncooperative techs, medics hustling between bays, cooks slamming pots and pans in what passed for a galley.

Every step was an unveiling of *Franklin's* inner workings— the heartbeats of countless systems syncopating into one determined pulse.

"Main Engineering, this way," he called over his shoulder as they navigated the innards of the omninought.

The Ensign was trailing him silently now; whatever fire had

been there was smothered by determination or perhaps resignation to fate—Porter couldn't tell which.

They reached Main Engineering—a cathedral of power—where engines, a mass of intricate circuitry, and a display of multi-colored blinking lights only few could understand. Porter paused at the threshold; even here, amidst the clean lines of technology, there was a striking beauty that commanded attention.

An eclectic crew manned the controls: a robust woman clad in a tank top and camouflage pants masterfully manipulated holographic projections, a middle-aged individual sporting a thick mustache reminiscent of Groucho Marx, and two senior men side by side, the shorter one not quite measuring up to his companion's shoulder, both exhibiting a decent grasp of the tech at hand.

Blunderton stayed quiet at his side as they took in the ship's impressive power-plant. A small smile tugged at Porter's lips despite himself—this ship would be home for now.

"Time to see just how spaceworthy she is," he muttered more to himself than Blunderton.

"Okay. So, where do we start?" Her voice had softened but carried an undeniable edge. Clearly, she was less than thrilled to dive into whatever abyss awaited them.

"With every bolt and panel," he replied, stepping forward into Main Engineering. "And we don't stop until this beast roars to life like she never has before."

Chapter 36

Halibart Shipyards

Ensign Roisin Blunderton

E nsign Roisin Blunderton followed on Chief Porter's heels, gripping her tablet against her chest while they wound through USS *Franklin's* serpentine corridors. A palpable urgency vibrated through the vessel, edging her nerves.

"Chief, we've got a problem with the atmospheric controls on Deck 12," a crewman called out.

He appeared to have been running, obviously looking for Porter. The crewman's face glistened with sweat, a black smear of *something* on his left cheek.

Porter barely glanced up from the schematic he was studying. "Reroute power from the auxiliary systems and run a diagnostic. I'll be there in five."

The man nodded, then sprinted off, disappearing behind a

bend in the corridor.

Blunderton suppressed a sigh as they changed course, heading for the nearest DeckPort. She'd lost count of the issues they'd encountered since boarding the battle-scarred vessel. It seemed like every corner they turned revealed another problem, another crisis demanding Chief Porter's attention.

As they stepped into the DeckPort, Blunderton's stomach lurched. She still hadn't gotten used to the disorienting sensation of being instantaneously transported from one part of the ship to another. Porter, on the other hand, seemed unfazed, his mind already racing ahead to the next task.

"Ensign, make a note," he said, his eyes still fixed on the schematic. "We need to replace the cooling coils in the galley refrigeration unit."

Blunderton nodded, tapping on her tablet. "Got it, cooling coils."

She couldn't help but feel a twinge of admiration for Porter's unflappable demeanor. No matter how daunting the challenge, he approached it with a cool, analytical precision that bordered on genius.

As they emerged onto Deck 12, they were greeted by a scene of controlled chaos. Crewmen scurried back and forth as they worked to bring the atmospheric controls back online.

"What's the status?" Porter barked.

"We've managed to stabilize the pressure, but the oxygen levels are still fluctuating," a young engineer replied, wiping his brow with the back of his hand.

Porter nodded, his eyes already scanning the control panel. "Increase the flow rate from the secondary tanks and recalibrate the sensors. That should buy us some time until we can replace the faulty components."

Blunderton watched Porter as he took command of the situation. He seemed to know exactly what to do... what his next move would be. *Show-off*.

A FEW MINUTES LATER, THE ALARMS FELL SILENT, AND the deck was bathed in the steady glow of the overhead lights.

"Not bad," she said flatly, struggling to conceal her begrudging admiration.

Porter glanced up, a hint of a smile tugging at the corners of his mouth. "Just doing my job, Ensign. Now, let's head to the bridge. I want to check in with VD and see how the rest of the crew is faring."

Blunderton felt a flicker of unease at the mention of VD, the hulking, tattooed man who seemed to be in charge of the ragtag crew. She cringed inwardly—like, who would want to be named that? There was something about him that set her on edge—a barely concealed menace that lurked beneath his gruff exterior.

As THEY STEPPED ONTO *FRANKLIN'S* BRIDGE—ominous in its quiet—Blunderton's gut tightened at what lay ahead.

"What's the ETA on our captain?" Porter queried.

VD eventually lifted his gaze from a glowing display; it landed heavily on them both. "That empty Mount there... that should tell you everything you need to know," he drawled with mocking clarity.

Porter exhaled loud enough for Blunderton to hear it from where she stood beside him.

"You mean to say....." Porter's voice trailed off as if words could dig them out from under this revelation.

VD leaned back into his chair, too casual for Blunderton's taste, as he surveyed them like bugs under a glass. "That's right —no captain for this jaunt. Well, other than you."

Blunderton suppressed a smart-assed retort. Her fingers craved a physical object to grip—a wrench maybe.

An awkward silence filled the space between them.

VD shrugged—a tectonic shift beneath those inked muscles —there was nothing controlled about this chaos anymore.

Blunderton couldn't keep silent any longer; words poured out like acid, deadly enough to eat through hull plating, "Who exactly set up this clown show?"

VD continued to look bored with the conversation, with Ensign Blunderton.

"What? You just going to sit there looking stupid?" she asked.

Porter sent a sharp glance in her direction.

VD snorted—a guttural sound that rumbled from deep in his chest.

She'd pushed his buttons—*Good*.

"Careful Missy," the big man said, his eyes going cold. "Yeah, I'm coordinating this clown show, as you put it. You don't like it, you can take a walk."

"Okay, okay. How about we take things down a notch?" Porter interjected.

Like a dog with a bone, the Ensign glared back at VD. "Really. You consider *this* having coordination?" She made a sweeping hand gesture showcasing the nearly empty bridge.

VD retorted without hesitation, "Seems like progress is being made to me."

A moment stretched thin between them before Porter stepped in. "I said, let's just move on."

Blunderton shrugged, still perturbed. "Fine, we're moving on."

Chapter 37

Halibart Shipyards, *USS Franklin*

Chief Craig Porter

Porter, having returned from the Engineering & Propulsion department, stepped onto the bridge. His thoughts were preoccupied with the tasks left on Blunderton's tablet... all to be completed today before the scheduled departure of *USS Franklin* from Halibart Shipyards—at midnight.

Blunderton had chosen a station to occupy, her gaze fixed on her datapad, the light casting stark shadows over her focused expression. Lists scrolled under her fingertips—ship systems were slowly, *too slowly*, coming back online—showing that a multitude of tasks were still undone. Her lips were a thin line, her manicured brow furrowed in concentration.

Porter bypassed her without a word, his resolve steeling him against the tension that knotted the air on the bridge. He settled into the Captain's Mount, its simulated-leather, cool and unwelcoming beneath him. This wasn't his usual seat, but with no captain and the ship in disarray, protocol was a luxury he couldn't afford.

"Stuff arrived," Blunderton announced without looking up.

"What stuff?"

"Your stuff," she said, tilting her head toward a stack of boxes, containers, a footlocker—and more mystery items cloaked beneath a tarp at the back of the bridge.

Porter, still sitting, glanced in that direction.

"Not sure what you had delivered, but there's been some peculiar sounds coming from that area." She cast a sidelong look at the piled heap of various items, then turned her attention to Porter.

He smiled, getting to his feet. "I bet Lucy's not too happy with me about now."

"Lucy? That a crewmember I've yet to meet?" Blunderton asked.

"Crewmember? I suppose you could call her that."

In one swift motion, he carefully lifted a case from the top of the stack, set it down on the deck, and then went back to the pile. While its top appeared level, there was an irregular shape beneath... all of it hidden by a canvas-like covering.

Porter noticed Blunderton's clandestine glances his way. Removing the tarp, there was a flurry of movement from what was now revealed as an oversized birdcage. Repeated loud screeches exemplified the feathered occupant's dissatisfaction with the situation.

The Ensign, obviously curious, now joined him at his side. Shoulder-to-shoulder, the two peered into the cage.

"That a parrot of some kind?" Roisin asked.

"Hyacinth Macaw."

The colorful bird tilted her head at them. Her golden beak

complemented her crimson, blue, and yellow plumage, making for a striking appearance. Lucy sat upon her sturdy-looking wooden perch, her azure feathers catching the overhead light. She bobbed her head slightly as she observed her surroundings, then brought her attention to the Ensign. With more than a glint of intelligence, the bird stared at Roisin with a playful intensity.

"She's beautiful," Blunderton said, extending a finger toward the bird.

"If you want to keep that finger, I'd suggest you not do that," Porter warned.

She hastily withdrew her hand as if touching a hot skillet. "So, Lucy bites, you're telling me."

"She doesn't know you... doesn't understand why you'd be poking at her like that. Once she feels comfortable around you, she'll let you touch her."

Porter leaned in. "Isn't that right pretty girl," he said in a baby voice. "I bet you're hungry. How about we get you some fresh water and a few Brazil nuts?"

He topped off the water dispenser from a plastic jug, then scrounged through several cases before coming up with a pouch of large dark nuts still in their shells. Presenting the open bag to the Ensign, he opened the cage door, and said, "Go ahead... offer her one of these."

"Uh, what about that whole wanting to keep all my fingers thing?"

"Lucy is ridiculously smart, she'll understand you're offering her food."

He watched Blunderton slowly withdraw a nut from the bag and tentatively present it to Lucy by extending an open palm—a large nut resting on her fingertips—just inside the cage's opening.

Lucy inclined her head as if pondering the proffered treat. Sidling nearer, she bent down and accepted the Brazil nut in her beak, then retreated several paces before crunching it down with a resounding *Crack!*

Chief Porter, your presence is requested within the Quansporter compartment.

At the abrupt, booming announcement from overhead by SARAH, Lucy let out a piercing shriek and began to flutter her wings.

Porter straightened and cocked his head. "Didn't think that thing was even functioning yet."

"It *was* on your list," the Ensign said quickly, referring to her tablet.

HE HURRIED ACROSS THE ROTUNDA WHERE THE still inoperable Gravity Well display would normally be showcasing the local star system. Then Porter strode into the Quansporter compartment, a wide grin spreading across his face as he took in the projected halo display.

"Well, I'll be... Coogong, you old worm! Didn't think I'd be seeing your scrawny hide anytime soon." He chuckled and offered up a fist-bump to the Thine, despite being a holographic projection. "How the hell have you been, you crazy scientist?"

Coogong smiled warmly. "Chief Porter, it is a most fortuitous reunion. Though I wish the circumstances were not so dire." His expression turned somber. "I'm afraid I bring troubling news regarding *Franklin's* manufactured wormhole capabilities."

Porter frowned. "Uh-oh, don't tell me we've got more prob-

265

lems. This boat's been through the wringer as it is. What's the damage?"

"My analysis indicates a critical power coupling in the aft section has been compromised," Coogong said gravely. "It's directly tied to the quantum field modulator that stabilizes the wormhole. Attempting a jump as is...." He shook his head.

"How likely will this issue present itself?"

"It may be as high as a thirty-five percent chance the field would destabilize."

Porter let out a low whistle. A destabilized wormhole was like asking for trouble.

"Thirty-five percent, huh? Doesn't exactly fill me with confidence." He rubbed the back of his neck. "And without that capability, we're dead in the water when it comes to linking up with Alpha Fleet. We're talking weeks, maybe months to get there at standard FTL."

Coogong nodded gravely. "Precisely the dilemma. You must choose—risk quick repairs and potential disaster or delay a week or longer at Halibart and ensure *Franklin's* systems are sound."

Porter scoffed. "A week? You know what Quintos has been tasked with, so you already know we don't have a week—hell, a day, to spare. Too much at stake. That fleet's counting on us." He paused, eyes narrowing. "Alright, Coogong, lay it out for me. What kind of duct tape and rubber band quick-fix are we looking at to shore up those odds?"

Coogong leaned in, his holographic projection flickering. "I've compiled the necessary specifications and calculations. It will require our combined expertise. If we start now, you should still be able to meet your midnight deployment time."

Porter nodded firmly. "Then that's what we'll do. Time to get our hands dirty, my friend." He straightened his posture. "I'm not about to be the reason everything grinds to a stop, not on my watch." He grinned wolfishly. "We'll tip those odds in our favor, just like old times back on *Hamilton,* huh?"

Coogong offered back a smile. "I would expect nothing less. Transmitting the data now. Please proceed aft and contact me when you are at the power coupling. We must hurry, it seems as though the fate of Alpha Fleet rests in our hands."

Porter, with Lucy perched upon his right shoulder, was situated at Helm. Ensign Blunderton was keeping busy, enlisting the help of a fellow crewman, moving the Chief's possessions from the back of the bridge into the nearby Captain's Ready Room.

Standing at the center of the bridge, VD cleared his throat. "This is the best I can do," he said with a scowl.

Blunderton came out of the ready room and made a face.

Porter observed the three ragtag individuals VD had hastily conscripted to fill critical bridge stations.

He arched an eyebrow as Ensign Blunderton strode closer with purposeful steps.

Hands on hips, Roisin appraised the motley collection.

"Scrounged up the best of the bunch," VD announced, gesturing toward the three wide-eyed crewmembers. "They can all work a command board, know a bridge station from a trash chute."

"Comforting," Blunderton said with ample snark.

VD went on, "This is Rigel Park, put him on the sensors and recon station. Lana Voss is your defensive systems expert, and Jansen Tycho can handle your comms station."

Porter eyed the trio, taking in their disheveled appearances. The wiry Rigel Park looked more like an elderly, indigent asteroid miner than a bridge officer, while Lana Voss' sinewy frame and circuitous tattoos gave her the air of a grizzled mechanic. Jansen Tycho, with his gaunt features and oversized uniform, seemed to embody the very definition of *makeshift*.

"VD, I appreciate you taking the initiative, but are you sure these are the best we've got?" Porter asked, offering up an apologetic expression to the newcomers.

The trio ignored the Chief's comment, their collective attention gravitating toward Lucy, the Hyacinth Macaw perched gracefully on Porter's shoulder.

"Look, Chief, I don't have a clue who's *best suited* for a starship's bridge," VD said defensively. "But I did my best to scrounge up some warm bodies who might actually know what they're doing. Take it or leave it."

Blunderton straightened, her verdant eyes glowering.

It was obvious to Porter that Roisin disliked VD, finding him offensive, while maintaining a mental tally of his perceived offenses. The Chief was reasonably confident she maintained a count of all of them—including *his*—so she could settle the score at a later time.

Porter chuckled, gesturing for the three new crewmembers to take their stations. "Fair enough, VD. I'm sure they'll surprise us."

He turned to the trio, his tone reassuring, "Alright, you heard the man. Park, you're on Sensors. Voss, you've got Defensive Systems. Tycho, Comms is yours. Let's see what you can do."

The three exchanged uncertain glances, but dutifully made their way to their respective stations.

While VD headed for the exit, Blunderton watched him with a skeptical eye, arms crossed over her chest. "Cream of the crop, huh?"

· · ·

He was going to miss his midnight deadline. Something SARAH was keen to remind him of every fifteen minutes. Seated at the Captain's Mount, Porter could tell Ensign Blunderton was uneasy, nervously patrolling the three occupied bridge stations like a persnickety mother hen. As it turns out, VD hadn't completely shit the bed—Rigel Park, Lana Voss, and Jansen Tycho were asking intelligent questions and at least seemed to be pressing the right buttons on their boards.

What Porter felt most concerned about was his lack of transparency with that critical power coupling. He, with Coogong's virtual assistance, had indeed patched the coupling and they'd done their best to test it, run thorough diagnostics. But there was no getting around it, a patch job is a patch job. In the final analysis, Coogong had not revised his grim 35% probability of catastrophic breakdown *if and when* they would venture into a manufactured wormhole. Didn't Blunderton deserve to know that? Maybe later.

Ensign Blunderton stood to Porter's left, her nose buried in the details of her datapad. "Going down the list... we didn't finish everything, but we've done all that can be done within our timeframe." She shrugged and looked to the Chief.

He didn't acknowledge Roisin; he needed to concentrate.

"SARAH, elevate the primary propulsion systems to *standby*," Porter commanded.

Immediately, what had been a nearly undetectable, subtle vibration coming up through the deck plates, was now becoming a far more pronounced *hum* indicating that the omninought's big drives had come fully online.

"Go ahead and release SpaceDock restraining clamps, SARAH, and prepare for departure."

The AI's acknowledgment was a soft chime in response.

And with that simple sound, *USS Franklin* shuddered as it embraced freedom for the first time in weeks. A collective breath held by those few souls aboard seemed to release as they felt the familiar lurch of the vessel easing out into open space.

Porter leaned back in the Captain's Mount and closed his eyes—praying to whatever gods watched over reckless engineers and their Frankenstein creations.

Silence. At this moment, it presented itself as an omen—a void where a soothing calm should have washed over the space... instead, it remained eerily hollow.

His eyes snapped open as alarms blared their protests through the bridge. "What now?" he muttered under his breath.

"Drives are spiking," Rigel Park announced, urgency sharpening his voice. "Radiation levels are fluctuating."

Porter let out a breath, his shoulders relaxed. "Ignore that. Those are false readings. Propulsion is fine."

Rigel Park, Lana Voss, and Jansen Tycho—all stared back at him.

Blunderton took in the trio, her face twisting into a disapproving scowl. "You heard him, we're fine." Then she shot Porter a *you-better-know-what-you're-talking-about* look.

"Now we've got an environmental surge in Deck 25—main circulating pump!" Crewman Park called out from behind.

Again, the three looked to Porter with anticipation.

"That one's real," the Chief said. "Tycho put a call into VD to take a look at it."

"Aye, Captain."

Ready to correct him, Porter decided to let it go. At least for the duration of this jaunt, he was Captain by default. And while this ship was barely held together with spit and baling wire, he had a feeling their problems had only just begun.

Looking over to Blunderton, he did a doubletake. *When the hell did that happen?* He glanced to his right shoulder—empty. Then he looked back at her. Sure enough, Lucy was perched there on Roisin's slender right shoulder, doing her little head-dipping dance... the one she does when she's happy. *Traitorous parrot!*

"We can't keep patching things forever," the Ensign said, her voice taut with strain. "There are still things on my list that should probably—"

"We'll do what we can for now; worry about those other things later," Porter said with resignation.

"But if we don't address these issues—"

Porter turned to face the young Ensign, his eyes locking onto hers. "Roisin," he said in a flat tone that left no room for argument. "It's just a list—we need to concentrate on taking this big hunk of steel from point A to point B... nothing more."

"What if we're intersected by—"

He raised a palm. "Don't! Don't even think about finishing that sentence. I get it. We're not battle-ready."

"Well, I hope the Grish will give us a pass if we cross paths with them," she said. The Ensign turned her attention to Lucy, exchanging a quick lips-to-beak kiss with the bird.

The bridgecrew, sparse as they were, labored in a frenzy as ship systems blinked in and out, like the erratic gasps of a faltering engine in the depths of a winter chill. Porter remained at the Captain's Mount and all he could think about was the next action he'd be taking—to generate a manufactured worm-hole. *Fuck.*

"Status?" he demanded through gritted teeth as another wave of alerts washed over them.

"We're holding... just," Blunderton replied tersely.

Another violent tremor rippled through *Franklin* like an earthquake breaking through asphalt.

The crew shared glances—fear and pleading—mirroring each other and then focusing on their temporary leader.

SARAH chimed in again from above—a litany of damages

that would dishearten saints. But saints weren't aboard USS *Franklin* today.

"It's time," Porter said.

All eyes swiveled to him.

Rising abruptly, he rushed to Helm and settled into the seat; he proceeded to input new jump coordinates for a manufactured wormhole.

"Time we see what this big, hobbled tub can do," he said quietly to himself. The Chief—the *Captain*— readied *Franklin* for the next aspect of this already perilous journey... while, hopefully, defying the odds in the process.

Chapter 38

Pleidian Weonan Star System
USS Washington

Captain Galvin Quintos

USS *Washington* navigated the distant outskirts of the Pleidian Weonan space with FTL urgency, having emerged from the wormhole four hours prior. Nevertheless, the recent anticipated clash between the Pleidian and Wrinnth forces had yet to materialize.

As we approached the star system, an unsettling silence had taken hold—devoid of the usual comings and goings of interplanetary commercial vessels, merchant freighters, or military assets. We had stumbled upon the remnants of a previous skirmish here—from the battle that took place a few days ago. I saw the ravaged vestiges of Pleidian and Wrinnth warships now adrift and lifeless.

There on the primary halo display, my gaze was drawn to

the luminous frontier of the Pleidian Weonan Star System. It was anchored by its two formidable, brilliant white, A-type stars.

As the omninought navigated the alien system, Xyralon emerged into view, resembling a molten cauldron with streams of lava sculpting deep canyons. Following that, we observed Vortraxia, a slightly smaller planet but rife with fierce storms, its atmosphere a dense tapestry of swirling clouds. My attention then turned to the vibrant blue world of Weonan, comparable in size to Earth, and our unwavering ally against the Varapin, Grish, and potentially the Wrinnth.

Once past Weonan, we moved on to its neighboring world, Barux, scarred by eons of asteroid bombardment; then Aquilaris, a water world veiled in mysteries within its depths; farther out within the system came Nebulon-IX, a gas giant adorned with vast rings and speckled with ice, rock, and the remnants of shattered moons. Finally, the system's outermost planets, Crysalis and Glacorium, languished in perpetual twilight.

What we hadn't seen, though, was any sign of Shawlee's Royal Guard, nor the invading Wrinnth.

"Captain, it looks like there's definitely been a *recent* battle here," the Ensign remarked, glancing my way.

My gaze shifted to Akari in response.

Leaving Tactical unattended, Lieutenant James headed over to Sensors and Reconnaissance; Ensign Lira pushed herself away to give the Lieutenant room to evaluate her readings.

Akari leaned over the display. "You're right, Ensign... they were just here." she said, shaking her head. "There's been a confrontation... not the obvious one that happened a couple of days ago... but something within the last twelve hours or so. Residual propulsion radiation, telltale Phazon Pulsar echoes..."

Lieutenant James straightened her posture and frowned in my direction.

But I had already connected the dots. "They made a run for it," I said. "It's really that simple. Shawlee's prime concern would be her homeworlds... this star system. With her Royal Guard crippled, she'd find a way to get the attacking Wrinnth as far away from here as possible."

"Not sure that explains why *Impervious* has gone comms silent," Chen said.

I thought about that. *Impervious* was the flagship of the Royal Guard, where Shawlee was certain to be situated.

"I wouldn't read too much into that," Akari said, retaking her seat at Tactical. "Maybe these Wrinnth have tech that can hone in on U.S. Space Navy communications."

I spun back to face Ensign Lira. "Those recent battle signatures you've picked up on. Any chance we can follow those, like breadcrumbs? Would at the very least give us a course vector to follow."

Lira's expression turned grim as she manipulated the controls. "I've already attempted that, Captain. But the local battlespace is cluttered with contradictory readings."

I heard the all-too-familiar, metal-against-metal clomping of a thousand-pound ChronoBot entering the bridge. Hardy came to a standstill at my right.

"You've been listening in on our conversation, haven't you?" I asked.

The robot paused, rubbing his nonexistent chin.

I knew Hardy well enough to know, his response was a diversion, an attempt to avoid incriminating himself. I was well aware that he had the irritating tendency to access the vessel's security feeds... as well as anything SARAH was monitoring. When it came to respecting anyone's privacy... he just didn't think in those terms.

Finally, the ChronoBot said, "I think you're going about this all wrong."

"Fine, smartypants," I said, "... then why don't you enlighten us with your grand wisdom on the matter."

Hardy looked to Akari. "Were the Pleidians and/or the Wrinnth cloaked?"

"That wouldn't be evident from the ship's residual signatures," Akari said, looking at her console, then turning back to the ChronoBot. "An invisible vessel still leaves at least some detectable indicators... that's why cloaking is excellent for evading long-range detection. Up close and personal, not so much."

Hardy continued to stare at the Lieutenant.

"God, I hate it when you do that," she spat. "Just say what you're dying to say."

"Built into every ship's *cloaking* algorithm..." He gestured with air quotes for the word *cloaking*. "... is a directive to substantially filter drive radiation exhausts, making ship-wakes minimally detectable. If you can capture those significantly reduced signature profiles, you may be able to hone in on them. If you're looking for breadcrumbs, those would be your best bet."

"He's right," Lira said from her station. "Based on the detectable, filtered-down drive radiation exhaust signatures, I'm taking a leap and assuming we have a course vector." She looked up to me and then to Grimes at Helm. "I sent you the coordinates to follow, Thom."

Grimes turned to look at me.

Considering we'd pretty much been chasing our proverbial tail here, I nodded to the Crewman. "Without any better leads to go on, let's give Hardy's suggestion a try."

Arms folded tightly across her chest, Akari's posture was

rigid—her lips pressed into a thin line. She did not look happy with that decision.

I smiled, "We'll give it three hours. That means you, Lira, SARAH, and Hardy have one job... use every tool available to us to find those ships."

The hours had stretched from three to six. Although *Washington* had not yet caught up to the warring parties, we had encountered sufficient clues to maintain our pursuit, assuring us that we were closing in on them.

ANOTHER HOUR LATER AND LIGHT-YEARS FROM THE Pleidian Weonan Star System, we'd lost the proverbial scent.

It was late and well past time for a shift change.

Reluctantly, I finally decided to allow the Symbio 3.0s back on the bridge... to trust them. The command was contingent upon one thing—if anything of importance occurred, I was to be pulled back onto the bridge immediately, at which point I would decide if I should bring back the rest of my day crew.

I genuinely attempted to sleep. I tossed and turned like a stranded fish on the deck of a fishing boat. This was turning into an issue—perhaps it was the moment to obtain something from Chief Knott that could render me unconscious. Then again, it's always unwise for a ship's Captain to be impaired by drowsiness-inducing medication.

Nighttime strolls offered a solitary comfort, not entirely

unpleasant. Loss accompanied me through these hours, a perpetual companion masquerading as a friend.

With a full cup of piping hot brew, I mindlessly turned the next corner at an intersecting passageway. There, I was startled by someone crossing right in front of me. Stumbling backward, I fumbled, half the contents of my coffee spilling down my chest and legs. Ready to reprimand my fellow nighttime wanderer to be more careful—to make some damn noise or something when coming to an intersection—all I could do was stare after the person with my mouth agape.

I knew her. And she did not belong here... not unless long-dead aristocratic Crytharan women had somehow been drafted onto the crew.

Lady Era continued briskly on her way, then, with a quick look over her shoulder, she gave me a bemused smile. *I have to be dreaming. I'm actually asleep in my quarters... right?*

Her now-distant laugh was like a whimsical nudge, meant only for me. *Not a dream.*

She made a left up ahead—Oh God, would she even be there when I made that same turn? Aberration or hallucination, it didn't matter, I couldn't lose sight of her. My feet slipped out from under me as I attempted the turn too fast.

Sprawled on the deck, covered in coffee, my gaze remained fixed down the corridor—scanning. Three simultaneous thoughts flashed into my head—one, this was *the* passageway within the Circadian Platform Deck G where the defective DeckPort was located; two, Lady Era was indeed gone; and three, Climbo was frantically pacing back and forth in front of the DeckPort's entrance.

As I lifted myself from the deck, the robotic pack animal pivoted in my direction while I approached. Wide-eyed, the automaton beeped and booped and looked from me back to the DeckPort.

"She got by you. Is that what you're trying to tell me?" I asked, wishing the stupid thing would just use its words.

Climbo answered with a rapid nod.

"Did she say anything before—"

Climbo was already shaking its head, no.

"And up until this point, nobody's crossed into that DeckPort?"

Another shake of the head.

Suddenly, a Klaxon blared. SARAH's voice filled the passageway:

Battle Stations...
Battle Stations...
All Essential Crewmembers
Report to Your Stations...

"Dammit!" My fists tightened until my knuckles turned white. The urge to lash out, to hammer a fist against the bulkhead, was overwhelming.

"Screw it!" I threw my now-empty coffee cup against the metal bulkhead, shattering it into a thousand pieces. Wide-eyed, Climbo went stock-still.

Without hesitation, I sprinted toward the DeckPort's entrance.

Chapter 39

Stepping out of the DeckPort and into the Rotunda, I noticed the Gravity Well display was active. Arriving dayshift crewmembers were hurrying toward the bridge. Glancing momentarily back at the DeckPort, a fleeting sense of relief washed over me for not being sliced in two. With that, I quickened my pace toward the entrance.

I must have been the last to reach the bridge, observing Grimes, Chen, Akari, and the others already present.

The primary halo display flashed with activity—alien warships, energy bolts crisscrossing the void—the scene made more frantic by that damn Klaxon's persistent blaring overhead. Yet, the crew remained standing, no one was rushing to their stations to address the looming conflict beyond.

I strode into the fray of still bodies and faces... as if caught in some kind of bewildered paralysis.

"What the hell's going on?" I demanded.

"That's exactly what I just asked. Has everyone lost their mind?" came a familiar female voice.

Like some prehistoric insect caught in amber, I was

suddenly frozen in the same unmoving stance as the rest of my crew. I gaped at the figure standing beside the tactical console.

Gail Pristy appeared perplexed, a deer in the headlights, yet she was the most captivating sight I had ever beheld.

Snapping out of my trance, I strode toward her, determined, unstoppable. She had time to take one dismayed step backward before I took her in my arms, leaned her over, and kissed her hard on the lips.

The bridgecrew gasped collectively. The audacity of my action seemed to shock the crew into a deeper silence.

The moment was electrified like a live wire wound tightly around our bodies. Time stood still.

I could feel Gail's eyelashes flutter against my cheek, her body tense, and then melt into the kiss. An arm came around my neck and pulled me closer. Our two hearts, pressed together, beat as one.

When we finally parted, breathless and dazed, Gail's gaze held mine with an intensity that shook me. "Galvin..." she whispered, her voice carrying a mix of reprimand and chagrin.

She scanned my face, her eyes searching mine for answers.

I couldn't help but remember the events that had transpired earlier—events that this version of Gail Pristy knew nothing about... how the original version of herself, walked into that DeckPort and was severed in half... and how I held her while she was dying on that threshold... and how admissions of love spilled from my lips. I took a moment to register this disparity, to understand that those awful moments and those declarations of love never happened to the Gail Pristy who was now standing before me.

I took a half-step back, still holding her shoulders. "I—"

But before I could explain myself or apologize for what might have been an overstep, SARAH's voice came alive...

Captain Quintos, there is an incoming transmission from Empress Shawlee Tee.

I met Gail's eyes once more, lingering longer than necessary, before turning away from her and moving toward the Captain's Mount.

"Put it through," I ordered, schooling my features into a mask of command, as I settled into place.

Beside the halo display that illustrated the tumultuous combat, a new halo projection emerged, revealing the distressed features of Pleidian Weonan's Empress. A sense of purpose seized the bridge as each crewmember hastened to their stations.

Pristy, the only one who remained where she was, watched the activity swirl around her. She looked about the bridge, her gaze settling on the halo display. Then her eyes rested on me once more in a silent plea for clarity.

"It's okay, Gail," I reassured her softly, "I'll explain everything. For now, just take a seat at Tactical 2, and don't worry about a thing."

"Empress, Shawlee." I greeted her, giving the Empress my full attention.

She appeared harried, yet I could tell the sight of me triggered a sense of relief, softening her face and shoulders.

"How in God's name did you find us?" She waved away her question. "As you can see, we've been discovered, again, by the Wrinnth. Been playing cat and mouse, but time's run out for my Royal Guard."

"How about we step in and deal with your infestation problem once and for all?"

A smile lit up her face. "I thought you'd never ask."

Ensign Lira, from Sensors and Reconnaissance, interrupted,

"Forwarding full battle sensor scan assessment to Tactical. We're looking at twenty Wrinnth warships—"

"I've got the data. Zip it, Lira... while I bring weapons online," Akari, already hunched over her board, cut in sharply.

"We need to focus on vulnerable hull targets, like that dreadnought's aft section," Pristy called out, her military instincts surfacing sharp as ever. "Phazon Pulsars, rail cannons, fusion missiles should be primed already!"

Akari shot her a side-eye, the corner of her mouth twitching in a half-smile. "Back seat driver," she quipped. "Say, how about you take another spin in that DeckPort, huh?"

Pristy, initially taken aback by the nonsensical comment, shrugged it off. "Hey, I still have a couple of maneuvers you've yet to see, Lieutenant."

Akari smirked and chinned toward the console. "Well maybe less talk then and more action, XO."

"Now now, children," I chimed in, adding a hint of levity to mask the strain. "There are more than enough enemy warships out there for everyone. Let's get to work."

I leaned back into the Captain's Mount, my fingers finding the familiar armrest controls, selecting the *Shipwide Announcements* touchpad.

"All hands, this is the Captain. As you are aware, we have gone to battle stations." The words came out steady, a calm before the storm. "Empress Shawlee Tee's Royal Guard is out there, tattered and battered, equipped with only barely-spaceworthy craft—they are quickly losing this fight. You should know the names of the allied vessels you'll be fighting for... *Impervious, Dauntless, Vanguard,* and *Stalwart*—each is a testament to the Pleidian's unwavering spirit and loyalty to their allies—us. But they are hanging on by a thread. Let's do them proud." I paused my announcement.

Pristy activated a new logistical halo display, this one

showing Royal Guard warship conditions and stats. There were also crewmember updates—hundreds of names scrolled by, too many with lines crossed through them.

It occurred to me, that this could just as easily represent what might be happening with Alpha Fleet right now within a totally different star system. A pang of guilt needled me for leaving, but I'd made a choice. I was here now—second-guessing myself served no purpose. I only hope this gamble wouldn't come back to haunt me.

I continued with my announcement, "We're not just fighting for the Pleidians," I told my crew. "We're fighting for *us*, for what could come next if we don't stand our ground here."

I cut the connection.

Akari elevated the ship's energy shields to maximum settings—causing the hull to thrum and vibrate around us. Throughout *Washington's* one hundred decks, thousands of compartments, and miles of corridors, the ship stirred to battle-readiness.

Glancing around, I mentally noted Hardy's absence. He typically would be at my side for an impending space battle such as this.

"Mr. Grimes, take us in slow. I want these Wrinnth invaders to see we're entering the fight... to take pause, to reconsider their actions today."

"Aye, Captain," Grimes responded, working the controls at Helm.

I glanced at *Impervious*, her once-pristine hull scarred and battered, yet she remained, fighting the good fight beside her sister ships.

"Mr. Chen, open a channel to the Captains of all four Royal Guard ships."

"Done. You're live, Cap."

My voice didn't waver. "This is Captain Galvin Quintos of

USS *Washington*. Captains, please be aware, we'll be coming in hot. This is as tight, close proximity battlespace as I've seen in a long time. The last thing we need here is to be crossing paths with one another. So, hold tight, and, if possible, bring your vessels to a full stop."

The display blurred as Grimes jumped us in, space stretching around us before snapping back like a rubber band released from tension. Twenty Wrinnth warships loomed around us, their silhouettes jagged against the backdrop of stars.

"XO," I said, catching sight of a hesitant-looking Pristy—perhaps echoes of that parallel life having met with an untimely death coming back to haunt her. "Coordinate with Akari on targeting sequences for every Wrinnth asset. *Washington* can walk and chew gum at the same time."

"On it," Pristy confirmed, snapping out of her momentary reverie.

Energy cannons charged with a low growl while fusion-tipped missiles whined in anticipation. Akari plotted firing solutions with a sniper's precision.

"Rail cannons locking on... targeting that nearest destroyer," she announced.

"Fire when ready," I commanded.

Washington trembled as countless rail cannons unleashed their wrath—innumerable rail spikes dispatched, brilliant flashes tearing through the void with the intent to inflict horrifying levels of devastation upon multiple warships simultaneously. One Wrinnth craft erupted in a blazing ball of fire. The charred wreckage was then spinning, somersaulting, off into the void. Another Wrinnth vessel, spewing atmosphere, limped away, sporting gaping wounds along its portside hull.

"Nice targeting!" Akari shouted, holding up a hand for Pristy to high-five.

But that small victory was fleeting; the Wrinnth suddenly

swarmed us like so many hungry sharks smelling bloody chum in the water. Where *Washington* was attempting to target multiple warships, the enemy was now totally consumed with targeting just one—*USS Washington.*

Crewman Davit's voice boomed from Defensive Systems. "Shields are getting hammered. Hull's glowing like a frickin' furnace!"

"Divert power to—"

Pristy cut me off. "That won't work! We're taking it from all sides. What we need is to get the hell out of this mess!"

"Helm! Jump us to the other side of this conflict," I ordered.

"You do that, and we'll lose our target acquisitions," Akari warned.

"Jump us, Mr. Grimes do it now!" I commanded.

Momentarily blurred and distorted, the primary halo display settled, now showing a new battlespace perspective.

Akari slammed a fist down onto her board. "See... we've lost acquisitions. Enemies rebounding! This is bullshit!"

"You need to shut up and do your job, Lieutenant," Pristy barked. "What the hell's wrong with you?"

Stewing, Akari let out a breath. "Sorry. Guess, I'm not used to sharing a station."

Tempted to weigh in on the back and forth, I forced myself to stay out of it. Pristy was the XO, this was her situation to deal with.

"Our shields are settling down some. Still hot enough to fry an egg on, but manageable," Davit said.

Incoming! Incoming!
Brace! Brace!

I had just enough time to catch a glimpse of the incoming missile's azure tail plume before all hell erupted around us.

I was thrown from the Captain's Mount as a thunderous explosion tore into *Washington*. Several nearby consoles were now fountaining bright amber sparks, while the overhead lights suddenly blinked out, leaving the bridge in darkness.

A moment later, the far dimmer emergency lights came on—providing just enough illumination for me to see several more of the bridgecrew splayed out on the deck.

"Report!" I yelled over the bellowing Klaxon and SARAH's continuous announcements.

"Looks like a fusion torpedo grazed our forward bow," Akari said. There was a trickle of blood making its way from her hairline down her temple.

I spun around to Damage Control, "Crewmember Soto, tell me just how bad that hit was!"

"Uh, bad, Sir." He shook his head as he scanned his board's indicators. "Hull breaches on Deck 33, Deck 34, Deck 35... we're venting atmosphere."

"Ensure all DeckGates have been activated."

"They were all automatically triggered, but I'm checking. Looks like eight have been secured for those affected corridors. And there's one that's too damaged to activate."

"Get SWM on it," I ordered. "And someone check in with HealthBay. I want to know injuries and fatalities ASAP."

"Being swarmed again!" Pristy said, now standing at her board.

SARAH's voice bellowed from above...

Damage Control teams to Deck 33, Deck 34, and Deck 35.

"Got all my target acquisitions back... firing solutions being calculated," Akari said.

I felt the trembling vibration of the rail cannons pulsing up through the deck plates underfoot—then the display flashed with scores of dazzlingly bright bursts tearing through the void —already causing devastating damage to the enemy ships.

At virtually the same moment, *Washington* was once again being targeted herself.

"They are most definitely not giving up..." Akari said.

"Neither are we," I retorted through gritted teeth.

The primary display flashed bright enough that I had to momentarily divert my eyes.

"That was another Royal Guard ship," Pristy reported. "Uh... *Vanguard,*" she added.

I watched as it broke apart in a kind of silent scream. My heart clenched at the sight, but there was no time for sorrow; we still had work to do.

"We've got incoming missiles!" Lira warned from Sensors and Reconnaissance.

"Dammit," I swore under my breath. "Someone check to see if SARAH's properly predicting impending strike zones this time around. We need shield modulations in place before we get blindsided again!"

"SARAH's on it," Pristy said. "Not sure what happened before."

I braced myself for the next salvo. *Washington* was sturdy, but even she had her limits.

"SARAH," I called out to the ship's AI, "I want DeckGates preemptively initiated prior to impact, let's be a little more proactive."

DeckGates now closing on Deck 5, 6, and 7.

Twenty minutes later we were still pushing back hard against the Wrinnth Fleet.

Another enemy ship fell prey to our continuous onslaught; then two more followed suit disappearing into oblivion. *Washington's* cannons roared in defiance against an enemy... an enemy who had clearly underestimated us from the start.

But numbers mattered in war—the Wrinnth ships pressed their numbers advantage despite their losses.

Stalwart took a direct hit and crumbled into space dust before my eyes. Two of their four were down... and that was two too many.

I clenched my jaw tight enough to crack teeth as I watched another clustered missile barrage, catching sight of their aft blue tongues of flame—no less than ten missiles heading toward us like death incarnate.

Incoming! Incoming!
Brace! Brace!

The impact rocked us violently; panels sparked and systems wailed in protest. Maybe we had bitten off more than we could chew—but I'd be damned if we let these alien bastards have the last bite.

Akari hollered from Tactical 1, "Look! Four enemy dreadnoughts and a destroyer... all lined up like ducks on a pond. What are the odds?"

"I'm on it. Bowlers are being loaded via their individual ramp-injectors now," Pristy said, a cruel smile tugging at the corners of her lips.

Used sparingly due to limited ordnance stockpile space, they were the most archaic, hell, primitive weaponry for the select few U.S. Space Navy warships equipped with Broadside cannons. They fire their twelve-hundred-pound bowlers, nicknamed for their visual similarity to massive-looking bowling balls and their strategically placed circular finger-like holes. Prior to impact, those holes are the dispersal element for magnesium scatter frags, which effectively weaken enemy hull armor plating a nanosecond prior to impact and allowing the giant explosive cannonballs to decimate anything—everything—they come into contact with. It was a rarity to find a ship's shields capable of withstanding that kind of impact.

"Bowlers are locked and loaded," Pristy said, looking back at me, waiting for the *go*."

"Do it, XO," I said. "Blow those motherfuckers away."

Boom! Boom! Boom!

Washington's big Broadside cannons thundered without taking a breath for a full five minutes. Undoubtedly, the big guns were already overheating—typically requiring ample time to cool down in between short salvoes.

Boom! Boom! Boom! Boom!

I had to give it to the Wrinnth... they really tried. In vain, they fired up their propulsion drives, put the proverbial pedal to the metal. But in the end, it was too little too late. Seeing the incoming, car-sized, explosive ordnances must have been an awe-inspiring sight. I didn't know much about the physical anatomy of the Wrinnth or what kind of attire they donned but I imagine, there was a lot of shitting of pants going on right before impact.

All five enemy warships blew apart in spectacular, ginormous balls of fire. We had delivered a crippling blow to the enemy ranks. With their formation a mess, scattering. What remained of the Wrinnth Fleet moved about in confused disarray.

My shoulders relaxed a tad as I watched. "Wait for it..."

Twelve seconds later, the ten remaining Wrinnth warships

were turning tail and fleeing the battlespace. Then, one by one, they jumped away without a trace.

I released a breath I didn't know I was holding and glanced around at my crew—faces slack with exhaustion and relief.

Then Shawlee appeared on the primary halo display once more—her eyes glistening with unshed tears as she stared back at me across the void that separated us but somehow felt closer than ever before.

"Galvin," she said softly—a myriad of emotions conveyed in one word—and all I could do was nod in acknowledgment. There was an unspoken bond between us—a bond forged through fire and blood and history.

She smiled faintly, looking at me with watery eyes. "We did it... together... again."

Chapter 40

USS Washington

Hardy

One hour earlier...

Hardy marched purposefully through the twisting corridors of USS *Washington*, the subtle whir of his advanced servomotors resounding softly off the bulkheads. Warning lights bathed the passageway in a pulsing crimson glow as he approached Deck 35. An ominous sucking sound—rapidly escaping atmosphere—was growing louder with each step.

Rounding the corner, Hardy's sensors detected the chaos unfolding. Crewmembers scrambled up ahead, their faces panicked as they fought against the pull of vacuum—he saw they were desperately trying to manually slide the malfunctioning DeckGate closed while the area was rapidly depressurizing—time was running out.

"Aw, hell. This isn't good," Hardy muttered, his Bostonian drawl laced with annoyance. Quickening his pace, he barreled toward the struggling crew, his 7-foot frame providing a sturdy bulwark against the relentless suction.

"Alright, kiddies, step aside and let the ChronoBot in the room handle this!" Hardy bellowed, his voice cutting through the din. He assessed the first problem. "As long as SARAH continues to try to close this thing, we're just fighting ourselves!"

He tapped into the ship's network and communicated with SARAH one-on-one, instructing her to stop trying to close an obviously mechanically jammed mechanism. Even above the roar of the escaping atmosphere, he heard the whine of the DeckGate suddenly stop.

"Okay boys, now let's try it again, giving it the ol' heave ho!"

Four SWM crewmembers got busy doing just that. The DeckGate groaned in protest, its massive panels straining against both the pull of the vacuum as well as whatever bend in the upper or lower slide track was causing the problem. The old adage, *if it doesn't fit, force it,* came to mind. Hardy leaned in and pushed, putting all of his one thousand pounds into it.

The DeckGate jerked several feet in the right direction, a good omen. But with that, the vacuum on the other side, the breached hull side, only increased.

"This isn't working, robot!" one of the maintenance workers yelled in frustration.

Sweat beaded on the crewmembers' brows as they continued to cling to any available handhold. Hardy knew that their lungs were burning due to the thinning atmosphere.

"C'mon, ya hunk of junk! Work with me here!" Hardy growled. The DeckGate shuddered, its progress agonizingly slow. Precious moments slipped away, and the crewmembers' vigor steadily dwindled.

Hardy watched in horror as a burst of sparks exploded from a nearby control panel. One of the SWM crewmembers, caught off guard, let go of the DeckGate and was immediately pulled through the breach. The man's dying cries were swiftly drowned out by the deafening roar of the decompression.

"Dammit," the ChronoBot muttered, his usually sarcastic demeanor altered by the situation's grim reality.

He discarded the manual strategy, redirecting his bio-mechanical processors to seek an alternate solution. The clock was ticking, and he realized it wasn't merely the SWM crew at risk but the entire ship.

The ChronoBot didn't require an atmosphere, the SWM guys certainly did. He internally cringed as he scanned their faces; they were turning blue from oxygen deprivation. Panic was an atypical response for the ChronoBot, but the severity of the circumstances was growing increasingly dire by the second.

"Alright, listen up!" he bellowed. "This has become a one-robot job. But first, I need to get you away from this giant vacuum cleaner nozzle. Everyone grabs onto me and holds on tight. This ain't gonna be pretty, but it's the only way we're getting you to safety!"

The three remaining SWM men, whose movements were getting more sluggish from hypoxia, looked at Hardy with confusion and desperation.

Without hesitation, the ChronoBot reached out with his chrome-plated limbs, enveloping the crewmembers, a quarter-back huddled up with his team. Bracing himself against the relentless pull of the vacuum, Hardy fought through it, cautiously retreating one slow step at a time, until the four of them were far enough from the DeckGate to release their grip and hurry to safety.

Once back at the DeckGate, Hardy commanded SARAH to reactivate the servos. Hopefully, now that the massive Deck-Gate had progressed further along its track, it would be simpler to coerce the structure forward.

Pushing, he growled, "C'mon, ya big bucket of bolts! Move your ass!"

SARAH was now speaking to him via the overhead PA system...

Hardy... the only means to close the DeckGate is to set it back onto its track. For that, you must be on the other side of the DeckGate.

He paused. "Did I just hear you right? You want me on the other side of this thing? The side that is venting out to space? Are you out of your—"

He cut himself off, seeing SARAH's logic. He could stand here all day shoving, but nothing was going to happen unless he could get this choo-choo train back on its track. "Crap!"

Hardy inched closer to the opening, meticulously sidestepping while clinging to the DeckGate's edge, battling the intensifying vacuum. He maneuvered himself around to the other side. As the unrelenting pull tugged at his legs, lifting them, he grasped for better handholds. Securing one for his left hand but not his right, his entire seven-foot frame was abruptly flung horizontally, resembling *long johns* flailing on a clothesline during a hurricane.

With a definitive jerk, he felt the DeckGate suddenly shift. Hardy realized that his considerable bulk, when added to the equation, had proven sufficient to dislodge the DeckGate, coaxing it back onto its designated track—where it was now commencing its sluggish progress toward the far bulkhead.

Dangling precariously, his massive frame thrashed; Hardy clung to the surface with just the tips of three metal-clad fingers.

Suddenly, the unrelenting force had won out. Hardy felt himself being violently dragged backward through the gaping breach in *Washington's* damaged portside hull. Tumbling head over heels in an uncontrolled somersault, he drifted helplessly farther and farther into the vast expanse of space.

Chapter 41

Pleidian Weonan Star System
USS Washington

Captain Galvin Quintos

I stood there on the bridge, my mind still reeling from the battle's ferocity, and Shawlee's transmission was still replaying in my mind.

Then SARAH's voice, always so composed, cut through the air...

> **Captain Quintos, I have an urgent message from beyond the ship.**

Before I could say anything, she continued...

> **It's Hardy... the robot requesting assistance. While**

attempting to repair a misaligned DeckGate, he was ejected into space along with another crewmember.

The SWM crewmember has perished. Hardy, although floating in space, appears to be undamaged.

Pristy winced, "After surviving such a contentious battle, that poor crewmember dies in some freak accident?"

I acknowledged her words with a subtle nod.

But irritation mounted as I realized the ChronoBot's mishap was becoming a pattern. It hadn't been that long since Hardy got ejected from a *USS Lincoln* airlock—there too he'd been blown out into the void of the Liquilid Star System... presumed lost forever.

Letting out a sigh, I said, "SARAH... where's Hardy now?"

"I got a fix on him," Ensign Lira said from Sensors and Reconnaissance.

Chen said, "Coogong is on his way up to the Quansporter compartment."

"See if you can hail Alpha Fleet. Get SitRep on their status, and coordinates where to intersect with them."

"Aye, Captain."

"Mr. Grimes," I said, getting to my feet. "Once we have those coordinates, lock them in, manufacture a wormhole, and get us the hell out of here."

The Helmsman hesitated, "Uh... you're not staying?"

"No, I have other pressing matters to attend to." I felt the others on the bridge looking at me.

"XO, Pristy, how about we take a walk? Undoubtedly, you're aware there's a... um... gap of time you need some help with, yes?"

She looked at me, stunned. Slowly, she too got to her feet. Glancing to Akari, she said, "You've got Tactical."

"Actually, she's got the Captain's Mount, for the time being." I gestured toward the exit. "Let's go."

Side-by-side we crossed the Rotunda without speaking. I slowed as we approached the DeckPort, Pristy moving ahead of me.

"You okay?" Pristy asked, looking back at me with a bemused look. "We're not leaving this deck."

"No... yes. Never mind." I moved forward closing in on the DeckPort, and said, "Deck 18, Violet Sector."

I stepped in holding my breath, then stepped back out—anxiously waiting for Pristy to follow me through. It took three seconds, which seemed like an eternity.

Seeing my expression, she stopped, and said, "Okay, this has to stop. You need to tell me what's going on right now."

I nodded. How do you tell someone that they had recently died—that what was left of their body, their other body, was lying within the chilly confines of the morgue?

We scanned the vicinity, catching sight of only a few passersby. I motioned toward an unoccupied nook just beyond HealthBay's auto-hatch, furnished with a cluster of benches.

"Let's take a seat."

But she didn't move. "Now you're scaring me. What the hell is going on? I mean it. Ever since I got onto the bridge, it's been like an ancient *Twilight Zone* episode."

"I know. Please... let's just have a seat and talk. Can we do that?"

Exasperated, she threw up her hands and headed for the nearest bench.

Taking a seat next to her, I let out a breath and collected my thoughts.

"Oh my God, you do know that I'm about to punch you in the mouth. Right? Spill it!"

"Fine!" I snapped back. "XO... Gail... you died."

"I died."

"It was a few days ago. A DeckPort mishap."

"If I died, I'd say it was more than a mishap."

"Yes... bad word choice."

She shook her head. "But. I didn't die. I'm here. We're sitting here on this uncomfortable bench talking."

I let a few moments tick by.

"No... you *really* did die."

My eyes slid over to the entrance of HealthBay. "There's a body in the morgue." I grimaced. "Your body."

I watched as the dots connected in her mind. "Oh... so, I'm not the original Gail Pristy..."

My shoulders rose dismissively, feigning an air that the XO was blowing the situation way out of proportion.

"Stop trivializing my death."

She stared off into nothingness as the implications of her situation were just now coming into focus. Then she frowned. "Wait. There are rules—no, laws that forbid doing what I think you did."

I pursed my lips.

"You haven't mentioned any of this to the EUNF... U.S. Space Navy Command?"

"They know you're dead. Know your, um, body, is lying—"

"Yeah, I got it. Prefer not to dwell on that fact right now," she said, growing more irritated. "So, how am I here? This doesn't make sense."

"We tried to bring you back right away, but the DeckPorts on

Washington are the new version. Updated, so that once someone walks into one of them, no longer will there be a duplicate, virtual version of the person kept in memory. It was suspected you were still alive, somewhere, within some indeterminate quantum plane... Let me tell you, Derrota, Coogong, Sonya, and even Kaelen Rivers were relentless in figuring out how to get you back. And, they had done just that with the help of the sphere. But, in the end, you still didn't walk out... not until later. Climbo was keeping a 24/7 vigil."

"Well, I'm here now. At least this version of me is here."

We stared at each other for a long time.

"That waiting period was rough. Hope, eventually, had turned to acceptance. Fate had made the decision for us—Gail Pristy was dead, and it was time to accept the inevitable. You have to understand, those who knew you—who had worked side-by-side with you—for so many years... well, it hit them hard. It hit me hard."

She looked away and shifted her weight on the bench, uncomfortable where this was going.

I continued, "I wasn't sleeping. Would spend my nights, for hours on end, just wandering *Washington's* corridors and passageways. I was a total wreck, Gail."

"So, how... ?"

"That last night during my nighttime wanderings, I saw someone. A woman."

"A crewmember?"

I shook my head. "No. It was Era."

She made a face. "Lady Era? From the sphere?"

"That's right."

"How is that even possible? How would a long-deceased person—a *virtual character*—from within that hold—"

"It was her, Gail. And she made it quite clear she wanted me to follow her. To be honest, I thought, being exhausted and sleep-deprived, I might be hallucinating. She was acting, what's the word... flirty?"

"She was flirting with you?"

"She was smiling, having fun. Like when you're kids and you're playing chase during recess? So, I chased her. Didn't have much else to do at three in the morning."

"Where did you chase her to?" she asked, her interest piqued.

I stared back at her, offering no response.

"She brought you to the DeckPort. The same DeckPort I... died in."

I nodded. "That's when I was called back to the bridge."

Pristy was now biting her bottom lip, deep in thought. "Lady Era must have shown me the way out. I don't remember that happening, but I know that's what happened. She saved me."

I slowly nodded. This was news to me... but it made sense.

Her eyes were on me; her lips twitched.

"But there's more to the story, isn't there?" Pristy asked.

Now would have been the perfect time for my TAC-Band to start vibrating, for SARAH to announce *Battle Stations*, or for Hardy to show up and make an inappropriate comment. But none of that happened.

She waited.

"Gail... after the accident, the other you... didn't die right away. What was left of you, lying on the deck outside the Deck-Port... we had time to talk. We told each other things that had gone unsaid for too long."

Her posture stiffened. Color rose in her cheeks. She averted her eyes, balling her hands into fists. She didn't want to hear what I was saying.

The Gail Pristy sitting next to me was a different Gail Pristy than the one to whom I had professed my love to while she was literally on death's doorstep. Her desire to shut out my words was palpable, yet the truth demanded voice. I parted my lips—

"There you are!" came a familiar, annoying voice. "There I was drifting along in space with all that wreckage and debris, when I had a thought..."

Hardy loomed over us first looking at me, then to Pristy.

"I've just interrupted a private conversation, haven't I?"

With a pained smile, Pristy looked up at the ChronoBot. "It's fine, Hardy. We were finished talking, anyway."

She rose from the bench without looking at me. "I have something I have to do."

"Where are you going?" I asked as she turned her back on me.

"I need to see..."

Oh no. "XO! Gail, that may not be such a good idea." My mind flashed back to the grisly scene—Pristy's body cleaved in half like a scene from a horror movie.

"Still. Something I have to do." She raised her voice as she started to walk away, "Alone!"

I glanced over to Hardy. "You do know you're an idiot, right?"

Chapter 42

XO Gail Pristy

She found HealthBay enveloped in hushed tranquility, its patients slumbering peacefully in the ward. Gail Pristy, however, found herself wide awake, her heart thrumming with a tumultuous blend of emotions as she grappled with the weight of her decision. Inner conflicts swirled within her, casting doubt upon the path she was about to embark on.

As she strode farther into the dimly lit compartment, a middle-aged, clean-cut medical attendant approached her, his brow furrowed.

"Hello..." His jaw went slack. All color left his face. "Um, I'm Vincent."

She was relieved he didn't extend a hand to shake.

His gaze darted toward the nearby auto-hatch leading to the

back of HealthBay, his confusion evident as he struggled to comprehend how the XO stood before him, alive and well.

Pristy, no stranger to the intricacies of a U.S. Space Navy ship of this size, had never ventured into its morgue. Leaving no room for negotiation and with steadfast determination, she said, "Thank you, Vincent. Now I need you to take me to the morgue."

The attendant just stared at her, fidgeting with something in the pocket of his lab coat. He clearly didn't want to fulfill the XO's command.

Ultimately, Pristy's influence prevailed. As an Executive Officer, second only to Captain Galvin Quintos himself, she reminded Vincent that her request was not a request but an order—to be followed without question.

Pristy trailed behind the attendant, her footsteps echoing through the metal corridor as he led her onto a winding passageway. Rounding a corner to the right, then veering sharply left, they approached another set of auto-hatches. A stark, nononsense sign hung overhead, its minimalist lettering set against the gleaming bulkheads: **SHIP'S MORGUE.**

They entered the chilly, sterile confines. Pristy's eyes scanned the compartment, half-expecting to see cadavers, cut open mid-autopsy, splayed out on the metal tables. Instead, she found the space clean, quiet, and softly lit, devoid of the gruesome work that sometimes took place within its walls. Gail Pristy's gaze swept across the compartment, where several imposing, autonomous MediBots lay dormant within their charging cradles; they appeared to be observing the scene with an unsettling, dispassionate vigilance.

Her gaze was drawn to the bulkhead where three rows, four locker doors each, dominated the wall.

Vincent, sensing her unease, made one last attempt to dissuade her.

"Please, XO... it might be best for you to return at a more appropriate time, perhaps accompanied by Captain Quintos himself?"

Ignoring his pleas, Pristy fixed her eyes upon the lockers.

Her voice firm, she said, "Which one holds the remains of..." She looked to Vincent, irritated. Did she really need to spell it out for the man?

The attendant reluctantly pointed to the bottom row. "Third locker from the left."

His fidgety mannerisms only served to heighten her irritation. With a curt dismissal, she ordered, "Get out. Leave, now."

Now alone in the morgue, Pristy's mind raced, her thoughts consumed by the unfinished conversation with Galvin on that bench. Why had she looked away from him, unwilling to hear the words she had longed for over the past decade? What had changed within her, causing her to rebuff the very affirmation she had craved? Was it because his words had not been meant for her, but for the one who now lay still before her?

Raising her palms, she yelled a firm, "Enough!" as if to banish the doubts that threatened to overwhelm her. With a deep breath, she released the metal latch and opened the locker door, revealing a sheet-covered form within. She pulled the drawer outward until it locked into place.

Swallowing hard, Pristy steeled herself against the dread that threatened to undermine her resolve. Remembering Galvin's words, she understood that the body before her had been grievously injured, cut in two by the *mishap* within the DeckPort.

Closing her eyes, she willed her mind to clarity before opening them once more. With trembling hands, she folded down the sheet, exposing the upper body of the figure before her. She had no desire to bear witness to the grisly injuries that had claimed this, *her,* life.

As she gazed upon the still form, Pristy found herself transfixed by the sight of her own likeness, eyes closed as if in peaceful slumber. A fleeting thought crossed her mind: *Is that what I look like when I sleep?*

Reaching out, her hand hovered in hesitation before finally making contact with the corpse's cold, lifeless chest, a stark reminder that never again would a beating heart reside within. At that moment, Pristy felt a profound sense of gratitude and reverence for the sacrifice that had been made.

Her eyes began to well, a lump forming in her throat. "Thank you for bringing us this far, Gail," she whispered, her voice thick with emotion. "Your sacrifice won't be forgotten, not ever. Going forward, you can rest assured that I've got this."

She knew Vincent was nearby and could hear him pacing about in the passageway. "Attendant, get in here and close up this locker." She spun on her heel and hurried out.

Chapter 43

Wormhole Transit — Deep Space
USS Washington, **Marines' Barracks**

Petty Officer Second-Class Aubrey Laramie

Aubrey's right fist pounded into Grip's upper arm, the meaty *thwack* fueling her relentless onslaught. Guttural snarls erupted from her throat with each hammering punch, the sounds reverberating through the Marines' barracks. Rivulets of sweat streamed down her flushed face, soaking her tank top. Across from her, Grip and Wanda traded wary looks, circling the seething Petty Officer with guarded stances.

"Easy there, Laramie," Grip's deep baritone rumbled, his hands raised in a placating gesture. "Maybe we should call it a night."

Aubrey's eyes shot daggers, her chest heaving with each

ragged breath. "Don't you dare," she snarled, shifting her weight to her back foot. "I'm not done."

Wanda's features sharpened, eyes locked on Aubrey. "You're losing it, Laramie. Rein it in."

With a menacing cry, Aubrey launched herself forward, her lithe form a blur of motion. Grip barely had time to react as she executed a series of lightning-fast kicks, her foot connecting with his forearm with a resounding thud. Undeterred, she spun low, sweeping her leg in a vicious arc aimed at Wanda's ankles.

Wanda leaped back, her face twisting into a scowl. "Enough of this bullshit," she growled.

Grip recovered his stance. He offered Aubrey a critical glare, then looked to Wanda with concern. "She's not listening, Wan. We gotta take her down before she hurts herself."

Aubrey seethed with a mix of rage and shame. The memory of her actions under the influence of Chaplain Halman Trent and that cursed fucking amulet replayed in her mind, each vivid detail stoking the flames of her fury. She could still see the looks of disgust, the whispers behind her back as she strutted through the corridors, her sense of self stripped away. *That wasn't me...*

And Captain Quintos... the mere thought of his disapproving gaze sent a fresh wave of shame crashing over her. She had admired him, respected him above all others, and now... now he knew the truth. He had seen her at her most deplorable, her most wanton.

Aubrey let out a primal scream and lunged at Wanda, her hands a flurry of strikes. Wanda parried the blows with practiced ease, her movements fluid and precise. Grip moved to flank her, his hulking frame poised to intervene.

Aubrey's mind was a whirlwind of rage and self-loathing, each memory of her actions under the amulet's influence like a dagger to her soul. She had been raised a devout Catholic, her moral compass forged in the fires of her strict upbringing. And now... now she was nothing more than a harlot in the eyes of her crew, her friends, her Captain.

The thought of Chaplain Trent's smug grin, his soulless eyes as he watched her descend into depravity, ignited a fresh wave of fury within her. She could still feel his clammy hands on her skin, his hot breath against her neck as he whispered his poisonous lies.

With a guttural roar and a fierce determination in her eyes, Aubrey delivered a relentless assault, each strike a calculated expression of her intent to inflict pain and exact vengeance.

As the two Marines parried her strikes, her kicks—Aubrey remained undeterred, relentless, her mind consumed by the need to purge herself of the shame and anger that threatened to consume her. She refused to be a victim, refused to let that soulless bastard win.

As the brutal sparring session continued, the bulkheads echoed with the sound of flesh striking flesh, punctuated by grunts and snarls of exertion. A single thought gnawed at her, motivated her, ever since she broke free of the cult's influence: she would make Chaplain Halman Trent pay for what he had done to her, no matter the cost.

Vengeance consumed Aubrey. This was the reckoning, the moment she'd unleash retribution. With a feral growl, she launched into a devastating sequence, her body moving with lethal precision. Her hand sliced through the air, fingers rigid, thumb tucked against her palm—a knife-hand strike aimed directly at Wanda's throat. The Tsuki Komi, a Krav Maga technique designed to crush the trachea, a move that should never be used in sparring, reserved only for the direst of circumstances.

Time seemed to slow as Wanda's eyes widened, her body reacting a fraction too late. She managed to partially deflect the strike, but the force of the blow still connected, slamming into her throat with brutal impact.

Wanda crumpled to her knees, both hands clutching at her neck as she gasped for air, her eyes bulging in shock and pain.

Grip roared in fury, his massive frame surging forward with terrifying speed. Before Aubrey could react, his meaty fist slammed into her shoulder with a sickening crunch, the sheer force of the blow wrenching her arm from its socket.

Searing pain exploded through Aubrey's body as she crumpled onto the mat, her vision blurred, a wave of nausea churning in her stomach. Through the haze of pain, she could see Wanda, still on her knees, her face contorted in a grimace of anguish.

"SARAH!" Grip's voice was loud, borderline desperate. "Contact HealthBay... Chief Knott... now!"

Aubrey's world spun, darkness encroaching on the edges of her vision. She fought against the rising tide of unconsciousness, her mind a whirlpool of regret and self-loathing. *Oh God...what have I done?* The barracks spun uncontrollably, then faded to black.

Chapter 44

Exiting Wormhole—Grish Territory
USS Washington, **Bridge**

Captain Galvin Quintos

I n the midst of a shift change, Pristy entered the bridge, her expression stoic, her eyes fixed ahead. She took her seat at Tactical without so much as a glance in my direction.

An awkward silence hung in the air, thick enough to cut with a knife. I opened my mouth to speak but quickly shut it, sensing the lingering tension.

Pristy leaned over to Akari at the adjacent station. "You're cleared to return to flight bay and rejoin your team, Lieutenant."

Akari hesitated, glancing between us, before nodding curtly. "Roger that, XO." She rose from her seat and headed for the exit, shooting me a perplexed glance as she passed.

I'd brought *Washington* to battle stations even before emerging from the wormhole. Our ETA was 75 light minutes, approximately 1.35 billion kilometers to the Grish Star System. This far out, there was little likelihood of an unexpected confrontation with hostile forces.

Chen had no sooner taken his seat at Comms when he relayed an incoming high-priority message from EUNF.

"I'll take it in my ready room," I said.

ADMIRAL GOMEZ FLICKERED WITHIN THE HALO display, his eyes were cold, lips pulled down at the corners—he seemed harassed, frazzled like he'd endured a stern dressing-down from on high. And that could only mean one person—President Cyprian Block himself.

"The situation has changed dramatically, Captain," Gomez began, his expression grim. "It seems EUNF comms transmissions have been compromised. The piglets... they're aware of Alpha Fleet's position—the Grish know exactly where they're holed up."

I felt my blood run cold at his words. "So, you're telling me our element of surprise has just been flushed down the toilet?" A knot formed in the pit of my stomach.

Gomez nodded solemnly. "Worse. The Grish Pinnacle Fleet has already begun mustering their forces. They'll be ready to strike within two days, maybe one."

My mind raced, calculating the potential ramifications of such a disastrous turn of events. We had planned to reunite with Alpha Fleet and *Franklin*, take care of Pinnacle Fleet, and then attack the Drakoria Star System together. But now the timeline was off. Alpha Fleet and *Franklin* would be on their own—their odds of survival just plummeted.

"And this ship... *Washington*? Do they know our current position?" I asked, trying to keep my voice steady.

"No. Of course not. Hell, as of two minutes ago, even I had no idea where you were." The Admiral almost smiled. "*Washington* is our ace in the hole, Captain."

I stared back at him quizzically.

Gomez continued, "You are to proceed directly into Grish space. Defeat their defensive capabilities, then bring your attack directly to the Grish homeworld of Drakoria. It's time for a little payback."

"Admiral..."

"I don't want to hear it, Captain. The President is adamant about this. Earth has taken it in the shorts multiple times now, and it's well past time the Grish come to understand the concept of cosmic karma."

I felt my jaw go slack at the prospect of *Washington* being deployed headlong into the heart of Grish territory, alone—all the while, Alpha Fleet and *Franklin* would be facing off with the full might of the Pinnacle Fleet.

"Sir, with all due respect," I managed, struggling to keep my composure, "Even if *Franklin* can reach the fleet's position in time, they'll be outnumbered by what? Two hundred ships to Alpha's less than fifty? Not to mention *Franklin* is less than battle-ready."

Gomez held up a hand, his features like stone. "I'm well aware of the tactical disadvantages, Captain."

"Sir... if you send in *Washington* to attack the Grish system on our own, you know as well as I do, we're not surviving that operation."

The Admiral's face remained hardened. "The new plan represents our best chance to strike a decisive blow into the heart of the Grish Empire, and do so while Pinnacle Fleet is preoccupied. The decision's already been made, Captain."

"Tell that to the crews of Alpha Fleet, Admiral," I snapped back.

It was evident by Gomez's expression he had just about as much lip as he was going to take from me.

"What I know is that I am your Commanding Officer. And as such, I expect you to carry out my command."

My gaze locked with his. "Sir, this new strategy... it's a guaranteed death sentence for *Washington* and her crew."

The Admiral's stare was resolute. "Undoubtedly, the Grish have already deployed Pinnacle Fleet to engage with Alpha Fleet. As far as the eggheads at EUNF can game-out, the piglet's strategic next move... the Grish will want to deal with a perceived, totally incapacitated, Alpha Fleet. They'll roll the dice, move to finish off the Alliance once and for all."

"Perceived?" I scoffed. "Alpha *has* been decimated!"

Ignoring my outburst, he said, "In any event, USS *Washington* will have an opportunity that may never come along again. A vulnerable Grish homeworld. Once you arrive in the star system, you'll concentrate on their defensive fortifications there in Drakoria space. And you'll be doing it without 200 Grish warships breathing down your neck. This is a narrow window of opportunity... one we cannot afford to squander."

I held my tongue, while my mind raced. So, while Alpha Fleet becomes sacrificial lambs to the slaughter, USS *Washington* embarks on a suicide mission of its own.

"War is hell and it's no place for the timid, Captain. You'll follow my orders and find a way to bring home the W. Have I made myself clear?"

"Crystal."

"One more thing, Captain. While this communique has been encrypted, any further deep space comms on the part of USS *Washington* must be curtailed. No one outside the hull of that ship, and I mean *no one*, can know your true whereabouts."

As I debriefed the bridgecrew, they were less than thrilled with the change of plan where the team of Alpha Fleet and *Franklin*, along with *Washington*, would be going it alone on their separate missions.

Chief Porter was, no doubt, onboard *USS Franklin* by now —perhaps already underway, having no clue that he was now taking part in a plan that was destined to fail from the get-go.

I'd watched as Pristy's posture stiffened, her expression going rigid. She was clearly incensed. She shared a close friendship with Porter, just as I did.

But I was a mere Captain, not an Admiral; it was my job to follow orders—no matter how distasteful. Still, I couldn't help but think... not only had Chief Porter's fate been sealed, but so had Alpha Fleet's and *Washington's*. A trifecta of a shitstorm.

I instructed Helm to maintain a steady course toward Drakoria. We would be running at sub-light speeds while cloaked. It was imperative we do nothing to bring undue attention to ourselves.

Twenty-five minutes later, my TAC-Band vibrated. It was Kaelen Rivers from Engineering and Propulsion.

"Go ahead, Mr. Rivers," I said, giving the man a bare modicum of my attention.

"You need to shut down ship-wide cloaking."

"I beg your pardon, Mr. Rivers. Have you been elevated to the lofty rank of Admiral? Because if you haven't, I don't take orders from you."

"Apologies. Look, we've got a starboard drive with readings quickly moving into the red. Suspect the Plasma Regulator

Module took some shrapnel from the last battle. Cloaking demands a crapload of resources from the propulsion system."

"And why is it you're telling me this? I believe Chief, uh..." I had to search my memory. "... Chief Hasselbaund is your Superior?"

"Come on, Hasselbaund's a tool. Said he didn't want to bother you with something so trivial. But he's both ignorant and wrong, a deadly combination for the Engineering Chief of a battle-damaged warship, an omninought, no less."

Tempted to tell Rivers it was a serious matter, bad-mouthing one's Superior, not to mention skirting that same Superior's direct orders... I didn't really know Chief Hasselbaund, but I had a gut feeling Rivers could be right... on all accounts.

I let out a breath, spun around and looked to the Engineering Station.

Lieutenant Commander Jorkins nodded. "I can corroborate that. Starboard drive's been acting a little wonky, Sir. Still within operating parameters, but... off."

Crewmember Davit shook his head. "Defensive Systems readings are all level. I'm monitoring the Stealth Shield Generator, no interruptions, nothing wonky."

River's voice blared from my TAC-Band, "You're not going to see a problem with the Stealth Shield Generator, Davit. It's an engineering issue, and the problem will be when that Stealth Shield Generator ceases to get power! Hey, if you don't mind *Washington's* big fat ass becoming suddenly visible at an inopportune time, like when we're going into battle, then go ahead... ignore me."

Pristy glanced partially over her shoulder but avoided making eye contact. "What do you want me to do?"

I stewed on it for several moments. "Shut it down, XO."

"Roger that," she responded flatly. "We're now visible."

Lira at Sensors and Reconnaissance perked up. "Three ships—"

"I got this, Ensign," Pristy cut in. "Three non-military freighters just popped into sensor range."

"Who are they?" I asked, getting to my feet.

Lira was ready with an answer this time before Pristy could chime in. "Grish signatures... their propulsion wakes are unmistakable on all three, Captain."

"Do they know we're here?"

"I don't think so," the Ensign said tentatively.

Pristy tapped at her board, "Sensor arrays on old freighters like that... probably haven't detected us, but it's just a matter of time—"

"Tactical! Destroy those ships! Stealth missiles. Do it—now!" I barked vehemently, making it clear, this was no time to ask questions.

Pristy didn't hesitate, silently following my orders. "Three stealth nukes are away, sir." But her right hand was still poised over her board. "Those are not military vessels. They're commerce ships. Hundreds of civilian lives onboard... belay that order and I can self-detonate those missiles right now."

I shook my head. "All it would take is one piglet comms transmission back to the Drakoria system. What then? Are you willing to put the lives of every crewmember onboard *Washington* on the line, just to ease your conscience?"

We held each other's gaze for several moments, then simultaneously looked to the primary halo display.

Off in the distance, three explosions erupted one after the other.

"Ensign Lira," I said. "Check and check again to make sure that there is nothing left of those three freighters."

"Those ships were unshielded. I assure you, all that's left out there is space debris, Captain."

318

"Helm, maintain course. XO, you have the Captain's Mount."

"Aye, Captain," she said coldly.

Heading for the exit, I bellowed, "And let me know if we run into any other vessels."

"Uh-huh, copy that," I heard her murmur under her breath.

Chapter 45

Grish Territory
USS Washington, **HealthBay**

Petty Officer Second-Class Aubrey Laramie

Aubrey stirred awake in HealthBay, initially disoriented... but then, the recent events within the Marines' barracks started to slowly come back to her. It was late, and the lights had been dimmed. Quiet as a tomb. Her shoulder was killing her as she scanned the ward for a nurse or maybe MedTech or even a MediBot. She needed to get something for the pain.

That's when she saw Wanda, asleep, neck bandaged, three beds over from her own. She inwardly groaned. *How will I ever face her again? Maybe I'll be asking for cyanide capsules instead of aspirin.*

She heard low murmurs over at the nurse's station. A couple of nurses were in deep conversation. Hearing the name, Trent, she was instantly on alert. She cocked her head and tried to listen in on the conversation.

"I hear he's pretty much staying squirreled away in his little Chapel," one of the nurses said.

"I guess it pays to know people in high places," the other one said. "I mean, how many people came through here, some seriously injured, all on account of that asshat."

Aubrey seethed inside, remembering what he'd done—what *she'd* done under his influence. The thought of that man still free to prey upon others...

Two figures suddenly rushed into the ward. It was hard for Aubrey to make out who they were at first, but then she saw that it was Sonya Winters and her Pleidian boyfriend, Ensign Plorinne. His hand was wrapped in a blood-soaked towel. Looked like a nasty injury. While Plorinne was ushered off behind the auto-hatch doors, Sonya turned to leave.

"Sonya!" Aubrey yelled in her direction.

Looking around, then seeing Aubrey, Sonya approached, looking a tad apprehensive.

"Aubrey?" Sonya came closer, took in the sling immobilizing the Petty Officer's arm. "I heard you were in here."

Aubrey winced, how many others had heard of her crazed actions, she inwardly thought. "What's wrong with Plorrine?"

Sonya smiled at that. "Oh, it's nothing, he got, um... injured up on the Symbio Deck."

Before Aubrey could respond, Sonya made herself at home and took a seat on the edge of her bed.

"I guess you're having a hard time with the whole Trent BS," Sonya said matter-of-factly.

Aubrey shrugged, not wanting to get into it with the teenager—a topic that all too easily brought up feelings of rage all over again. "If your uncle had done his job and thrown that dirtbag in jail a long time ago, I wouldn't be lying here, nor would Wanda. And then he lets that deranged pervert out of his cell... what the—"

"Is that what you think?" Sonya scoffed, cutting her off.

Aubrey didn't back down. "Yeah, that's what I think." The Petty Officer's voice dripped with venom. "That scumbag deserved to rot behind bars for life. Your uncle botched it, and now we're paying the price."

"That's bullshit and you know it. My uncle's hands were tied by EUNF bureaucrats. Truth is, you don't know what you're talking about. It wasn't my uncle that chopped Wanda in the neck, it was you."

Someone across the ward shooshed them.

With a bitter laugh, Aubrey shot back, "Right, orders. Because that's what matters when someone tries to kill you. Look, Sonya, I respect the chain of command as much as the next person, but there comes a time when you have to do what's right, not what you're told."

"It's easy to judge when you're not the one making the tough calls," Sonya retorted, now nervously flexing her fingers. "I don't think you have any idea how a ship's captain has to weigh his orders against the consequences. Anyway, like I said, you don't know what you're talking about."

"That again. Whatever you're alluding to, you should just spit it out. But at least I'd have a conscience, Sonya. It's not just about orders; it's about protecting your crew."

"Really? That's what you're going with? So, you're all about protecting your fellow crewmembers, huh?" Sonya's eyes shifted to the incapacitated Wanda several beds over.

Aubrey's foot twitched, resisting the impulse to give the insolent teenager a firm kick off the mattress.

The teen's expression became even more resolute, Aubrey had to admit, the way she defended her uncle was somewhat admirable.

Sonya continued, "It's not as black and white as you make it out to be, Aubrey. Trent may be out there right now, but the Captain's doing everything he can to bring him back."

"Yeah, right," Aubrey said with a roll of her eyes. But then her face softened. *What the hell is wrong with me? Taking it out on this kid?*

Getting to her feet, Sonya looked around the ward. She lowered her voice, "Can you get out of here?"

Taken aback, Aubrey said, "What? You mean... like right now?"

"You'd be back here in thirty minutes, tops. I promise."

Aubrey didn't answer.

Sonya made an overly sympathetic pouty-face, and used a baby-talk voice, "Ahh, does the Petty Officer need more time to rest from her little booboo?"

With that, Aubrey was throwing off her covers and sliding out of bed. She was a little wobbly on her legs and her recently dislocated shoulder was screaming *bloody murder,* but she pushed through it, swallowed hard, and straightened up.

Sonya made a face and glanced down at Aubrey's loose-fitting gown. "You may want to re-tie that gown... your naked ass is hanging out the back."

FIVE MINUTES LATER, HAVING SNUCK OUT OF HealthBay, hurrying through several passageways and multiple DeckPorts, Aubrey continued to follow Sonya. Finally, she found herself entering the ship's Symbio Deck. Expecting it to be as quiet as the rest of the ship, she was surprised to hear all kinds of strange noises. Weird. They sounded... animalistic.

"What's going on in here?" she asked, trying to keep up with the youthful, nimble Sonya who was several strides in front of her.

"We've had some time on our hands, so we've been making some mods... several of the Symbio creatures have exhibited mobility issues in the past. We're just getting some of the kinks out of the fabrication process."

Darkened lighting cast shadows across the *backstage* area of the Symbio Deck, revealing row upon row of partially assembled creatures. A half-formed Triceratops hulked in one corner, while the unmistakable shape of a baby dragon loomed nearby, both unmoving sentinels in the stillness. Aubrey suppressed a shudder as she surveyed the eerie bio-mechanical breeding grounds, an unsettling factory floor of artificial life.

A blur of movement flashed across Aubrey's vision, no more than twenty feet away. "Fuck! Did you see that?" the Petty Officer shouted, her voice echoing off the bulkheads.

Sonya smirked. "Don't be so dramatic. That's Cleo."

"What's a Cleo?"

They had reached the entrance to a closed auto-hatch. Sonya turned and looked past Aubrey, her eyes searching. "Uh... It's a Deinonychus."

"I don't know what that is," Aubrey said, not liking the sound of it.

"Well, they're a larger raptor species, at least compared to Velociraptor. They have distinctive sickle-shaped claws on their hind feet. They lived during the Early Cretaceous period."

A chill ran down Aubrey's spine. "And there's one of those—"

"Deinonychus," Sonya volunteered.

"Yeah, that, is running around loose in here?"

Sonya looked unconcerned as she entered a code onto an old-fashioned keypad device. The auto-hatch slid open. Sonya stepped aside, "Come on in."

Aubrey hesitated, taking one last glance around the Symbio Deck. "Your boyfriend. His injured hand..."

Sonya shrugged off the question, "Yeah, Cleo can be a tad... cantankerous at times. Come on in, no dinosaurs are lurking around inside my vault."

Aubrey stepped into the sanctum, a subtle amber glow filling the space. It was dominated by blinking halo displays, humming technology, and an azure glow emanating from the myriad of consoles and incomprehensible gadgetry that surrounded an obsidian workstation. As the holographic projections flickered with esoteric codes and symbols, the electric atmosphere permeated the chamber as if its very molecules thrummed with potent computational power waiting to be unleashed by the teenage hacker's deft hands.

Sonya splayed a hand to the open ergonomic chair. "Sit."

Aubrey did as told, wincing from an abrupt sharp pain in her shoulder.

Leaning in over her workstation, Sonya tapped one-handed, bringing up what looked to be some kind of high-up perspective security feed.

"What am I looking at?" the Petty Officer asked, ready for the girl to just get to... whatever she was up to.

Sonya queued up the security feed, and Aubrey leaned in, her eyes widening as the scene unfolded.

"This is from the ship's brig. You tell anyone that I have this feed, and I'll unleash Cleo into your quarters while you're asleep."

"Whatever," Aubrey said, attempting to sound unconcerned.

She now watched as the scene came alive within the narrow passageway. Both Quintos and the Chaplain were there. *Shit,* she could almost feel the tension between the two. Riveted, she watched the Captain suddenly close the distance between them, then slapped the Chaplain hard across the face before seizing him by the collar.

"Holy crap!"

"Keep watching," Sonya prompted.

Captain Quintos was now dragging the struggling Chaplain down the corridor while landing several punishing blows to the back of Trent's head.

Aubrey and Sonya exchanged a quick glance.

She watched as the two reached what she could now see was an entrance to an airlock chamber. Aubrey's breath caught in her throat. Quintos hurled Trent into the open airlock like a rag doll, then slammed the hatch door shut—trapping the man inside. She could imagine the alarm's shrill whine piercing the air, swoosh sounds as the chamber began depressurizing.

Aubrey felt her jaw drop open.

Trent pounded on the hatch door's transparent view panel, his eyes bulging with terror as he gasped rapidly thinning air.

Quintos' hand hovered over the button that would, without a doubt, eject Trent out into the vacuum of space.

Wide-eyed, Aubrey unconsciously placed a hand over her mouth. She could see Trent's lips forming frantic pleas as his movements were becoming more and more sluggish.

"Oh my God, he's going to kill him," she said with a gasp.

Only then, when the Chaplain was on the verge of losing consciousness, did Quintos reengage the airlock's re-pressurization sequence. Trent collapsed hard onto the deck, gulping down precious oxygen.

"So... Aubrey. As you can see, my uncle didn't just let him off with a slap on the hand," Sonya said with an *I told you so* expression. "He did his best to make the perv pay."

Chapter 46

Alpha Fleet Rendezvous Point
USS Franklin

Chief Craig Porter

T he bridge of *USS Franklin* hummed with tension as the halo displays blinked to life, revealing the stern faces of Alpha Fleet's surviving Captains. Craig Porter suppressed a sigh, bracing himself for the inevitable onslaught of hostility. He could already sense the disdain radiating from the holographic projections, a tangible force that seemed to permeate the very air they breathed.

Ensign Roisin Blunderton stood at his side, a petite statue, her emerald eyes narrowed in defiance. Porter had come to appreciate the young officer's fiery spirit, even if it did occasionally border on insubordination.

Aware that communications traffic might have been compromised by the Grish, he announced, "This is Captain Craig Porter of *USS Washington...*"

He had instructed SARAH to send an encrypted sub-level message out to the fleet in parallel—informing the fleet officers that he was, in fact, Chief of Engineering, Craig Porter, and the omninought that was fast-approaching their fleet was not *USS Washington,* but *USS Franklin.* He was sure they'd been briefed on the switch and would be going along with the open channel ruse.

"Requesting formation approach vectors," Porter continued, his voice confident and... well... sounding 'captainy'.

It took a few moments before a series of scoffs and derisive snorts greeted his words, prompting Blunderton to stiffen even further.

A grizzled officer filled the display... wavy, gray locks atop a craggy-featured face.

He looked familiar but Porter couldn't place him. Squinting, he could just make out **Captain Longmont** engraved on his gold-plated name tag. Seriously, *who wears a name tag?*

Contempt cut deep lines across Longmont's face as he leaned in, lips curled in a sneer. "Your identity, *USS Franklin,* and purpose are no mystery." Longmont's voice took on a deeper condescension, "Just ensure you don't plow into any of our ships... and we'll be grateful." He allowed a dry chuckle to punctuate his words.

So much for keeping *USS Franklin's* undercover mission hidden, Porter thought.

The conversation took an acrimonious turn as a halo display projected a far younger-looking Captain.

"An Engineer masquerading as a Captain?" the youthful officer interjected. "That bodes well for your piloting prowess," he sneered, his voice dripping with sarcasm.

Blunderton bristled beside him. Under her breath, she murmured, "I know that asshat. Captain Griffin. Pretty boy who thinks he's God's gift to all humanity."

Porter raised a palm, silently cautioning her to hold her tongue. He had no intention of allowing this briefing to devolve into a petty squabble.

"And since our esteemed Fleet Commander Quintos is not able to grace us with his presence... I suppose we're stuck with what we get, that right, *Chief?*" Griffin spat.

The challenge hung in the air, thick and oppressive, but Porter refused to take the bait. He was a seasoned veteran, not some fresh-faced cadet eager to prove his mettle. There again, the Grish could be eavesdropping on every word, systematically dismantling whatever half-baked scheme had been cobbled together.

By now all of the halo displays were populated, not a friendly face among them. "With all due respect, Captain Griffin," Porter began, keeping his tone level, diplomatic. "I have zero interest in jumping into the middle of a pissing contest. This omninought was deployed here to support Alpha Fleet, correct? And as you say, we've got a fleet of Grish warships bearing down on our position. Maybe it's best if we don't squander this time with infighting?"

Voices rose, overlapping into a litany of dissent as the Alpha Fleet Captains volleyed for control, accusations flying like shrapnel.

Another Captain appeared large on one of the halo displays. Either he was sitting closer to the optics or he had an abnormally large head. He was squabbling with one of the other Captains, about something... halo displays talking—sniping—to halo displays.

SARAH had taken it upon herself to put the Captains' names and titles on their respective displays. A Captain Felix

Pettigrew, whom Porter had crossed paths with previously, seemed to have just joined the party. He had a pinched face with a ruddy complexion ravaged with acne scars. He appeared to be arguing with the big-headed Captain.

Pettigrew's gravelly voice lashed out, spraying the air with spittle. "Question my tactical judgment? I've led more campaigns than you've glimpsed stars in the void, you impudent fool!"

Another Captain, a female, uttered a lethal flurry of insults, taking the attention off of Pettigrew.

"The Cat Lady," Blunderton whispered.

Captain Liu's large green eyes flickered against the jet-black bob that framed her face. She jabbed a long, slender finger at the display. "Stow it, Pettigrew. This is not your operation. How about you take that tin can of a shipwreck of yours and shove it up your ass."

Porter had to chuckle at that one.

The bickering continued. Porter shook his head in disbelief. They were like a pack of rabid dogs fighting over a bone, oblivious to the hungry pack of wolves lurking just outside the door.

Blunderton stepped forward, her eyes blazing with conviction. "Captain Porter is right!" she yelled loud enough to override the others. "And yes, I said *Captain* Porter. He is the one seated within the Captain's Mount. And, if I am not mistaken, this omninought has been designated Alpha Fleet's flagship, yes? So how about you stop wasting precious moments on these petty power struggles?"

Porter's breath hitched. A lowly Ensign had just rebuked a gaggle of egocentric Captains. He attempted to keep his expression neutral.

But as the cross-talk subsided, stern, reddening faces, looked to Blunderton.

Porter steeled himself, bracing for the impending storm. He gazed up at Roisin, ready to reprimand the Junior Officer, but hesitated. There was nothing about her uniform, no markings, no stripes, no name tag, nor rank designation, that gave away her status within the U.S. Space Navy hierarchy. What she did have, was Porter's Macaw still perched upon her shoulder. And as ridiculous as that should appear to, well, anyone, it was also a bold statement in and of itself.

Glancing between the myriad of halo projections, Porter wasn't seeing the outrage or indignation of just a few moments ago... now, he was seeing a sea of faces awash with cowed indecision. He had to fight the urge not to laugh.

The sudden change in mood wasn't lost on Blunderton, either. She and Porter exchanged another look.

He read in her eyes, *Can I just go with it?*

He nodded. *In for a penny...*

She turned to face the assembled Captains, her words ringing with the clarity of a shipboard Klaxon. "Keep in mind, this Captain..." She pointed to Porter. "... was hand-picked by Fleet Commander Quintos. Between the two of them, they have labored over and acted upon more strategies and tactics than most of your sorry lot will ever know. I propose we follow his lead and start planning for the battle to come."

Porter stopped himself mid-grinding of his molars. His pasted-on smile felt as fake as the Ensign's last statement. *Oh boy, she'd just taken things a little, no, a lot, too far.*

Two full minutes had passed. A hushed silence fell over the bridge as Blunderton's impassioned words still echoed off the bulkheads.

At last, Captain Longmont gave a curt nod, the fight

draining from his eyes. "Very well, Chief... *Captain* Porter. The floor is yours. What's your plan?"

As if a searing hot cattle prod had just been shoved up his keister, Porter straightened his shoulders while sending a *now you've done it*, glance over to Blunderton. Vibrant feathers fluttered as Lucy, the duplicitous macaw, pranced a spirited jig atop her perch on the Ensign's shoulder.

SARAH had assured him communications were being triple-encrypted. He could speak freely.

"The plan I'm laying out won't be a walk in the park..." he said, stalling while his mind raced.

Unease slithered across *Franklin's* bridge, an ominous precursor to potential calamity. High stakes loomed, leaving Porter to improvise hastily, grasping at straws with each breath.

The interim Captain went on to outline his strategy, his words punctuated by the occasional dismissive snort or derisive chuckle from the still somewhat skeptical Captains. But as he delved deeper into the intricacies of his plan, a hush fell over the assembled officers, their expressions shifting from derision to grudging respect.

"... AND THAT'S WHEN WE'LL UNLEASH THE FULL might of *Franklin's* Phazon Pulsar cannons," Porter concluded, his voice resonating with conviction. "With the Grish Fleet divided and their defenses compromised, we'll have a narrow window to turn the tide on their considerably greater numbers and superior firepower."

Captain Liu of USS *Sentinel* leaned forward, frowning in contemplation. "It's a bold plan, Captain Porter, I'll give you that. But what about our dwindling munitions reserves? some of us are already running dangerously low on rail munitions."

A murmur of assent rippled through the other Captains, but Porter held up a hand, silencing their protests.

"I've already accounted for that," he said, his eyes glinting with a hint of triumph. "*Franklin's* armory coffers of rail spikes are relatively full. Captain Blunderton has already initiated the quansporting process to share our reserves."

It was still a rarity for U.S. Space Navy vessels to have quansporting capabilities—especially older ships such as those making up the bulk of Alpha Fleet.

His eyes caught Blunderton's. She looked momentarily shocked; clearly, Roisin was caught off guard at hearing Chief Porter call her *Captain*.

Porter continued, "We have a new prototype weapons system, courtesy of our Thine allies. Code-named *Singularity Lances*, these bad boys pack enough punch to crack open a Grish dreadnought like a mallet slamming a tin can."

Blunderton's eyes widened. She leaned in, her voice a hushed whisper. "I've heard rumors about that tech, but I thought they were still at the theoretical stage."

Porter allowed himself a small smile. He'd had plenty of time over the last few days to delve deeper into both *Washington's* and *Franklin's* Omninought-class weapons' capabilities. He doubted even Quintos knew about this one—highly classified Thine technology killer armament. There was the possibility that the weapons weren't quite ready for prime time—maybe it was still in the testing phase but from what he'd determined—looking at the blueprints and inspecting the actual hardware—the turret-mounted gun should work.

Captain Longmont cleared his throat, his expression guarded. "I have to admit, Captain, your plan has merit. But there's still the matter of command structure. With Quintos absent, we need a clear chain of authority. Will it be you in charge, or... um, Captain Blunderton there taking the lead onboard that flagship?"

All the color drained from Ensign Blunderton's face.

Momentarily stymied, Porter said, "No, um, we've discussed that, and I'll remain in the Captain's Mount going, uh... going forward."

One by one, the other Captains nodded their assent, their expressions ranging from reluctant acceptance to outright admiration.

Porter found himself at a loss for words, his gaze shifting from Blunderton's unwavering stare to the assembled Captains. Against all odds, this woman had managed to unite this fractious rabble, if only for the time being... but that was something.

"Alright, then," Porter said, his voice gruff but tinged with a hint of pride. "Let's get to work. A Grish Fleet is coming our way and we've got preparations to make."

With the comms connection cut, Ensign Blunderton stepped in front of the Captain's Mount, and with hands firmly on her hips, she glared down at him. "Captain fucking Blunderton!?"

Porter waved away her words dismissively, "It's fine. Hell, by the time this battle has come and gone, and in the unlikely event that any of us are still alive... no one will remember you or your name."

Her eyes didn't waver from his. "In the history of the Maritime Navy, nor Space Navy, a lowly Ensign has never been promoted to Captain in one fell swoop. Not ever. It's not done!"

A nervous laugh escaped Porter's lips. "Come on, Roisin... you know you're not really a Captain—"

A scorching glare bore into him. "You've handed me fake Captain's bars, Porter. Impersonating a commanding officer? That's a cell in Space Navy lockup for two, three decades."

His hands rose, palms outward, feigning capitulation. "Consider it handled." *Shit, how do I get out of this one?*

Blunderton continued to stare, unmoved by his declaration.

Porter swiftly shifted gears. "For the present, Ensign, a mountain of tasks demands our attention."

She raised her voice as she stormed off, "Yeah, well that's *Captain* Blunderton to you, Chief."

Chapter 47

Entering Grish Territory
***USS Washington*, Rotunda**

Captain Galvin Quintos

I leaned on the railing of the Rotunda, my hands gripping the cool metal as I stared into the Gravity Well's oversized 3D projection. The light show before us was mesmerizing —exoplanets, moons, and the central star of the Drakoria system painted swirls of light and shadow across the attentive faces of my bridgecrew. I'd requested Derrota, Coogong, and Hardy, along with several department heads, to be present as well. Perhaps as a not-so-subtle jab, my executive officer opted to position herself at the farthest point away from me along the railing's curve.

A heaviness settled in my chest, an increasing disquiet as we confronted the calm before the tempest. One fact remained undeniable—our chances of making it through the next day were slim to none. No matter how I tried to sugarcoat it for my crew, how self-assured I appeared and sounded about our impending mission, the inescapable reality was, well... reality. *USS Washington* had been deployed to this star system to plunge a dagger into the very core of the Grish Empire—when in actuality, this would amount to little more than a doomed attempt at making a point. Earth, the Alliance, was losing this war. Sure, eliminating the Varapin threat had provided a temporary boost to our spirits, yet it couldn't erase the stark reality—the Grish Empire's power had grown exponentially, leaving us irrevocably outmatched.

A grim reality settled over me as I gazed at Gail Pristy's silhouette against the viewport. The old adage mocked us—*all good things must come to an end.*

I inwardly scoffed. No, cruel fate had snatched away what might have been between us before it even had a chance to grow. The unforgiving universe delighted in dashing hopes before they could take root. Any flicker of possibility between Gail and I had withered, extinguished by the harsh reality bearing down upon us.

Buck up, you miserable sap! came my inner voice. The harsh words echoed in my skull. I wrenched away from the railing, squared my shoulders, and plastered on a mask of confidence and unflinching optimism.

Derrota stepped forward to the podium, his demeanor studious yet unmistakably tinged with a hint of awe. I could almost feel the cerebral gears turning in his head as he addressed the crew in the Rotunda, the Gravity Well casting an ambient glow over his features. His discourse began as I fixed my gaze on the fiery heart of the Drakoria system projected before us.

"Once we arrive, we'll see that at the center of this celestial fortress beats Drakoria's Sun." Derrota gestured to the menacing red supergiant on display, his words measured, his anxiety contained beneath a layer of scholarly poise. "The giant red star's corona, while impressive, serves as a warning of the star's immense power."

Derrota's words carried weight, the ambient glow from the celestial behemoth lending an ominous undertone. Fiery tendrils licked outward, a harbinger of the star's destructive capabilities. An invisible force tugged at me, the red super-giant's gravitational influence distorting the fabric of space itself. I don't think I'd ever witnessed a star quite like this one—oppressive yet awe-inspiring.

He continued, his sing-songy Mumbai accent soft but clear, "Closest to the star resides Xendari, a scorching testament to what lies too near the star's wrath. It's an implacable, fiery sphere, its very crust appearing as if it's in a constant state of meltdown."

"That was almost poetic," Pristy said, giving Derrota a playful smile.

Derrota's gaze lingered on the next icy sphere, lips pressed together in a solemn acknowledgment of Nortuum's frigid mysteries. "An unrelenting glacial world," he uttered, "where harsh, inhospitable conditions hold dominion. Hardly a tempting vacation spot."

Hardy interjected, "Towering navy-blue ice formations and ghostly, shifting, ammonia clouds. A wonderful place... if you're a penguin in a spacesuit."

The Gravity Well shifted focus, and with it, Derrota's narra-tive moved to Voraxia. "Volcanic activity on a planetary scale—it churns and regenerates ceaselessly. Any craft that strays too close would undoubtedly meet its demise under Voraxia's crushing gravity and relentless flame."

I leaned in, could just make out the lava rivers crisscrossing Voraxia's violent surface.

"And this inviting sphere is called Calydon. In reality, it's a forbidden primordial world, which remains off-limits even to the Grish. A prehistoric landscape with the equivalent of Earth's dinosaurs. From what we've gleaned from Grish data records, centuries earlier, inter-planetary travelers had brought baby creatures back to their homeworld of Drakoria, later causing catastrophic loss of life as full-grown dinosaur creatures rampaged towns and cities, the Grish populace becoming their breakfast, lunch, and dinner."

Having set the stage with the layout of the star system, Derrota yielded to Hardy, who came forward for the next part of the presentation. Shifting bulky chrome and whisper-silent servos, Hardy moved up to the lectern.

"The system's defensive network—" Hardy's booming voice seemed to fill the entire Rotunda and for once conveyed the seriousness of the situation.

The Gravity Well changed perspective, zooming out so the entire system came into view. Red icons, one after another, popped into view at what seemed to be random locations. I figured there must be dozens of them.

Zooming in on one of the dots closest to Drakoria, it became evident we were looking at a space station of some kind. Ominous-looking with its top-mounted turret cannon—the sheer size of the thing made me involuntarily swallow.

"These Star Guns," Hardy continued, "are part of a highly advanced planetary defense system—AI-controlled with integrated evasion and offensive capabilities. That means these bad boys can move. Their photon shield arrays and kinetic energy cannons make approaching them, well... an act of suicide."

The display zoomed in even more, the matte black construct taking on a foreboding silhouette against the distant, amber-colored world beyond.

"And how many of these things are floating around in this system?" Pristy asked.

"Exactly fifty," Hardy said. "One for every state of the Union, if anyone's feeling nostalgic for home."

Mesmerized, I gazed into the Gravity Well's hauntingly life-like hologram. The Star Gun construct provided an ominous silhouette—its massive cannon depicted an unsettling clarity that posed an undeniable danger that even an Omninought-class Warship such as *Washington* dared not dismiss.

Hardy took a step back, letting us know he'd finished speaking.

My mind spun with tactical options. Sure, introducing a formidable omninought into this battlespace, would cause devastating havoc in the system—but I kept coming back to those fifty big Space Guns. We were, simply put, going to be outmatched no matter how I looked at it.

I stepped up to the lectern where I met the gazes of my crew, their expectant expressions a sobering reminder of the daunting challenge before us.

Hardy's faceplate lit up with a Hiroshima-like explosion. "Is it too late to turn back? Or maybe just surrender now and forgo the whole space battle nonsense?"

Nervous laughter rippled through the crew, somewhat easing the palpable tension.

I said, "Thoughts? Recommendations? Now's the time to speak up, people... other than Hardy's, anyone else's suggestion will be listened to."

Pristy spoke up first, "Those Star Guns... Hardy said they're AI-controlled cannons—a networked matrix. Can't we breach that network? Hack into it?"

I heard Coogong's voice, but him being so short, I couldn't see him among the crowd. "That is a possibility we have been pursuing. Unfortunately, it has not been as fruitful as we would like. The Grish maintains a dynamic threat response firewall that uses advanced algorithms and technologies to adapt its security measures in real-time, providing near-perfect protection against breaches."

I scanned the crowd for the little Thine scientist but soon gave up. "Bring Sonya into the mix, she's—"

Suddenly, Coogong's close proximity voice startled me, "She's already a part of the team, Captain."

How Coogong had so quickly moved—was now standing a mere foot away from me—I had no clue. His friendly worm-like face stared up at me through that amber-colored Ambiogel liquid sloshing around in his helmet.

"Good to know," I said. "Keep me apprised of your team's progress." I looked to the others. "Anyone else? Don't be shy... speak up."

Ensign Lira, often overlooked for her quiet demeanor, cleared her throat. "It seems to me those big guns are overkill—"

"That's kinda the point, isn't it?" Crewmember Davit chided sarcastically.

"Let her speak, Mr. Davit," I said.

I actually agreed with Davit but I wanted to give Ensign Lira the respect of hearing her out.

"Those Star Guns are here for one purpose and one purpose only... to take out warships like *Washington*, right?"

I nodded at the obvious.

"And while there is a smattering of Grish security vessels here, typically, there would be an entire fleet. Something akin to what the Royal Guard within the Pleidian system had been, yes?"

Dismissively, I said, "Undoubtedly. Knowing what's coming from the alliance, the Pinnacle Fleet has mobilized multiple smaller fleets into that one armada." I was ready to move on from Ensign Lira and looked to the others.

341

"No, Captain, you're missing my point," Lira said with surprising pushback. "Star Guns are not designed to ward off smaller attack vessels. Those would have been allocated to their on-the-move security forces. Their version of a Royal Guard."

I stared back at her, my interest now somewhat piqued.

She said, "Well... onboard *Washington*, we have hundreds of Arrow Fighters. With a combination of smart missiles, *and those Arrows...*" she let her final words trail off in a higher pitch, allowing me to connect the dots.

The large compartment went as quiet as a church.

"Go on," I urged.

Her voice was steady despite all eyes suddenly on her, "We could recalibrate the Arrow Fighters' reflectors to scatter their approach vectors. It's like hurling a handful of pebbles at a window—too many signals for them to track, disguising our real attack angle."

"Yes... we can blitz those big guns!" I bellowed. "Dammit, Ensign you're absolutely right! We... no, I, was thinking way too big. *Washington's* brawn isn't going to defeat the enemy here, it'll be the nimbleness of our Arrows!"

I opened my mouth to speak but Captain Wallace Ryder beat me to it, "I'm on it, Galvin. Give me a few hours to come up with a workable strategy, to meet with my squad leaders. We'll be ready to present it to you soon." Ryder spun on his heels and headed for the DeckPort.

Did I think we actually had a chance to prevail here? No. But this just might turn out to be one hell of a fight.

Chapter 48

Alpha Fleet Rendezvous Location
USS Franklin

Chief Craig Porter

Within the span of three hours, interim Captain Porter had completely rearranged the Captain's Conference Room into what he now referred to as his Logistics & Mobilization Nexus. Porter was a visual thinker. He did well with physical models—tactile representations over impersonal digitized holographic projections. And right now, the space was filled with a dozen or so scaled-down facsimile miniatures. If someone were to drop by, say, for a visit and didn't know what was transpiring, they would think Porter was a toy maker, or maybe one of those centuries-past Walt Disney Imagineers. The conference table was laden with small, intricately detailed spacecraft. Dreadnoughts, battle cruisers, frigates, and space carriers. In fact, what was laid out on the oversized conference table was Alpha Fleet.

Ensign Blunderton hurried into the compartment looking flushed, forehead moist with perspiration, and out of breath. Like him, she had been going non-stop. Having learned how to utilize *Franklin's* Quansporter compartment, she had been literally jumping between Alpha Fleet vessels, meeting with ship officers and department heads, basically giving everyone Porter's marching orders—those orders that would prepare the fleet for what was coming.

Blunderton, sans Lucy—who was currently back in her cage —took in the array of small U.S. Space Navy, Thine, and Pleidian warship models. Her brows arched. "Wow!" She reached for the largest of the toy-like vessels, *USS Franklin,* and held it up close to her face, scrutinizing the incredible detail. "So real looking... What's the scale of this thing?"

"Well, in this case, since *USS Franklin* is five miles long, that model in your hand represents a scale of approximately twenty-six thousand four hundred to one. So, since the model is one foot long, it equals twenty-six thousand four hundred feet of the actual spacecraft."

Suddenly, the wiry, scraggly, white-bearded, and looking far-too-old-for-active-duty, Rigel Park, entered the compartment. He was carrying a large plastic container that the man was just barely able to see over the top of. Park deposited his load onto the table with an exasperated exhalation. "That should be the last of them," he said, wiping the sleeve of his shirt across his brow. "There should be forty-eight in total. Oh, and VD says *Franklin's* primary replicator unit is starting to overheat. That the thing wasn't designed for an operation of this magnitude."

Porter considered that. Of course, it wasn't. Just the same, the massive piece of equipment, referred to as a large-scale replicator unit, or LSRU, was unlike anything else ever launched into the depths of space, maybe with the exception of the identical unit aboard *USS Washington.*

Housed within a compartment approximately the size of a football field, the sprawling, inter-connected pieces of hardware, representing one gigantic unit, could rapidly restore even the most intricate and multi-faceted ship components, sometimes within a matter of hours or days. A game-changer for a warship often light years from the nearest shipyard facility.

"What are you doing? Dump them out on the table, Park." Blunderton said, falling into her faux Captain's role far too easily for Porter's taste. But the old spacer did what was asked of him without complaint—dumping out another dozen or so spacecraft miniatures.

Immediately, Porter got to work, examining each of the scaled-down ships. "These are pretty good. Better than the last batch."

"Why does it matter," Blunderton commented with a shrug befitting a pre-teen. "It's not like anyone's going to actually be flying around in these little things."

Porter held up a battle cruiser in front of her. "As discussed, these models are scaled-down versions of the originals, right?"

She nodded but made it clear by her expression that she didn't care. "We're not going to be putting miniatures out in space. This seems like a waste of time. Time we don't have."

Rigel Park dug into his left ear with a gnarled fingertip, eyes darting between the pair like a pickleball spectator. "Yeah... VD reckons we'll miss your deadline."

Porter glared at the old man. "This isn't my deadline. The Grish are coming! Whether we're ready or not! Personally, I'd like to be as prepared as possible."

Blunderton tossed *USS Franklin* back onto the table. "Keep doing whatever you're doing, I'll deal with VD."

He watched as Ensign Blunderton, with Rigel Park close on her heels, hurried from the compartment.

Ensign Roisin Blunderton

Even with the advent of DeckPorts, it didn't guarantee instant access to every nook of the sprawling omninought. Certain areas remained tucked away, segregated from the ship's vital departments by winding detours—a deliberate separation from the well-trodden routes. The Replications Department took up three separate and equally large compartments... strategically positioned on Deck 6, nestled just aft of the midship section yet still within Violet Sector's bounds.

Multiple corridors converged upon its cavernous interior. A flight bay-style energy field breached the port-side hull, granting direct access to the void beyond. It made sense... let's say one of the ship's house-sized Broadside turret booths needed replicating, you'd need a means to maneuver the thing out of the ship, right?

Ensign Blunderton made her way to the first of the three chambers, mentally preparing herself for what lay beyond the double auto-hatch doors, knowing the activation of the LSRU unleashed a horrific deafening roar. Before going in she stopped at an ear-shield dispenser kiosk. One did not venture into the compartment without first placing hearing protection headphones over one's ears.

She winced as she stepped into the cavernous chamber, the deafening noise assaulting her ears despite the cumbersome hearing protection. She clamped the bulky half-domes tighter against the sides of her head, but the relentless din still pounded mercilessly at her eardrums. *Christ! Who designed this thing? It's like a medieval torture device.*

She spotted VD up on the machine, one that resembled a 19th-century steam locomotive, albeit one that was five times the size. She grimaced, taking in the big man's sweat-drenched shirt and the equally drenched red bandanna tied around the top of his head. The sleeves of his denim shirt had been torn free revealing tree-trunk-sized biceps and Popeye-sized forearms.

Her skull pounded from the perpetual roar. Gritting her teeth, she clamped her palms tighter over the headphones, yet the ceaseless barrage still battered her eardrums. One hand rose, waving frantically to catch VD's eye amidst the racket.

Her gaze followed the hulking figure scrambling across the oversized contraption, never still—a carnival freak with super-human stamina. Those tree-trunk-sized arms continued to yank levers and spin metal wheels in a ceaseless flurry of motion.

Finally, he saw her down below, scowled, and then shut down the LSRU.

"Oh my God," she gasped, directing an annoyed expression toward the machine. "How can you stand working in here!"

"What do you want? This shit's not going to get done by itself!" he shouted, gesturing to the big contraption.

She noticed that he continued to yell as if the LSRU was still running. She figured the man's eardrums were probably shot.

"Need an update for Porter. When will we be seeing a full-scale replication?"

He stared down at her like she was mentally challenged.

A beat later, VD looked up toward the portside energy field and splayed his hands in an overly dramatic gesture. "All you had to do is take a look! I've got three ships fabricated, two frigates, and half a destroyer!"

Not expecting that, Blunderton spun around and hurried over to look out through the blue-hued energy field into the vast void beyond.

Wide-eyed, her lips spread into a broad smile. If she hadn't known better, she would have sworn she was looking at a U.S. Space Navy Frigate... hundreds of yards long, half of that length, wide. The ship was brimming with pivoting gun turrets, and hundreds of glowing porthole windows; there was no way that ship wasn't real—wasn't authentic. Sure, Porter explained that the models were made of a flexible material, a specialized polymer composite—that they had been designed to resist temperature extremes, radiation, and even micrometeoroid impacts. But she hadn't expected anything like this.

She looked back up to VD. "How...?" She took in the big machine and shook her head.

To her surprise, the man actually smiled. "As you know... this LSRU is the fabricator. It spits out the inflatable balloon parts, or sections, into the next-door compartment where Tycho is ready to start inflating them with a hydrogen gas mix. Then those sections, pretty much light as air, are maneuvered off to the third chamber where Lana Velcros them together. Because of size constraints, the final assembly of all the balloon parts is done outside the hull by a team of maintenance droids."

She noticed Porter had entered the compartment and was headed her way.

He joined her, now both facing out to deep space. A swarm of maintenance droids scurried about, assembling an array of decoy starships, their metallic limbs working with meticulous precision.

A FULL MINUTE WENT BY BEFORE SHE TURNED her emerald eyes upon him.

"Chief Porter," she said, her voice tinged with skepticism. "Do you really think this ruse will fool anyone, let alone Grish Command?"

The sandy-haired Chief stepped closer to the energy field, his gaze following the intricate dance of the droids. A wry smile played upon his lips as he turned to face her. "It's worked before, Ensign."

Blunderton arched an eyebrow. "Enlighten me."

Porter's expression took on a faraway look. "During World War II, just before the Allied Invasion of Normandy, the allies employed a bold trickery. They constructed remarkably lifelike, inflatable decoy tanks and positioned them strategically across the English countryside."

Blunderton narrowed her eyes as she leaned in, captivated by his tale.

"The Germans, ever vigilant, fell for the ruse," Porter continued. "Their intelligence reports indicated a massive buildup of Allied Forces in the southeast, prompting them to divert troops away from the actual invasion site."

A slow smile crept across Blunderton's face as she pieced together the implications. "And the real invasion force landed unopposed."

"Hardly," he said with a shake of his head. "Normandy was a meat-grinder of a battle. Estimates suggest that allied casualties during the Battle of Normandy, which lasted from June 6 to August 25, 1944, were somewhere between 225,000 and 250,000. That figure includes killed, wounded, and missing in action."

"I had no idea," she said, deflated. "Is that what we'll be looking at? Unfathomable losses like that?"

"I hope not... possible though. But there again, our trickery just might succeed. Each of these decoys will be emitting false radiation signatures from non-existent drives, defensive shield emissions, and even ship-to-ship communication traffic. From a distance, the Grish will be detecting a fleet—an armada—larger than their own, evenly distributed into several attack groups. It should be a sobering realization for them."

Blunderton turned her gaze back to the void, watching as the droids meticulously connected and attached decoy ship sections.

He continued, "We need the Grish to do the one thing they rarely, if ever, do in battle..."

"And what is that?"

"Divide their armada. The Grish typically rely on over-whelming might, favoring brute force over strategic maneuvering."

She pursed her lips, considering what he was saying.

"Next, the smart move would require the piglets to use the element of surprise for their attack. To do that, they'll need a coordinated, simultaneous assault on each of the three Alpha Fleet battle groups."

"But only one will be real?" Blunderton asked, skeptical.

He shook his head and smiled. "Nope, the real *Franklin* and Alpha Fleet assets won't be any where near the decoys... not at first."

"Now I'm totally lost," she said with a sigh.

"Good, let's hope the Grish will be equally lost," Porter said. "Alpha Fleet, all 32 vessels—"

The Ensign jumped in, cutting him off, "My count has Alpha Fleet at 45 vessels."

"You've got some old intel, Ensign." Porter took a deep breath, then let it out. "Yes, what remained of the fleet after coming up against Prowess Fleet was 45 vessels—but take off the three of those out for repairs. Another ten were lost in a previously fought battle with the Grish, leaving 32."

She shook her head. "Against the Grish's—what? 200 warships?"

Porter stared back at her with a disapproving scowl. "I don't have time for doubts and second-guessing Ensign... you going to let me finish with the details of the plan?"

Blunderton nodded. "Go ahead. I'm all ears."

"Alpha Fleet—all 32 vessels—and *USS Franklin* will be cloaked and poised to unleash hell's fury at key strategic locations... and while the Grish are thinking they're being clever... sneaking about, preparing their coordinated three-pronged offensive on our fake flotillas—"

A slow grin spread across Roisin's lips as comprehension dawned. "They'll never see us coming until it's too late."

Porter matched her expression, offering back a wry smile. "Uh-huh, by the time those swine fuckers realize they've been duped, we'll already have them by the throat."

She looked at the Chief, clearly the man was wickedly smart. How he'd conjured up this battlespace chess match so quickly, amazed her. There again, he may be a total fool when it comes to actual tactical thinking. He's an Engineer by trade, not a seasoned starship captain.

"What about *Washington*? They're coming back to join the fight once they're done with whatever it is they're doing. That's part of the plan, right?" the Ensign asked with a heightened enthusiasm.

"We plan, God laughs," Porter said wryly.

"Well, let's hope you've accurately predicted the Grish's mindset," she said, her skepticism back. "That's a lot of moving parts. And a whole lot of assumptions on your part being made..." she added, her hands now repetitively, nervously, smoothing down the front of her uniform.

Porter chuckled, his voice tinged with a hint of mischief. "Ah come on, have a little faith, Ensign. Sometimes, all you can do is throw a plan together, calculate for a few contingencies, and hope for the best."

As the droids continued their busy work, Blunderton forced herself to think positively. To mentally push away all those invading whispers of dread now swirling around in her mind.

Chapter 49

Entering Grish Territory
USS Washington, **Chapel**

Chaplain Halman Trent

T he murky confines within the Chapel's back office were shrouded in an oppressive silence, save for the faint hum of the halo-emitter and the occasional crackle of static. Trent, leaning back in his chair, legs casually extended with his feet up on the corner of his desk looked up to the flickering display, his fingers tracing the contours of a small, ornate, 6-inch by 6-inch square box, resting on his lap. The box's wood surface was engraved with arcane symbols, a testament to the Chaplain's darker proclivities.

Trent's mind drifted back to the moment he had acquired his latest macabre treasure—a tiny, delicate golden hoop earring, plucked from the ear of Lieutenant Gail Pristy after she had fallen under the sway of his amulet. The memory of her pained cries as he had wrenched the jewelry from her lobe sent a shiver of perverse delight through him.

As a shadowy silhouette materialized on the display, Trent's lips curled into a sardonic grin. Cloaked in darkness, with only faint streaks of light hinting at a presence, the figure remained inscrutable, an enigma shrouded in obscurity.

"Ah, my friend," the Chaplain began, "I trust you bring news of our... mutual endeavor?"

The man's features remained obscured, but Trent could sense the underlying tension in his voice. "Indeed, Chaplain. The pieces are falling into place, but I must caution you—the stakes are higher than ever."

Trent's chuckle was flat—there was no hiding the dislike he had for the man. His fingers deftly plucked a small gold post, a piercing, from the box. The sway he had held over his minions was intoxicating, and he was prepared to do anything to get it back. "Underestimate me at your own peril," Trent said, his tone as cold as space itself.

The man leaned forward, a band of light catching the steely glint in his eyes. "Do not forget, Trent, that my continued support hinges on your ability to deliver. The U.S. Space Navy must be crippled. Captain Quintos, his crew... ensure they will be too preoccupied to interfere with our designs."

Trent pressed the small post between his thumb and forefinger, the sharp point biting into his skin. He was already growing bored with this conversation. "Oh, I have a plan that will not only shatter crew morale and decimate their pathetic unity but also render them incapable of stopping us."

The man's face twisted into a grotesque mask. "Care to enlighten me, Chaplain?"

Trent felt a depraved warmth envelop him as he plucked a lock of auburn hair from the box, twirling it between his fingers. His mind flashed to Aubrey's athletic, naked silhouette.

Cinched together with a tiny blue ribbon, he brought the lock of hair up to his nose and inhaled deeply. "Inheritors of Tenebrosity—my flock of devoted followers are dispersed throughout the sector... and they're patiently waiting."

The man's eyes narrowed as he nodded, his expression hardening. "Ha! From what I've heard, your influence has been squashed. And recent, shall we say, missteps, aboard *Washington* have attracted unwanted scrutiny on you—on *our* objectives. Remember... we have eyes, ears... everywhere. Some here believe your usefulness has... expired."

"If that's a threat, I would think again. A temporary hiccup does not change things. My influence is simply simmering, ready to reach far beyond the confines of this ship or even this star system," Trent said, his voice full of malice. "Or have you already forgotten how easily I infiltrated the highest echelons of the EUNF?"

The man leaned back into the shadows, his expression unreadable. "Perhaps."

Trent's fingers caressed around the lock of hair, a distorted smile spreading across his face. "With the Inheritors' network in place, we are on the verge of sowing the seeds of discord and mistrust throughout the Alliance. Imagine the chaos, the infighting, as once brethren start to turn against themselves."

The man's fingers were now drumming against the surface of an out-of-view desktop. "You've been short on details on how you propose to accomplish that."

Trent carefully returned the ribboned strands of hair to his box of treasures. "There lies your indispensable role, my friend. I will need further access into encrypted networks, codes, protocols—the very lifeblood binding the EUNF's strategic influences."

The man seemed to be weighing this latest request. "That can be arranged." The man leaned forward, the light momentarily catching his gaunt features. "But be warned, Trent—further failures, embarrassments, the consequences will be... severe."

Trent's eyes smoldered. He wanted to strike out at the pompous fuck. Instead, he said nothing.

The halo display flickered, and the connection severed, leaving Trent alone in the dimly lit compartment. He sat there, the box clutched tightly in one hand, a distorted sense of triumph coursing through him. Quintos and his crew had no idea what was coming, and by the time they realized the true extent of his machinations, it would be too late.

Trent lifted the box and studied it with an almost childlike fascination. He sat like that for a couple of beats while his thoughts raced.

In the meantime, he had other business to attend to... up there on the Symbio Deck. Another day, another trophy. Maybe young Sonya Winters would be offering up something more than a simple piece of jewelry, or a lock of hair... something a little more interesting... a fingertip, perhaps?

Chapter 50

Petty Officer Second-Class Aubrey Laramie

Aubrey stepped out of the steamy shower, droplets of water clinging to her toned body. Glancing around the utilitarian space of her junior officer's quarters there within the Circadian Platform Decks, she muttered, "I don't belong here."

Her stomach was still twisted into knots at the memory of her actions under that bastard Chaplain Trent's influence. Even now, days later, she felt her cheeks flush—shame and guilt poised to suffocate her. She closed her eyes as a vise tightened around her chest. Her mind flashed back to the barracks. *Oh God... what the hell had I been thinking?* One minute she's sparring, the next she's viciously attacking Wanda, one of her shipmates... her friend.

Aubrey grabbed a towel and furiously rubbed it over her damp skin. Facing the others after her actions seemed an impossible task. News traveled through the ship faster than the Bubonic Plague ravaging medieval Europe.

Aubrey's Olympic archery skills and position as a Junior U.S. Space Navy Officer felt like a distant memory. The strong, disciplined woman had been reduced to an unthinking marionette, dancing to the tune of a sadistic puppeteer. There again, Trent had been made to pay, well... somewhat. She thought back to Sonya's cubby hole tech station, the security feed where she witnessed Quintos' decisive confrontation with the man. To think she had dismissed him as soft on exercising necessary punishment. The Captain had revealed himself as someone willing to go to extremes to protect his crew. Aubrey had misjudged Quintos. His actions ignited a newfound respect within her, as well as a desperate need to prove her worth.

Aubrey was more convinced than ever that her life needed a reset. As she dressed in a fresh Petty Officer's uniform, she surveyed her quarters with a shameful shake of her head. *I really don't belong here.*

Without allowing another thought to worm its way into her resolve, Aubrey took a deep breath and strode purposefully out of her quarters. She needed redemption, a clean slate, and she wasn't going to find it by wallowing in self-pity.

Her brisk pace didn't falter as she approached the nearest DeckPort. Hesitantly, she said, "Blue Sector, Deck 34 — Marines' barracks." It was time to right her wrongs, and there was no better place to start than with Wanda.

Approaching the taller, brawnier woman, Aubrey braced herself for the confrontation, fully expecting Wanda's wrath. To her surprise, Wanda's response held a hint of understanding.

"I know what it's like to be manipulated," Wanda admitted, her still raspy voice laced with empathy. "Trent's amulet had you under its control. You were angry. That wasn't your fault,

Laramie. What matters now is how you move forward from here."

Aubrey was taken aback by Wanda's compassion. The words unlocked something inside her, and she found herself opening up about something she'd been contemplating... her desire to make a career change. "I want to join Max's Marines."

It seemed as though Wanda hadn't heard her.

"Maybe here I can prove my worth. Better atone for what I did under the Chaplain's influence. What do you think? I could undergo the necessary training... earn my place among your ranks."

Wanda paused, her eyes taking on a faraway gaze. "That's a tall order." She gave Aubrey a stern look. "You do know you outrank Sergeant Max as a Petty Officer, right? And you're Space Navy, not a Marine. We don't just hand out memberships."

Aubrey's heart sank as her dreams of a redemptive life's reset seemed to slip away. But Wanda wasn't done.

"Talk to Max," she said with a shrug. "He makes the rules for his team. If anyone can make an exception, it's him. But don't go in half-cocked. Do your research first."

Three hours later, Aubrey spotted Max in the barracks break room. He eyed her warily as she approached, clearly still fuming over her attack on Wanda.

"Sergeant, I'm glad I found you," she began, nerves making her mouth dry. "I... I wanted to apologize. There's no excuse for what I did, but—"

Max cut her off, tossing his empty coffee cup into the trash. "You think you're the first to injure one of my crew?" He smirked. "Get over yourself, Laramie. Grip, Ham, Hock,

Wanda...hell, even me. We should install a revolving door to HealthBay with how often we end up there."

His dismissive attitude struck a nerve, and Aubrey opened her mouth to retort but the words died in her throat. Indecision paralyzed her.

"What the hell's wrong with you?" he grumbled, brushing past her toward the exit.

Aubrey swallowed hard, forcing down her pride. "I want to become a Marine!"

Max stopped but didn't turn around.

She pressed on, her voice steadier than she felt. "I belong on your team, Sergeant. It's the only place on this ship where I truly fit in."

Slowly, he turned to face her, studying her with an appraising look. "You're an Officer, college-educated, and academy-trained. But you're no Marine. You haven't paid the price in blood, sweat, and tears."

As Max made a move to walk away, desperation drove Aubrey to blurt out, "I have precedence!"

He paused, his expression making it clear he didn't care about whatever technicality she thought she had.

But she didn't back down. "You can make me an honorary Marine under the Navy-Marine Corps Joint Integration Program." Aubrey recited the details Sonya had helped her research, the words tumbling out in a rush. "Select Space Navy officers can be nominated to undergo Marine training and serve under Marine guidelines. If I complete it successfully, I earn the title Marine Corporal to solidify joint operations."

A crease formed between Max's brows as he processed this. "That's a real thing? You're not bullshitting me?"

"No, Sergeant, it's real," Aubrey affirmed. "The Captain would have to sign off, but—"

"Okay, I'll look into it," Max said flatly, cutting her off. He studied her face. "But let me make one thing clear, Laramie. If I put you through Marine training, it'll be the worst few weeks of your life. The word *misery* won't even begin to cover what you'll go through. Be sure you know what you'll be signing up for."

Aubrey met his stare unflinchingly. "I can take whatever you dish out, Sergeant. My mind's made up."

A beat of tense silence stretched between them before Max's lips curved into a rare smile. "Then consider this your one shot at redemption, Laramie. Don't waste it."

Relief washed over her, bringing with it a surge of determination. She would prove herself worthy of the honored Marine ranks, no matter how grueling the path ahead. Squaring her shoulders, Aubrey offered a sharp salute.

"I'm ready, Sir. Bring it on."

"We'll see," Max scoffed, then turned and headed off.

As she pivoted on her heel and strode off in the opposite direction, Aubrey couldn't deny the roiling storm of emotions warring within her. Aubrey felt both purpose and trepidation, but she pushed aside her doubts about what lay ahead.

The final hurdle remained—persuading the Captain that this decision served both the interests of the U.S. Space Navy and her own military trajectory. A grin tugged at her lips. *Am I really going through with this? Become a Marine?*

Chapter 51

Captain Galvin Quintos

I paced the bridge, my boots echoing a rhythm that matched the pounding in my chest. Tension cloaked every inch of the compartment, a thick, palpable fog. We all knew the weight of what was to come; ultimately Earth hung in the balance, balanced on the razor's edge of the decisions I would be making today.

My eyes flicked to the main halo display. The vivid tactical rendering of the Drakoria Star System sprawled across the oversized projection, a projection incomprehensibly dominated by two Grish dreadnoughts. Dreadnoughts that were not supposed to be here. The fifty unmanned Star Guns, sure... but not dreadnoughts. *Shit!*

"Obviously, the system is anything but defenseless," Pristy observed grimly from her tactical station. Multiple small sensor displays cycled, as the XO worked her control board. "For Lira's plan to work, we need a new angle."

My jaw tensed further. What slim prospects we had for triumph had plummeted into the realm of the impossible. I opened my mouth to speak, but SARAH's crisp voice cut through the tense silence...

Captain Ryder indicates all Arrows are cued for deployment and on standby...

Deck plates trembled beneath my feet as *Washington's* big drives spooled up.

Lieutenant Hargreaves said, "Captain, all five squadrons—Shadowstrike, Thunderbolt, Nightwing, Sunburst, and Ghost-wind... poised in our three flight bays."

I nodded. 375 Arrow Fighters with engines idling, eager pilots awaiting the *GO* command, more than ready to tear out into the void. I thought of Captain Wallace Ryder and Lieutenant Akari James. Would this be the mission one or both of them would never return from? I inwardly chided myself. Thinking like that was never a good idea.

I rubbed at the scruff on my chin. Our opening salvo awaited my command, the first act in what promised to be a merciless confrontation.

The awareness of the dreadnoughts had altered the battle-field calculus irrevocably. Skulking unseen as phantoms in the shadows was a luxury we could no longer afford. Revealing our position became an unavoidable necessity—we must drop our cloaks, announce our presence to the hulking leviathans, and open fire without hesitation. Even a moment's pause, the slightest wavering, risked allowing one to slip away and guar-antee our downfall.

All eyes turned to me, the weight of their gazes like the crush of a neutron star's gravity. I straightened, squaring my shoulders as I turned to Grimes at the Helm Station. "Tell me you'll be able to thread the needle—short-jump us right in between those dreadnoughts?"

Grimes met my gaze, unwavering. "No problem, Captain."

A flicker of relief broke the grip of tension. I pivoted towards Pristy. "What's it going to take to bring down two formidable warships at once?"

Pristy's expression tightened, her eyes calculating. "One at a time would be preferable."

"That's not an option," I shot back. "Either ship escapes, and we're finished. It's both or nothing."

It seemed as though the entire bridgecrew held their breath. Then Pristy nodded. "Broadsides could do it. But firing both sides simultaneously... We risk the reactors, the drives, everything."

My gaze snapped to Lieutenant Commander Jorkins at Engineering. "Tell me we have the capacity to pull this off."

Jorkins's fingers flew over his console, numbers, and scenarios flashing. After a moment, he looked up, his face grim. "If we stagger the volleys ... port-starboard, port-starboard, we might avoid overloading ship systems."

I felt a muscle twitch in my cheek. "Okay, well... that's at least something. Coordinate with XO Pristy. Make it work."

I strode over to Lieutenant Hargreaves at Flight Control. He was bent over his station, eyes fixed on the myriad of displays in front of him.

"We're about to jump into the fire," I said as serious as a heart attack. "Not a whole lot of room to deploy the Arrows. Tell me it's still doable."

Hargreaves frowned, reflecting the same uncertainty that Jorkins and Pristy shared earlier. But then, something shifted. "If Grimes truly hits his mark... like dead center between the two... and if our pilots can launch and fishhook their rapid deployments... doing so without slamming into those dreadnoughts....."

Hope sparked in his eyes. "Yes, Captain. We should be able

to make that happen."

I nodded, a new surge of adrenaline hitting my bloodstream. Could we pull this off? Deploy our fighters in a daring strike, then cripple the dreadnoughts with precision strikes from our main batteries?

The odds were against us. Any misstep and *Washington* would be obliterated before our pilots even left the flight bay. The mere thought of it tightened my throat, so much so that I found myself running an open palm over my Adam's apple.

Pristy glanced my way. She lowered her voice so only I could hear her, "What's with the indecision? You've already determined that making a quick retreat isn't an option. That making that concession would domino... with Alpha Fleet's inevitable defeat, the Pleidian and Thine worlds soon to follow. Then—"

"Earth. Yes, XO... I'm well aware of the potential dismal chain of events."

Two figures on the bridge had maintained silence. Derrota, stationed at the science console, was engrossed in calculations only he understood. And Hardy, standing statue-like beside the Captain's Mount—was uncharacteristically taciturn, his usual light-hearted banter absent.

"Hardy? Care to throw your two cents into the hat?"

With that, animated, bright red dice repeatedly began skittering across his faceplate, their numbers tumbling with every roll. A cacophony of casino jackpot chimes lent a multi-sensory layer to the exhibit.

Hardy said, "Best not to play the odds, Cap. I assure you, they're not good. We should strike and strike now. What are you waiting for? A written invitation from the piglets? Maybe an engraved smart missile, one with a nice ribbon tied around its nose?"

He may be a smart-ass robot, but he did have a point.

Chapter 52

Alpha Fleet Rendezvous Location
USS Franklin

Chief Craig Porter

Porter sat hunched over his console in the faintly illuminated Captain's Ready Room, his sandy-blond hair disheveled from the countless hours spent pouring over tactical plans and simulations. The faint hum of the halo-emitter and the distant thrum of *Franklin's* drives provided the only soundtrack to his late-night vigil. Unaccustomed to the archaic act of typing in an era of 3D video halo displays, Porter's fingers moved clumsily across the keyboard, his hunt-and-peck method... a slow, painstaking process as he tapped out a final message for Quintos—a missive that would, undoubtedly, remain unread until it was too late.

Porter's mind raced as he wrestled with the weight of his own doubts. He wondered if the plan he had so meticulously crafted, the one that hinged on deception and misdirection, might be unraveling before it had even begun. He felt it in his gut... that Grish Pinnacle Fleet was looming ever closer, a relentless tide of destruction that threatened to engulf them all.

The Chief knew he needed to record his thoughts, albeit electronically, to provide a measure of finality for his old friend and Captain, Galvin Quintos. He was disheartened that they could not communicate, leaving them both in the dark at such a pivotal time. But it was essential for Quintos to grasp the extent of Alpha Fleet's endeavors. To comprehend the depths of Porter's resolve to cripple as many Grish forces as he could, despite the stark reality that it would likely prove a fruitless endeavor... especially if his friend would not be able to join them later in the fight.

The message began with a simple greeting, a brief preamble that belied the gravity of the situation:

Galvin,

If you're reading this, then I fear the worst has come to pass. I wanted to take a moment to share my thoughts with you, to offer some insight into the decisions I've made and the reasons behind them. I hope that, in some small way, this will provide you with a measure of comfort and understanding.

Porter's fingers paused, hovering above the keys as he gathered his thoughts. He continued, recounting the events that had led them to this fateful juncture:

The preparations for the Grish have been nothing short of Herculean. Ensign Blunderton and I have worked tirelessly to coordinate with the Alpha Fleet Captains, finally securing their agreement on a unified course of action. VD and his team have labored without rest, constructing decoy assembly sections and piecing them together with the aid of an army of droids. Our original goal was to build two hundred ultra-realistic, sensor-defying warships that would mimic the ships of Alpha Fleet. However, we fell short by 25 decoys, as the five-mile-long USS Washington-class Omninought decoy proved far more time-consuming than anticipated. Even so, the decoy fleet that has been assembled is an impressive sight to behold.

As he typed, Porter couldn't help but feel a sense of pride swell within him, a fleeting glimmer of hope that was swiftly extinguished by the cold, harsh reality of their predicament. The plan, as ingenious as it was, was riddled with flaws and uncertainties, any one of which could spell doom for Alpha Fleet and the countless lives that hung in the balance.

Ensign Blunderton has been instrumental in coordinating with Alpha Fleet Captains. The cloaking of the 'real' Alpha Fleet vessels, ensuring that their drive emissions, shields, and radiation signatures are minimized to prevent detection. Those ships that are not cloaking-capable have been interspersed within the decoy armada, much to the chagrin of their Captains. We will have them strategically placed, keeping a wide berth, so that any decoy explosions do not impede the fleet's mission. The Captains were skeptical at first, but, eventually, saw the logic in this strategy and reluctantly agreed to the plan.

Porter leaned back in his chair, his eyes scanning the words he had written thus far. He knew that he needed to convey the gravity of the situation, to impress upon Quintos the enormity of the task that lay before them. He steeled himself, summoning the resolve to continue...

I fear that our efforts may not be enough, Galvin. As you know, the Grish are cunning and ruthless, Pinnacle Fleet, undoubtedly, will be a force to be reckoned with. I've done everything within my limited powers to ensure some semblance of success—which, admittedly, isn't saying much coming from an Engineer... not a seasoned battle captain. Truth is, I cannot shake this gnawing feeling of doubt that has taken root within me, which very well may be from that questionable burrito I had replicated at lunch. I can only hope that, when the time comes, our deception will be enough, at the very least, to buy you some time... to conquer whichever enemy you will be facing. And if you can't make it back here to join me, well... Godspeed to us both.

As he wrote these words, Porter couldn't help but feel a sense of despair wash over him, a dark and all-consuming wave that threatened to drag him beneath its depths. He forced himself to continue, determined to see this message through to its conclusion...

I want you to know that... whatever the outcome, it's been one hell of a ride. I've been proud to serve alongside you and the rest of the fleet. You're one of the good guys, Galvin. I hope you find what you're looking for. And I mean that personally... beyond the endless demands of the U.S. Space Navy.

Yours sincerely,

Craig

With a heavy heart, Porter signed off on the message, then allowed his finger to linger over the SEND key for a moment. Before giving it another thought, he hit the DELETE key, instead.

"Fuck it, let the pieces fall where they fall... "

He rose from his seat and made his way to the bridge. He pushed aside his doubts and any lingering premonitions of defeat. It was game-time.

THE BRIDGE OF USS FRANKLIN HUMMED WITH anticipatory energy, thick with the weight of expectation, as if charged particles glistened between consoles—giving the compartment a pulsing life of its own.

Porter and Blunderton stood shoulder-to-shoulder, their postures rigid with expectation. Both were spellbound by the primary halo display before them. One hundred and seventy-five gargantuan faux Alpha Fleet ships splayed across the star-studded canvas of space. Each vessel appeared as a titan of war, bristling with the latent potency of weapon turrets that gleamed under the caress of thousands of glowing porthole windows—intermittent running lights blinked on and off in sequence, a hypnotic morse code of readiness that spoke volumes of the latent power readying to be unleashed. These silent behemoths, split into three mighty phalanxes conveyed an authority that, deceptively, was both regal and menacing—a mock fleet so devilishly realized that it just might send a ripple of trepidation through the ranks of their adversary. *Franklin's* own doppelgänger was there among them—the magnificent replica a dominating presence that dwarfed the others.

Chief Porter's chest swelled with pride as he considered this scarce crew's profound achievements. His gaze flitted toward Blunderton, her eyes blazing an emerald hue, mirroring the awe inspired by the mock fleet before them.

The real Alpha Fleet was cloaked and lying in wait—backed off as far as possible—their drive emissions curtailed to the very minimum and shields lowered to avoid any chance of detection. They too had broken into three distinct groups, each mirroring their respective decoy counterparts. Now, all they could do was wait and hope.

As the hours ticked by, the tension on the bridge continued to mount, a mounting pressure that threatened to snap at any moment. Finally, after what felt like an eternity, SARAH's voice filled the bridge, her calm, measured tones announcing the slow advance of the Grish Pinnacle Fleet.

The enemy ships were also cloaked, their approach as silent and deadly as any cautious predator would be stalking its prey. The bridgecrew held their collective breath, their eyes locked on the logistical halo display—phantom icon representations on the move.

It was Blunderton who finally broke the silence, her voice a triumphant cry that echoed through the bridge, "Yes!"

The halo display, updated in real-time, showed the Grish Armada, some 200 warships were now splitting off into three definitive groups—each advancing for an attack on a respective assemblage of decoys.

Porter's plan had hinged on this critical moment, the one action that would determine the success or failure of their entire operation. He had insisted on minimal comms traffic, relying instead on the fake comms signals generated by the decoy ships to maintain the illusion of a genuine U.S. Space Navy Armada. The secret signal to attack the Grish would be USS *Franklin's* own commencing of Phazon Pulsar, rail cannon fire, and deployment of smart fusion missiles.

As the Grish finalized their ghost-like advance on the decoy fleet, unaware that they too were being invisibly stalked, Porter waited, sweat beading on his forehead. He knew that the moment of truth had arrived—the instant when the enemy would be the most distracted—and with a little luck, would be more confident than they should be.

The Grish attack came in a simultaneous three-pronged assault—missiles and railgun fire raining down on the decoys and several real warships. Porter's voice cut through the chaos, his order to SARAH to commence firing on the unsuspecting enemy, a clarion call to arms.

"It's game-time," Lana Voss murmured. Her sinewy frame and intricate circuitry tattoos gave her a badass vibe.

The rest of the real, totally outnumbered Alpha Fleet,

followed suit, their cloaked vessels jumping in practically on top of the enemy as the three clusters of U.S. Space Navy, Thine, and Pleidian warships unleashed a withering barrage of firepower. USS *Franklin*, as planned, moved throughout the battlespace unrestrained, unleashing everything the less-than-fully operational omninought could throw at the enemy.

The battle that ensued was ferocious, a maelstrom of fire and fury that seemed to engulf the very stars themselves. The Grish caught off guard and reeling from the sudden onslaught, quickly lost several dozen warships in the opening salvo. However, it wasn't long before they realized that they had been duped, their initial shock giving way to cold, calculating wrath.

Reorienting their massive warships, some of which measured a mile or two in length, was no easy task. It required both time and distance, precious commodities that were in short supply. But soon *Franklin* bore the brunt of the enemy's countermeasures. The big omninought, the largest vessel amongst Alpha Fleet by far, soon became the target of choice for the Grish, their relentless barrage quickly taking a heavy toll on the ship's defenses.

The skinny old veteran, Rigel Park, stood up from his station and gave the halo display a two-handed middle finger bird. "Fuck you piglets!"

An overhead Klaxon blared. SARAH's voice, once a steady and reassuring presence, now rang out with urgency as she announced one breached deck after another.

Porter's skeletal bridgecrew scrambled between stations, their movements a blur of efficiency borne from a singular focus. No words were exchanged, none were needed—they operated as a singular entity, unified in cold determination to withstand the onslaught.

· · ·

THE BATTLE RAGED ON, AND PORTER COULDN'T HELP but wonder if their efforts could... possibly... be enough to turn the tide—or if they were merely delaying the inevitable. Too early to tell.

The fate of Alpha Fleet, hell, the Alliance, hung in the balance, teetering on the edge of a knife. As *Franklin* continued to fight, her hull groaning under the relentless assault—acrid-smelling smoke now hovered a foot off the deck plates. Porter clung to the hope that their sacrifice would not be in vain, that their actions would be enough to ensure the survival of those they had sworn to protect. What he did know... this once proud and formidable omninought was literally being torn, apart piece by piece.

Precariously seated at Tactical, Porter gripped the edges of his console, his knuckles turning white as he witnessed the unfolding destruction before his eyes. Suddenly, the battle had taken a devastating turn, Alpha Fleet was being systematically decimated by the relentless onslaught of the Grish Fleet.

Blunderton, seated upon the Captain's Mount's armrest, gasped—USS *Capital Fight*, a once sleek and powerful dread-nought had burst into a tremendous fireball—falling victim to three in close-pursuit enemy destroyers, with their relentless, overwhelming firepower. She realized with the fall of that dreadnought, Captain Longmont would have perished as well. No time to reflect on losses.

Porter's attention turned to a barrage of plasma fire tearing through another U.S. Space Navy vessel, USS *Foresight*, it seemed as though her shields had crashed—bolts of enemy fire were slicing into her hull like a hot knife through butter. *Foresight's* power-plant flickered and then died, leaving the once-mighty vessel adrift and defenseless. A final volley of railgun fire from a Grish battle cruiser ripped through her mid-ship, undoubtedly obliterating her bridge, and like USS *Capital Fight,* just moments prior, the warship was engulfed in her own equally magnificent ball of flame—silencing her valiant crew forever.

Jansen Tycho, his normally gaunt features even more haggard-looking, hurried over to another station. "We got an out-of-control fire raging on Deck 23."

Lana added, "SARAH will initiate fire suppression—"

"Uh... no, that wasn't fixed back at Halibart," Tycho said ruefully.

As Alpha Fleet wreckage tumbled and drifted lifelessly, the Grish turned their attention to USS *Dragon Fire*. Porter knew the warship's Captain, Vince Garrity. Garrity was a seasoned veteran and, as such, he maneuvered with skill and precision, attempting to evade the onslaught. But the enemy's firepower was simply too overwhelming as fusion smart missiles quickly gained on his attempt to flee the pursuing frigate—*Dragon Fire* seemed to absorb the strikes... but soon the enemy's force buckled the ship's armor plating like a stepped-on soda can.

Porter could only imagine the ensuing chaos unfolding within *Dragon Fire's* corridors as DeckGate bulkheads automatically slammed shut, sealing off breached sections—sentencing scores of crewmembers to the cold vacuum of space. Despite the momentary reprieve, the ship's main reactor finally succumbed to catastrophic inflicted damage—detonating in a brilliant flash that consumed *Dragon Fire,* this time in a blinding sphere of superheated plasma.

Porter's heart dropped as he continued to witness the battle's apparent conclusion—this fight was almost over.

SARAH was, for the most part, fighting this battle. The ship's AI was far and away the most advanced, quantum-level tech to ever come out of EUNF's think-tank labs. Not so much having given up, more like resigned himself to the inevitable— Porter took a seat at the Captain's Mount, while, next to him,

Blunderton remained seated on the armrest. Neither spoke—what was there to say?

He'd released full helm control of USS *Franklin* to SARAH as well. The ship moved within what was commonly referred to as *the fog of war*. Reminiscent of the trench warfare of WWI, where heavy mist, along with smoke, obscured the battlefield to the point that one could hardly see who they were firing at—friend or foe. The battlespace here within the void wasn't much different. A virtual scrapyard of dead and dying blown-apart warships, some venting atmosphere, others charred beyond recognition. And then there were the tumbling frozen bodies—Grish, Human, Pleidian, and Thine...

Ensign Blunderton suddenly stood up, took a step closer to the primary halo display.

Porter too had been taken by surprise by what seemed to be unfolding before them. *Franklin* had picked up speed and was accelerating within the battlespace at a breakneck, unsafe, heart-pounding velocity. Another turreted cannon, almost as large as one of their Broadside cannons, had come alive.

She looked to Porter, "Is that the one code-named, *Singularity Lance?*"

All he could do was nod, and watch. His stomach lurched as the massive ship's engines rumbled the deck plates, inertial dampeners struggling to keep the extreme g-forces at bay. Klaxons continued to blare and echo off in distant corridors.

Ensign Blunderton staggered, having to grab onto the Tactical Station for support—while Porter dropped heavily back into the Captain's Mount. All had their eyes locked onto the primary halo projection—on the nightmarish scene unfolding before them. Debris and twisted wreckage from fallen ships tumbled past in a blur like cosmic shrapnel, reminders of the perils they now hurtled toward at reckless, ungodly speeds. But none of that could distract them from what else was happening.

Franklin—no SARAH—was *somehow* taking the Grish forces by storm. The Singularity Lance, along with each Phazon Pulsar and rail cannon on the ship, had been activated—all were firing.

Every one of the bridge's halo displays had come to life. Each video feed provided a different vantage point of the ensuing battle.

VD's hulk-like frame slowly rose from his seat. "There's a target lock on every remaining Grish asset."

Porter already knew as much, seeing the bright green bounding boxes strategically snapping into place over the enemy ships.

"It's happening so fast..." Blunderton said. "It's as if SARAH's been... possessed."

"I don't care if she's been possessed by Satan himself, as long as it doesn't stop," Porter said.

The numbers climbing on the logistical display held Porter's stare, enemy casualties rapidly mounting and at an unbelievable pace. This battle was quickly coming to an unexpected conclusion.

Chapter 53

"Mr. Chen, open a shipwide channel."

After a moment, the Comms Officer nodded, "You're live, Captain."

"This is your Captain speaking..."

I paused, now second-guessing the rehearsed speech I'd prepared. Sure, it was filled with all the trite motivational buzz-words. Assurances that we'd faced tough times before and not just survived, but prevailed. Declarations of *USS Washington* as a titan among vessels, possibly the fiercest the Alliance had ever produced. Proclamations of unwavering confidence in my crew...

I now looked at my bridgecrew. My eyes coming to rest on my XO. I briefly wondered what thoughts were behind those pretty blue eyes. What did this version of Gail Pristy want out of life? And did that include me?

"This is for all the marbles, folks," I said. "It all comes down to this day, this hour... this moment in time. As the battle before us commences, I want you to remember something. Yes, of course, remember your loved ones back home, wherever home is for you, but I want you to remember yourself as a young child. The impractical, hopeful, and probably naive, expectations you had for your future. Some of you may have wanted to follow in a parent's footsteps and become a fireman, a doctor, or maybe be amongst the crew of an intergalactic starship. Now I want you to imagine that same child lost, wandering a desolate, ravaged dark world on the brink. Where Armageddon had arrived and stolen every man, woman, and child's dream. That is what the Grish want for you. That is what awaits that beautiful blue jewel of a world we call home amongst the stars lightyears away from us now."

I hesitated once more. Looked up to Hardy—where he stood stoic, contemplative. "Hardy, do you have anything you'd like to add to the crew?"

"Not much. Think you covered things fairly well. Just that it's high time we introduce ourselves to these pig-faced sons of bitches, let them rue the day they ever fucked with the Alliance."

"And then there's that too," I said with a crooked smile. I signaled for Chen to cut the channel.

"SARAH, bring us to battle stations."

A Klaxon wailed down from above.

Battle stations...
Battle stations....
All personnel prepare for battle.

I spun around, making deliberate eye contact with each of my bridgecrew. "You got this people."

Spinning back forward I let out a measured breath.

Pristy was looking back at me. With the ghost of a smile, just loud enough for me to hear, she said "And you've got this too, Captain."

"Mr. Grimes..." I said with gusto, "Jump us into position."

No sooner had the words left my lips than the starfield on the viewscreen distorted, folding in on itself as *Washington's* jump springs engaged. In a matter of moments, the blackness resolved into a scene of profound trepidation.

Two massive Grish dreadnoughts hung suspended in the inky void, their hulls adorned with ranks of gun turrets glimmering like obsidian fangs. Beyond this imposing vanguard, off in the distance, a constellation of crimson beacons winked ominously—the mighty Star Guns, whose inescapable targeting systems were primed to skewer any approaching vessel.

Despite the doom-laden vista, my heart swelled at the flashing status lights indicating the imminent launch of the Arrow fighter squadrons. A smile played across my lips as the first telemetry data began filtering through. Ready or not, this battle was underway.

Chen's voice cut through the tension as he spoke to the squad commanders. I could just make out faint voices, the excited banter, Arrow pilots giving each other shit. I might have even heard J-Dog and Ballbuster in the mix.

My gaze was suddenly locked onto the fiery plumes trailing behind them, brilliant blue and amber flames slicing through the emptiness as the first crimson Arrow Fighters rocketed out from the primary flight bay. My heart missed a beat, it only took a fraction of a second for me to assess their trajectories—their velocity was far too extreme to make the abrupt fishhook maneuver. I wanted to scream for them to throttle down, to yell out loud enough so that my voice would carry through *Washington's* hull, out into the soundless void, and into each of their cockpits. But no words escaped my open mouth.

The hush of held breaths was shattered by piercing cries of anguish as those first Arrows failed to execute the maneuver, plowing into the obsidian flank of the portside dreadnought in a cataclysmic bloom of fire and debris. For an interminable moment, the bridgecrew could only gape in mute horror.

The following Arrows adjusted and compensated, making the near-impossible maneuver, avoiding a similar catastrophe by mere feet. In rapid succession, the squadrons from each flight bay launched into the heart of the now erupting crossfire. With breathtaking precision, they wove through the deadly onslaught, accelerating into elaborate starburst attack patterns to unleash fury on their awaiting Star Gun targets.

"Arrow squadrons: Shadowstrike, Thunderbolt, Nightwing, Sunburst, and Ghostwind, initiating maneuvers," Lieutenant Hargreaves announced from Flight Control.

"Broadsides coming online!" Pristy's shout shattered the stillness as the first tremors of *Washington's* primary weapons spooling up reverberated up through the deck plating.

"Enemy dreadnoughts rail cannons are coming online!" Davit called out from Defensive Systems. "Shields at maximum!"

The ultra-realistic three-dimensional halo display made me flinch, fists clenching white-knuckled, as plasma fire lances slashed toward us, only to erupt incandescently against our ship's rippling energy shields.

"Firing portside Broadsides!"

The deck juddered underfoot as *Washington's* primaries roared in a deafening rhythm. I watched, teeth clenched, as the first salvo detonated squarely along the all-too-close dreadnought's armored flank. Geysers of plasma and shredded armor vomited into the void, trailing tails of flickering light—debris and bodies tumbling in the cyclonic wakes.

Although still in one piece, one enemy warship was done—down for the count.

Yet as raw cheers of defiance burst from the crew, retaliatory strikes pounded *Washington* from the one remaining Grish dreadnought. Plasma bolts and swift rail projectiles ignited *Washington's* shields in vivid energized spasms of stress.

"Starboard Broadsides!" I snapped the order, but the words withered on my lips as Pristy was already shaking her head, jaw set.

"Down! Starboard Broadsides offline!"

SARAH's dispassionate announcement joined the din of chaos...

Multiple hull breaches across starboard flanks. Damage control teams responding...

Lurid status graphics came into view across the auxiliary halo projections as the omninought twisted and bucked under a renewed onslaught. A visceral wave of dread washed over me, the gravity of our predicament taking hold.

More halo displays flickered to life at Pristy's command. Shadowstrike Arrow Squadron was now engaging the nearest Star Gun fortification. The cockpit camera feed instantly had me mesmerized. For a moment, I wanted to be out there, hands on the controls, at one with a nimble fighter, in the thick of things.

It was a duel, reciprocating crimson and azure energy bolts of plasma scorching through the darkness in a blinding frenzy. At the heart of the battlefield, the swarm of angry Arrow Fighters jutted and twisted in complex, ever-shifting geometries as they dueled with the towering lone Star Gun.

"Captain!"

My attention was still locked onto Shadowstrike's fervorous attempt to take out the big gun.

"Galvin!"

Pristy's shout lanced through the miasma of my darkening thoughts. "Railguns are down! We've got Phazon Pulsars taking up the slack but they're already redlining!"

Acrid smoke was now drifting onto the bridge—the haze making my eyes burn. Trying to swallow, my throat felt scorched as if I'd inhaled a lungful of hot embers. A glance around the bridge told me that others, closer to the point of origin, were more drastically affected; some crewmembers were clutching their throats, collapsing at their stations.

"Dammit! Incapacitate that dreadnought. Aim for her drives—one full-on blast. All starboard Phazon cannons. XO, calculate a firing solution and make it count."

"Already on it."

Pristy's deft hands flew across her tactical board while coordinating via Chen to the gunnery teams keeping the big, overheating, energy cannons operational.

"Ready on your command, Sir!"

"Stand by....." I raked my gaze across the primary display, eyes locked onto the aft section of the enemy warship. Without a doubt this move will have been anticipated, my counterpart, the Grish Captain similarly staring back at *Washington,* no doubt snarling, *Go ahead... take your best shot, human.*

"Fire," I said, my voice barely loud enough for my XO to hear me.

Simultaneously, the Grish dreadnought fired its own concentrated salvo of plasma bolts, but not toward our aft section, our drives, but toward *Washington's* towering Circadian Platform—they were targeting our bridge.

The sheer magnitude—the intensity of crisscrossing weapons fire—was both daunting and thrilling.

"Their shields are holding. But ours are too," Pristy said.

I stood, moved in close enough to the primary display to touch it. "Give me a new firing solution. Concentrate there. On the dreadnought's venting arrays, here, here, and... here!"

"Okay, I'll need a second," she said.

The first azure lances flashed outward, a rippling stutter of *Washington's* Phazon Pulsar Cannons assailing the new targets.

"Grimes! Get us moving! We need some dist—"

But the crewman's grimace cut me off. "Can't do it, Sir. The dreadnought's adjusting its position—it's maneuvering to maintain a parallel course."

The overhead Klaxon blared. SARAH's voice droned on with ominous efficiency. Another deck had just been breached.

I stifled a curse, dread and desperation filling my mouth like bile, while my eyes scanned multiple halos. I settled on the logistical readout. The ship had sustained damage in excess of thirty percent across various sectors, and the true test of our endurance had not even commenced.

Perspiration now glistened on Grimes's forehead as the Helmsman struggled breathlessly to distance us from the enemy dreadnought.

"Jorkins!" I yelled, "Have Engineering and Propulsion divert auxiliary power to our jump springs. This trading punches crap isn't working."

The young Engineer's reply was funereal. "Negative, Sir. Jump springs share power with our downed Broadsides. We're restricted to sub-light maneuvering for the time being."

I swallowed hard, feeling the first icy trickles of fear snake down my spine as the totality of our plight settled in. We were cut off and crippled, facing down a capital-grade dreadnought while desperately trying to neutralize a network of unmanned, semi-intelligent defense platforms designed to slaughter everything in their path.

I stole a glance at Pristy, the XO's face a rictus of intensity and focus. Even as her console strobed with cascading warnings of incoming weapons fire, she was still attempting to gain a tactical advantage over the enemy.

I knew the answer before the question left my lips. "Fusion tipped missiles?" I uttered, the words scraping from my throat like shards of broken glass.

"Negative!" Pristy shook her head, sweat-slicked wisps of hair whipping across her brow. "What are you crazy? Way too close for nukes!"

Suddenly, a tremendous concussion shuddered through the bridge, staggering some crewmembers, while pitching me off my feet.

Davit's panicked voice cut through the bedlam like a banshee's wail. "Starboard shields at twenty percent and falling... Venting atmosphere..."

I pulled myself to my feet and surveyed the scattered bodies out in the Rotunda. Crewmembers had been flung across the expanse, several of their corpses now smoldering. The air filled with screams and smoke as the sound of DeckGate bulkheads was now sealing off breached sections.

It was bordering on being too late, but it was time for desperate measures. I didn't think it would even help at this point... but we had to try.

"Hardy," I said. "I've got Max and his team standing by in the Quansporter compartment. Get over there. It's time you and the team make a little unannounced visit to our neighboring dreadnought friends. You know what you have to do."

Hardy was already moving towards the exit, the big robot's footfalls ringing like the peals of a death knell.

I called after him, "I want live feeds!"

Hardy didn't reply, just continued his implacable stride toward the ravaged Gravity Well beyond. I just hoped the Quansporter was still operational.

I wrenched my attention back to the unfolding catastrophe splayed across multiple halo displays. Arrow squadrons had managed to neutralize a mere seven of the enemy Star Guns—doing so at the cost of thirty Arrows. Plasma salvos continued tracking with remorseless, inhuman precision.

Ryder's voice, tinny but resolute, crackled across the comms amid a barrage of static. "...found a solution... the regulators! Target the power regulators at the base of each turret! It'll take no less than five consecutive strikes to bring a Star Gun down!"

As if to underscore Ryder's words, the latest casualty tallies flickered into gut-wrenching existence—only two hundred and twelve Arrows remained operational out of the initial force of three hundred and seventy-five.

Pristy swung around to face Jorkins, her face contorted into a snarl of reprehension. "What do you mean, limited power? Get your fat ass over to E&P. You need to personally tell them to reroute power from the tertiary grid. Point a tagger at them if you have to, dammit! We need power to our starboard side or we're all screwed. Got it!?"

Jorkins recoiled from the XO's tirade getting to his feet. Stumbling, he sprinted for the exit as SARAH's implacable voice continued to rattle off a litany of damage reports:

Structural compromises across Deck 12 through Deck 17. Sealing off affected sectors...

I watched almost dispassionately as the logistical display updated with further Arrow losses.

"What the...?"

The words were barely out of my mouth before I realized

what I was seeing. Hardy's faceplate camera was transmitting directly to the primary halo display. The big robot moved with the same implacable strides, flanked by Max and his Marines. Dark figures, armed with heavy shredders, moved through the corridors, their forms illuminated by the flickering amber lights and smoke.

SARAH had their superimposed names following along as if tied to them by invisible strings.

"What the hell!" I balked.

As if seeing her name wasn't enough, Laramie's graceful, slender form stood out amid the armored bulks of Grip, Wanda, Ham, and Hock. I felt a surge of anger at the sight, realizing the young Petty Officer must have stowed away with the team despite my express orders not to.

The team moved fast within the enemy dreadnought. All five of Hardy's plasma cannons had been deployed from their hidden compartments—suddenly coming alive in a torrent of brilliantly energized flashes as an armed team of Grish combatants came into view at an intersecting corridor. Suddenly, more and more piglets were pouring in from three sides, their weapons fire so bright Hardy's video feed momentarily distorted. The team was taking it from all sides, with nowhere to escape. Sudden ordnance detonations flashed with the ensuing engagement. More than a few piglet bodies went airborne.

Hardy's cannons thundered, the staccato of their discharge audible, albeit muted, from the halo display. At one point, catching Max's feed, I caught sight of Hardy's faceplate... there, a whimsical game of Pong was in progress—two white paddles jutted up and down vertically, batting a lone dot... back and forth it went across the black background.

"Idiot," I said with a smirk.

An ominous tremor came up through the deck plates. *Washington's* battered frame shuddered and groaned under one more relentless barrage. My breath hitched as I caught sight of the omninought's undulating aurora of her shields blinked out completely, *Washington's* armored flanks now laid bare to the merciless turrets and guns of the Grish dreadnought.

"Damage report!" I could barely hear my own words over the rising thrum of hammered bulkheads and explosive decompressions.

Crewmember Soto's reply at Damage Control was curt and utterly without hope. "We're open to hard vacuum across forty percent of the outer hull. Structural integrity is failing."

SARAH's voice rang out, for once tinged with what could only be desperation.

All hands...
Brace for impact...
All hands...
Brace for impact...

I caught sight of a torn-away ship section—not sure if it originated from omninought or dreadnought—cartwheeling end over end, wreathed in tongues of escaping atmosphere. As if in slow motion, the exposed structure with partially exposed decks, passageways, and corridors, tumbled ever closer. I instinctively took a step away from the primary display.

Pristy said, "Yeah, go ahead, take a step back. Sure, that'll save you."

A chuckle nearly escaped me in the bizarre calm of disaster. My gaze locked on the colossal chunk of metal grazing the Circadian Platform's flank, where our bridge nestled. With a resounding *CLANG,* the impact sent me sprawling. Sitting on the deck, I watched the behemoth deflect and spiral off into a new path.

I could hear Pristy calling my name. She pointed at one of the halo displays. And in that interminable moment, with the darkness closing in around us, I saw Hardy's form through the swirling pall of smoke. Max's feed was back, and piglet bodies were... well, everywhere. Clearly, the enemy had not been prepared for being boarded.

Max was issuing orders to his team, then the Sergeant removed something from his pack. Grip did the same. I saw that both were now holding explosive ordnances.

Max's voice was cool, calm, and all business, "Approaching the bridge now... just a heads up, Captain... if you're catching this feed. We're going to drop off some gifts for the kiddies and amscray the fuck out of here. Coogong, be ready to quansport us out of here on my mark."

Coogong's voice came next, "Roger that, Sergeant."

Max, his voice much louder now, yelled, "Coogong! Get us out of here!"

All but one of the 12 halo displays flickered and went dark.

Grime's voice broke in, "We've got jump springs back online!"

"Get us out of here, Helm!"

The enemy dreadnought was already aglow—like a mythical fire-breathing dragon, suddenly consumed by its own internal combustion. The Grish beast was erupting, exploding before our eyes—just as *Washington* was being consumed within its radiating hellfire.

And then... we jumped.

Epilogue

Drakoria Star System
USS Washington

Captain Galvin Quintos

our days later, *USS Washington* wasn't going anywhere. Her hull was riddled with innumerable breaches along her starboard side, resembling a block of Swiss cheese more than an Omninought-class Warship. Critical departments had sustained heavy damage, including Engineering & Propulsion, Environmental Control, and Weapons Systems, just to name a few. But like her sister ship, *USS Franklin*, having an on-board replications facility down on Deck 6, allowed for repairs to get underway now, versus the necessity to be towed to the nearest starbase. I seriously doubted *Washington* would be salvageable in the long run— which I found sad, she had performed admirably, beyond anyone's expectations.

But my heavy heart went further than just the ship—during the ordeal here within the Drakoria Star System, 253 valiant souls aboard *Washington* had perished, and nearly 100 Arrow pilots met their eternal drift into the abyss.

Stationary just beyond Drakoria Star System's farthest outlying world of Calydon, that forbidden primordial exoplanet, *Washington's* crew remained on high alert. Lone piglet warships, even battle groups, still lurked beyond the star system. With that said the interstellar legions of the Grish, once a match for the Alliance's prowess, now laid waste across the cosmos. Their foremost triad of fleets—*Prowess, Torrent, and Pinnacle*—had been decimated. With what *Washington* had accomplished here, added to that of Alpha Fleet, with *Franklin* at the vanguard at the rendezvous point—we had dealt the decisive strike, the coup de grâce, to the once mighty Grish war machine.

Yesterday's arrival of USS *Franklin* into the system along with what remained of Alpha Fleet, a mere 15 warships, had prompted a wave of exhilaration through the crew.

Chen played a prerecorded congratulatory communique shipwide from Admiral Gomez. Raucous cheering filtered in from somewhere beyond. Gomez let the crew know that every nation was already gearing up for Alpha Fleet's eventual homecoming. That and word had spread—retrieval of the *Statue of Liberty had* only fueled the frenzy dirtside. A grand unveiling ceremony was penciled in for later in the year, Lady Liberty's reforged form would grace the New York skyline once more. Gomez went on to say that after decades of relentless war, and hard-fought victories across the cosmos, Earth's two most formidable enemies had finally been beaten down to a mere shadow of their former glory.

Soon after Admiral Gomez ended the announcement, Chen informed me that President Block would be calling in within the hour. That I was to assemble my direct-report officers and be ready to discuss the plight of the Grish homeworld of Drakoria.

HEAT SWAMPED THE CAPTAIN'S CONFERENCE Room, a testament to the Environmental Systems' persistent malfunctions. Hardy deemed Climbo's presence essential. So, the ChronoBot stood next to the mechanical mule, in contrast to the rest of us, who were tightly packed around the table.

Pristy had opted to sit next to me at the table, an encouraging sign that things may be thawing between us, while Chief Craig Porter took the seat on the other side of me. Stephan Derrota and Coogong sat across from us. Others around the table included Captain Wallace Ryder, Lieutenant Akari James, SWM Chief LaSalle, HealthBay Chief Knott, and other U.S. Space Navy personnel, including, Kaelen Rivers, Petty Officer Second-Class, Aubrey Laramie, and Ensign Roisin Blunderton, who I'd never met, but Craig had requested her presence. Just now entering the compartment were Sergeant Max Dyer and Chaplain Halman Trent, who most definitely had not been invited—at least by me. Another attendee, though not visible at the table, was my niece Sonya, undoubtedly perched in her upper deck niche, her ears surely tuned to the meeting through a hacked security feed. I had no issue with her listening in, provided our conversation didn't delve into sensitive depths.

The festive mood prevailed as we waited for the caller of this meeting, President Block, to appear on the halo display. It had been years since my friend Craig Porter and I had caught up, I'd missed him. As the arrival of President Block was close to an hour late, Craig was provided an opportunity to elaborate on what had transpired on *USS Franklin*, how his few, less-than-conventional, crewmembers had pulled off the impossible.

That's when Craig's eyes swiveled to the auburn-haired

Ensign, sitting quietly, not making conversation with anyone else. Then his gaze shifted to me. "Galvin... not everything that transpired those few days was, shall we say... by the book."

I hitched a shoulder, "I'd be the last person to be a stickler—"

"No, man... this eclipses your penchant for dismissing a ChronoBot's shenanigans or even your penchant for cycling through warships more often than the rest of us change our socks."

I felt the urge to object but I stayed quiet. *I change my socks far more often than I go through warship assets.*

He continued, "Galvin... things onboard that ship were crazy. It was a miracle we'd even made it to the rendezvous point to intersect with Alpha Fleet."

"Impressive job," I remarked. "Your actions could very well have altered the war's trajectory. That's all in my report to the higher-ups. Brace yourself for some well-deserved recognition, maybe even a step up the ranks."

"I couldn't care less about any of that." His eyes flicked back to the woman with emerald eyes. "When we arrived at the rendezvous point, the fleet was a mess. The infighting was like nothing I'd ever witnessed. There was no way this group of misfits was ever going to come together as a cohesive team."

"Obviously, you changed that. Brought them together."

Porter made a face. "Me? *Pfft.* It wasn't me... It was her. They listened to Blunderton."

As I assessed the Ensign, undoubtedly now aware of my scrutiny, she was smoothing out wrinkles on her already perfectly pressed uniform with the palms of her hands. I'd seen repetitive OCD behavior before—the young woman was clearly dealing with some issues.

"The thing is, she may have led a few of the skippers to

believe she was, well... a higher-ranked officer. Um, a Captain, in fact."

I found myself momentarily at a loss for words. "She impersonated being a U.S. Space Navy Captain?"

Porter didn't bother answering, simply letting out a resigned breath.

I lowered my voice, "Does anyone else know?"

He nodded. "Yes... well, probably. We'll see if any of the Alpha Fleet Captains run a complaint up the flagpole. Galvin, she could be looking at a court-martial. Hell, she could go to jail. I could too."

I sat back and let all that sink in. Craig was right. The two of them were, well, fucked if this got out. There again, I'd probably done worse. Hadn't I left my U.S. Space Navy commission to become a rogue pirate for several years? But I always had Empress Shawlee Tee on my side. I honestly didn't see any way out of this for the two of them.

Momentarily startled, I heard a crackling in my left ear. Like all U.S. Space Navy personnel, I'd been surgically outfitted with an auditory comms implant right out of the Academy. But they'd proven to be more annoying than useful, TAC-Bands becoming the preferred communications means over the years. Most of us have long forgotten that the devices were even present.

Sonya was speaking to me. No hello. No, excuse me, this is your niece speaking. Just Sonya being Sonya...

"I may have a solution to your friend's dilemma."

Knowing she was looking at me via a security feed, I simply raised my brows.

The teenager chuckled, "You know what's weird about that Ensign... she's like, beyond a recluse. Very few friends, if any. No GalacticWeb social media presence..."

"What's your point?" I asked.

As both Porter and Blunderton looked at me, I waved a dismissive hand.

"I can make her a Captain."

I glanced upward, seeking the security camera monitoring my movements. Spotting it, my gaze sharpened, silently warning Sonya to proceed with caution.

"I'm already tapped into her government personnel file. It's sparse. Almost as if she's gone out of her way to stay anonymous, a ghost."

I whispered, as if that would make a difference, and said, "I don't like this..."

I could hear Sonya's tapping fingers. "This is going to work. Now, there is zero chance a lackluster Ensign, just three years out of the academy is going to suddenly skip six rank grades to Captain. That is, unless... she'd actually enlisted two years prior to that. So now she's a young-looking twenty-nine-year-old. And, lo and behold, she's proven herself on multiple occasions, saving a shuttle crew of four from dying in a vacuum breach. And did you know she took down a Varapin Cyclone Death Fighter single-handedly? That was some great Shredder shooting on her part. Let's see... this is interesting, she came up with an attack strategy that led to the allied invasion of an enemy starbase. Oh, and finally, Blunderton now has more hand-written letters of recognition than General George S. Patton in her file."

The halo display at the center of the table flickered. I had a feeling the meeting was about to start. Under my breath, I said, "I don't know about this, Sonya..."

But she was still talking. "What I suppose is most shocking about this stellar officer, is that with all the medals and accommodations, rank promotions... they've been held up by EUNF red tape and bureaucratic bottlenecks. And while she's been hard at work as an 'acting' U.S. Space Navy Captain, she needs

Admiral Gomez to do his damn job, sign the paperwork—paperwork that just so happened to land within his virtual mailbox this very second."

I felt a cantaloupe-sized knot forming in my stomach. "And none of this will ever come back to bite you, or me, in the ass?"

Again, both Blunderton and Porter looked at me.

"I have no idea what you're talking about. Your fingerprints aren't anywhere near this. I was never here talking to you about it. Bye Uncle person, and by the way, you now owe me big time." She clicked off.

I looked to Porter. "It's taken care of."

Blunderton's repetitive wrinkle-smoothing motions had become more pronounced.

Looking at her, I said, "It's now just a paperwork mishap. Don't make me regret what's been done here... Captain Blunderton."

The woman's captivating green eyes blinked several times as comprehension set in. Her face drained of whatever color it had had previously. She looked to Porter and then back to me. "Thank you, Captain. I promise... I won't let you down."

THE HOLOGRAPHIC FORM MATERIALIZING AT THE table's center wasn't President Block or Admiral Gomez, but Empress Shawlee Tee herself. Gone was the combat suit hugging her frame from our previous encounter.

Guilt washed over me. I was unable to communicate with her. Find out if the Wrinnth had returned to finish her—her homeworlds—off. To say I was relieved she emerged unscathed would be a gross understatement.

I heard a surprised intake of breath from Blunderton. Barely audible, she commented, "She's so beautiful."

Empress Shawlee Tee of the Pleidian Weonan Empire was

indeed a striking beauty. I took in her softly glowing blue-hued skin. Her unique oval head, open in the center like an elegant torus, intelligent eyes along the outer rim and her nose and mouth gracefully positioned at the lower edge. Her long blonde hair reminiscent of a human woman, was currently worn long, cascading over her shoulders.

Her eyes scanned the faces around the table, coming to rest on mine. "Captain Quintos... Galvin." Her smile widened, her eyes glistened, looking ready to overflow. "How many times in one lifetime can I thank you—the way you always seem to come along, helping save the day."

I shrugged. "Well, we were in the neighborhood."

A flurry of chuckles rippled around the table.

"And Chief Porter," she continued. "Thank you for stepping up and destroying Grish's Pinnacle Fleet. The hoops you must've jumped through, well, it's nothing short of miraculous."

His cheeks colored as he absorbed the compliment.

"All of you. Thank you from the bottom of my two hearts. You will be in my—*all* of Pleidian Weonan's—thoughts and prayers for a long time. Bless you."

She tilted her head, a bemused expression on her lips. "I suppose Captain Quintos, you'll be requiring a new Omni-nought-class Warship to replace *Washington*?"

Before I could answer, the Empress's majestic form had faded from view.

President Block's craggy, frowning face took her place. I'd already spoken to the President several times these last few days, so I wasn't all that sure why this officer's meeting was even necessary. But it wasn't for me to second-guess the Commander in Chief.

"Let me get right to it, people. We have some hard choices to make. None of them are pretty. All are necessary."

"What kind of choices?" I asked, perplexed.

Pristy rolled her eyes. "Maybe if you stop talking he'll tell us." She gave me the hint of a smile. "Go ahead, Mr. President. We're all ears."

"Thank you, XO Pristy." Block looked to be choosing his next words carefully. "The United States operates as a Federal Republic. A Democracy. I work for that Republic, as do you. America and the other nations of Earth have suffered greatly at the hands of our enemies. The Varapin and the Grish. And while we are on better terms with the Varapin. They *did* apologize... for whatever that gets us. The Grish have not. These United States have made it abundantly clear that the Grish need to pay for what they have done."

There were nods and murmurs of agreement all around the table.

"Good. It looks like we have agreement in that regard," Block said.

I narrowed my eyes. "What exactly does this have to do with us, Sir?"

"Today. Within hours, all major cities, government facilities, and military bases on Drakoria are to be wiped from the face of that world."

No one spoke. No one so much as scratched their chin.

"Mr. President, taking counter-measures against an enemy's military infrastructure is one thing—"

The Admiral looked me dead in the eye. "Regrettably, my reference to our democratic way of life didn't extend to the workings of military command."

Pristy and I exchanged a look. Neither of us liked where this was going.

"Sir. We don't operate like that. It was horrendous when the Grish and Varapin attacked civilian locations on Earth, and it would be just as horrendous for us to do the same here."

The President's voice was stern. "War is never pretty, and

it's high time you all remember something—" He leaned forward, locking eyes with both me and Pristy. "Unless we unleash a hellstorm on those Grish bastards, they'll just regroup and come at us twice as hard next time 'round."

Stephan Derrota squared in his seat—his pained expression was mirrored by most of the others around the table. He lifted a hand, "Sir... Mr. President?"

Block's typical expression of annoyance softened some looking back at the mild-mannered scientist. "Yes, Stephan, you have a question?"

Derrota hesitated, then asked, "Can it be up to us? To the crew of USS *Washington* on how that... um, hellstorm as you put it, is unleashed upon the masses?"

The President contemplated on that for a moment. He shrugged. "This is best left to your military officers. I suppose it would be acceptable for those there on the front lines, so to speak, to come to that determination. But to put it bluntly, we are looking for retribution in kind. None of us can forget, that Earth lost millions over the course of this war. I want this done, and I want this done today. Have I made myself clear?"

Blank stares and a few slow nods answered back.

"Excellent. Block out."

Minutes after President Block's projected image had faded into the ether, no one spoke for three full beats.

"Stephan?" I finally asked. "Why were you interested in the methodology we'd be using for the attack on Drakoria? I know this aspect of serving on a U.S. Space Navy warship makes you uncomfortable...."

He nodded, "To say the least. Still, the President makes a good point. I was just wondering if there was an alternate means of dispensing, um... justice. You know, without deploying fusion-tipped missiles, or firing Phazon Pulsar bolts into city centers. All of which is quite extreme."

I winced at how barbaric that sounded coming from my friend.

"You have a better idea, Stephan?" Pristy asked in a sympathetic tone.

Coogong, who had remained quiet up until now, was nodding his head. His Ambiogel-filled helmet sloshing about some. It seemed as though the Thine scientist had already figured out where Derrota was going with this.

The halo display had reverted to its screen-saver mode, now projecting the majestic worlds within the Drakoria Star System illuminated against the contrasting total blackness of space.

Derrota gestured towards the system's outermost world, nearest to *Washington*. "Calydon. A prime example of untamed nature left to flourish unchecked. It makes one wonder what Earth would be like, had the dinosaurs survived. Could humans and dinosaurs have coexisted?" The scientist shrugged.

Engineer Kaelen Rivers scoffed, "Uh, no. Not a chance. Humans would be little more than a T-Rex's hors d'oeuvres before dining on a meaty triceratops, or maybe a few Velociraptors."

"Ick," Pristy said, making a face.

It took me a second, but I got there too. "What... really? You can't be serious."

Derrota nodded, seemingly not bothered. "Allows for nature to take its course. Some would say a more humane alternative to deploying fusion missiles or Phazon Pulsar fire into population centers."

Hardy stepped forward, his metal hand coming to rest on Derrota's shoulder. With a tilt of his ChronoBot head, he said, "So let me get this straight, we'll be quansporting herds of Calydon's dinosaurs onto Drakoria?" Turning to Kaelen Rivers, he added, "I like it... piglet finger food for Jurassic lizards!"

The End...

Stay tuned, the next USS Hamilton *book is already in the works!*

Thank you for reading USS Washington-the Black Ship. *If you enjoyed this book, PLEASE leave a review on Amazon.com —it really helps!*

To be notified the moment all future books are released, please join my mailing list. I hate spam and will never ever share your information. Jump to this link to sign up:

http://eepurl.com/bs7M9r

Acknowledgments

First and foremost, I am grateful to the fans of my writing and their ongoing support for all my books. I'd like to thank my wife, Kim—she's my rock and is a crucial, loving component of my publishing business. I'd like to thank my mother, Lura Genz, for being a tireless cheerleader of my writing. Others who provided fantastic support include Lura & James Fischer, Sue Parr, Charles Duell, and Stuart Church.

Check out my other available titles on the page that follows About the Author.

About the Author

Mark grew up on both coasts, first in Westchester County, New York, and then in Westlake Village, California. Mark and his wife, Kim, now live in Castle Rock, Colorado, with their two dogs, Sammi, and Lilly.

Mark started as a corporate marketing manager and then fell into indie-filmmaking—Producing/Directing the popular Gaia docudrama, 'Openings — The Search For Harry'.

For the last nine years, he's been writing full-time, and with over 40 top-selling novels under his belt, he has no plans on slowing down. Thanks for being part of his community!

Also by
Mark Wayne McGinnis

Scrapyard Ship Series

Scrapyard Ship (Book 1)

HAB 12 (Book 2)

Space Vengeance (Book 3)

Realms of Time (Book 4)

Craing Dominion (Book 5

The Great Space (Book 6)

Call To Battle (Book 7)

Scrapyard Ship – Uprising

Mad Powers Series

Mad Powers (Book 1)

Deadly Powers (Book 2)

Lone Star Renegades Series

Star Watch Series

Star Watch (Book 1)

Ricket (Book 2)

Boomer (Book 3)

Glory for Space Sea and Space (Book 4)

HOVER

-

Heroes and Zombies

-

The Test Pilot's Wife

-

TheFallen Ship

The Fallen Ship: Rise of the Gia Rebellion (Book 1)

The Fallen Ship II (Book 2)

-

USS Hamilton Series

USS Hamilton: Ironhold Station (Book 1)

USS Hamilton: Miasma Burn (Book 2)

USS Hamilton: Broadsides (Book 3)

USS Hamilton: USS Jefferson –

Charge of the Symbios (Book 4)

USS Hamilton: Starship Oblivion –

Sanctuary Outpost (Book 5)

USS Hamilton: USS Adams – No Escape (Book 6)

USS Hamilton: USS Lincoln – Mercy Kill (Book 7)

USS Hamilton: USS Franklin - When Worlds Collide (Book 8)

USS Hamilton: USS Washington - The Black Ship (Book 9)

USS Hamilton: USS IKE - Quansport Ops (Book 10)

ChronoBot Chronicles

Printed in Great Britain
by Amazon